AISEAL MÓR WAS BORN IN
AUSTRALIA OF IRISH PARENTS AND
GREW UP SURROUNDED BY THE
TRADITIONS OF STORYTELLING AND
MUSIC THAT ARE SO MUCH A PART
OF THE GAELIC CULTURE. AS A CHILD HE LEARNED
TO PLAY THE HARP, A SKILL THAT HAD BEEN
PASSED DOWN THROUGH HIS FAMILY OVER
MANY GENERATIONS.

HE GAINED A DEGREE IN PERFORMING ARTS
FROM THE UNIVERSITY OF WESTERN SYDNEY IN
1990 AND HAS SINCE WORKED AS AN ACTOR, A
TEACHER AND AS A MUSICIAN.

CAISEAL HAS JUST COMPLETED WORK ON A
COLLECTION OF ORIGINAL COMPOSITIONS, ALSO
CALLED 'THE CIRCLE AND THE CROSS', CURRENTLY
DISTRIBUTED THROUGH POLGRAM (CATALOGUE
NUMBER A1S2).

THE CIRCLE
AND
THE CROSS

CAÍSEAL MÓR

ARROW

An Arrow Book
published by
Random House Australia Pty Ltd
20 Alfred Street, Milsons Point, NSW 2061

Sydney New York Toronto
London Auckland Johannesburg
and agencies throughout the world

First published 1995

Reprinted 1995

Copyright © Caiseal Mór 1995

National Library of Australia
Cataloguing-in-Publication Data

Mór, Caiseal, 1961–.
The circle and the cross.

ISBN 0 09 183089 3.

I. Title.

A823.3

Cover design and all artwork by Caiseal Mór.
Typeset in 10/11 point Palatino
by Midland Typesetters Pty Ltd, Maryborough, Victoria.
Printed by Griffin Paperbacks
Production by Vantage Graphics, Sydney.

for

nancy

ACKNOWLEDGEMENTS

ITHOUT THE SUPPORT AND ENCOURAGEMENT OF MY LITERARY AGENT, SELWA ANTHONY, I WOULD NEVER HAVE BEEN ABLE TO COMPLETE THIS WORK. I CAN ONLY THANK HER SINCERELY FOR HAVING FAITH IN ME AND THE NOVEL.

MY PARTNER NANCY PUT UP WITH ME WHILE I WAS GETTING THE DRAFTS TOGETHER AND THEN READ AND RE-READ EACH DRAFT AS I FINISHED IT, ADDING COMMENTS AND GIVING ME AN IDEA OF WHAT WORKED AND WHAT DID NOT. SHE PROVIDED AN OBJECTIVE POINT OF VIEW WHENEVER I NEEDED IT. I DON'T THINK I COULD EVER THANK HER ENOUGH FOR ALL SHE HAS DONE.

MANY THANKS ALSO TO DOUGLAS WHOSE ADVICE AND COMMENTS ON DETAILS OF HISTORICAL ACCURACY AND FLOW OF THE NARRATIVE I FOUND INVALUABLE. HIS POSITIVE COMMENTS ALWAYS SEEMED TO COME WHEN MOST NEEDED.

I WOULD ALSO LIKE TO THANK JULIA, MY EDITOR, WHOSE ENTHUSIASM FOR THE NOVEL AND CONSTRUCTIVE CRITICISM MADE THE TASK OF ACTUALLY WRITING THE BOOK SO MUCH EASIER AND ENJOYABLE.

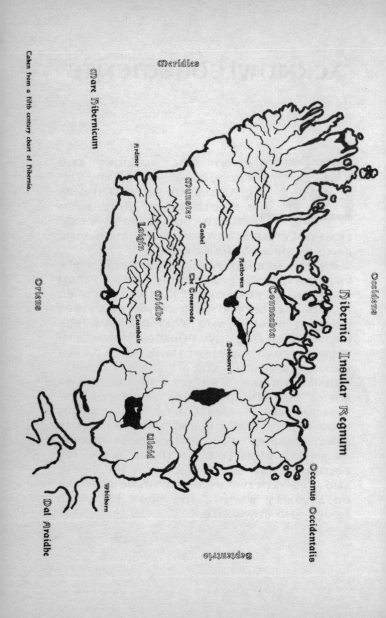

Taken from a fifth century chart of Hibernia.

Meridies

Mare Hibernicum

Oriens

Occidens

Hibernia Insular Regnum

Oceanus Occidentalis

Septentrio

Ardmor

Munster

Caisel

Rathowen

Laigin

The Crossroads

Midhe

Teamhair

Connachta

Doharui

Ulaid

Whithorn

Dal Araidhe

PROLOGUE

ear the wind wailing down a chimney on the darkest night of winter. Sit at the fire warming flesh that has blued in icy air. Rest eyes that ache, feet that are weary. Listen to the homely sounds of neighbours preparing meals in the cottages nearby.

Imagine, if you will, a dry-stone dwelling that is empty save for the silent long dead souls who keep watch over the house. Across a cobbled courtyard spring water struggles up through stone pipes into a granite trough worn smooth in the great passage of years since the first Gaels set it there.

Snow lies heavy on thatch. Ice hugs doorsteps. Golden lamplight escapes from cracks in wooden window shutters. Sweet peat smoke scents a chill breeze that enfolds the tiny settlement, gathering sounds and lifting them into the night.

An old song-maker, chanting in the style of her ancestors, raises a keening cry lamenting the long absence of summer. The hills around hear the notes and pass them down the valley, adding the muffled tunes of their kind. They remember other winters and other races who have long since left this place to pass eternity in Tir-Nan-Óg, the land of the everliving.

Here, amongst these folk who called themselves the Feni, was I born and there passed my first years on this Earth.

A traveller chanced by that place some ten years ago. He told me what he saw. The houses are now ruined shells. The timber is rotted and the hearth-stones lie cold. The people are all gone. They live only in my memory.

I have not, in all this time since, returned to the valley of my ancestors. Now I am too old and the journey is too dangerous. I can only dream that I am home and hope that my yearning heart will be satisfied one day.

Oh, but when I dream it is not always of winter's bite. I dream also of the clear air at summertime. I dream of the ordinary daily tasks that everyone in the clan hold had duty to share.

And there is one scene that unfolds itself to me in sleep-travel time and again. A child is dutifully chasing the goats at sunset to bring them in to the safety of their enclosure. He has yellow hair and a soft, easy laugh. He is slender and his eyes are deep-set and dark-ringed. He knows each goat by name and one or two he addresses as equals. From them he has learned his first lessons in respect.

His feet follow a hoof-beaten dirt track down the side of a small grass-covered knoll toward the round hillfort that his people call the dun. The goats march before him, breaking into a trot at the sight of their home, knowing that shelter and water await them there.

The boy does not notice the farmers or labourers or even the people of his own clan working within the low walls. He does not smell the supper boiling at the cooking fire. He cannot hear the greetings of his friends or the gentle rebukes of his mother.

His head is full of the words of the storytellers.

In private delight, he brings to mind every expression, every gesture that he has witnessed, striving to recall all he can of the old tales. He is truly a dreamer. He would leave his home tomorrow, if he could, to be a poet.

That young dreamer still lives strong in me.

But surely I am speaking to you of some things a little too soon. There will be time enough for that part of the story later.

This tale really begins at the far end of the same valley where a trickling stream narrowed before pouring into a pool. At that place, a roughly-built rock ford reached the sand on the other side of the water. And there, almost smothered by blackthorn bushes, lay the beginnings of a road.

This was no ordinary road. To me and my clan this was *the* Road.

It was our link to the world beyond. It was our lifeline, our protector, our procurer of rare goods. We revered the Road for, you see, we lived at one of those rare places where it came to an end.

In these times there are few people living who could tell you more than rumours and whispered half-truths of the origins and history of the Road. I alone remain of those who ever knew the larger part of the tale.

Beyond our valley, towns and cities and palaces and empires erupted like springtime seedlings from the edges of the Road. The taverns groaned full of travellers who wandered it; the markets hummed at its side just as the hives of worker bees buzzed in their all-consuming labour.

This Road brought all together: the farmer, the soldier, the journeyman, the merchant, the priest, the king, the lowly beggar. The Road served all, yet mastered each, for it drew travellers then as I imagine it draws folk still, spurring their curiosity to set out for lands that lie beyond the well-worn comfort of familiarity.

Would that you ever find yourself walking the

Road, trudging without purpose, seeking some journey's end, I give you this warning. The Road is a living being. She is an enchantress and She has a long reach.

She may at her whim lead you to the edge of the world, into the lands of light. Aye, and She could as well set you on the paths that reach only into the darkest corners of this Earth.

The Road holds within Her an unseen current that will drag you to Her holiest shrines. There She will reveal Her mighty triumphs, each greater than the last, each a song of Her splendour. In that moment when you are caught up by the travel-trance you will become lost to all your fellow beings, though you may well be surrounded by them.

For my part, there have been times, many times, when the will to continue on the long Road almost deserted me. There came a day, once, when my body lay battered, exhausted and near-dead and my soul yearned for the quiet respite of the lands beyond life. In all that suffering my only constant companion was the Road. It was She alone who could carry me forward to a safe-haven or to disaster, as was Her whim.

These days I rest often and travel little. I have a room in a town, in a country far from my homeland. In this time I have no leisure to journey, but the spirit of the Road still returns to taunt me. She fills my mind with part-recollected, part-imagined scenes from my wanderings, dangling before me enticing visions of what might have been or what yet may be.

Last night She came to me in my room as I sat strumming the harp before the fire. Yester's eve marked the time of the Great Festival that my people called Beltinne or the Fires of Bel. The folk of this country celebrate that feast in a different manner from the tribes of Eirinn. Here the people mill around the market cross and sing and dance and when they are too tired or too drunk they return home to their beds.

As the sounds of their merrymaking drifted in through my window, I wandered into the realm of soul-flight. I lifted up, leaving my body behind, and sailed high up over the stone-tiled town only to float gently down again in the midst of the thronging crowds. There before me a small drama unfolded.

A child's toy boat was swept along by the gutter-stream. Faster and faster it sailed until the heart-broken youngster could keep up no longer and was left crying in vain for his tiny craft. The cleverly carved treasure disappeared in the swirling whirl-pool of a sewer grate, ever bobbing along toward the river, out of the sight and knowledge of mortals. My mind's eye observed what happened after.

The building torrent of the flood carried the fragile ship out to meet the lapping waters of the blue depths. Far, far, ever seaward, sailed the toy. Through storms and calm it voyaged to be washed up by the tide one morning in another country where a child, not unlike the fellow who mourned its loss, found the boat, admired the workmanship, cherished the possession of it, but never guessed how long it had travelled nor whence it came.

In that vision rests the mystery of the true nature of the Road. Lost wanderers such as myself are like unto that toy boat lifted up on the wave crests of the Ocean of Being to glimpse at distant harbours from dizzy heights, only to be plunged down once more into the swell of the surging salt water before the eyes can fully focus on the horizon.

As the years continue to unfold, these trance-journeys come often to replace my clear memories of the old days. So many names and faces are lost now forever in the murky oblivion of forgetfulness. Yet I remember now, and will remember beyond this life, the dream-tales that first led me on my quests. I will remember the storytellers and their harps. I will remember the man who first spoke to me of the Road and I will remember our first meeting and our long friendship.

I will remember also the cherished gift he gave me at my initiation. The gift of a name.

I am called Mawn.

ONE

n a bleak steel-grey day, when the sunlight managed only to dimly light the world, the Sea put out its callous fingers of briny spray and threw them around a tiny vessel that foundered in the foam-capped fury. It gathered up a great trough of water with which to swallow the fragile craft. But the Sea was only teasing. This was a game it played often with the unwary. This was the Ocean's amusement.

Palladius the Elder gripped the gunwale of the boat with his long wiry fingers and, standing as best he could, bellowed with the strength of one who knows his cause is just, 'See, Brothers, how the Devil taunts us?'

Another wave crashed across the bows, filling his mouth with salt. The old man gladly took up the challenge, his face full of fire. 'Do not falter at your oars, Brothers, for the Dark One cannot harm you if your spirit be pure!'

The five other men shook the icy water from their faces. One or two sought reassurance from their comrades, but they all pulled hard at their oars, goaded on by the threat of drowning in the fearful tempest.

The wind, baying like a pack of wild demonic dogs, tore viciously at their hair and clothes. Palladius, the light of his green flaming eyes piercing the very air, held a silver crucifix high over his head and strained to raise his curse above the din of the roaring sea.

'Be still, thou fiends of the waters!' he shouted. 'You cannot delay the coming of the Word to this land.'

'For the love of God,' screamed Linus, the rain whipping his face and stinging his eyes, 'sit down and keep your hand on the tiller or we'll all be drowned.'

Slowly Palladius turned his gaze to the wiry young man who cowered in the bow. 'Still your tongue, boy,' he snapped, 'or by all the Saints, I'll tear it out with my own hands. Can you not see that the Devil has you in his grip?'

Linus was deathly white with fear, the fine bony structure of his face haggard and drawn. For a fleeting moment the two men's fierce glares met across the short space that separated them. Then another great wave intervened and it broke their hold over one another.

With frightening swiftness, a broaching squall lifted the boat up and twisted it askew. Somehow the exhausted crew kept her upright.

'Pull on your oars, you faithless bastards!' cried Palladius, emptying all the air from his lungs in a delirious rage.

Declinu looked around at his bishop, trying to catch what was said, but all he heard over the noise of the gale was a furious mumble. Palladius let the cross fall back around his neck and gripped the side of the craft with bleeding hands and whitening knuckles.

'Lord hear our prayer,' muttered Declinu. 'Holy Mary, Mother of God, the Lord is with you ... ' Another blue-grey roller grabbed the vessel and he forgot his entreaty for the moment.

The ebbing, foamy flood seethed and rolled, back

and forth. Then the wind dropped suddenly as if in answer to the bishop's curses. But the Sea had not yet vented all its passion. A monstrous ridge approached the boat, dwarfing it in a mass of water taller than a tree. A colossal mountain of a wave it was, towering over them and speaking of their doom. It rumbled onward dragging the boat from a watery valley up to a breaking peak so that the men all clung tightly to their seats or to one another.

All except the bishop.

He alone remained standing, defying the Ocean as if he were locked in mystical single combat with it.

When the monster had passed by them Declinu noticed that Seginus was no longer in the seat beside him. In panic he spun round in his place to seek him out. But his worst fears did not materialise. The young man was safe. He had been washed into the bow and sat there clinging to his half-brother, whose olive skin made Linus seem that much paler.

Then Declinu's attention focused on the stern. Donatus was there gesturing excitedly but his words could not be heard over the ferocity of the storm.

'There!' spluttered the old scribe. 'There! Land! Thank God, we're saved!'

Declinu looked where Donatus was pointing. Sure enough, there was land not far off, but no safe landing place. 'Rocks!' he howled, half-standing in terror. 'We'll be smashed to pieces!'

'Shut up, you bloody coward!' returned Palladius, a deadly threat in his speech.

The wave under them broke abruptly into streaking foam and Declinu saw nothing but white, and tasted nothing but salt, and his nostrils filled with water that trickled down the back of his throat making him gag. With the sleeve of his habit he tried to wipe his face and lost his handhold; then he felt himself being wrenched up from the craft and turned in his seat. The air was knocked out of his body. His head thumped heavily against an oarstock, but his leg caught around a loop of rope and he was able to haul himself back to his place. He grappled around blindly for his oar. It was gone.

In seconds Declinu's vision had cleared enough for him to see Donatus kneeling at the back of the boat in absolute fear, his bulk stabilising the craft as it was buffeted from behind.

Palladius had his crucifix raised again. There was madness in his eyes and the sea water streamed through his grey beard. 'You will not stop me!' he cried in defiance of his unseen foe.

When the next swell broke across the wooden vessel, Declinu heard the loud crunch of timber cracking. Before he could call out, the air exploded in a burst of spray and splinters. Seginus was gone; Linus was clinging desperately to the shattered bow, and Donatus, the wordsmith, was weeping as he thrashed the tiller about fruitlessly.

Only Palladius seemed truly unmoved by the frightful scene. Beside him knelt the youngest monk, Isernus, with his bright blue eyes streaming tears. He gently kissed the carved form on the bishop's crucifix and moved his lips silently in prayer.

Declinu searched for his rosary. 'God, I am only twenty-three years on this Earth—' He had only managed those few words when the rocks rushed forward to meet him and he was dragged under the sea. Desperately he strained to hold his breath, to stop the water filling his lungs, but his head did not find the surface and he could feel himself weakening.

The next thing he knew was the scraping shock of being washed up a pebble beach by the surging tide. Then the Ocean grabbed at his legs, trying to claim him again. In desperation he dug his hands into the ground and struggled to crawl up the steeply sloping shore. Despair filled his heart for he sensed that he was losing the fight, sliding back into a cold blue grave. Then suddenly he felt a hand grasp one wrist, then another. He threw his head back to behold Seginus and Linus pulling at him with all their might. They dragged him clear of the water as quickly as they could, not wishing to tarry long enough to chance being ripped back out to sea themselves.

Two other men, still stunned by the rough landing, lay further up the beach out of danger of the Ocean's grasp. Twisted timbers and ropes and provisions were scattered all around. Pieces of cloth torn from the sails were spread out on the pebbles.

Seginus helped the half drowned monk up to where the others were lying and then went back to his task.

The first thing Declinu did when he realised he was safe was cross himself. That done, he coughed up a large quantity of brine. When his lungs were clear he looked about him. Donatus lay on his left, bruised and breathing hard, but alive. To his right was the motionless body of Palladius lying face up, mouth open wide. Declinu rolled over to examine the bishop closely, but at that very moment Seginus came and dumped another monk on the pebbles. It was the boy, Isernus.

As if to mock them further the rain began to pelt harder and the biting wind tore at their soaked black vestments. One by one, as they all realised that it was only by some miracle they had all survived, they knelt and pressed their faces to the land in thanks.

'Praise be to God,' whispered Donatus, 'and bless our bishop and take him into your bosom.'

'One day surely,' boomed Palladius still lying face up, 'but not this day.'

The bishop was calmly staring at the sky as if he were studying it. There was blood pouring from his long nose but he was otherwise unharmed. High above, a single cloud parted briefly and the light of the sun streamed down upon the beach before them like a sign from God.

The stunned brothers salvaged what they could of their possessions and made their way up the beach toward the long stems of green standing at the edge of the wind-blown rocks. They were all soaked through. Their bodies were chafed by the salt; their minds numbed by the constant battle they had fought to survive this journey. All of them were pale and gaunt from lack of sleep and solid food.

Above the stony shoreline where the grasses grew, they gathered, standing in a circle, heads bowed. In turn, each man pulled back the black woollen cowl from over his face to reveal the shaved tonsure of a Roman monk.

When they were settled, the grey-bearded bishop acknowledged them, signing round the circle to them one by one. Their eyes stared back at him cold, exhausted and relieved.

The old man took his shepherd's staff from Linus, who had recovered it for him, and struck the metal tip hard into the moist soil. 'This land is claimed for the Church of Rome and for the bishop of that city His Holiness, Pope Celestine,' he announced. 'As the evangelical overseer appointed to this country by His Holiness, I banish all evil from this place. From this day forward it is a Christian land and I, Palladius, am its first bishop.'

The brothers all solemnly knelt, crossed themselves and joined in a prayer led by the tall missionary.

'Pater Noster qui es in caelis sanctificetur nomen tuum . . .'

When their hasty but heartfelt thanks were done, they dragged what was left of the boat ashore. The remains of the vessel that had barely kept them safe for many days upon the raging sea would now be butchered to serve as their shelter this first night on the land. They would have to wait until the light of morning to build a more permanent structure out of beach stones. Night would soon be upon them and for now they were content to rest again with the solid ground beneath them and the sweet smell of the soil of the Earth in the air.

After the shelter was erected, they built two fires: one high and dry near their lean-to and another on the seashore near the watermark where they had landed. When that was done they gathered to bless their refuge and to receive instructions from their leader.

'In gratitude for a fair voyage,' decreed the bishop, 'and a safe landing on these wild shores, we will give the dark hours over to a vigil of prayer. Each brother is to take a turn on the beach where we came to land, facing east in homage to the Holy Mother of Christ, the Blessed Virgin Mary Star of the Sea. We will implore her to watch over us and the future success of our mission to this island.'

Then they all ate a little of their meagre rations and lay down to rest a while.

Just after the midnight hour, when it came to his turn at the vigil, Declinu rose and nervously placed his sandals on his feet, tightly binding the leather straps. He took his Gospel and beads from the waterproof case in which he carried them and made his way hesitantly to the place where they had landed. There he found Seginus by the fire, finishing a round of the novenae and gravely crossing himself.

Declinu waited a moment for his brother to rise and then blurted, 'Was everything quiet?'

'Yes, of course,' replied Seginus, somewhat surprised at the question. 'Save for the roar of the ocean, which I may never entirely banish from my ears.'

'What I mean is,' Declinu looked around to check that no-one would overhear what he was about to say, 'I have heard tell that this land is full of evil spirits and demons.'

'And I have heard it called 'The Sleeping Land', added Seginus. 'At least that is what the Roman galley captains called it—Hibernia. It certainly seems to be sleeping soundly tonight,' he quipped. 'And soon so shall I!'

'There is a story that the folk of this land fought a long and bloody war against the spirits of the island until finally they made a truce with them,' whispered Declinu, beads of sweat glistening on his forehead. 'It is said that the demons still secretly walk the land and capture the spirits of those who stray from the company of others. Once they have the victim's soul ensnared they take it to their palaces deep underground and keep it forever as a slave.'

Declinu looked up and down the beach and added dramatically, 'But they always leave the body of their prisoner to be found brutally battered

14

and foully scorched by the fires of Hell.' His eyes widened so that Seginus could clearly see the dark irises against the whites.

'I have heard that too,' nodded Seginus in agreement.

Declinu, seeing that he had his brother's attention, continued. 'The people who live here are just as strange as the demons with whom they share the island. There was a man in the monastery at Our Lady's who had been taken captive by the natives of this country. He told me that there are cannibals on these shores who collect the heads of their victims and keep them nailed over the doors of their houses. He also said that there are powerful magicians among these folk who, by merely reciting a verse, can kill another man even over a great distance. And that these same evil magi can turn themselves into any shape they choose—bird, fish, tree, or even the wind itself.'

Seginus was now listening intently. He had travelled to many countries and, for one of so few years, he knew much about the world. His father had been a cohort commander in the Twentieth Legion and had often spoken of his adventures and all that he had seen of the world beyond the influence of civilisation. Seginus had heard many tales but he had not heard this story. 'Go on,' he insisted.

'They play upon lyres,' continued Declinu, 'such as they have in Alexandria, but these instruments are full of enchantment, for with them the magi can put a girl to sleep or stir a man to war or send yet another helpless victim to the kingdom of the demons. Even the women in this land are hardened warriors and they are the equals of their menfolk in battle.'

Seginus only just managed to stifle a cynical laugh. 'My dear friend, do not take everything you hear as if it were written in the Gospels. What manner of people would allow their women the same rights as men? That is against creation. It happens nowhere on Earth.'

'But Julius Caesar writes that the Briton tribes called their women to war during the occupation of that land.'

'He was a pagan and an exaggerator.' Seginus smiled indulgently at his comrade and slapped him across the back, leaning in close to speak softly. 'If the women of this land come looking for you tonight, tell them you'd rather face their demons. Good night to you. And God bless you.' Seginus laughed loudly and walked back up the stony foreshore to the shelter, still amused at his friend's gullibility.

Declinu was somewhat put out by the other monk's remarks but quickly forgave him and took out his prayer beads to begin his part of the vigil. He was a pious soul, though a very superstitious one. Before him the Hibernian Sea was like a great expanse of slowly heaving ice lit by the shimmer of the full moon. Waves still crashed onto the beach, heavy and relentless.

Declinu arranged his Gospels on a small prayer mat and then draped a cloak around his shoulders. Kneeling, he crossed himself and began to pray fervently and loudly. Somehow the sound of his own voice seemed to banish any thoughts of malicious spirits and murderous Hibernian women. But it did not dispel the feeling that nearby there was someone or something watching him very closely. And that whoever or whatever it was had no particular love of Christian monks.

Although the familiar words of the 'Ave' consoled him, still he was plagued by the uneasy feeling that at any moment he could be snatched away to become a hive worker in some Hell on Earth.

After the passing of about an hour he ceased his chanting to take a drink of water and to throw some wood on the fire. He stood up, stretching his limbs, and found that his arms and legs were streaming with sweat: he had spent the greater part of his watch so far in a tense state of abject fear.

'This is ridiculous,' he thought. 'I have been sent here to convert the savage heathen to the cross. It is stupid of me to be afraid of the shadows when I have much more to fear of the living people of this land to whom I am to minister.' He laughed at himself a little, disquieted by his own lack of faith, then went back to tending the fire.

As he poked the coals with a long piece of driftwood, a breeze rose suddenly from the sea. It caught his cowl and ripped it over his face so that his vision was obscured. As he was righting it he heard a voice behind him, though he could not make out any words. Just as quickly as the wind had lifted, it dropped again, and all was perfectly still.

Declinu pulled the hood back over his head and looked up and down the beach. Nothing stirred. Telling himself that he was imagining things, he knelt down to rake the fire again.

Suddenly, behind him in the grasses near the beach, there was a loud crack like a branch snapping under a great weight. Declinu started so that he almost fell backwards. Quickly recovering from the shock, he concentrated all his senses on the spot from whence he thought the noise had come. For a while all was still again, then he heard the steady beat of footsteps on the pebbles.

Now he was sure that someone was approaching. Instinctively Declinu moved to put the fire between him and the walker. He stared in the direction of the noise, straining to see through the night.

In moments a dark figure appeared striding across the strand. The frightened monk struggled to make out if the shape were real or imagined. Eerie shadows pulsed around it, or were there other demons nearby?

The figure picked up its pace, its footfall much louder now. As it got closer, Declinu watched the outline of the monster grow to an enormous size. It became more and more hideous. There were great folds of flesh hanging from its body, and where a head should have been there was only a solid black lump. He thought back over all the books he had read and all the paintings he had seen of the Devil's servants. This was far worse than any of them.

Declinu had the presence of mind to cross himself. He took a deep breath, preparing to call out for help. But his voice would not do his bidding. His throat was paralysed by fear. He felt his limbs begin to shake violently. The monk clutched at his breast, sure that his heart had stopped and certain that he was under some kind of evil spell.

He moved to grab a brand from the fire and lash out at his attacker, but he knew that a slightly built man like himself would have no chance against a demon from Hell. Nevertheless, he determined to attack it. He gathered his wits and stepped toward the fire. As he did so, his footing slipped and he tumbled onto the crunching stones, taking his weight painfully on his hands.

In the next second the figure had reached him. It stopped only a few paces away and lifted a gloved hand to its face, drawing the covering slowly away. Declinu forced himself to look up and then choked back a scream.

Two small familiar eyes reflected in the firelight. They were full of wonder and they were the eyes of Linus the half-brother of Seginus. Declinu breathed out heavily in relief but could not immediately master his tongue.

'Hello,' Linus said. 'Are you awake?'

'Of course I'm awake!' answered Declinu indignantly. 'I am stoking the fire.' He was deeply embarrassed by his fear and was determined not to let his nervousness show.

'I could not hear your prayers so I thought perhaps you had fallen asleep. Would you like some company?' asked the young man.

'Not tonight, Brother,' came the sharp reply. 'I am supposed to be keeping the vigil.' Declinu stood and shook himself.

'Are you tired?' asked Linus.

'I could sleep for a week. It has been that long since I rested without any interruption,' Declinu sighed.

'Then you go to bed,' offered Linus. 'There's no sleep in me. I'll take your watch.'

For a moment Declinu seriously considered the proposal. He realised that he had been working himself into a state because he was so exhausted. 'Will you be able to keep the watch?' asked Declinu, obviously not believing that the younger monk would stay at his post.

'Of course I will,' replied Linus, showing a little hurt in his tone. 'I cannot rest anyway. There is something about being in this land that makes me feel quite strange. I find I can't even close my eyes for excitement. I can't wait for morning so that I can begin exploring this place. Go to bed and I'll wake Isernus when it's time. The bishop need never know.'

At the mention of Isernus, Declinu began to suspect that Linus had some other motive for offering to take the vigil. Almost everyone in the party had noticed the friendship that had developed between him and Isernus in the months before their departure. The two had been very discreet and not gone too far in expressing their affections, but the bishop would have flayed them alive had he discovered what Declinu knew to be the true nature of their feelings.

'Surely you would rather be asleep on a night such as this,' urged Linus, in his soft reassuring voice. 'Are you not spent from the long voyage? Go to bed and I will pray that you rest well.'

Despite his reservations Declinu began to give in. The thought of a warm, dry blanket wrapped around his frozen bones was very enticing. And the company of his brothers sleeping nearby would surely make him feel safer. He was weakening to the idea.

'A little rest surely would not hurt anyone. I would be better able to perform my duties tomorrow,' he told himself.

'Very well, Brother, thank you for the few extra hours of sleep,' he said finally.

Then guilt shook him a little, as it often did, and he decided to give Linus a friendly warning. 'I beg you not to get caught. Remember, you are not in Rome now,' he whispered. 'Here Palladius is the law and he would rather see you dead than find you were engaging in ... yes, well ... sinful activity. I think you take my meaning, Brother.'

'Good night, my friend,' said Linus gratefully. 'I won't betray your exhaustion to the bishop, fear not.'

'Just do not involve me! If Palladius discovers

you breaking the code it will be none of my doing,' protested Declinu. 'Good night.'

He pushed roughly past Linus to go to bed. Declinu had only gone ten steps when he began to regret his decision. But he was tired, irritable and more than a little fearful and he just wanted to rest. So he made his way quietly to the shelter and carefully moved around to the open end of the upturned boat and lay down without so much as a sigh, so as not to disturb anyone.

As he drifted off into an uneasy slumber he thought he saw Isernus rise and leave the little refuge, but Declinu was sinking into a deep and troubled sleep and he did not take too much notice.

TWO

rother,' repeated the nervous Donatus, 'Brother Declinu, wake up!'

'I'll rouse him soon enough,' boomed another voice.

Declinu felt the biting cold spread across his shoulders and face as Palladius tossed a bucket of sea water over his head.

'Are you with us?' bellowed the bishop.

'Yes, I think so,' stuttered Declinu. He struggled to focus for a moment, then he saw Palladius looming over him and realised that he had overslept. 'Yes, your Reverence, I am awake.'

'Then be so good as to tell me where you spent your apportioned time during the vigil last night,' demanded the bishop.

'I was relieved by Brother Linus,' said Declinu sheepishly.

Palladius looked at him with obvious disbelief, the corners of his mouth curled in contempt.

'It is true, I swear it,' pleaded the startled monk. 'You have only to ask Linus himself.'

'Would that I could,' said Palladius without any trace of emotion, 'for he lies now amongst the ashes of the fire. He has been most cruelly slain.'

It took a few moments for the enormity of the statement to hit Declinu. He tried to speak but all that came out was a confused, 'What?'

'Brother Linus is dead,' repeated Palladius,

slowly speaking each word so there could be no misunderstanding.

'How ... did ... it happen?' sobbed Declinu, holding both hands over his cheeks. 'Was it the demons?'

'Demons?' screeched the bishop, grabbing Declinu roughly by the top of his habit and hauling him to his feet, 'What demons?'

'The demons who steal the souls of the innocent,' stammered the monk, as if the answer were obvious. 'The demons who scorch the bodies of their victims in the fires of Hell.'

Palladius grasped Declinu by the sleeves, striving to hold him still enough so that he could see into his eyes and tell if the younger man was hiding anything. After a few moments he leaned in closer so that their noses almost touched, and grunted, 'Come and see to your brother who has departed us.'

Declinu stared up at him in alarm. The bishop's face seemed more gaunt and severe than was usual, even for him.

Palladius held him uncomfortably close and hissed into the monk's ear, covering the side of his face with spittle. 'My son, if you have a confession to make, you should do it before we reach the body. Then at least God will smile on you for your repentance.'

'By all the hosts of angels, you can't think that I had anything to do with ... ?' Declinu began, but he ran out of breath and fell silent.

When they reached the place where the vigil fire had been, a body, charred and lifeless, lay strewn face-down in its midst. The coals were as dead as the monk who lay in the ashes.

Isernus and Seginus were kneeling on the beach in silent shock. Donatus followed a few moments later, taking up a position at their sides.

When he could bring himself to look closely on the horrible sight, Declinu observed that the legs and head of the corpse were strangely untouched by the flames but the torso was black and still smoking. He did not immediately recognise this gruesome body as that of Linus. Indeed, at first he refused to believe it was the boy. Then the breeze cast the stench of singed flesh toward him and Declinu collapsed on the pebbles in a fit of distressed retching.

It took Declinu a long while to recover, but when he did, he lifted his head to gaze again on the awful sight before him. 'It is the work of demons,' he muttered.

'Aye,' agreed Donatus, 'the fabled devils of Hibernia. They have scorched him black with their fiery breath.'

'The Devil walks here, that is certain,' began Palladius, 'but I'll wager he cloaks himself in human form.'

As one, the small band shuddered and genuflected.

'Lord, what horrors await us in this land?' moaned Donatus.

Seginus approached his half-brother's body and leaned over to raise it out of the fire pit. As he rolled the corpse over, the other monks gasped in horror, muttering prayers at the terrible sight that was revealed. The eyes of the lifeless monk stared directly into the sky, frozen by terror at the instant of death. One hand clutched at the handle of a long knife which pierced deeply into the blackened chest, the other held a string of rosary beads.

'That is his own blade,' wailed Seginus, tears falling from his eyes. 'Our father gave it to him when he was a boy.'

Isernus was beside himself with grief. Doubled up and crouching among the rocks, he wept loudly and uncontrollably. Palladius allowed the boy to continue for a few minutes but then his patience deserted him. He turned coolly and struck him hard with the back of his hand, sending him sprawling to the ground, senseless.

'Prepare the body for burial,' he ordered. The bishop then let his gaze fall on Declinu. 'You, Brother, come with me!' The command was full of menace. 'You and I will recite the holy offices for the soul of our dear friend.'

He turned and marched up the beach. Declinu followed obediently, trying to match his master's gait. As he caught up, the older man spun round to face him.

'What happened?' he demanded.

'I do not know what you mean,' replied Declinu, stunned.

'Don't waste my time, young man, tell me exactly what happened or by the grace of God you will suffer for it!' hissed Palladius.

'I do not know,' insisted the monk, '. . . well, not exactly.'

'So you do know something.'

Declinu looked at his master, saw the determination in his sharp features and decided to tell him some of what had transpired during his watch. 'It is my fault,' he began. 'I was weary, and Brother Linus offered to take my place . . . I did not think that the demons would take him. God alone knows I would rather have been roasted alive over the spits of Hell than see that poor lad suffer the way he did.' Then he related most of what had passed between him and Linus the night before.

'So, you claim that you slept and saw no-one else

rise last night?' inquired Palladius when Declinu had finished.

'That is so, my lord,' Declinu lied.

'Then it is almost certain that the poor fellow was burned alive by the Devils of this land.' Palladius spoke the words almost to himself, but he seemed satisfied, even relieved, with his conclusion. 'It is a lesson for us all that we must be ever vigilant. He could not destroy us all at once on the sea, so Satan will try taking us one by one.' Palladius turned his face heavenward as if searching the sky for an answer. After a few minutes of scanning the clouds he cast his gaze once more on Declinu. 'Now we must see to the funeral of our first martyr,' he announced solemnly.

Declinu was more than a little disturbed by the phrase 'our first martyr'. He had his own suspicions about exactly what had taken place on the beach after he went to bed, but the demons of Hibernia stilled seemed very real to him. He felt easier with assigning a supernatural explanation to events than facing the notion that one of his companions might be implicated in so foul a deed.

The brothers worked hard the rest of the day, transporting small slabs and larger stones up onto the grass where a space had been cleared for a tomb. It was the bishop's idea to mark the site with a great church in honour of Linus, but for the time being a rough cairn would have to suffice. There were now only five of them after all, and one of their number was over sixty years old, so they could not hope to build an elaborate memorial.

It was late afternoon when they eventually placed the last stones on the top of the great pile and dispersed along the beach, each alone, to pray and prepare for a midnight Mass for the dead.

A new fire was kindled after they had all

returned at the appointed hour. Incense, miraculously rescued from the shipwreck and so doubly valuable, was set to smoking all around the monument. Throughout the preparations for the ceremony Declinu eyed his companions carefully, trying to spot any sign of fear or guilt or remorse. But it seemed there was only genuine sorrow—and fear—on their faces. Had he but known it, they were each watching him also. Donatus never once took his eyes off Declinu, staring at him the whole time with anger and dread.

Seginus was infinitely more subtle. He remembered well his conversation with the monk before his own watch ended. 'If he is a servant of the Devil, why did he not strike me down when he had the chance?' he asked himself. 'He knows too much about the ways of Satan and of the evils of Hibernia. It stands to reason that he had something to do with my dear brother's death, if he was not responsible for it himself.'

During the preliminary prayers and invocations each brother held a lighted prayer-candle before him. Enhanced by the tiny candle flames, shadows flickered across their faces, giving their features an eerie otherworldly look.

'Truly fearless, truly fortunate martyrs,' began the bishop's prayer from the writings of Tertullian, 'called by God to glorify the name of our Lord Jesus Christ. If any of us would truly honour and adore the Lord these are the models for him to follow—' There was as usual no emotion in his voice as he recited the liturgy.

Declinu noticed a twitching muscle on the face of Isernus. 'Or was it,' he wondered, 'the candlelight playing tricks with his vision?'

'—martyrs of the Mother Church,' continued Palladius.

Isernus was craning his neck up toward the stars and he had dropped his candle down to his waist. His eyes were hidden from everyone's view.

'The same Holy Spirit is active now as was in those times, the omnipotent God the Father and his Son, Jesus Christ, our Lord, whose glory and power are boundless.'

Declinu detected a teardrop running down the young man's cheek. Isernus was quietly weeping.

Suddenly the prayer ended and Declinu instinctively crossed himself.

'*Dominus vobiscum,*' Palladius intoned.

'*Et cum spiritu tuo,*' answered Declinu.

'*Requiéscat in pace,*' ended Palladius.

'*Amen,*' chanted the chorus.

'Now share the blessed sacrament,' began the bishop. 'When they had gathered with the Lord ...' Declinu shut the rest of the words out and wished for morning, but the service for the dead was long and elaborate and continued most of the night, only drawing to a close when dawn was almost upon them.

The monks had fasted all the previous day and by the time the mass was over Declinu was desperately trying to quieten his noisy gut. Yet, out of respect for his late brother in Christ, it was a long time before he lifted his eyes from the rough pile of stones wherein the body now lay entombed. His instincts told him that all was not as it should be. He examined the immediate area with his sharp eyes. Something was certainly amiss. The long shadows surrounded only three figures.

Isernus was gone.

Dismissing himself as politely as possible, Declinu quickly combed the nearby territory. He went first down to the beach and then to the fresh water stream close by but could find no sign of the young monk. Finally, in desperation, he went reluctantly to Palladius full of concern for the grieving boy.

The bishop listened to what Declinu had to say then shook his head gravely and placed a hand on the monk's shoulder. 'It pains me to think that the lad is so distressed,' he said. 'You should go to find him and see that he does not harm himself.' But the care in the older man's eyes disguised his true thoughts and as Declinu ran to do his master's bidding, Palladius followed at a safe distance so that he could observe the monk without being noticed. 'There is some evil here,' the bishop told himself, 'and this monk will lead me to it, I am certain.'

Unsure where to begin his search Declinu decided to try walking the woods on the coastline around about, but he held little hope of finding the boy.

It was past mid-morning before he thought he caught sight of his young companion in the far distance standing on the top of a hill, silhouetted against the sky. Just as Declinu began to focus on him, Isernus raced headlong down the opposite side and the monk could no longer see him.

Declinu sprinted toward the hill. He had only gone a short distance before he was breathless but he feared to slow his pace in case he should lose sight of the distressed brother for too long. He would not want to face Palladius with the admission that he had found Isernus only to lose him again shortly after.

Despite his haste, it was a long time before Declinu reached the top of the hill. Staggering and at the point of exhaustion, he struggled to regain his breath, but the scene that unfolded before him took it away again.

Not a hundred paces away stood another hill,

smaller than the one upon which he stood. Its earth was gouged into the shape of a great coiling serpent that wrapped itself many times around the base of the mound. At the top of the hill there was an oblong wooden palisade, shaped to resemble the head of a dragon. Within the defences there were many circular buildings. Smoke issued in long streaks from the roof-holes of houses. And in the centre of the settlement a large crowd of people had gathered.

Declinu's legs gave way beneath him and he sat down in astonishment, mouth agape. 'All this day and the previous we have been camped but a short hike away, and yet none of us had any idea that there was a village of natives so near to us!' he exclaimed.

Eventually remembering that he was meant to be seeking his brother, he got himself up off the ground to make after him. Then he recalled the death of Linus and thought better of approaching the village. He did not wish to fall into the hands of savages who might well be able to conjure up fire demons.

He wrung his hands. 'I must go to the bishop with this news,' he said aloud, turning to head back to the beach.

A tall bearded figure appeared without warning out of the bushes nearby. 'You will not have to go far,' remarked the bishop. 'What news have you?'

Declinu was stunned to find Palladius standing so close to him and no word would pass his lips. He could only gesture dumbly at the village.

Palladius studied the hillfort long and hard, talking often to himself; finally he turned to face Declinu. 'Well, it is clear to me that we must make contact with these people sooner or later,' he said pensively, 'and since the boy Isernus has not yet returned we will go and ask their help in finding him.' He looked to the sky. 'It is coming again tonight. We will return to the beach to gather our things and then set out again before the dawn.'

Palladius set a cracking pace back to the lean-to shelter and the other monks. Declinu could only follow him in bewilderment, but he was certain there was some reason for the bishop's abruptness, other than the fact that it was the fashion in which he addressed most people.

When, later, he revealed news of the village to his followers, Palladius declared, 'I will keep the vigil myself this night at the grave of Brother Linus. Those of you who would join me may do so.'

All of them caught the inference that they had no choice in the matter and bowed their heads in acquiescence.

'Seginus,' demanded Palladius.

'Yes, lord,' answered the monk.

'You will light the vigil fires at the resting place of your father's other son.'

'Thank you, my lord.'

With that the brothers dispersed to make ready for the night, to prepare provisions for the evening meal and to gather wood and water for the dark hours.

Declinu, however, remained with Seginus after he had lit the fire, the pair sitting cross-legged opposite each other.

For a long time the two men sat in silence. Finally it was Seginus who broke the silence. Turning to his companion, he said, 'Perhaps this truly is a land of evil demons, Brother. But it was the hand of man that struck my half-brother dead. I swear that I will find the one who did it and he will suffer for his crime. Now Isernus is gone also. Could it be that he has fallen to the same hand?'

Seginus looked at Declinu with such hatred in his eyes that Declinu felt not just that he was accusing him, but that he was threatening him also. Declinu brushed the comment off, trying to change the direction of the conversation. 'When I left your brother he was in good spirits. And we should be thankful that he has gone to his rest with a clear conscience and into the bosom of Christ.'

Once again Seginus looked at his companion, but this time his expression was cynical and full of bitterness. 'You and I both know that he was not as pure as he should have been. He has gone to his just reward, that is certain. But he was too young to suffer so grim a death. The one who did this will pay for his barbarism, I swear it.' Seginus spat these last three words with a venom that was clearly aimed at the other monk.

'Are you accusing me?' gasped Declinu in shock.

'I am saying to your face what the others are already whispering behind your back.'

'Don't be absurd,' laughed Declinu nervously. 'Do you really believe that I could kill two of my companions? Would I have gone in search of Isernus if I had wanted him dead also? Do you think that I am capable of stabbing your brother, dragging him into the fire and then calmly going back to bed afterwards as if nothing had happened? Would I not have blood on my hands? Would I have been fool enough to remain under the dominion of Palladius and risk the penance he would surely deal me?'

The tense silence that followed told the monk that Seginus was not impressed by anything that he had heard.

'You are seeking in the wrong direction, Brother,' asserted Declinu.

'Perhaps you are right,' conceded Seginus. 'Very

likely the hand that struck him down was that of a heathen savage, and if so, I will atone for my brother's death with the conversion of all the Hibernians to the faith or,' he went on, 'with their blood.'

Declinu was always disturbed by fanatical talk. He had often heard priests in Gaul talking this way and it made his stomach turn. He had never been able to imagine the gentle Christ of the Gospels condoning such sentiments. As was his way he chose to ignore the comments, yet the words had made him intensely uncomfortable. He knew in his heart that there was more to this than a simple, brutal slaying by wild natives.

He did not want to speculate too much further for he was not ready to face the other possibilities which gave him even more discomfort.

The two men returned to their silence. Eventually, tired of sitting beside the brooding Seginus, Declinu stood up and walked down to the beach.

The tide had covered the spot where Linus had been killed and now was receding again, but there was still charcoal spread about indicating the general area where the fire-pit had been. He went over and poked about with a piece of driftwood at the tiny blackened pebbles that lay there, not searching for anything in particular but letting his thoughts drift back to the night when Linus had been killed. He turned the wet stones over and over, revealing charred splinters and uncovering scorched shells.

Among the dead coals Declinu suddenly noticed something poking through the surface, which sparkled brightly. He dug around deeper for it with his hands and finally found a piece of blackened, burned, leather thonging with a delicate silver cross entangled in it. At first he thought he had found a piece of jewellery belonging to Linus. Then he remembered that Linus always wore a robust cross made of bronze. They had buried him with it.

Declinu put the object in his pouch and checked that no-one had been watching. He threw the piece of driftwood into the sea and strode back up the beach toward the shelter. It was nearly dark and he wanted to avoid any more conversations with his brethren on this particular evening so he went straight to his position at the vigil without eating.

'The hours pass slowly in meditation,' noted Declinu to himself after the first measure had been spoken. He wanted nothing more than to end this night so that the dangerous quest they were on could draw closer to its resolution. All the remaining brothers were chanting methodically and twitching their beads through their fingers. Declinu knew that each of his fellow monks had the same thoughts as he.

He glanced at each of his companions around the circle one by one, trying to discern who was concentrating and who was not. Seginus was certainly deep in contemplation, of that there was no doubt. Next to him, Palladius sat poised like a lion seemingly at peace, yet like a sleeping cat, ever ready to strike out at the unwary. Beside the bishop, Donatus, the overweight old monk who taught writing and reading, was gradually succumbing to sleep.

From out of the corner of his eye, Declinu glimpsed another figure close to Donatus and realised there was one too many men gathered at the fireside. A cold shiver of fear travelled down his back and across his legs. The memory of the first night on the beach flashed through his mind.

'Is this Linus returned to haunt us?' he thought.

Shaking slightly, he turned to better see the man seated between Donatus and himself.

The fellow was small and dark-skinned. It was Isernus.

'Brother, you have returned to us!' cried Declinu in relief.

All the monks stopped short and looked up in amazement.

'I have,' replied the young monk.

Palladius rose slowly to his feet watching the young Isernus all the while. 'Where have you been?' he asked sternly.

The monk stuttered an answer. 'I wandered long in the hills in my grief and there I met one of the people of this land, who took me before the local chieftain. Brecan is his name. He has sent me back asking that you accompany me to his hall. He has prepared a feast and would welcome you all as honoured guests. I have told him of our mission and he wishes to hear the Word and perhaps to take the holy Chrism.'

The bishop stared at Isernus intently for a moment; then he gently put out his hand as if to touch the monk's brow in blessing. Isernus bowed his head and Palladius, taking advantage of his position, punched him hard in the face, knocking him off balance. 'Do not leave my sight again without permission!' he roared. Then he turned to the others and, assuming a calm voice once again, declared, '*Deo grátias*. God is watching over us,' as he made the sign of the cross. 'Collect your things, Brothers,' he continued triumphantly, 'our work has begun at last and we have much to do.'

The four monks rushed to do his bidding, gathering their books, their holy vestments and all else that the sea had allowed them to retain. When they had their gear, they began the long hike through the darkness to the Hibernian village. They followed well-worn paths and so the journey was not as difficult as Declinu's walk had been earlier that day. In the time it took for Declinu to recite the first twelve psalms under his breath they came to a broad track that cut through the woods.

He had chanted two rounds of the rosary when he realised that there were at least twenty warriors escorting them on either side of the path. The Hibernians moved in absolute silence through the underbrush, rarely stirring a branch or even a stalk of grass.

Before Declinu could allow panic take hold of him, the little party turned a sharp bend in the path and walls loomed suddenly out of the darkness. A tall wooden rampart made of sharpened logs surrounded a low hill. The line of the barricade was broken only by a pair of heavy oak gates that swung open as if by magic when the monks approached.

Firelight spilled from the hearths of thirty round thatch dwellings that were spread around the inside perimeter of the fort. The ground sloped up from the outer walls toward the central building on the top of the mound. They were led by their escort around the hill to the right, gradually spiralling their way toward the top even though a path led there directly.

As the warriors closed in around the monks, Declinu managed to get a closer look at them. Each wore a long moustache; the older men had leather plaited into theirs. They wore their hair long, tied back and woven with yarn to keep it out of their faces. Their upper bodies were bare but for twisted gold neck-pieces, which Declinu guessed would weigh almost twice as much as his Gospel.

Every warrior had clear bright eyes and tanned bodies and they all stood a head taller than him at least. He noticed that their trousers looked, at first glance, to be made of wool, with brilliant colours incorporated in the design, but in fact the material was much finer than wool and it had a sheen to it that was unlike anything Declinu had ever seen. A few of the men had dark blue circular motifs etched onto their arms and what looked to be paint on their faces. Most were barefoot, though some wore sandals similar to the standard issue of the Roman legions. The only weapons they carried were javelins, but they were longer and heavier than any Declinu had ever seen.

Women were rushing out to see the monks now and Declinu was surprised to find that some of them were dressed in exactly the same manner as their men. One young fair-headed woman had bare breasts and the young monk quickly averted his gaze, pretending not to notice. Other women were dressed in long robes, their hair knotted with gold and silver wire.

The spiral journey took them around the whole village, so by the time the door to the central building was in sight, Declinu was short of breath. He glanced behind him. 'Everyone from miles about must have gathered to see us!' he thought, for behind them all the people of the settlement were tightly packed, jostling to catch a glimpse of the monks.

He heard the people talking with wonder of their guests. He was relieved that he understood some of their speech. His long hours of study had not been in vain.

The door to the chieftain's hall was a cured cow hide. A warrior pulled it aside and a short fat man carrying a long, intricately carved staff greeted them within. The building was circular with a roof that formed the shape of a cone. Declinu tried to make out how high the ceiling was but the darkness engulfed it. Massive beams supported the sides of it yet the covering seemed to be made only of reeds. There were skins, furs and linen-hangings decorating the walls. And the hall was full of smoke from the hearth fire.

The man at the door spoke to them in broken Latin. 'Welcome to the house of Brecan.'

Declinu leaned in close to the doorkeeper. 'Who taught you to say those words?' he whispered in his rustic Gaelic.

The man pointed at a thin dark-haired figure who stood behind his chieftain and said, 'Cieran, Bardagh.' Then he led them to seats on benches that had been set aside in the centre of the hall around the fire. A large, slightly overweight man with a yellow beard that showed a hint of greying stood politely and waited for them to take their seats. He was obviously the chieftain known as Brecan.

The one called Cieran sat on the left side of Declinu, and Palladius took his place on Brecan's left. It was part of Declinu's task to translate as much as he could of the evening's conversation.

Although all of the monks who had come with the bishop had studied what little could be found in the libraries of Gaul and Britain concerning the languages of Hibernia, Declinu knew more than any of them. He had spent nearly six months as the student of a Breton monk called Kallan, who had himself passed many years among the southern tribes of the island and so knew a good deal of their speech.

Kallan had often described the Hibernians to him: their brutality, their boasting and their feasting. He had spoken of their love of stories and songs and music. He had told everything that he could recall of his days as a captive.

'We are come to this land as emissaries of His Holiness Celestine who is, by the grace of God, the Lord Bishop of the Holy Roman Church,' declared

Palladius. Declinu translated his master's words.

'You are welcome here,' proclaimed the thin dark-haired Cieran. 'Brecan, chieftain of the southern tribes of the Soghain, welcomes you.' The man spoke perfect Latin without a trace of any regional accent.

'Where did you learn to speak the Roman tongue so well?' enquired Declinu once Cieran had returned to his seat.

'I was a student at the Druid universities in Alban and Armorica. Latin is spoken by many of the scholars there.'

'But you have no accent! You speak it better than the Pope himself,' said Declinu, diplomatically using broken Gaelic so the bishop would not understand.

'I was once a resident at the monastery in the Isle of Glass. An old Druid there taught me how to speak the foreign words clearly.'

'A Druid in a Christian monastery!' gasped Declinu in disbelief. 'It can't be true.'

'In that part of Britain there has always been a deep friendship between the old ways and the new. The holy Christian brothers share their houses with the travelling Druids of our people. I have often told Brecan of the Christian ways and he views Christ as a great hero at least equal to any in our legends. He wishes to hear the full story from you and your bishop. I will translate if you like and together we can present the story to him.'

'But you are a pagan priest!' protested Declinu. 'How do I know that you will translate exactly what the bishop says?'

'I am sworn to truth. It would be unthinkable for me to change your meaning or pervert the heart of your teachings. Besides, I have heard the tale and it is a good one.' Then Cieran laughed a little. 'But

I am no priest, not as you know them. We do not have priests. I am a storyteller. My role is that of keeper of history and law.'

Declinu nodded, not quite understanding.

'That is my role in life. By our ways everyone has a part to play in the community,' resumed Cieran. 'The chieftain has duties that he must perform before he may exercise his rights. For example, he is entitled to wear clothes of five colours. I, as a bard, am entitled to four. A king may wear six. The High-King may wear seven.'

'The king?' began Declinu astounded. 'High-King? You have kings?'

'Of course we do. How do you think the land is governed?'

'I thought you were all savage.' With that comment he realised he had gone too far and bit his tongue.

'Do not worry,' Cieran reassured him, 'I believed the same of Romans, until I met one.'

As they talked, food was brought to them on large bronze trays and the hungry brothers ate their fill. Brecan, his wife and his daughters all waited patiently for the bishop's story. The warriors too came into the hall and Declinu noticed that they had left their weapons outside.

When he had eaten, Palladius, speaking through Declinu and Cieran, began the story of Christ. Throughout the tale Brecan occasionally interrupted the narration to question some detail or to call for more drink and food, but for the better part of the evening the chieftain sat enthralled as the tale unfolded.

Cieran, concerned as he was for keeping the tale pure in its essence, conferred often with Declinu on the exact meaning of a certain word. In the end the night proved to be not long enough for a full account of the early Christian church but Palladius told of their own adventures since departing Britain. As the dawn approached he ended with an account of the unexplained murder of Linus.

Brecan was deeply moved by all that he heard and ashamed that one of the heroes of this saga had died only the night before last and within the boundaries of the country of the Soghain. He rose and bowed low to the monks and then he motioned for his warriors to gather round him. With backs to their guests they engaged in a heated discussion; then he and his soldiers left the hall as the first light streamed under the cow hides.

'You see,' explained Cieran after they had left, 'he is personally responsible for the death of your companion because as strangers you fall under his protection. The law demands that he pay you a fine for the murder, though we know not who committed the crime. Such a custom is called the payment of an eric.'

'But he was not even aware of our landing!' protested Declinu. 'How could he hold himself responsible for the misfortunes that befell us?'

'It is the law and the custom,' answered Cieran. 'He must make a payment to you in compensation for your companion's death. Also your bishop has proven to be a very brave and honourable man. The journey that you undertook was extremely dangerous and yet he did not take the opportunity to boast of it.'

'Are we to be permitted to stay here then?' asked Declinu.

'Brecan's advisers will meet today and discuss the matter,' answered Cieran in a diplomatic tone. 'I will then advise Brecan on what course of action is best.'

He offered a glass of liquor to his guest and then

returned to relating Brecan's predicament. 'Each person in our society has a certain value placed on their life,' he explained. 'If they are injured, or insulted, they or their family may claim recompense from the injurer. Your party, however, presents a unique problem. Usually the fine would be paid out in cattle, but you have no land on which to keep cows, so we will need to agree on some form of compromise.'

Declinu watched the young man as he spoke. His gestures were flowing and expressive and there was a gentleness about him that Declinu found reassuring and calming. He spoke with authority and yet with humility and this was what impressed Declinu most. The Roman brother found that he was quickly developing a respect for the Druid; he even felt that had circumstances been different they might have been great friends, for they were kindred spirits. But Declinu knew that he could not afford to get too close to the Hibernian. Palladius would certainly not approve.

'For the time being your bishop will be given the chieftain's own house in which to rest. In a few hours we will summon him and give our judgment. You and your brothers may rest in my house until then.'

'Thank you,' said Declinu sincerely—his head was by now spinning from lack of sleep. So much had happened this day that he was a little confused by it all.

Cieran led the brothers to comfortable quarters that were really just a smaller version of the chieftain's hall and Declinu slept soundly until he was called for a meal just before noon. Palladius came to join them at Cieran's house.

After a prayer of thanksgiving they ate of the foods provided for them and talked while they waited for the expected summons.

Seginus reasoned that they should try to escape from the fort while they could.

'They are savages,' he asserted. 'Worse than animals.'

'Animals do not speak Latin quite so well,' observed Declinu.

'Mark my words, we will regret the faith we place in them,' rejoined Seginus, full of anger. 'They have already been responsible for one death, how many more of us must perish at their hands?'

'You have spent too long among the Saxons,' interrupted Donatus. 'They truly are untrustworthy savages.'

'But they have the same laws and customs as us and they came to the Cross in their hundreds!'

'Eventually,' admitted the old scribe, 'but, as I recall, it took three auxiliary legions to persuade them.'

'They are an honourable and proud people,' said Seginus with rising indignation. 'As the people of Rome were before they let themselves get fat on the generosity of the church!'

'How dare you speak to your elders like that?' shouted Donatus, barely containing his rage at the ill-concealed insult.

Palladius brought his fist down heavily on the table. 'That is enough!' he bellowed. 'What more did the Druid say to you?' he asked, turning to Declinu.

'He told me that they felt responsible for the death of Linus.'

'So they admit it!' interrupted Seginus.

Declinu ignored this latest outburst. 'Cieran says it is their custom to compensate victims of crime,' he continued, going on to explain the situation as he understood it.

'I will ask the chieftain for land to build a

church,' declared Palladius after he had heard what Declinu had to relate, 'and then I will offer him the Chrism. In the meantime, go off and seek solitude and guidance, all of you. I will not have you bickering at a time like this.'

The brothers bowed to their bishop and quickly left him to sit alone in the house of Cieran.

As they were going their separate ways, Declinu caught the attention of Isernus.

'Brother,' he called, 'may I walk with you?'

'Of course you may,' Isernus answered warily.

Declinu drew level with his companion. 'I have noticed your strong feelings over the death of Linus,' he began tactfully.

'He was my friend,' snapped the younger monk. 'I trusted him more than any other man on Earth.'

'And did he betray that trust?' queried Declinu, boldly testing his theory.

Isernus stopped in his tracks and grabbed at Declinu's shoulders. 'What do you mean? What are you saying?' he yelled.

'Quiet,' urged the other monk. 'Not here. We will go somewhere where no-one can hear us talk.'

He turned the young man by the shoulders and pushed him along before him. They quickly left the village and followed the path toward the beach. It was a long walk and so it was unlikely they would be followed, but Declinu kept stopping to check for the sound of footsteps behind them. He had not forgotten how Palladius had followed him when he had been searching for Isernus. Neither of the two spoke until they had nearly reached the cairn of stones which marked the grave of Linus.

'Why are you bringing me here?' spluttered Isernus.

'So that you may make your peace with him,' answered Declinu softly but firmly. Then he took

44

the silver cross from his pouch and held it out before the trembling Isernus.

The young man looked at the cross, his face suddenly losing its colour. Then stumbling across to the mound, he knelt down among the stones that were arranged to spell out the name 'Linus' in narrow Roman letters.

'Is this yours?' asked Declinu. 'I found it among the ashes of the vigil fire.'

'Brother,' Isernus replied, 'will you hear my confession?'

'Yes, of course I will, my friend,' answered the older monk in relief. 'How have you sinned?'

'He told me to meet him on the beach,' began the boy, breaking into a sob. 'I did not know ... I mean, we were friends!' The tears rolled down the his cheeks. 'He grabbed me but I didn't realise what he wanted to do until he tried to tear off my robe. I panicked ... I didn't understand ... He was my friend ... The leather thong that held my cross must have snapped in the struggle. He was mad with lust. I fought him hard but he was stronger. Then I felt the knife he kept in his belt ... As we grappled I took it ... I only meant to scare him off, but before I knew what had happened he was falling forward clawing at the hilt ... There was blood everywhere.' Isernus broke down and pushed the heels of his hands into his eye-sockets, wailing uncontrollably. 'How can I live with myself? I have murdered a sainted martyr!' he sobbed.

'You will do penance, but no-one save God and myself will ever know of your crime, I swear it,' promised Declinu. Then he sat down beside the boy and put an arm round his shoulders and Isernus fell into his confessor's lap until the sorrow had subsided.

THREE

recan, who was the chieftain of the tribes of the people of Soghain dwelling in the Kingdom of Munster, determined, as was his right and duty, to grant to Palladius and his successors both land and cattle, and the freedom to build a church and dwellings for his followers. In this matter, as in most matters, he regarded himself as being very shrewd indeed. Brecan prided himself on always planning ahead. He was famous for it.

But his counsellor, Cieran, did not immediately perceive the true purpose of his chieftain's plan. As was the duty of an adviser, he pressed Brecan to consider the long-term effect that this decision would have on his own folk.

'You heard the story they told, of the man hung on a tree by his enemies,' reasoned Brecan, 'who became a god as a result, and rose from the dead.' His full moustache wafted over his lips in time with his speech. 'It is clear to me that Christos is a hero and the son of a god. Indeed, he himself may well have been a god on Earth.'

'The Christians believe not that he is *a* god but rather the *one and only* god.' argued Cieran.

'*A* god or *the* god, it could not possibly harm us to be under the added protection of Christos.' Brecan did not pursue the point; he saw by the Druid's skeptical expression that Cieran was not

46

particularly impressed by this argument, so he decided to let him in on the deeper reason for his decision. 'These people have voyaged over the perilous sea and faced death a hundred times to reach here. Do you think that there will be no others who will come? If we turn them away now, what will happen when thirty of their kind arrive on our doorstep? Who will tend to them? Who will feed them?'

Cieran did not answer him. He was striving hard to follow Brecan's line of thinking.

'As the situation stands it is my responsibility to recompense them for the death of their companion, and to clothe them and feed them, and that is placing a huge burden on the whole village. But if I grant them land and cattle now and then one day thirty more of them wash up on the beach, it will be the bishop who must provide for them, for they are his clanspeople.' He smugly waited for Cieran to give his approval of the reasoning.

'That is true enough, under the precedents of the law,' stated the Druid, 'but surely only the King of Munster can give such a grant to foreigners.' He ran the fingers of his left hand over his shaved forehead in a commonly recognised sign among his kind which indicated that while he did not necessarily approve, legally his chieftain was in the right.

'The King of Munster is not here, I am. And a decision must be made. While we wait a month for an answer from the Rock of Cashel we must still feed them. They will do us no harm if we treat them fairly and who knows their god may prove to be a better provider than most of the others we have sacrificed to!'

'Palladius would have you become a sworn follower of Christ.'

'I see no harm in that,' said Brecan, sweeping his hand through the air as if to dismiss the importance of it.

'You may not find the bishop very accepting of our ways.'

'I have been chieftain here for a mere twenty years. Our ways have not changed in a thousand. Do you really believe that these men will make any real difference to our lives?'

'If I were you, Brecan,' began Cieran, trying to put his view as diplomatically as he could, 'I would pray to the new God that it does not.'

In the next weeks both Brecan and Cieran took daily instruction from Palladius and the other monks in the ways of the Roman Christians.

Brecan devoured the tales of tribal leaders guiding their kin through the desert, of evil despots who brought about the suffering and destruction of their people when they refused to accept the rulings of the One True God, and most of all the tales of the miracles and parables of Christ.

Cieran was too learned in the ways of his kind to accept all the tales as absolute fact; he also knew of the Greek convention of allegory. More importantly, however, he was suspicious of the bishop's true motives. Despite his reservations, though, he began to understand the hidden messages in all that he was told, the subtle morality that lay behind all the stories. He spent many hours debating with Declinu and eventually realised that there was little essential difference between the teachings of Christ and the learning of his own folk.

'You speak often of your laws,' enquired Declinu

one morning as they sat together in the sun, 'may I read them?'

'The laws are not written down,' replied Cieran. 'They are remembered word for word. Our ancestors knew the danger of written words. Once a law is put down in black and white it is open to interpretation, since the inflection, the mood, the inner meaning can only be transmitted by an orator.'

'But any law-keeper could add his own shades of meaning to the laws!' protested Declinu.

'No. We are bound to keep them perfectly preserved in our memory. We do not interpret the laws. We keep them safe. We guard them. It is the kings and High-King who must ensure they are justly implemented.'

'But a king could choose to exercise the rulings of a Druid in many ways that might not reflect the true spirit of the law,' rejoined Declinu.

'Then he would be replaced.'

'Replaced? Who in Hibernia has the power to remove a king from his throne?'

'Our kings are elected each year by the free men and free women of each kingdom. And they must pass many tests before they are installed. Finally the Druid Council of the Wise at Teamhair must approve the election and appointment according to the rules of kingship. An unjust king would not gain any advantage from bending the law to his own ends, for he would quickly be summoned to appear before the Druid Council and might be impeached even before the end of his term. The High-King is elected by the lesser kings to oversee the defence of the whole of the land. He must also be endorsed by the Druid Council.'

'What is this Druid Council that you speak of?' asked Declinu. 'You have not mentioned them before.'

Cieran laughed. 'You are worse than a little child with all your questions!'

Then he realised that he was enjoying teaching Declinu what he knew and that he was developing a genuine liking for the monk.

'The Great Council is made up of twelve senior Druids, men and women. The High-Druid presides over the Council. He or she is generally a very old and learned member of the poetic order. The High-Druid is not empowered to make major decisions alone, only to keep the peace between all others on the Council.'

'I believe that is what the early Christian fathers had in mind for the cardinals,' mused Declinu.

'They also preserve the treaty that our folk hold with the people of Danu,' added Cieran.

'The people of Danu?' gasped Declinu. 'Aren't they the race of wizards who lived in Hibernia before your people?'

He was interrupted by the loud ringing of a bell across the settlement calling the monks to prayer. 'Goodness! That's the Angelus. It is midday! The bishop will boil me down for a soup if I'm late to devotions.' Then a thought crossed the monk's mind. 'Will you join me at Mass, Cieran?'

The Druid smiled broadly. 'I have been wondering how long it would take for you to ask me. It has been nearly a moon since you arrived among us.'

They walked silently together to the temporary wooden chapel that lay just outside the perimeter of the settlement. Declinu was growing day by day to love his new home. His hosts were generous with their time and their wealth, though it could only be counted in cows. There were rarely any disputes in the community and those that did occur were settled quickly. Everyone trusted each other and revelled in sharing their good fortune with as many of their neighbours as possible. The worth of people was not just something rendered in terms of how many cattle they owned; each person was valued for his or her individuality.

'In the monastery, the air is full of rebukes and criticism,' thought Declinu as they walked. 'Often the most gifted Christians are forced to take to the life of a hermit in order to avoid conflict with their superiors. There is constant penance, punishment, corruption, dishonesty. Priests purchase high office as if a full purse was the only qualification required for a man of God. In these days, where in all the Church lies the love that Christ spoke of?'

As they passed by the door of one of the houses that lay lower down the slope, a woman came out and placed a warm bundle wrapped in linen in Declinu's hands. 'It is the bread for your sacrifice,' she explained.

Declinu thanked her, and they passed on. 'There is more Christian love here in the hearts of these heathen than there has been in Rome for nearly four hundred years,' he realised.

As they neared the chapel they found Palladius waiting for them. 'You are late,' he said simply to Declinu, ignoring his guest. 'This is becoming a regular occurrence. In penance you will fast for seven days, letting nothing but the Holy Sacrament pass your lips. And you will pray at the altar of the shrine of Linus every day for twelve hours. Now go to your services.'

Declinu bowed in acquiescence and handed the sacred bread to Palladius. Then he went to gather his Gospels and prayer books and set off to the beach at the stone chapel that held the tomb of Linus. If he was nurturing a love of the Hibernians he was also beginning to recognise in himself a hatred of Palladius.

'It is the influence of the heathens,' he rebuked himself, 'that lets such thoughts enter your head about your Holy Father and teacher.'

But then he had to admit that he had long regarded the bishop with some distaste. He would never forget the way he had looked at Linus that day of the storm. There was something devilish about Palladius. He crossed himself. Such thoughts were heresy and he resolved to pray for guidance.

Cieran remained for a while at the door beside Palladius but said nothing. In the end he did not enter the chapel as he had planned. He departed to take the long way round to the beach.

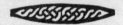

On the seashore, on the very spot where the body of Linus lay forever under a covering of stones, the brothers from Rome eventually replaced the little stone chapel with a fine church. It was not a grand edifice such as those they had all seen on the continent; their whole church would not have filled a chapel of one of the European churches. It was built of stone because that was the most readily available material on the rocky beach. Palladius constructed his first ecclesiastical monument not necessarily for permanence, but certainly for effect. The altar slab that marked the tomb of Linus was designed to be the focal point of the whole structure and the long narrow windows of the church were positioned to throw light down upon it throughout the day.

Brecan supplied the labourers; the bishop supplied the inspiration. The two became fast allies, although Palladius referred to their relationship as a partnership. He saw Brecan merely as a means to an end, a way to keep a foothold on the island and to establish a foundation for future expansion.

Brecan the Chieftain quickly came to look upon the little stone house of God as a great achievement. He fully expected to be remembered as its builder in songs and stories. In the end, that was all that was really important to him.

There had not been any wars in his lifetime in which to earn glory or show valour. Unfortunately for Brecan's adventurous spirit, Leoghaire High-King of Eirinn had begun his reign well, and before him, Cormac had ruled long and justly. There had been twenty years of peace: no call for real warriors or real deeds. So Brecan could only listen to the old tales of bravery in the evening by the fire and imagine himself a hero.

Not that he was completely unknown. In his youth he had been famous for his strength and his boasting. Famous, too, for the table that he laid for guests. But it was never enough for him to be a fine host. He was growing old now, and more than a little fat. He tired quickly and sometimes his wife found him dozing by the fire at midday, digesting a meal. The chapel was perhaps his last chance to make a lasting mark.

When the Chapel of the Cairn was completed and the high Mass said at its altar, Palladius set the next phase of his plan into operation. On the first anniversary of the death of Linus a wondrous miracle occurred.

By chance, Palladius and Seginus were praying together in the chapel, sharing the midnight vigil, when Linus himself, accompanied by none other than the Blessed Virgin Mary, appeared to them and instructed them on how to go about evangelising the rest of the country. The Sainted Martyr

Linus also made some rather flattering predictions regarding the future status of the local chieftain, Brecan of the Soghain.

'Very astute for one so recently introduced to sainthood,' thought Declinu when he heard what Linus had revealed. 'A pity that he was not so gifted a diplomat in life.' Then he realised that he was being very unjust. 'Perhaps there is some truth in it,' he conceded.

Brecan certainly seemed to think so. And not long after the holy visitation, just to confirm the new exalted status of Linus, a miracle healing took place. For a month Brecan's youngest son had suffered a strange malady that caused him to vomit and faint. The sickness came in spells lasting a few days, after which he would be fine again for a short while. After four weeks he was so weakened by the loss of fluid that everyone was certain he would soon die.

When it seemed there was no other hope, Palladius convinced Brecan to allow the boy to be taken to the altar for prayers to be chanted over his body. Brecan gave his approval, thinking that the boy would die anyway and that it would not hurt to try.

Within a day of being laid on the altar, the lad was running with the calves in their enclosure, and the illness did not return. Palladius quickly announced that Linus had intervened on behalf of the boy and cured him. This incident finally convinced Brecan that he should succumb to pressure from Palladius and he approached the bishop begging to be Christianed.

At a solemn ceremony he accepted the Word of the Gospels, had the demons exorcised from him and finally took the holy Chrism. Following his example, most of the clanspeople from all around the settlement eagerly lined up to join the swelling ranks of the converted.

Miracle healings became more and more common in the chapel and the place became known as Ardmór, the Great Cairn. Brecan achieved a degree of fame, which suited him well enough, he became known as the guardian of the relics of Saint Linus. But, for Palladius, Ardmór was only a stepping stone and he quickly outgrew it. One day, not long after Brecan had taken the Sacrament, Palladius declared his intention to leave for Teamhair where the High-King held court.

'I am going to convert the Emperor of this island to the faith so that the whole country will more readily accept the word,' he announced.

Considering his ambivalent attitude to the regular appearances of Linus and the Virgin Mary, Declinu was a little surprised to be nominated abbot of the new monastic settlement in the bishop's absence. Isernus, a man who went out of his way to keep his opinions to himself, was put forward to be his deputy. Seginus and Donatus were commissioned to go north with Palladius.

When the implications of the bishop's decision hit him, Declinu discovered that he was not at all upset to see either Palladius or Seginus leave. He had come to admire his hosts and to respect their way of doing things. The bishop, however, continually referred to them as heathen, even when speaking of the most devout among the people of Brecan. Declinu by now considered Palladius a narrow-minded and unjust man, who was at times vicious and ungodly and whose behaviour was a regular embarrassment to him.

As for Seginus, Declinu knew him to be bad-tempered and abusive, treating all the Hibernians with a contempt bordering on outright hate. He rarely spoke to any of them, unless in rebuke, or to harangue them about the evil of their pagan ways.

Declinu could not see what was so bad about their customs. They were an honest and trustworthy people. They had a code of law and honour that was certainly not Roman in its inspiration, but it was in some ways a fairer system. They valued highly the skills of artists and musicians and poets. They respected the rights of others and protected and sheltered strangers. Palladius, on the other hand, trusted few people.

'At last I will be able to do things without feeling the cold breath of that old crow on the back of my neck,' thought Declinu. 'I will be able to work closer with my good friends here.' His companionship with Cieran crossed his mind. 'I will no longer live in fear of retribution.'

Then he suddenly appreciated how much he had begun to think like his hosts. They despised restrictions and revelled in the opportunity for creative endeavour. 'At last I will be free of that dry, withered scold.' He laughed aloud at the rebellious nature of his thoughts and then crossed himself and resolved to confess this latest sin to his confidant, Isernus.

'Isernus. Now there is a miraculous transformation,' thought the new abbot. 'He has changed from the shy soft-spoken brother I first met in Gaul, to a well-rounded confident man, quietly proud of his own achievements. He has worked tirelessly for this community through the times of hardship and disease. He has gained their respect and admiration. They treat him as a man born to their country, an equal.'

Through all the trials of the previous year Isernus had managed to keep secret the terrible murder of Linus and the circumstances that led to it. None knew save his confessor Declinu. Isernus had overseen the construction of the church and had spent every spare moment of his life in earnest prayer. Only Declinu was aware that this was the penance he was performing for his crime.

Palladius, Seginus and Donatus left for Teamhair on the day after the feast of the Resurrection.

'I will send you word upon our arrival,' Palladius reassured Declinu, 'and I will send letters to Rome. But you will report directly to me only. Do you understand?'

'Yes, Lord.'

'Very well.' He touched the abbot's head and exclaimed for all those present to hear, '*Pax vobiscum.*'

The fifty or so people who had gathered at the edge of the settlement responded as one voice, in their own Gaelic tongue, 'And also with you.'

Two further years were to pass before the community at Ardmór heard so much as a word from Palladius, though Declinu had sent written reports to Teamhair regularly, and penned many other requests for an answer to his letters. He had finally, out of sheer desperation, sent a messenger to find the bishop; but the courier never returned nor was he ever heard of again.

When a rider finally reached the abbot at his little community, there was great excitement and many of the lay people gathered to wait for the news that he carried. His servant searched the whole community for him, missing the obvious places but letting everyone know what was happening. 'Abbot Declan! Abbot! Where are you?'

Declan, as he had come to be known by his flock, knelt before the altar of the chapel, signed the cross and then walked briskly out into the morning sunshine.

A stranger was standing near the gate house talking to Isernus, gesturing passionately and raising his voice in what could only be taken as anger. One of the new young monks, a boy from the village, came up to the abbot and tugged on his sleeve.

'Abbot Declan, there is a messenger for you. He has come from the seat of the High-King!' the boy cried excitedly.

'Thank you, my son, I see already that we have a visitor. Bring him into the eating hall and fetch him some bread and mead.'

The boy rushed down to the stranger, almost tripping in his haste, spoke his words and then disappeared to prepare the food. Declan walked into the eating hall and sat at a long bench to await his visitor. He did not have to sit long. A man bearing a sword and wearing heavy travelling gear burst into the hall a short while later, dropped his bag and turned to the abbot.

'You've done well for yourself!' the stranger exclaimed. Then he kicked a chair aside and hollered, 'Well, have you no welcome for your brother in Christ?'

It took some moments for Declan to recognise Seginus Gallus. The months away had changed him somewhat and he had grown too. His clothes were also quite different. He was no longer dressed as a monk.

'Brother, two years have certainly transformed you!' The abbot stood and held out his arms.

'And you. Is it Declan they call you now?' asked Seginus.

'It means one who works hard.' Declan modestly brushed his hand past his face, dismissing the compliment the Hibernians had paid him.

'Why have you not written of all your achievements?' demanded Seginus, gesturing around him at the eating hall but meaning the progress the community had made in general.

'But I have, Brother. It is you who has not written to us,' answered Declan, confused.

A cloud passed across Seginus' face as if he had suddenly realised something that should have long been obvious. 'Damn! Damn that Leoghaire to Hell's fires!'

The visitor slammed his fist into the door and then gave the wall a mighty kick with the toe of his boot. 'I should have known not to trust him!' he yelled.

'Brother, what are you talking about?' asked Declan.

'The High-King must have been intercepting our messages. That is why we have not heard from you for so long. We were fed a rumour that the southern tribes had risen in rebellion and killed all foreigners and servants of the High-King, but now I see it was a lie to keep us in check. Damn!' He sank down into a chair. 'These savages follow no rules of war that Rome would recognise.'

'War!' Declan repeated the word in horror. 'What are you talking about, Brother?'

'Have you not heard? The High-King Leoghaire has declared that all the followers of Palladius are to be banished from Eirinn. Some of our converts, feeling that the judgment was hasty, initiated a revolt against the ruling. The hostilities rapidly escalated to the point of open warfare within a few short weeks. It has been a bitter campaign. Many good Christians have been slaughtered by these

Gaelic bastards!' He punched his fist down on the table in disgust.

'Our army has suffered several terrible defeats and twice Palladius narrowly escaped capture. He sent me here to see if either you or Isernus had managed to survive and if so to enlist your help.'

'I will help you in whatever way I can, Brother, but I am only the abbot of a small community,' stated Declan. 'If it's warriors that you need you must speak with Brecan.' He thought carefully for a moment about all that he had been told and then added, 'Why would the High-King want to banish us all? What has happened to make him take such action?'

'There are heretics at the court, Pelagians and Copts. They have the High-King's confidence and have plotted against us from the very start.'

'When did all this come to pass, Brother?' queried the abbot, still in shock at the news.

'The war has been going on for some six months. We were virtually imprisoned in the royal enclosure for over a year before that. Finally the bishop could take it no longer and we made an escape.'

'You escaped from a royal palace? Were there no guards?' Declan remembered his teacher Kallan's story about hostage-taking, but he said nothing of it to Seginus.

'King Dichu of the Kingdom of Laigin came to our assistance. He is a Christian king now. It was a desperate fight and we only just managed to get away with our lives. Donatus is dead. The long imprisonment was too much for him.'

Declan crossed himself and silently wished eternal rest upon the old scribe. However, he got the distinct impression that not all the facts were being presented to him.

'What do you seek from us then, Brother? How

may we be of assistance?' asked the abbot.

'I want all your Christian warriors,' explained Seginus. 'I will take every able-bodied man we can lay our hands on. Isernus is to come with me also.'

'Isernus! But who will help me here?' protested Declan. 'I cannot run this outpost alone. And what if the High-King should come searching for you? How do we defend ourselves with all the warriors gone to fight in the north? And what of the cattle, who will tend them? And the ploughing and planting?'

'That is not up to me,' insisted Seginus. 'These are the orders of Bishop Palladius himself. And I can assure you that Leoghaire will not bother to send troops to the south. A High-King has never before successfully entered the Kingdom of Munster by force, and his army cannot spare the manpower at the moment anyway. Palladius is supporting Dichu of Laigin for the High-Kingship.'

Declan was incensed, realising the bishop was playing politics to further his own ends. 'What if I refuse to allow my flock to be dragged into a war?' he declared defiantly.

'Don't be a bloody fool! Palladius would wipe you off the face of God's Earth! In these last two months I've seen him hang men whose only crime was that they neglected to bow their heads on entering a chapel. I would not like to be even the Abbot of Ardmór if Palladius were your enemy.'

Declan turned his head down to look at the floor. Anger began to burn in him and he was struggling to control himself and think clearly. As soon as he had quieted himself sufficiently he placed the palms of his hands flat on the table before him with his arms outstretched. He breathed slowly and deliberately, mastering his emotions and curbing his tongue from uttering any insult.

When finally he spoke, his voice was determined and quiet. 'Leave us in peace. We have prospered since you went off to Teamhair and the people are coming to our community in droves. This news could well turn them against us.'

'Obviously you do not understand the urgency of the situation,' snarled Seginus. 'If Palladius is banished from Eirinn, so are you! Then where will your people come for guidance?'

'I have not wronged the High-King. He will not seek to punish me,' returned Declan.

Seginus groaned contemptuously. 'You always were a bloody coward. I will never forget the first night we spent here in this Godforsaken land. Your cowardice is the only reason my brother lies now rotting under a hill of beach pebbles in a poxy chapel at the far end of the Earth!' He made a sweeping movement with his arm.

'Now that I have time to look about me, I can see that you have become more savage than even the heathen Gaels. I am going to speak with Brecan, then I will return to see if you are still of the same mind. But really there is nothing left you can do to counter the bishop's orders. Isernus will be coming with me when I leave tomorrow no matter what.'

He once more slammed his fist into the wooden trestle table and it shook violently. 'God help you when this war is over because I promise you that Palladius will hunt you down and then you will die the death of a heretic.' He got up from his seat, grabbed a hunk of bread and stormed out of the room, leaving Abbot Declan to ponder his future.

In the early hours of the next morning Isernus and twenty warriors of the Soghain, led by Brecan in his finest ceremonial armour, mounted their horses and prepared to leave Ardmór. The chieftain had quickly and eagerly agreed to go with

Seginus. It was perhaps the last chance he would ever have to take part in any sort of adventure.

Declan waited patiently at the gates to the settlement as the warriors rode out, blessing each and praying for their safe return.

Finally Seginus drew his horse level to the abbot and let the mare stand for a short while. When Declan did not initiate the conversation, Seginus only said, 'You are decided then? You will not even send food and clothes or any other aid to support the cause?'

'I will not support insanity no matter what form it takes,' answered Declan. 'We came here to conquer with the Word not with the sword. My conscience will not allow me to aid you. Palladius is perverting the spirit of our mission by becoming involved in the political disputes of this kingdom. And you are ignoring my wishes as abbot of this community.'

Seginus spat. 'We'll see if you speak so when they put a rope round your neck.' Then he spoke loudly for all to hear. 'By the authority given to me by the bishop of this land, Palladius, I declare you, Declan, so-called Abbot of Ardmór, to be heretic and anathema. Any that harbour you or assist you are libel to the same penalty that you will surely face when this war is ended—death!'

Then he leaned over in his saddle so that only Declan would hear what he said next. 'May I return soon to carry out the sentence!'

The envoy of Palladius turned his horse and rode off at the head of his small force. Isernus looked back at his friend, confused and powerless to change the frightening course of events. With genuine regret he waved a cautious farewell to his peaceful life.

Abbot Declan stood by the gate, broken-hearted

that, after all, their work was likely to end in a deadly conflict. 'Maybe that was the meaning of the omen that was sent to us on our first night in this land. Perhaps we failed the test in our first hours on this island,' he thought.

He recalled ruefully that the life of Linus could have been saved if only he, himself, had not been so willing to give in to temptation. If he had not listened to the clever arguing of Linus, that monk would still be among them. Then perhaps none of what later came to pass would have been possible. Perhaps even this war may not have come to be.

He pulled the heavy wooden gates shut behind him, turned on his heel and went inside to compose a letter to Pope Celestine in Rome. On his way he called to his steward, 'Fetch me my horse and enough provisions to get me to Teamhair!'

FOUR

n the seat closest to the fire sat a young-looking man of perhaps thirty years, sipping mead from a wooden bowl. He wore the simple dark-blue woollen wrap of his order over a plain, undyed tunic. It was not any of these badges, though, that so obviously marked him as a filidh. Only an initiated poet travelled the land with harp and Brandubh cloth. Only a greatly respected storyteller sat in the warmest part of the house before sunset.

Olan, the wife of his host Midhna, busied herself making loaves for the evening meal. The sweet aroma of yeasted dough spread through the dwelling, delicately spicing the air.

With reverence the man set his carved bone and earthenware playing pieces on a painted linen before him. He placed the little High-King in the middle of the cloth and closely grouped the other four white kings around that centre piece. At the edges of the linen he put the earthen pieces, leaderless and desperate. They soon stood in groups of three, guarding the four holy houses of Summer, Winter, Autumn and Spring. They were known as the Brandubh: the Ravens.

Within moments, in the secret manner of a Druid, an intangible part of him had begun to focus itself on the task at hand. The ritual chant that he was recalling for summoning the ancestors to bear witness to the game was ancient beyond reckoning.

His lips began to move, mouthing the words of the Blessing of the Brandubh, a liturgy he had repeated many times. His grey eyes sparkled in the firelight and his blue-black hair shone.

A child of the household, full of an infant's curiosity, made a spirited attempt to climb onto his knee, slipping as she did so. With one arm he caught her up in a smooth, graceful sweep. He set her down again on the floor before a cry of dismay could even pass her lips. Then he patted her on the head indulgently and returned to his contemplations.

Although the sky was still lit by the dying sun, in the firelight this little corner of the cottage already seemed trapped in the depths of night. The blue-clad wanderer who was reciting the archaic consecration of the Brandubh could, for all the world, have been some Faery being locked in contest with an invisible opponent.

In due course he finished the blessing and then sat patiently awaiting his summons. His mind closed to all the activity around him and he began to induce a deeper state of relaxation throughout his being.

His very presence at this fireside sent waves of excitement rippling from the doorstep of the house, through the settlement and out to the people working in the fields. The news of his arrival passed on the breeze from one clan-holder to another. It had been many months since a Druid, filidh, brehon or bard had visited this settlement. These people were hungry for the wisdom, words, tales and summons that he brought to them. The full cycle of a year had gone by since a poet of his standing had last shared the hearth of Midhna's clan. This night the whole community, nearly thirty people, would crowd around a fire in the fallow field, suffering any discomfort to hear his words.

In the metal forge, Midhna, the man of iron, and his two eldest sons worked on, finishing the craftwork for two sets of plough harnesses.

A sturdy oak-built paling housed the bellows and its fuel-fed fires that near two hundred years of constant use had marked with layers of soot and scorched caked ash. The forge no longer produced swords, arrowheads and helms as it had during the clan wars of three generations before. Now the descendants of Maoile the Giant, who first fired the forge, cast nails, needles and iron rings. The heavy hammers fell on sickles, hunting knives and farm tools. It was hot, demanding labour. The semicircular hearth set in a pit lined with stone remained one of the few left working in the kingdom of Munster. There were only a handful of able smiths still remaining in the land of Eirinn. The steady pump of the leather bellows, the ringing beat of the hammer, the searing flames and choking smell of white hot coals, this was Midhna's inheritance.

The ironworkers looked toward ending their toil for the day. The cool reward of the evening's merriment beckoned. Brother Sun made ready to depart on his journey to the lands over the Western Ocean. The smith's sons, Cen and Beoga, stoked the forge for the night, uttering a song of thankfulness to the miracle of fire while their father collected buckets of charcoal and stacked it all against the stones in the fuel room.

Throughout this night, as with every night time out of memory, one member of the team would remain on watch in the forge to stoke the fire and ensure that it did not spread to the roof-tree and thence engulf the whole building. This night the duty fell to Beoga and he was sullen at missing the chance to hear Gobann the Filidh speak.

Elsewhere, the young men and women whose work was less taxing collected fallen timber for the building of a bonfire. A night such as this would surely be warm and dry and the evening could be given over to tale-telling.

In the midst of all the activity, Gobann stirred from his meditations by the fireside. 'It is time,' he announced in a detached manner. Standing, he bowed to his hostess and, leaving the Ravens waiting in place to begin their game-play, he moved toward the low door.

Stopping just outside, he searched the sky for his silent companion: She who watched over him on this Earth. He found her resting, deep in the darkening blueness that would soon be evening. She was bright, defiant and alone, as ever the first of the stars each evening to reveal herself to the Earthfolk. With a formality that bespoke sincere homage, he clutched his hand to his breast and spoke.

'Greetings to you, Queen of the Night, radiant Even-star. Watch over my work in this place.' Mind and soul he was preparing to perform a difficult and painful duty.

His thoughts strayed to imagining what life may have been like had he not taken the Druid path, had he not been sundered from the kindred that he loved and not been promised to poetry and to truth.

'There is too much to prepare,' came his inner words of self-discipline, 'too much at stake for you to allow any self-indulgent thoughts to steal your attention at this time.'

Thus reprimanded he turned, smiling, to face the waiting clanspeople. He spoke in the soothing tones of the storyteller's craft and his clear, resonant voice bounced off the stone walls of the clustered round-houses to echo in the small courtyard. 'The First Star is the traveller's guide. Those who know her station in the heavens are never lost.

'The First Star carries within her spirit the yearning that reunites all who endure the pain of separation from their kinfolk. She is the unstoppable force who brings them together again, over the distance of oceans or of lifetimes.'

By habit and design Gobann allowed none of his true thoughts to betray themselves to his audience, but the bitterness groaned deeply in the back of his mind, teasing cruelly, saying, 'That at least is the theory.' No sooner had the emotion formed into thought, than Gobann suppressed it and outwardly removed any expression from his face. All the many years of his crafting would need to be brought to bear in the next few days. The circumstance touched too close to his own experience and it threatened to open old wounds.

He turned to face the Even-star once more, seeking to bathe himself in the feeble distant light. After a few moments, without taking his eyes from the night-sky, he spoke. 'This is the theme of the tale of the Leaving of Oisin.'

People were now rushing ahead of Gobann to take up positions at the edge of the field, fearing that a story might begin without them. The loss of one word would be a grief to any of them, so rare and precious was the tale-weaver's gift.

Gobann was not one to hasten. He knew well his art. For the tale-telling to be effective he must wait until the right moment to commence. He certainly would not begin any speech before reciting the welcomes and the graces. Besides which, his host had not finished work for the day and might be some while yet.

The poet took the opportunity to stroll at an unhurried pace down the cow track that led from the courtyard to the field. As always a group of younger children tagged along close behind him.

'I can risk offence to no-one,' he gently reminded himself. 'One wrong word, any sign of doubt or insult, and my task will be that much the more difficult.'

Ahead of him lay the place of meetings. His eyes scanned the assembly as he tried to put names to faces. Near the main trestle tables sat the family of Scéolan the weaver. Gobann's gaze was irresistibly drawn to the old man's long gnarled fingers.

'Each profession carries a mark,' he thought. 'The weaver wears reddened eye-sockets and clawlike hands from a life spent before the loom. The farmer sports bowed legs and browned skin, the legacy of long exposure to wind and weather and back-breaking labour. The blacksmith shakes ashy soot from his hair with callused hands that have grown to fit the hammer. But what of the storyteller?'

In his quietly confident way he returned a friendly greeting to a familiar face as more thoughts took form. 'In time what marks a filidh to his profession? By what blisters can a farmer gauge the worth of a poet? Will any of these folk ever even glimpse the scars that come of lifelong severance from the simple pleasures of a settled existence? Can they see the bruises that result from devotion to learning and to the ancient ways?'

His eyes fleetingly searched the sky again. 'Since the days of childhood, I have only known the stories of the Triads, the ancient Gaelic legends. I have known only the sounds of the Harp, the loom of the music-maker. I have known only the sacred Laws of the Great Store, the Seanchas Mór. I have dreaded nothing but the harsh rebukes of my teachers. But I have not suffered real hunger or want. I have been well cared for by my guardians. Yet there are times when I still wish that I could be free to be the son of a farmer.'

Someone gave a shout nearby, startling the poet from his thoughts. It was a boy of five with sandy yellow hair and a mud-splashed face. There was such joy, such excitement in those eyes and in that voice that Gobann could only smile broadly in reply.

'So young and fresh,' he thought, 'ready for to hear of wondrous deeds from far-off days. A bright face not yet lined with care or worry or fear. Children should be allowed their freedom,' his spirit screamed, 'not bent to the will of their elders.' Instantly he was ashamed of himself for entertaining such a thought, for he was well aware that he lived a life free of the hardship that was the lot of all farming folk.

The words of Lorgan Sorn, his teacher, came to him. 'Children who have not known the ravages of suffering and hardship are the brightest souls of all.' He knew, despite his inner rebellion, that there was no better life than that of a Druid.

A rush of images raced through his head, undisciplined and scattered. He struggled to maintain some control over them. Truly the task at hand was to be harder than he had expected. He fought to focus on what was happening around him. Searching the crowd, he noticed his host approaching at last and forced all his attention onto him.

From the back of the small crowd Midhna the blacksmith made his way through chattering relatives and neighbours, giving a greeting here, a word of sympathy for the grieving there. Hurriedly removing a large leather apron from around his stout belly, he went straight up to his infirm uncle, the master who had taught him the art of the smithy.

Slowly, respectfully, he bowed and touched the

man's forehead with a blistered palm. Empty eyes stared back. There was no sign of recognition. Midhna was coming to accept what all others in the village knew too well. 'That one will not be long with us,' he told himself. 'It is a miracle that he survived the winter.'

There were other informal exchanges with well-wishers as Midhna approached the central table. He was a little out of breath after the brisk walk and the ensuing pleasantries. Finally he reached Gobann who smiled warmly at him. Shyly Midhna turned away from the poet, reaching for a jug of water to conceal his reddened face. After a few quick gulps he began to recover. He remembered the words of his uncle, 'One should always be relaxed when greeting the travellers', but he always had difficulty dealing with strangers.

Midhna's glance bore an unspoken apology for his lateness as he called the gathering to silence. He did not have to ask twice.

'The Valley of the Dobharcú honours the learning of Gobann, son of Caillte of the clans of the Dál Araidhe.' His large graceless hands formed the signs of welcoming. He passed his guest a wooden mead cup. 'A hundred thousand welcomes to you!' The assembly echoed the chief and enthusiastically gulped honey-mead from similar cups.

As was the custom, Gobann took a small sip then handed the cup back to his host. Midhna drank deep, refilled the cup, and in a moment Gobann held it in his hands once more.

The poet raised the little vessel above his head with both hands and said, 'A blessing on the work of the people of this place.'

He swallowed the brew and the pleasant warmth of the thick spicy liquid clung to the back of his throat. Satisfied that hospitality was served, people took to their places.

Gobann allowed himself to be led to a bench behind a long oak table. Once settled there, he returned to his silent observations with the patience that was his hallmark. Midhna drank another, deeper draught, sucking the liquid from the bowl in undisguised delight. This was a night for storytelling and laughter!

From the hearth of each little round-house the scent of roast meat, freshly warmed bread and barley broth spread out to the tables. Gobann breathed deeply, his lungs devouring the heady odour of the feast. He felt his stomach turn with the desire for food.

Midhna looked to the poet, his expression communicating an unspoken question and, nodding his acknowledgement, Gobann raised his right hand to his breast. All became silent. When he saw that he had their undivided attention, Gobann rose from the bench to speak.

'In the name of the houses of learning, and the Court of the High-King at Teamhair, I bring you the good wishes of the Great Council of the Drúi.' He paused a moment to allow them all to take in what was said. 'In the name of Leoghaire, High-King of Eirinn, and with the blessings of the Chieftains of the Feni, I bring you tidings of the world beyond the Valley of the Black Otter.'

'We are all eager to hear your words,' said Midhna, picking up on his cue, 'but first, refresh yourself, share the last of the winter store with us and drink your fill of our honey-mead. Leave the cares of your office for a time. You have departed the Road and now you may rest.'

Gobann thought, 'With all my heart I wish that I could.' Smiling, he placed his left hand on the shoulder of his host and said, 'I thank you, master ironsmith. You and your folk are well renowned for welcomings,' he raised a cup of mead and the smile broadened, 'and for the potent waters that you teach your bees to brew! If I drink much more of it I will have no choice but to rest!'

The whole group laughed raucously at this little joke. It was well known that strangers to these parts could rarely match the locals in a bout of serious drinking, especially if Midhna supplied the mead.

'This valley is famous also,' he continued, 'for the fine poets who spring from the well of your heritage.' He paused and all went quiet, listening intently to his every word. 'Fondly and with great respect is remembered among the Druid Council the wit of your maternal grandfather, Cianan of the Sweet Melody. Truly was the sound of his harp a gift to this world from the gods.'

The assembly rose together and raised their cups to the sky, each drinking in proud silence to the memory of that honoured bard. Only Midhna of all of them sat subdued and emotionless.

Gobann cast his gaze over the crowded tables and added, 'There may be another here among you more talented than ever he was. May the gods help you to recognise and nurture such a one.'

Midhna managed to take the poet's words in good spirit and as they were intended, as honourable compliments. Outwardly he mirrored the delight of his kinfolk. Inwardly though, he was bubbling with a rage that threatened to show itself. He tried to turn his mind to something else, but could not. 'All I remember of that old man,' he recalled to himself, 'was a talent for hard drinking, abusive speech and idleness!'

Midhna felt suddenly uneasy. His face reddened.

He wondered if the poet had somehow heard his thoughts. He opened his mouth to speak, but Gobann was already talking to him.

'How many children have you now?'

Midhna picked up a jug and moved to the end of the table to serve his clansmen, answering in as casual a manner as he could muster, 'Two strong lads who work with me and five healthy girls.' As an afterthought he added, 'Of course there's the other lad. Not fit for work. He's not right in the head, you know. Yes well,' he said, voice trailing off, 'you know a bit about him.' Gobann only nodded.

Olan suddenly appeared bringing two large steaming pots, each brimming with barley broth, to the long wooden table where Gobann sat. She carefully placed one before Midhna and another in front of his guest. Then, with a round-faced hearty laugh, she dolloped a helping into Gobann's bowl and bade him enjoy.

This feast was not likely to be anything grand, the poet knew that, but there was a festive mood. People were beginning to release some of the tensions built up during the long confinement of winter.

Next passed around on great earthen platters came loaves of fresh grainy bread and slabs of that day's batch of creamy curd-cheese. The clamour of thirty country folk vigorously consuming their evening meal did not distract Midhna from the discomfort of hearing his grandfather praised.

'Only those who did not really know him call him Cianan of the Sweet Melody,' thought Midhna. 'To his family he was Cianan the Wanderer, Cianan the Lazy Drunkard.'

Butter was passed up the table in a glazed bowl. As the bowl came to him, Midhna took his knife and gouged out a piece of the delicacy, dropping it into his soup. It began to melt away before his eyes, forming a fatty skin across the top of the broth.

His thoughts continued. 'Cianan brought poverty to my kin. The forge lay silent for three seasons because of him. He left my father and his brother, my mother and all the clan for the glory of a courtly life. Those hard times were the worst in living memory.' He noticed that Olan was sitting now beside him, pushing him up the bench. He moved slightly for her. 'If it were not for my uncle, my teacher, the smithy would be silent now and we would be scratching bark from the trees to feed ourselves in the cold months.'

Midhna drank a cup of mead straight down, filled it again from a stone jug and looked at Gobann. The poet was engrossed in a discussion with Niós over the untimely deaths of some of his finer calves.

'What could this harper know of Cianan? He is surely too young to have known him.' Midhna watched Gobann's face as he talked. The poet was enthusiastically agreeing to accompany Niós to the fields in the early morning and to check the state of the hay in stock.

'All for poetry, for words,' thought Midhna. 'Pretty phrases don't till the fields. You can't persuade a bull into plough-harness with legends. Harpers daren't strike the forge hammer for fear of their delicate fingers!'

An old bitterness was rising in the blacksmith. He ate his broth slowly and observed with disgust that everyone present looked on the poet with awe. Even his son, Cen, was sitting soft-eyed soaking up Gobann's every phrase.

The words of the poet flashed through his mind.

'There may be another . . . ' The voice echoed for a moment in Midhna's memory, then the full meaning struck him like a body blow. 'This harper means to take one of my sons with him when he leaves! That's what he meant! How dare he! I will not lose either of them to the storytellers.' With that vow he brought his fist down on the table with the fiery force of his outrage.

All those present went quickly silent and all eyes turned to him in surprise.

For a moment Midhna was still too angry to realise that he had been impolite; then he yelled, 'More mead,' and most of his kin took it to mean that the blacksmith intended to get very drunk and they returned to their feasting.

Midhna stared at his beloved son Cen with fiery eyes. Observing the blacksmith's expression Gobann realised his task would not be easy.

Cen was only seventeen summers on Earth and would soon take over the running of the forge. He was so like his father that the older folk sometimes mistakenly addressed him as Midhna. Before many more years he would surely be a master of the craft, an ollamh. He was strong and a natural leader. The other young men always waited to hear his opinion and more often than not took his view or followed his advice. If Cen were to leave for Teamhair, he would be sorely missed.

At the end of the bench sat Beoga, resting a while before taking his watch at the forge. 'He has a rare eye for beauty,' thought his father, 'and the skill of a much older man. In fifteen years he has already surpassed his elders. Those intricate patterns and spirals of his, the way he turns items of mundane household use into crouching ravens or goat-headed beasts of the myths, truly mark him as a man of iron. In time with diligence,' thought

Midhna proudly, 'he may even be the better crafts-man of the two.'

The youngest of his sons had not yet begun his life of work at the forge. He had always been a sickly child and he was too small and frail to be anything but a hindrance to the elder smiths.

Midhna glanced at the lad. 'Maybe Mawn should join his brothers this season. He has never shown more than a passing interest in the working of metal. His body is too slightly built to lift the tools. He prefers his own company too much. He only ever speaks to ask some fool question or another.'

Midhna realised that he had never greeted the boy's enquiries with any real seriousness. 'A nine-year-old places importance on subjects that a grey-beard has long since forgotten about,' the blacksmith reflected. He resolved to give the lad more of his time, wondering whether perhaps the sickness had passed.

His thoughts had drifted on to the future, brood-ing on the grim possibilities, when suddenly Gobann, having finished his meal, was pushing the dishes away calling for his harp. Scéolan the old weaver who sat close to the main table breathed a knowing, 'Ahhh!' The children ran to kneel at the poet's feet. All talk hushed to a low murmur. All eyes focused on the visitor.

'Boy!' said Gobann, looking directly at Midhna's youngest son, 'fetch me some water.'

Mawn stood, startled, and ran to the house. His mother was lifting the harp in its otter-skin bag onto her shoulder when the boy bolted through the door into the gloom. He quickly grabbed a wooden jug and dipped it deep into the water barrel. Holding the jug steady, he followed Olan back to the tables.

Gobann noticed them approaching. 'The saying

goes, "It is hard to tell a story without a drink." ... Well it usually means brewed drink. My throat welcomes this cool, sweet water after the strong mead of Midhna.' He took the jug from Mawn and drank from it. Then he reached down to where Olan had placed his harp bag and removed the precious instrument from its covering. Tenderly he sat the harp on his lap and began the process of tuning the solid brass wires that were its strings. As he did so, he spoke softly to each wire in turn, coaxing them into harmony with their neighbours. No-one listened to what he said for the air was full of the rich bell-like tones of the harp which sailed with the sparks of the fire into the purple ceiling of the night.

Mawn sat lost in a music trance. He had only once before seen such a harp and that was some time ago. A two-headed salmon carved into the forepillar, one face toward heaven, the other toward earth, cast the gaze of its jet-black eyes upon him. Intricate knotwork patterns laced around the soundbox and along the curved tuning board. Fiery sparkles caught the boy's attention. Set into the forepillar were three large gems embedded in silver mounts, each stone as clear as a mountain-fed stream in spring. The brass wires reflected the firelight and seemed to be of pure gold and to exude an ancient magic.

Eventually, after what must have been an age to the waiting audience, Gobann ran his fingers down the full thirty strings, making one final check, and then he began his tale.

'At just such a feast as this,' he began, 'Oisin of the bright face, the son of Fionn, sat among the company of the Fianna.' The poet's fingers lightly touched the wires now in imitation of archaic, courtly music. The harp began to hum gently.

'Fionn MacCumhal was the greatest warrior of those times. You all have heard of his feats in battle, of the honour of his band of heroes and of their strength and valour.'

Gobann's long shaped fingernails pulled lightly on the wires. Occasionally he would touch the vibrating brass with the back of a nail, setting it buzzing wildly. The poet glanced at his host and noticed that he did not have Midhna's full attention. The man was staring into space but idly splintering the table with a meat knife. So Gobann ran his fingers down the wires again and the blacksmith started out of his daydream. After the ringing of the harp died down the poet continued the tale.

'Fionn lamented to his son of the sad and sorry state that had befallen the warrior band. The great soldier was now in the autumn of his life. Old age and infirmity kept him often at home. Too many of his brave companions had passed into the Cauldron of Rebirth to take another time on Earth or, worse, had succumbed to the torment of advancing years.'

Gobann glanced quickly at Midhna and was now satisfied that the smith was listening intently. None could resist the harp-call.

'A filidh sang in that hall of the glories past, of a time when the Fianna were famous for valorous deeds and battle fury. He sang of the adventures of Conan of the Heavy Hand, of the reign of King Oiliol, of Táillc son of Treon and the battle of Cnoc-An-Ar. Then the filidh sang of Diarmuid and Gráinne and that sorrowful memory put a melancholy mood on Fionn. The renowned fighter resolved that they should not spend their days wasting away in old age but should once more ride out in search of adventure. Fionn bade the company to rise from their sloth and to take to the hunt with him. They mounted their steeds and set out. Oisin rode beside his father, holding the banner of the Fianna aloft. And before going very far the dogs picked up the scent of the Queen of the Deer-people.'

With the skill of a master harper Gobann brought forth from his instrument the sounds of horses and hounds hot on the heels of a wild white hind. Everyone sitting before him knew the story of this mystical animal and how, many times, Fionn had pursued her to no avail. The deer's appearance in the tale was also the recognised sign that something otherworldly was about to happen.

Many in the crowd now closed their eyes, submitting to the power of the music, seeing better in their mind's eye how the Faery beast ran before the hunt.

'All that day and the next, Fionn and the Fianna hunted the snow deer, sometimes losing, sometimes closing pace with her. They crossed the plains of Cill-Dháire and through the land of the Dési. At the setting of the sun on the second day of the hunt, all the party were exhausted and wanted to rest. So they halted and the hind rested too, just within their sight, at a place where the western ocean meets the rocky strand. There on a low cliff between the edge of the forest and the roaring sea they lit fires and waited the coming of the First Star.'

Among the poet's listeners those who had earlier witnessed his words concerning that star now exchanged knowing winks. Gobann sensed the Even-star gently enfolding his soul in her light as he spoke. He drew strength from the companionship of his star-friend, feeling his spirit begin to lift to the realm of storytelling. He ceased to be merely repeating phrases learned by rote. Drunk with the inspiration that poured into him through his sky-bound helper, he breathed each sequence of the tale now as if it were part of his very fibre.

This was the way of his kind. Each member of the Druid order had a spirit guide, a soul-friend. For him the Evening Star was the key that unlocked the sacred magic of his craft. She reached into the depths of him. She gave him the power to pluck images out of the storehouse of his mind and speak them.

The merest thought of her spoke to his spirit of all that had ever been dear to him. Her appearance each evening was as important to him in this life as anything was allowed to be.

'As the star rose bright as silver across the sea,' Gobann continued, 'a woman stepped out of the cool sea onto the rocks.' The poet's hands evoked an old Faery tune from the harp. 'The warriors knew her for one of the Tuatha-De-Danaan.'

Gobann's audience barely stifled 'oohs' and 'ahhs' at the mention of the seldom seen Faery folk. He waited for their excitement to subside a little, then continued the tale.

'She wore a queenly crown over flowing golden tresses of silken hair. She was dressed in the fine dark green of the people of the woods and her cloak was embroidered with silver threads. The first rose at summertime was never as red as her full lips when they moved to speak; no spring water as clear as those eyes. Her fragrance was of fresh honey, her voice rang as sweet.'

Gobann, as always, nearly lost himself in this part of the tale. He knew a woman who reminded him of this Queen of the Faeries and so it was easy for him to breathe life into the description of her. Síla's face burned in his memory. She had long ago captured his heart completely. 'If she came to me now and asked me to go with her I would not hesitate,' he thought.

A filidh has many skills and this poet had acquired more than most. In the telling of a great tale there was more craft needed than just a knowledge of the story. Each bard spent seven years learning the verses word for word. Only then could a storyteller be expected to keep the legends alive. A bard might study twelve years before being awarded the title of filidh.

Gobann still regularly spent long hours practising his recitation, walking the roads talking aloud to himself. He was famed across the five kingdoms for his rendering of the great tales.

When next he spoke his voice had a feminine quality that had his listeners believing indeed that the beauteous Faery Queen stood before them.

'"Niamh of the Golden Hair I am called. I come to ask of you, Fionn MacCumhal, a gift." Fionn could only answer, "Name it, Lady", for he was awed by the light of her beauty. "I would that you name for me one of your companions as my husband."

'Fionn replied, "Would that it were I, Lady, but surely he is younger and stronger than I will ever be again. Name him and if he should agree then you may take him." '

The poet paused and assessed the audience. They were bound in the spell of his words. ' "I am the daughter of the King of Tir-Nan-Og, the Land of Ever-Youth, where the trees bear fruit of gold and silver, and the water is as potent as mead. Beauty and joy live there always for under magic bonds no pain or mortal suffering can afflict the souls who call that place home and no-one ever dies. The one that I summon must come with me to that land and live, never to return to his kinfolk unless he rue the day he first saw me."

' "Let me only know the one that you have chosen," said Fionn, "and I will release him to you."

'She raised her eyes toward the young man who stood beside Fionn and said, "He is known by the people of the Gael as Oisin of the bright face. He is your son." '

Around the gathering of attentive listeners, mouths dropped open, women gave little gasps, men shook their heads. In the far distance a low roar of thunder rolled across the Earth, intensifying the atmosphere.

'Never,' continued the poet, 'had Oisin encountered such a one as this woman and he resolved to go with her to her country, despite the bonds she placed on him against his returning. For in the short time since he had first seen her, he knew that his path was no longer the same as that of his father's clan. He knew that he was promised to another life.'

Gobann ceased his tale for a second to sip at his water. There was an underlying reason for this simple act. It was to make clear that the main message of his tale was in the last words he had spoken. And the point was not lost on Midhna.

'Oisin gathered his possessions and mounted a white stallion,' continued the poet, 'which Niamh led to him. She mounted the war horse behind him and after short farewells the two rode off across the wave crests toward the horizon.

'It was not long after that Fionn fell ill because of the loss of his beloved son. Each day he would sit at the water's edge waiting and hoping that his son would return or send some message. But no white horse ever came and Fionn withered with sadness and died. And as for Oisin, he has never returned, but dwells still in the Land of Youth in joy with his lover until the world changes.'

All were silent, contemplating the bard's words. They rewarded Gobann with the greatest honour they knew, the withholding of their own speech.

Midhna found his head buzzing with confusion and anger. The quiet intensified as another minute slipped by. A flash of lightning lit the horizon; clouds surged across the sky, suddenly blocking the moon from sight.

People returned to their meals, eager to finish before the coming downpour forced them inside. Midhna struggled to speak, to open his mouth and make a sound, any sound to break the silence of those around him. He knew that such an action would be in breach of hospitality but his fury simmered at the arrogance of one so young, one so obviously new to the bardic profession, demanding such a silence.

Gobann felt the unrest rise in the big man seated beside him. He sensed also the hopelessness, the frustration. He decided it would be very dangerous to push the boundaries of hospitality too far, lest the emotions of his host begin to erupt. He spoke directly to his host. 'I am tired. May I suggest that we adjourn to your house and play at the Brandubh before sleeping?'

Midhna nodded and, relieved, called the feasting to an end.

fIVE

he storm sent a first raindrop down to strike Midhna on the cheek as he and Gobann reached the dwelling. Within the cottage the hearth fire crackled and spat. In front of the fireplace on a low table, the game board had waited since Gobann had set it there at dusk.

Olan bundled her children off to the great bed they all shared and then busied herself making sure there was mead and broth enough for the traveller and for her husband. Midhna took his seat on a three-legged stool, relieved to be away from the sharp ears and prying eyes of his neighbours.

Outside, a fierce wind rose and howled over the thatch roof. The woodsmoke could not escape through the ceiling hole and began to build up in the room. Thunder resounded along the floor, deep and ominous. Rain pelted in varying waves of intensity, blown by harsh gusts against the outer walls of the dwelling.

Locked in an adjoining enclosure, a young goat cried in fear of the tempest. Another goat lay in strewn hay in a corner of the dwelling, allowed to sleep with the family because she was nursing a newborn kid. Mawn approached her quietly and sat softly stroking her nose. He placed his fingers on the space between her eyes and brushed them slowly down over her nostrils. No-one but the nanny goat noticed him.

Olan finished her tasks and bid goodnight to her guest. Then she too went to bed, knowing that Midhna had something on his mind and that it would be best to leave him in the company of the Druid.

Gobann mumbled a few more words over the Brandubh, threw a small log on the flames, and sat leaning heavily against the stone retaining wall of the fireplace.

'The choice is yours,' said Midhna, searching for a cup from which to imbibe his mead.

'I will take white,' sighed Gobann and he leaned over to make his first move.

The blacksmith smiled at the poet, seeing through Gobann's strategy almost before he had decided firmly on what it might be. Midhna was an acknowledged expert at this pastime. Satisfied that the game would be an easy victory for him, the blacksmith relaxed and said, 'I find I must apologise to you, Poet.'

Gobann stopped breathing for just a moment, unsure of his host's meaning, and raised his eyes to meet the blacksmith's. He was careful to make no move and to say nothing that might give away his thoughts.

Midhna waited for some reply and when none was offered he continued. 'I had no idea that you were so gifted as a tale-teller. I once knew another who was so gifted, but she paid for her talent by also suffering the future-sight. It made her life hardly worth living.'

The poet raised his eyebrows slightly; he was clearly impressed with the smith. Taking a spoonful of broth from the pot over the fire, the poet emptied it into a bowl. Then, placing the bowl on the floor before him to cool, Gobann picked up a slab of honey cake in his long wiry fingers and broke it in two. As he did so he casually remarked, 'I knew your mother well, you know. She cared for me when first I travelled to Teamhair. That is who you were referring to, wasn't it?' Then he stuffed a piece of cake into his mouth and chewed.

Midhna moved uncomfortably on his wooden stool. A old woman's face flashed before him: a kind caring face, the face of his mother. He remembered how she had held both of his elder sons at birth, blessing them with her tenderness. She had already passed on by the time Mawn had been born. The mead was beginning to loosen Midhna's tongue. 'I sometimes suffer the sight myself,' he confided.

'Do you?' asked Gobann. 'And how exactly does it feel?'

'It feels as if I can almost reach out and touch far-off people and places.'

'Almost?' repeated Gobann. 'Then you are perhaps also gifted. I did not know, but I shall certainly be more careful around you in future,' he joked.

The poet picked up the soup bowl and took a mouthful of broth. Midhna dropped his eyes back to the Brandubh board. After a moment the blacksmith made a move, effectively blocking Gobann's attack.

'How often does the sight come to you?' enquired Gobann.

'Now and again,' replied the blacksmith guardedly. He pretended to be concentrating on the game.

'And does any other of your bloodline suffer from it?'

'I don't know. We do not speak of such things.'

Gobann chewed silently.

Midhna took advantage of the resulting pause in

the conversation to change the subject. 'Tell me, what news of the kingdoms have you, Poet?'

Gobann looked into the dark eyes of his host, swallowed the broth loudly and replied, 'War. There is war between the High-King and Dichu the King of Laigin. The High-King has the upper hand at the moment but old Leoghaire will need luck to gain any more ground.'

'War! How did that happen?' exclaimed Midhna. 'I thought there was a truce and that the peace would last many years yet.'

'As did many so believe. And it is not for the want of Leoghaire's efforts to maintain the peace, but even he cannot forestall war forever. Strangers have come from a far country, from a place called Rome. They, like the White Brothers who came from the desert, are followers of the Christ. These Christians, however, wear black robes and claim to be sent by the God of Christ to put the whole of Eirinn under the domain of their bishop in Rome. Their leader is one called Palladius. He is a Briton from Alba or Gaul, I am not sure which.' Gobann paused for breath, leaning over the table to make his next move.

'Leoghaire gave the Romans a welcoming and showed them his hospitality,' Gobann stopped for a moment, striving in his poet's way to present all the facts carefully and fairly, 'for the coming of the Christ was foretold by the Druids and the White Brothers have lived amongst us since the days of King Cormac Mac Airt. It was Cormac who allowed those first Christians leave to stay in Eirinn. He even became a student of their philosophy. Through his interest they were permitted to teach their doctrines as long as they vowed not to try to coerce people to their faith. The good brothers kept that promise these two hundred years and only accept converts to their faith who come of their own free will.

'Palladius, however, claims that the White Brothers are actually servants of an evil god called Satan. This Palladius has declared that since they do not bow to Rome they are a corrupt branch of the Christian faith, and that they are only waiting for the day that this Satan will come laying Eirinn to waste so that they may rule over us unopposed.'

Midhna made the sign of banishment and muttered a blessing on his homeland. Then when he thought the poet was not looking, he slyly picked up one of the ravens and made his next move.

Gobann noticed the subterfuge but pretended he had not. 'As it turned out, Leoghaire was very wise to distrust the Romans. He placed them under bonds of their word not to leave Teamhair until a debate could be held between the White Brothers and the Black.'

Midhna picked up from the Brandubh board the little carved bone piece that represented the High-King. He studied the workmanship as Gobann spoke.

'When the debate began to go against him, Palladius broke his word and took refuge with Dichu, the King of Laigin, who is sympathetic to the Roman doctrines. And so it is that Leoghaire is forced to make war on the whole kingdom of Laigin for harbouring law-breakers. Dichu also fancies himself as High-King, no doubt. I have not had word for some days now as to how the conflict goes, but messengers came to Teamhair just before I left there with news that Leoghaire had taken two hundred hostages in a battle on the Great West Road. That should delay Dichu's ambitions a while. I have many friends among the White Brothers and I fear how this may end. Their ways are, after all, not so different from ours.'

Gobann noticed Midhna handling the Brandubh piece. He picked up a cup, took a sip of mead and then carried on his tale as if he were teaching one of his students back in Teamhair. 'I find the Romans, however, hold no common philosophy with the Druid Council. They sit many hours each day on their knees praying to their god in silence. They wear thick, poorly made robes that they do not wash but allow to become disgustingly filthy. And it is said they sleep but a few short hours each day. I have heard their songs. They are very sad and overlong but I do not know what they sing about: I cannot understand their speech and do not care to.'

Midhna moved in his seat again and placed the little king back on its square in the centre of the board. He had heard enough of the world outside; it had not eased his mind one bit. He dimly perceived that Gobann was playing a game with him that somehow mirrored the Brandubh, though the pieces were made of thoughts and words, not of bone and clay.

He felt his impatient anger rising again. And just as Midhna became aware of his feelings the words began suddenly and unexpectedly to spill from his mouth; he could not seem to hold them back once the barrier was broken.

'One such as you does not travel across Eirinn to a tiny village on the edge of the kingdom during a time of war just to tell stories of Faery queens and explain barbarian philosophies to an ignorant blacksmith. Tell me and tell me plainly, what brings you here after so long an absence?' He had spoken slowly and deliberately at first, but the sentiments gathered their own momentum and by the time he had finished they were gushing forth from his mouth like a waterfall in flood.

Gobann coughed a little to clear the crumbs from his throat. 'I have offended you, I am sorry. I have breached your hospitality through my poor judgement. There are more urgent things for you and I to discuss, it is true. First let me say, I truly wish that there was some way I could make this easier on you.'

'And that the task had not fallen to me,' he added in his thoughts.

'Yet it is my duty to follow, as it is for each of us, the path that is laid out before me. You are a fortunate man, Blacksmith, for you have a degree of freedom in choosing your path. There are others, such as the one I came here to find, who have a road chosen for them. They may fight against their destiny with all their might, but they will find their lives following a direction long ago set out for them. Or in their next life they may find the tests are made even harder.'

Midhna looked toward the earthen floor, contemplating what the poet had said, waiting for him to announce which precious son must be surrendered. The room remained still but for the spitting fire. Across the fields the wind suddenly rose again, sharply mimicking the wild cry of a Faery ban-sidhe.

The blacksmith examined the ceiling, avoiding the poet's eyes, reassuring himself that the roof would hold out through the night, keeping a check on his outrage. Then he made another sign to banish the spirits of the Sidhe-Dubh, the dark Faeries, and tossed a few drops of mead into the fire, muttering another blessing.

Gobann added his own words and, observing his host closely, gauged that the time was ripe to move close to the heart of the matter.

'I have found in the past few months that my

own life has taken a different direction. It is something that I am not enjoying very much at all. You
see, I did not always suffer the future-sight. It is a
new and frightening experience for me. Wisely do
the legends call the Faidh a sickness, an affliction,
a curse. It is a lonely burden to bear and few really
understand it. When I was a lad I was separated
from my kindred to spend my life training to
become a bard. Though I have spent almost every
day since then developing my gifts, it has taken
many years for my real talents to develop. Be sure
that I will care for the boy with the understanding
of one who knows what it means to be alone.'

Gobann tried to read the older man's thoughts
in the lines of his leathery face and the rhythm of
his breathing but Midhna gave no clues to his what
his feelings might be.

'I know that this is difficult for you, but try to
think of the lad,' Gobann continued. 'With his
talents he cannot possibly stay here, that is for
certain. He is chosen, he is marked to the path of
the Drúi. And many souls like him are called for
the great fights that are to come. This Palladius is
just the first of many invaders who will try to
change our people to their ways.'

The wind whipped around the overhanging
thatch outside and whistled loudly. Midhna picked
up a small log in one large powerful hand and
leaned forward to place it among the flames. Then
he picked up his mead cup again.

'It is said that one should never come between a
man and his family or a man and his mead,' replied
the smith. 'My two sons are more important to me
than my very life. When I am dead it is they who
will keep the forge firing. Their sons will carry on
the smithy after them and only in that way will I
be sure that the future is prosperous for all my

descendants. Would the training of one boy make as much of a difference to the Council as it would to me? And what makes you think that I would gladly let either of them go from my hearth and agree never to see him again?'

Gobann paused to measure the blacksmith and sensed a storm rising in the man to equal the one that was spending itself outside. The features of his face, Gobann noted, were reddened and his brow was furrowed from the effort to remain calm. But Gobann was now certain that the task would, after all, be easier than he had expected.

He turned in his seat to face Midhna and after a few moments he slowly, clearly declared, 'You are rightly concerned for your two eldest sons, Midhna. I will not part you from either of them. It is your youngest, the one called Mawn, that I seek to take with me.'

The blacksmith drew a loud, sharp breath through his teeth. He shuddered as if the poet had thrown a bucket of ice water over him. This was certainly not what he had expected. 'Who would have thought that the sickly one might be of any interest to the Druids?' he asked himself in wonder. Then he noticed a gleam in Gobann's eye and remembered that he had seen that same look many times in the eye of his youngest son.

'Why would you have one who is ...' Midhna searched for the right word and lowered his voice to a whisper, 'stricken, when you could choose between one of two healthy and bright young men?'

Gobann smiled. His hand found the silver sun wheel that he wore on a leather thong round his neck and he fingered it gently as he replied. 'What you call *stricken*, my kind calls *gifted*. It is true that his health has not been good since some years, but I think we both know there is a good reason for that. One who is as naturally talented as Mawn sees the world in a thoroughly different way to those who do not possess his insights. He may be Faidh for all I know. Though, understanding what that means, I pray that he is not. Even so, I have a feeling from what you have said that he may be more valuable to the Druid Council than we realise.' His hand let go of the pendant and it fell back under the folds of his shirt.

Midhna could not help but notice the silver amulet for it was a symbol of high office only awarded to those who exhibited the deepest devotion to their calling and rarely worn by one so young. He looked at the poet in a different light and suddenly found that he had a great deal of respect for him.

And he was relieved too. He was facing the truth, a truth that he had denied to himself for many years. 'I have never understood the lad,' he confessed, breathing easier. The great burden slipped from his shoulders with every word.

'His mind is not right. I don't know what to do with him. Last summer I found him seated in the topmost branches of the rowan tree near to the Road. He was sitting there singing . . . just singing, mind you. He fought me hard when I tried to bring him down. All he could say was, "I am calling to the bright ones." I thought the Faery folk had gotten hold of his soul. After I dragged him home, he refused to speak. It was days before I got more than a peep out of him. I cannot see a happy future for him amongst the soot of the forge. He would be a danger to himself and to others with his daydreaming.'

Midhna's voice cracked a little with emotion. 'Perhaps the best thing for him would be the life of a Druid,' he conceded. 'There are already those who say he should have been drowned at birth and talk quietly about him behind my back as if he were a bad omen.' Midhna stopped short and bit his lip, unsure if he had said too much. He did not wish to offend Gobann, no matter what.

Again the gale rose outside. The blacksmith looked across the room to the dark corner where Mawn now slept curled up by the goat. He lowered his voice so that his son would not hear, 'The boy's habits are strange. It is not unusual for us to find him sitting in the middle of a haystack in summer talking to himself. He never takes food with the family but carries his dinner to the grain store and sits there amongst the barley, eating in silence. At first I used to beat him in the hope that I could knock some sense into him but it made no difference, only that he stayed away longer with the goats each day, so in time I began to ignore his ways.'

Midhna placed his cup on the floor and took up another small log turning it over in his hand. 'There is one other thing I should tell you.'

'Yes,' said Gobann expectantly.

'I am sure that he has the future-sight. He has at times told us of events that had not yet come to pass, and each time his word has proved correct in every detail. And there have been occasions, too, many of them, when he has suffered much the same as my mother once did.'

'How was it with her?' Gobann enquired with sincere sympathy.

'A fit of screaming and howling, followed by hours of fever and visions.'

The nanny goat stirred in her sleep and her kid bleated loudly, waking Mawn who sat up in the hay rubbing his eyes and yawning. The two men looked at each other and silently agreed to speak no more about this subject in front of the boy.

Gobann was satisfied with all that he had heard. 'The house is at rest now,' he whispered to his host, 'and you also should take sleep. I can tell you nothing more of Mawn's future or how he may fare, for that was foretold by another, but I promise you that I will care for him as if he were my own son. Go to your rest now. Tomorrow we will speak again.'

Despite his own reassurances to Midhna, Gobann felt an uneasy shudder move down his spine, as if in speaking of the future he had promised too much. He shrugged the feeling off but as he made to rise from his seat, a small spark flew from out of the fire and landed smoking in his lap. Instinctively the poet brushed at it with his hand. The tips of his fingers caught the corner of the table and scattered Brandubh pieces across the floor. Both men quickly got down on their knees to retrieve them.

When he was sure that all the pieces were on the table again, Midhna got to his feet slowly and then helped Gobann to stand.

'More than half of what you have told me this night, Poet, I do not fully understand,' admitted the blacksmith, 'and less than half of the rest is of any real concern to one such as me, but I feel I must trust you Gobann son of Caillte. I pray that my son serves you well, for with what of the sight I have, I fear your task may be long and difficult.'

'Mawn will be well cared for, do not fear. Now sleep! I will tend the fire. Leave me to my thoughts for a while.'

Midhna nodded respectfully and went to his rest. He lay down with his face toward the corner where Mawn was sleeping and in a short while he was slumbering, uneasily but with the soundness of one who labours hard.

Gobann was not in the mood for disciplined

thought this night and so he let his mind stray a little. Before his eyes the Brandubh pieces were scattering themselves across the floor again and again. 'An omen of the future?' he asked himself, letting his body relax and sink forward on the stool before the fire.

'Perhaps there have been too many sleepless nights followed by too many days of rough roads and hard weather,' he thought. 'Perhaps, the life of a travelling Druid no longer suits me.'

Whatever had brought on this feeling of exhaustion was now wearing down his willpower and he began to drift into a dreamlike state. An overwhelming feeling of despair clawed at him. The impulse to float away from his body was very tempting and soon it became difficult for him to concentrate on remaining conscious. His eyes were wide open but he was not walking in the world that they saw.

His gaze was still directed at the fire. As he watched, the flames licked around the logs and took on twisted half-human shapes. Hideous forms dressed in long black robes danced out of the hearth and swiftly surrounded him, their mocking cackles echoing in his head. In the next instant Gobann felt himself being lifted out of his seat by these creatures of the flames and led out into the night. They carried him effortlessly and brought him down to where tables still stood from the evening's storytelling.

As they got closer to the feasting place, their fiendish laughter became harsher and full of malice; their thin bony fingers gripped the poet's wrists tighter, cutting the blood flow. They bore him to the bench where earlier in the evening he had sat beside his host. Just as they placed him down at his seat, the bonfire exploded in a deafening hiss, as if a barrel of water had been poured on it. The creatures swirled around in the smoke and then melted into the furnace once more.

Faces took form in the coals of the fire: some healthy vibrant beings; some horribly deformed. And there were others that seemed to rot before his eyes, the flesh peeling away in great sheets. He began to notice then that some of the faces were familiar to him. The inhabitants of Midhna's village had become players in his dream.

By his side, Midhna grinned a repulsive smile. Sharp, pointed teeth protruded through bloody gaps in his grey lips. Scéolan the weaver was now a shrivelled old Raven. He still had the basic shape of a man, but had developed the features of a black carrion bird. An orange beak snapped loudly shut, clicking with menace. The weaver picked up a piece of meat with long pointed talons and tore the morsel to shreds. Then, holding his head back, he swallowed the flesh, gurgling with pleasure. Gobann was fascinated by the transformation. He had heard of Druids who had shape-changed into other forms but the thought of taking on the attributes of a beast terrified him and he muttered a prayer to all that was holy that he would never have to suffer that fate.

Suddenly a man who the poet knew was not of the village walked briskly through the smoke and approached the high table. Gobann barely recognised his teacher, Lorgan Sorn, but he knew the friendly expression in those eyes only too well. Lorgan came to stand before him, staring blankly at his student. Seeing the face of one he loved calmed him down a little and he tried to convince himself that this was just a dream brought on by exhaustion and overwork.

Gobann shifted his gaze to the field. The grey-blue smoke began to move rhythmically. Then the thin wisps began to take on other forms. In moments, stark gaunt figures filled his sight. They danced in a circle, slowly at first, then moving faster and faster, spiralling in toward the bonfire. Three of them, all women, threw themselves screaming into the flames as their comrades watched, gliding above the ground in silence.

As Lorgan's ancient face moved to block Gobann's view the old teacher underwent a hideous change. First the eyes were drained of their colour, like the lifeless orbs of dead fish, the flesh around them as cold as marble. Then dry earthen lips moved to speak, opening in a gust of foul breath. From each corner of the mouth a vile yellow liquid trickled, running down the pointed chin.

The old man was urgently straining to communicate in a rasping, hollow voice,

'Any who live alone, long only for mercy,
The mercy of rest among their own people,
The ways of the exile are harder than words can
    tell.
I am alone. As you will be.
Each day at dawn I speak to myself. I give my
    thoughts utterance.
For there are none living now to whom I would
    freely speak and tell my heart's desire.'

Gobann listened intently, blocking all of his other senses, trying to understand what was being imparted to him.

'The lad will need to learn to curb his mind, to wait
    for the right time to speak,
For he will be cut off from his countrymen,
Separated from his kin by far distance of Time and
    Tides.'

Lorgan continued to chant breathing deep and loudly. His lungs sounded the death rattle.

'He will remember well his friends, they will fill
his mind,
When strangers cry out "Mawn" he may not recall
that was once his name.
And he will search the faces of the men and women
who sit at their hearths.
And though he will only see shades of what once
was, he will hear their songs and music forever.
If you teach him well, Gobann.'

The poet heard his name and answered instinctively, nodding his head. Instantly a sharp pain stung him across the brow and the air filled suddenly with shouts. Hundreds of people appeared from the darkness, running wildly into the scene. The bonfire became just one small blaze in the centre of a large village engulfed in flame. Near to where the gate of the feasting field should have been, women and children scrambled down an embankment towards the crashing waves of an ocean.

Somewhere the unmistakable clash of iron sword against wooden shield was growing in intensity. A stench of burning flesh carried on the breeze. Battle cries rose in fury nearby. A bloody fight would soon be upon these poor defenceless souls.

Gobann touched his forehead. He felt the bristles across his brow where his head was shaved ear to ear in the Druid fashion. His fingers brushed a bruised lump. There was blood on his hand. He struggled to remember how he had been injured but only felt dizzy and weak. Through the throbbing in his skull he forced himself to look around and take in his surroundings. All around him there was despair and horror.

He sat cross-legged in the middle of a group of huts. The blue cloak that he always wore was torn and mud-stained and wet with blood. Warriors ran by him in fear, throwing down their weapons as they fled. Gobann tried to control his breath and calm himself. 'This is not the village at Midhna's forge,' he told himself. 'This is a vision. This is some other place that exists only in the future.' He moved to stand but he foundered. His legs were powerless to raise him.

A young man came running wildly out of a nearby hut clutching a beautiful gold cloth. Gobann grabbed him by the tunic as he pushed past, begging the youth to help him stand. The strange fellow stared at him for a moment full of fear, uttered some words in a harsh guttural language that Gobann could not recognise, then ran off in the direction the other villagers were headed. The poet observed the strange young man until he disappeared from view. Then out of the corner of his eye he caught sight of a familiar shape.

Between two rough mud-brick buildings he saw a harp lying on its flat back in a puddle. It was not, he noted with relief, his own beloved instrument. This was a much poorer and simpler example. An armoured warrior approached the harp and kicked it gingerly, as if he expected it to leap up at him and attack.

This warrior was unlike any Gobann had ever seen. His clothing was a unique mixture of styles and materials. He wore trousers under leather armour, but they were of a very poor quality cloth. His feet were bare. His flame-red hair was knotted on top of his head in an untidy bundle, and where a twisted torc of gold should have hung around his neck, he wore instead a plaited beard, weighted down with silver trinkets. He was certainly not a Gael.

The stranger gave a piercing high-pitched cry of defiance and he fumbled with something at his belt. In a moment both of his hands gripped a long-handled wide-bladed axe of the type used in Eirinn to split flat, even slabs of wood for the roof-tiles of the houses of the nobility. He raised it high above his head, swung it around behind him and brought it crashing down on the harp.

The tiny instrument splintered and shattered, crying out in its agony as the tension of the music wires was suddenly released. Coolly the strange warrior withdrew his weapon and quickly checked the blade for nicks. Then he once again gave the dead shell a kick.

A white-robed man, his face concealed by his attire, appeared from the doorway of the building closest to where the broken harp lay. He walked calmly toward the warrior, his elbows tucked in at the sides and palms uppermost in the universal sign of prayer and of peace.

Gobann breathed in deeply, intending to call out a warning, but his voice was not quick enough in coming. In an instant the warrior again raised his weapon above his head. The blade whistled down, smashing onto the man's collarbone. There was a sickening crunch. The poet, paralysed by the shock of the bloody murder, could only sit drowning in the revulsion of what he saw.

The axe brutally split its victim across the chest to the stomach. A thick red stain spread swiftly across the white robe as the already lifeless body inside collapsed. Using a bare foot for leverage, the warrior pushed the crumpled carcass off his weapon. He lifted the axe above his head once more and swung it around. The blade sliced through the air splashing tiny drops of blood across the ground. Satisfied, the foreigner stuck the handle back in his wide belt and entered the nearest building. Gobann soon heard screams from within.

More warriors like to the red-headed one came running from between the buildings, setting afire those that were not already burning. They seemed not to notice Gobann. As they passed through the scene, they changed subtly in appearance, throwing off the forms of men and taking on the abstract guise of the pieces of his own Brandubh set. They were becoming Ravens.

In the midst of all this clamour, a small procession appeared weaving its way through the frantic setting. Two figures dressed in long black cloaks bore thick, lighted candles before them. They were followed by a man holding a gold jewel-encrusted box and another carrying a folded red cloth of velvet. Of the last two figures also robed in black, one was only too familiar to Gobann. He wore a short pointed hat and carried an oaken staff on which was mounted a large silver cross.

The poet screamed at the man at the top of his lungs, 'Palladius!' but his voice was lost in the commotion, and the Roman did not hear him.

The crash of heavy timbers succumbing to flame sounded to the right of Gobann. Palladius and his retinue disappeared in the resulting billows of spreading smoke.

Gobann did not have a chance to figure out where the monks had gone before a call rose through the chaos somewhere behind him. The voice was well-known to him and he felt relieved to hear it.

'Master Gobann!' shouted the young man. With great effort, Gobann twisted his torso around to look at the caller. He was a man in his twenties, fair of hair, with green eyes. On his shoulder he carried the bag that had held Gobann's harp since his days as a novice. The otter-skin covering was discoloured slightly but there was no doubt that it was his.

'I have her here,' said the youth. 'Now we must leave!'

'I cannot go,' answered the poet, and he found himself grasping the shaft of a long, oaken arrow that protruded from his chest. 'You must leave me. Save yourself and the harp, my son. She is yours— you have earned the right to bear her.'

Gobann looked the fellow in the face and remembered the young man's name, though it was one he felt he had never really spoken. 'Mawn,' he gasped.

As he watched, the face changed, growing quickly younger, until in an instant a boy's eyes stared back at the poet. The lad was no longer carrying the harp bag, he was holding a jug of water.

'Yes, master, I am here,' he said.

The world began to spin violently around Gobann. He felt as if a great weight had been placed on top of his head. There was a weakness in his neck that made his chin fall on his chest. All the confusion of battle ceased, the light died down, and he smelled only burning broth.

For a brief moment he was back in the valley of Dobharcú, sitting at the hearth of Midhna on a three-legged stool. The face before him was not distorted nor fearful. It was that of the blacksmith's youngest son.

'Master, it is I, Mawn. Don't you recognise me?'

Gobann made to reach for the jug, and then the world grew dark and he fell forward onto the hearthstone.

six

urrough slumped in his father's great oak chair. His right hand lay along the armrest. His forefinger traced back and forth across the intricate designs carved deeply into the timber. His feet scuffed the floor before him and his head was resting with his chin on his chest.

The ceremonial duties of a prince did not agree with him. He preferred to be outdoors attending to the practical business of helping to govern the kingdom. As soon as he had entered the room he had discarded his armour, his blade, his long grey brat-cloak and all the decorative trinkets that were worn at court. Now he closed his eyes and pushed his back into the seat, letting out an anguished but subdued sigh. The muscles on his freckled face began to relax. His well-toned warrior's body ceased its unsettled movements and he slouched further into his seat.

Outside his chamber there was a tentative cough and then another which signalled an end to his short rest. The youngest son of King Eoghan of Munster half turned in his seat as the door to the chamber squeaked noisily on its hinges and pushed his red hair from his face. A figure dressed in dark-blue robes entered. Murrough forced himself into an upright position, expecting to receive another envoy from Teamhair.

'Rest, my lord, and sit back, it is only an old counsellor come to hear your worries. You need not be formal with me,' said the visitor.

It took only a moment for Murrough to recognise the voice of his father's counsellor. 'Cathach! Where in the name of the Morrigan have you been? Have you not heard the news? Dichu is marching!'

'I have heard and know perhaps a little more than you, but as a member of the Druid Council I have other duties than those I perform at court. In the Oak College at Cnóc Pocan there was an important debate at which my views were sought and that matter took precedence over the politics of the kingdoms. May I sit down? It has been a rather strenuous few days and my weary bones do not take the saddle as well as perhaps they did thirty years ago.'

'Of course, rest yourself here at my side.' The prince pulled in a seat for the old man then he took the mead jar and placed it on the table before his friend and adviser.

Cathach allowed himself a moment to settle into the high-backed chair and to draw his cloak about him, then reached for a cup and spoke as he filled it.

'There are many warriors on the Road,' he stated matter-of-factly. 'More than one would expect for the settling of such a petty dispute.'

'The petty dispute has grown, I fear. The High-King is furious. He has raised all the warriors of Eirinn, but every footman in the land with some grievance on him has taken arms with Dichu and that Roman.'

'It will take more than Palladius to turn the tide of the people. He is too harsh, too cruel; he has no real support. Would you follow a man who puts folk cruelly to death merely for speaking the ancient tales?' asked Cathach.

'Of course not!' snapped Murrough. 'But he has many sympathisers.'

'Mostly outlaws and mercenaries I have heard. An ear that hears only the sound of silver coins jingling can be sympathetic even to an unjust cause.'

'Nevertheless, there are many marching in his army,' pressed Murrough.

'Do not worry too much about Dichu; his time is at hand and he will not see the new year. And as for the Christian, well, the tide will surely turn here toward the Romans, as it has elsewhere, but not for many years yet.' Cathach's voice was calm and confident. 'Palladius is not the conqueror. His time in Eirinn is to be only short and he will quickly be forgotten. His deeds, no matter how horrendous, are nothing compared to ... ' Cathach stopped himself. 'One day another will come and we must be ready for him.'

'How do you know this?' the younger man demanded.

'I do not ask you how you go about the business of being a Prince of Cashel and so you should not ask me how I come by my trade,' asserted the old man. 'But have I ever told you anything that did not come to pass?'

'No,' admitted Murrough.

The old Druid clasped his hands in front of him and his face lit up with a self-satisfied smile. On his lap his twisted fingers curled around each other like the branches of an aged tree. 'Then trust that the Druid Council is well informed. If you concentrate on your duties, I may be more able to see to mine. You have much to learn and many tasks to perform in the future. The new invader will likely come in the time of your kingship.'

'My kingship? It is by no means certain that I

will be ruler of Munster. My brother Morann Eoghanacht is better known to the people than I and he will surely be elected.'

'Morann will take the Druid path. You will lead Munster.'

Murrough took a moment to let this sink in. 'Why are you telling me this? Are you trying to fill me with false hopes?'

'Who would want to be a king?' answered Cathach quietly. He unfolded his fingers again one by one and there were loud cracks as the swollen joints settled again into place. 'The duties of a provincial ruler are great, as are the burdens. It is not something to aspire to if you would have a happy and peaceful life. Nor perhaps a long one. Do you think that the power you will wield will be any compensation?'

The Druid waited patiently for a reply.

The prince, brooding, gave none, so Cathach answered for him. 'You would be wrong to think so. Such power may too easily control you. You could well become a slave to it. Beware!'

Murrough looked his adviser squarely in the eye, 'Will you still be my counsellor?'

'Only the passing of time will reveal that, my boy. Have you not learned the Brandubh well enough to play without your tutor always watching over your shoulder?'

The old man laughed, teasing his student. 'For the moment I will remain in your service, but I, too, am nearing the end of my days in Eirinn. But enough talk of that for there are other more important matters that I think you should consider. First of all there is the issue of the community of Christians who have established themselves in your kingdom. Brecan, the chieftain of those parts, has sent troops to side with Dichu.'

'What! One of my own kindred?' exclaimed Murrough. 'Well, that's easily dealt with. I will send a force to teach him something of loyalty. He and his people will suffer exile.'

'Do not be too harsh, Lord. You may need their support later. Perhaps simply dealing with the ringleaders would be enough.'

'Yes, for the moment,' agreed Murrough. 'But treason is treason and I must not let it pass unnoticed.'

'That, anyway, is of minor concern. There are two other matters that you should decide right away,' continued Cathach. 'We have already spoken of the rowan tree near the Cashel crossroad. It seems certain now that Dichu will try to seize it as a symbol of sovereignty.'

'I have placed a sizeable guard on the tree,' Murrough reassured him.

'Then double it,' asserted the Druid, 'for we must not allow it to fall into the hands of this destructive Roman priest who has Dichu's ear. Oak groves cut down and burned may one day grow back, but this tree can never be replaced. It comes from a time when the Earth was an entirely different place and there is not another like it. The Danaan Princes have sent an envoy to Cnóc Pocan to remind the Druid Council of our obligations under the ancient treaty between our two peoples. One of those obligations is that we keep safe the Quicken Tree. We dare not neglect its defence or we stand to lose the goodwill of the Sidhe folk. And I do not need to tell you what that may mean.'

'Surely the Danaans are no longer a force to be reckoned with?' exclaimed Murrough.

'Speak not too loudly, boy,' Cathach rebuked him, 'for you do not know what you are saying!' Then he instantly regretted his sharp tone with the prince. 'I must try to remember that he is no longer a lad,' he told himself.

'The Danaans are and always were a mystical race,' he informed the prince, 'and they have many ears.'

Murrough had heard the tales of the Tuatha-De-Danaan many times but he never tired of listening to them. He loved hearing about their ability to change their outward appearance, their talent for music, their magic, their great age, their relations with the humankind; everything that he heard he soaked up like a dry sponge.

'When our people came to Eirinn over a thousand years ago,' Cathach explained, 'there were bloody battles between our two races. They had the magical arts as their weapons and our folk had only the mastery over iron. There was a long stand-off and there were many losses in that war. Not until Amergin, the bard of the Gaelic folk, pronounced judgment and terms for a truce did the fighting cease. Even with an official peace between our peoples there have been sporadic outbursts of violence ever since.' The old man noticed that Murrough was taking in every word and so he did not hesitate to continue.

'Under the terms of the truce, the Danaans took every part of Eirinn that was below the ground and the Gaels took all that was above. They then used their wisdom to cast a series of spells that separated the two domains by a thin magical curtain. In this way travellers may still pass between the two realms, ours and theirs, but most folk cannot even perceive that there are two separate lands. They were, as I said earlier, a race of wizards and they knew the secrets of immortality. Their memories are long, much longer than many lifetimes among our folk. And so the peace is delicate. We must not provoke them in any way or the resulting war would be far worse than you or I could possibly imagine.'

Murrough tensely grasped the arm of the chair on which he sat. He was about to speak, but Cathach cut him short and came directly to the next topic on his list. 'Then there is the Druid Gobann, whom you may remember. He has in his charge a young boy. This lad has been chosen for great works by a council of Druids representing our peoples and the Danaans. We have been labouring together on a plan that may save our land from the evils that have befallen most other countries at the hands of the Romans.'

'I have heard that the Vortigern of Britain has invited Saxons into his lands to protect the realm from the savage tribes of the north,' added Murrough.

'It is hard to say who is more savage, the Saxons or the northern Cruitne. At least the Cruitne have music, so they cannot be completely barbaric, but if it is true that there are Saxons already in Britain, then events are moving much faster than any of us could have imagined. The sooner we secure the lad's safety, the better we will be prepared. Take him into your household for a while. Hide him as you see fit, but do not speak of his true fate to anyone, save me alone. I cannot stress to you enough that a great deal is in the balance, the lives of many that are not even yet born may well be at stake, and there will surely come a time when your fate rests entirely in this boy's hands.'

'You say that there will come a conqueror to Eirinn one day, so why are we bothering to resist now? To be sure we need only sit back and wait. What have we to gain by struggling against our inevitable fate?'

'*Nothing* is inevitable, my boy! What we will gain is time. Time to ready our world for the coming of new things. With time we will change the outward shape of ourselves so that later we may go unnoticed within the new world, just as the Danaans did before us. Only in that way will our tales, our history and our music live on into the next millennium. Many of us will wear the guise of Christians, but we will in truth be keepers of a much older path. The folk of Gaul were not so prepared and now few people live who can even speak their tongue, let alone recite the histories.'

'Who is this boy?' asked Murrough. 'How can he be so important?'

'He will be merely one of a small band of Druids who will carry our messages to the next generations. He will be a Wanderer.'

Murrough had only ever heard Cathach speak once before of the Wanderers and then it was when the prince was but a boy himself. He was beginning to understand the urgency of the situation. 'A Wanderer is only ever appointed in the most dire circumstances!' he exclaimed.

'That is true,' answered the Druid. 'This is such a time.'

'He will have a great responsibility to bear.'

'He will not bear it alone. He will be joined by another child who even now is preparing to take her vows as a novice Druid,' explained the old man with genuine sadness in his voice.

The prince put his cup heavily down on the table. 'I will send two riders to find the poet Gobann and his boy.'

'You must seek them at Rathowen in three days' time if they survive the great battle there.'

'Battle! What battle? Dichu is a full week's march from Rathowen,' protested Murrough.

'That is the final piece of news I have for you. Dichu is marching east toward Teamhair. He obviously hopes to catch Leoghaire off guard.'

'When did you learn this?' asked the prince.

Cathach smiled a slow wide grin and said, 'Just now, my lord. A rider from the Princes of Connachta brought the news.'

Murrough leapt to his feet and wrapped his cloak about him. He snatched up his armour, hastily slinging it in a bundle over his back. 'Leoghaire will need every able sword hand, I must hurry.'

'I, too, will be coming presently,' shouted Cathach after Murrough. 'I will be bringing my grand-daughter Sianan to witness the fight.' As an afterthought he added, 'Do not forget that you must find Gobann!'

But Murrough was already calling for his horse. Cathach could only hope the prince had heard that last reminder.

'Mawn ... Mawn!' A woman's voice cried out across the yard. 'Mawn, get the goats out of their pen before you leave. Your sister will take them again today.'

Gobann the Druid, son of the poet Caillte, woke from a deep, sound sleep. The high-pitched voice of a young girl took over from the woman and spurred the braying and complaining goats out of their enclosure. The poet lay on his stomach amongst a pile of straw, covered in blankets and skins. Feeble rays of sunlight penetrated the dusty dwelling. Olan sat stirring a great cauldron full of milk, which hung from a beam on an iron hook over the fire. All else was still.

Peaceful.

'If only I could stay here,' thought Gobann, 'and become part of this village and disappear from the rest of the world.' He turned his head and noticed a boy dressed in a fine green travelling cloak standing at the foot of the bed. His fair hair was cut short, his face washed and at his feet was a rolled blanket bound with leather to form a carrying strap.

It was Mawn.

'Will we be leaving today, master?' he said simply.

'Are you so eager to depart this place, boy, that you wait my waking in readiness for the journey?'

Mawn did not answer. He only widened his already broad smile.

'Then you may begin your duties, if you are willing.' Gobann fumbled around about him searching for the harp bag. When his hand found it he motioned to the boy. 'Let's see if you are strong enough to lift it.'

Mawn knelt down and tenderly hoisted the harp onto his left shoulder. It was much heavier than he expected but he stood very still so as not to show any discomfort.

Gobann was impressed with the lad's resolve. 'I know you were listening to the conversation between your father and myself,' said the poet. 'Has anyone yet asked you what you would do, whether you wish to stay here with your family or trudge the Road with me?'

Mawn sighed slowly and shook his head.

'Then what's it to be?' Gobann pressed. 'The paths I walk are dangerous and tiresome. The learning I will give is demanding and requires of you diligence and persistence. You will need to learn to put your own feelings aside for the good of others.'

Mawn nodded, not quite understanding the full implications of this.

'You will be little more than a servant to me at first, until you have proved your worth, and you will doubtless resent many of the tasks I set you.'

The boy listened, weighing up the consequences of his decision. The leather strap of the harp bag was already beginning to cut into his shoulder. He wavered for a moment.

'In time we may be friends and equals, but for a time you will have to bear many hardships alone. If you prove to be, as I believe you are, chosen for the Druid path, you will one day be just as I am, a traveller, a poet, a keeper of the histories.'

Mawn stroked the harp bag with his right hand, but uttered no sound. His fingers followed the patterns of knotted bands that decorated the tanned covering. His memory was straining to recall the details of the harp's decoration.

'You must decide this willingly. I cannot force you to a life of hardship. And if you would rather remain here, I would not blame you. I must tell you that you and others of your generation have a great and difficult task ahead of you. I was sent to find you and to teach you so that you might be better prepared for the future.'

Mawn stood as tall as his slight frame would allow. Deep in his soul the light of poetry burned fiercely. That Gobann could see plainly.

The boy held the older man's gaze, drew a deep breath and answered, 'I want to be a harper in the court of the High-King. I want to see all the people there at Teamhair. I want to be a bard.'

'Then so shall you be. And may the gods bless your ambition,' replied Gobann. 'Now you must say farewell to your kinfolk and I, too, must make ready to depart. I will give you only the time it takes for me to wash and dress.'

Thus dismissed, Mawn carried the harp bag outside and placed it near the stables beside all the provisions that the community had gathered for the two travellers. Then he went to see each of his family one by one as he was bid.

Gobann dressed and scrubbed himself in a trough outside the house. His body was sore and his limbs stiff. He had slept well but still he felt drained, as though he had been on a long journey without stopping to take rest. He was tying the long black strands of his hair in a knot at the back of his neck when Midhna approached, sweating and filthy from the forge.

'I give you gifts of food and two jars of mead,' he declared. 'Use them wisely.' The big man broke into a laugh, and took the poet's hand in a rough but friendly grasp.

'Trust me, I will!' answered Gobann, holding his head in mockery of the sickness that strikes those who partake of too much honey-brew. The two men clasped their arms together then and each looked sternly at the other.

'Are you recovered?' enquired Midhna.

'I think so,' replied Gobann, 'but my body is tired and aching as though I did not rest at all last night.'

'Poet,' began the blacksmith cautiously, 'you have been abed three nights since the feasting.'

'Three nights?' Gobann stood dumbstruck, trying to remember. 'Three nights ... Why did you not wake me?'

'We feared to disturb you after ... after ... what befell you.'

'I suffered the Faidh?'

117

'You did and in much the same way that my mother suffered it.'

'Then I have stayed much longer than I had intended. I must leave. Now!'

'Peace be with you, Bard,' offered Midhna, his face suddenly expressionless and cold, but he took Gobann's hand in a friendly manner.

'And also with you, Blacksmith,' returned the poet, but his mind was already on the Road.

Midhna let go his hand-hold, turned, and purposefully strode back to the forge. No-one else came out to say goodbye. That had been Midhna's task alone.

Gobann sat down on a bench facing the blacksmith's house to lace his boots. The Faidh was a thing that could drain the strength of the mightiest warrior, he knew, yet still he had not been prepared for the full effect of a visit from it. Then he remembered that he had seen the moment of his own death. It did not frighten him in the least but the vision clearly told him that he had only an allotted time in which to complete his task.

'Three nights!' he muttered to himself in disbelief.

Across the courtyard the poet could see a figure standing in the shadow at the window of the house. It was Olan, checking to see if the two were gone. When she noticed him looking at her she pulled the shutters closed and dissappeared. The poet understood only too well the great loss that she was feeling as her youngest son prepared to leave his family forever. Pushing the pain away again, Gobann finished with his riding boots and walked across to the horses. He loaded the stores and tied up his travelling gear.

Slinging his harp securely across his back, he mounted his old grey mare. There he sat waiting for Mawn as his horse stamped and turned impatiently. She was not happy to be leaving the valley either, but for her it was the moist green grass of Dobharcú that was on her mind.

Presently Mawn appeared from across a field. He strode toward his horse and climbed onto the saddle without a moment's hesitation and without a sound.

A word or two of encouragement and Gobann spurred his mount on. Mawn followed. Neither looked back and neither spoke. They rode slowly out of the valley beside the stream until, at length, they came to the little ford. Visible on the other side lay the beginnings of the Great Road. Here Gobann halted.

The horizon was a swelling mass of grey-black cloud swirling like the smoke of a forest fire. A storm was rising out over the sea and Gobann knew it would be upon them by early afternoon. The daylight was already taking on an eerie luminescence. The poet's horse pulled around to gaze once more on the lush valley.

'It seems that there is at least one mare in Eirinn who is broken-hearted for parting this place. Well was she named Drugal the Unwilling.'

The horse turned again hearing her name and neighed loudly. Seeing the smile light on the lad's face Gobann took a more serious tone. 'This is your last chance, boy. When you cross this stream and take to the Road you will leave the valley forever. It is not too late, even now, to turn around and ride home.'

'Where are we riding to first, lord?' Mawn asked without any sign of regret in his voice.

'To the Dun of Rathowen a little to the north. There we will bide a while with my dear friend who is the chieftain of her people and shares a place with me on the Council of the Wise.'

Mawn sat for a moment breathing in the crisp air of the valley one last time, then he turned his horse about and spurred it hard across the ford.

Gobann waited a second longer. He considered riding back. He knew the people would welcome his staying in this place. He felt that he could live a long, peaceful life here honoured by his neighbours.

'I must speak with Cathach about all that has happened. It is all too fast, too intense. What if I cannot fulfil all the tasks that are placed before me? By staying here so long I may have broken the terms of my quest prohibiting me from remaining more than two nights under the same roof. If I have failed the test I may no longer be acceptable as a candidate for the office of High-Druid. Damn the Faidh if it has ruined all our plans.'

At the top of the rise, on the other side of the brook, Mawn was galloping toward his destiny. Gobann shut out his fear, his reservations and his regrets, and remembered his duty to the boy.

He kicked Drugal lightly to encourage her to cross the waters. She waded over indignantly, splashing about as much as she could. Gobann tried not to notice.

SEVEN

n the low earth wall that formed the outer parapet of the Dun of Rathowen stood the woman known to her people as Caitlin. She was tall for a woman of her race and her face was showing the effects of many days without sufficient sleep. But for all that, she was justly known for her beauty.

That morning she had bundled her long brown hair into a bun and fastened it with a bronze pin. The wind teased at it though, and many strands were now loosing from their bonds and blowing about her face. Her bright green eyes searched the road that wound from the west. Clouds that had brought three full days of rain threatened again to empty their burden on the land. The chill air reddened her lightly freckled cheeks.

Wrapping a rust-red wool brat tight about her body, Caitlin turned to take shelter at a watchhouse before the downpour. The first drops thudded into the ground as she reached the gate. A guard was huddled under the entrance anticipating the worsening weather.

Caitlin brushed past him to stand by the fire in the centre of the small hut. As she shook out her cloak another man in rough leather armour and helm pushed past the sentinel.

'Scouts have sighted their army,' he blurted. 'They are hardly a day's march from here. It is sure they wish to make for this stronghold.'

He waited for a reply. The woman splayed her fingers out over the fire, warming them, stretching them. She stared into the coals, but made no sign of acknowledgment.

'Did you hear me?' he insisted. 'Dichu and his force are upon us.'

'I am sorry, Fintan,' answered the woman softly. She tore her gaze away from the flames and sought out the young warrior's eyes. 'I was thinking of Gobann. He has not yet returned. It is over a week since he set out and his destination is less than a day's ride from here. I fear that he may have been taken.'

'Pray that he has not,' said Fintan solemnly. 'It is said that the Roman, Palladius, is killing all Druids and burning all harps. A week ago at the Black Grove his followers skinned two men and a woman alive before the whole army.' The young warrior shuddered at the thought. 'The Grove was burned and the ground trampled and salted so that nothing will ever grow back.'

'How well are we prepared for their coming?' asked Caitlin, moving to sit on a low stool and spreading her cloak across her knees.

Fintan took his seat on another stool. He kept a respectful distance but was close enough that their words could not be overheard. Leaning in to speak, he noticed droplets of rainwater in her hair and he breathed deeply the pleasant scent of the dried herbs in her pouch.

'All the ditches have stakes mounted to prevent horses entering save where we would wish them to. Thank the gods for this rain; it has slowed their march and softened the ground a little so we have been able to place the spikes close together. I fear that they will not withstand a determined attack though.'

He watched the lines on her forehead move in a frown of concern. 'The farmers around about are still burying their surpluses,' he continued, 'but that task should be ended by evening. I have seen to it that water is collected in every available vessel as you ordered.'

He dropped his voice instinctively as the guard shuffled about in the doorway. 'All the sick and infirm along with every child below the age of ten summers are being taken south to the caves near the loch. I have sent riders to Teamhair and to Cashel but I fear that help will be too late in coming.'

'And what of the stores of food for the round-house? Are they prepared?'

'Aye, every grain we could find within a day's ride. And all the mead from the district to warm the wounded. Is your work finished, lady?'

His voice was a little harsh. Caitlin took careful note. She knew it was not that he resented being ordered about by her—he had enough experience of her to realise that this was her way in times of necessity—but she thought he might be a little hurt by her coldness and she rebuked herself for it. 'When the job is done I will speak with him,' she told herself.

'My work is nearly complete, but for the collection of the herbs of healing,' she said, answering his question, 'which I will do on the morrow. Arm your warriors, Fintan, and all the men and women of the district. Send out your fastest rider to Cnóc Pocan to the Druid Grove there. It may be that Gobann has made for that haven and I must know if he is safe. In the meantime tell your scouts to look for two bards travelling together on the Road.'

'Two? I thought the poet always journeyed alone.'

'No more,' stated Caitlin. 'Now he has a charge. They must both be kept safe at any cost.' She observed the bags under Fintan's eyes and knew that he had not rested for many hours. 'And get some sleep,' she added lightening her tone, 'what good is a champion to me if he cannot stay awake at his post?'

Fintan rose slowly, stretching his legs but always watching the young woman before him. It was said that she was descended of the Danu queens, and he could see why, for she had a regal air about her. 'One cannot help but do as she bids,' he thought.

His eyes strayed to the line of her breasts and he decided, 'If, gods grant it, we live beyond the next Moon I will make this woman my wife. Even though she were the highest Druid in the land I would have her for my own.'

'Your gaze betrays you, Fintan,' said Caitlin softly. 'Go now.' She quickly stood to face him and touched his cheek with her lips.

The warrior blushed hotly and wound his cloak about himself as he made to leave the hut. Such was his nervous haste that he bumped the door-frame hard with his shoulder and swore.

Caitlin smiled, leaning back against the wall watching after him as he left.

'If we live beyond this Moon then it is you who will be mine,' she promised him in her thoughts. Still smiling, she moved toward the fire once more and shut her eyes. Allowing the half-sleep of a warrior to take her, she pushed her stool back against the wall. Outside, the grey daylight dimmed as dusk came over the land. The bird calls ceased for the night and all was quiet. The hours passed calmly by.

In the dark, thunder mumbled across the cold Earth. Caitlin opened her eyes, unsure whether she had heard anything significant. A horse neighed loudly and hooves clattered across the causeway below. There were curses, challenges.

'Horsemen!' she thought.

She stood quickly, the muscles along her spine locked solid from sitting too long. Gathering her senses she stepped outside.

The guard was gone to the forward post to reinforce defences should the riders prove hostile. In his hurry he had foolishly left behind his iron shield. Caitlin made a mental note to chastise him about it later and climbed the embankment to peer across at the forward defences. She could just make out three riders. They were halted at the outer rampart. The spears of many warriors were aimed at their bodies.

Fintan stood between the horses, his sword unsheathed. Caitlin could hear words raised in anger but could not make out if it was Fintan addressing the riders or if it was the voice of one of the strangers.

Unexpectedly one of the them threw down his sword and scabbard and dismounted his horse. He was immediately surrounded by spearmen. He took the reins and led his horse toward the entrance to the hillfort with an escort close around him.

The other two strangers turned and galloped off as fast as their horses could carry them. Caitlin knew instinctively that this man was the enemy: one of the followers of Dichu or, worse, one of the servants of Palladius. She skittered back down the bank and headed for the round-house.

She had not expected that Dichu would be willing to talk terms, the man had a reputation for butchery in battle. Her heart beat hard and fast. 'Perhaps they have Gobann and the boy. All our plans may be ruined before they have a chance to bloom.' She made her way swiftly along the paved path, but her legs could not carry her fast enough.

Only as she reached the doors of the stone fort in the centre of the defences did she realise that it had been raining heavily and she had been drenched to her underclothes. Hastily she entered and made for her chamber. There she quickly changed into dry linens.

'The cloth is worn and old and the colour faded but it will have to do,' she told herself. 'Better to be dry and in tatters than to be looking like an otter fresh from the lake.'

She combed out her hair and found her silver neck-band. Downstairs she could already hear men's voices and smell meat being cooked. 'That is good,' she thought. 'Give him the best we can offer, Fintan, then he will think we are well provided.'

She fastened her cloak-pin to her skirt and went down the winding stairs to the feasting hall. In the shadow of the doorway at the foot of the stair she stood concealed to observe the visitor.

'I will talk to your lord, if he be of noble birth,' the stranger insisted, 'but to none other.'

Caitlin had placed herself well behind the man, but even so she could plainly see that his clothes were not those of the common folk of Eirinn. His shirt was deep blue and of a thin material that flowed and shone as he moved. His boots were knee high and jet black. His thick trousers were double-stitched down each seam with leather thonging and they were of fine white calfskin. A long scarlet cloak lay discarded across the back of another chair and on the floor was a helm of shining steel with long red feathered plumes arranged along the top.

126

Roman.

'Do you understand?' the stranger was saying to Fintan. 'I ... will ... speak ... to ... none ... other.'

Fintan noticed Caitlin in the shadow of the stair-well and coughed, embarrassed.

'Lady,' he began, 'this is Seginus Gallus, an envoy from the Bishop Palladius. He seeks audience with you.'

Seginus turned in his seat to better see Caitlin. He had a man's body but a boy's face and his skin was smooth and dark.

'I am Caitlin Ni Úaine. I am a Druid and a judge,' she said slowly.

'I don't care if you're the Holy Mother of Christ herself, I have orders to deliver my message only to the chieftain of this dun.' Caitlin noticed his accent and the difficulty he had with pronunciation. He was clearly a foreigner.

'I am of the clan Úaine and a Brehon judge. I am the chieftain of this dun.'

Seginus stood slowly in disbelief. He stared at Caitlin, trying to discern if she was joking. The colour left his face for a moment. And then he laughed. 'No wonder we sweep the heathen before us! A woman! Chieftain!'

Then he rounded on Fintan. 'Do you know that the Holy Scripture teaches that women are weak and are meant to be tamed by men? Women are evil creatures sent to defile the Earth with their lust! Men were created to keep the sins of their kind in check. Have you no shame to be ordered around by a mere female?' This last comment was said with such venom that the words spat forth from Seginus' mouth in a gush of saliva.

Fintan put his hand upon the hilt of his sword. Caitlin shook her head at him. He squeezed the

127

pommel with white knuckles but then loosed his grip.

'She is our chieftain and you are in her hall,' said Fintan, barely controlling the fury in his voice.

'In my country she would be serving us wine and we would be playing dice to decide who beds her this night.'

'Still your tongue,' commanded Fintan, 'or you will learn to do without it!'

The Roman muttered something in his own speech and then laughed again, louder this time. Grinning with contempt, he coughed a ball of phlegm into his throat and spat it toward Caitlin's feet. The vile substance cut a low arc as it flew across the room.

Caitlin could only watch in disbelief. She had no idea that foreigners were capable of being so foul.

Before the fluid had touched the floor Fintan raised a ready fist and punched the man to the ground. He stood over the Roman, one foot pushing the olive-skinned face into the dirt.

'Let him up,' said Caitlin firmly. 'I'll not see hospitality broken even for an ignorant wretch such as this. Let him up but do not allow him to make another move like that.' She stood over Seginus and spoke slowly to him. 'Do you hear? If you behave like a dog you will be sent back to your master with your tail between your legs.'

Seginus twisted his head around under the warrior's heel and looked at her. He had been surprised by the blow and he was winded. 'Savages,' he thought. Then he spoke. 'Very well, but you have broken the laws of hospitality with me. When Bishop Palladius hears—'

Caitlin cut him short. 'The good bishop is a Romano-Briton. He does not recognise our laws, much less live by them, so I do not think he would bother to quote them to me. In any case, does your own teaching not advise you to turn the other cheek when an enemy strikes you and then that you should be gracious unto them? Do not presume to threaten me, young man. You are in my country now and I am a chieftain of the clan Úaine.'

Fintan reached down and effortlessly dragged the Roman up by the collar of his fine blue shirt. The stitching tore loudly. Seginus fell back into the chair, grasping at the split seam.

Seeing the fellow once more seated, Caitlin walked calmly across the room to find a chair. She came to where the Roman cloak lay draped across her seat. Without hesitation she pushed it to the floor and sat in the place it had occupied.

'Now, you may tell me,' she said, 'what message this bishop of yours would send to me.'

Seginus rubbed his jaw where he had been struck. He shook his head to clear his wits. 'She is no more than a farmer's daughter,' he thought contemptuously. 'By the blessed Apostle Paul, her clothes are no better than a milkmaid's!' He noted the stern faces around the room, though, and realised that any of these warriors would gladly slice a Roman head off if she bade it.

Caitlin coughed loudly, waiting for a reply.

'I have travelled hard and would speak better with a full belly,' he said playing for time.

'Very well,' replied Caitlin, turning to Fintan. 'Fetch him meat and drink but nothing special, just whatever the ration is for today.'

The warrior took his cue and went to the kitchen to gather the best of everything that was in the store. 'Let him believe we eat like the High-King in Teamhair. That'll make the bishop think twice about besieging us,' he reasoned.

'Are you a Roman?' Caitlin asked Seginus coldly as Fintan left the room.

'I am the son of a Roman officer and a woman of the province of Gaul.'

'Your people would call you a bastard then?'

'I am a holy brother in the service of Christ. It matters not who my parents were. I am devoted to the one true God. The God of Love who will bring me one day to paradise.'

'Is your god the god of war also?'

'He has called on me many times to fight against the evil one and in this land there is much that is the handiwork of the servants of the Lord of Darkness. Many of your people still worship idols and springs and trees and rocks. So I am sent like my brothers in Christ to show your folk the way to Heaven.'

'From what I know of the Bishop Palladius, he has already showed many of my people the road to that place, and then sent them swiftly on their way,' she said not bothering to hide her disgust.

Seginus took a small wooden cross from under his shirt. He was angry at the accusing tone of his host. 'She is a heathen,' he reminded himself. 'She is not worthy of my anger. Let her hear the Word. Others more proud than she have embraced the faith.'

He got down on his knees and holding the cross above him said, 'Sister, since you will not hear the words that I offer you, at least listen to the word of God. Then you might save yourself and your kindred. Accept the holy teachings of Christ. Let me Christian you into the fellowship of the Holy Cross. Do this and you have my solemn promise that when my bishop comes here tomorrow, and with him the warriors of Dichu, they will pass over this place and leave you in peace.'

'Eternal peace,' he promised under his breath.

'But, Roman, I have long known the teachings of Christ. I was taught to honour your faith by my tutors. I have taken the wine and bread also and shared the house of the white-robed Brothers of Christ.'

'They are the servants of Satan!' hissed Seginus. 'Heretics!' He made the sign of the cross and Caitlin noticed that he did so in a different manner from the White Brothers.

Seeing this, she took a few moments to observe him more closely. His black hair hung lank and greasy and he smelled heavily of sweat. It was obvious he had not washed for many days. And there was something else about this man. His eyes moved swiftly round the room, never focusing on one point for more than a few seconds. It was as if he had lived too long surrounded by danger and treachery. His outward distrust of all people gave him the air of a feral creature. He was frightened and skittish, like a fox brought indoors for the first time.

'Sister,' continued Seginus unaware of Caitlin's scrutiny, 'these men you talk of serve not the King of Peace, but Lucifer himself, the fallen servant of God. I have been told that Druids are wise, so I beg you listen and accept now the learning of the words of the Gospels.'

Tenderly he kissed the cross and laid it down before him. From his shirt he took a small package enclosed in leather. Slowly he unbound the fastenings which held the parcel closed and unwrapped a book.

Caitlin had no interest in such things. She had seen many books at Teamhair but she could not read and did not desire to learn how. Her patience was wearing thin.

'Save your breath, Brother, here is your meal,' she interrupted as Fintan entered bearing a full platter of food.

'You say you were told that Druids are wise,' she asked, 'is that why Palladius has them skinned alive?'

'Most Druids are servants of the Devil and if they will not renounce their evil master for the faith of Christ, we have no choice but to dispatch them to Him for His judgment.'

'I am a Druid,' she remarked, 'and I will not submit to you.'

'Then, Druid, you will surely die and then you will burn forever in the fires of Hell,' replied Seginus calmly.

'Is that the nature of your message from Palladius then?' demanded Caitlin.

The Roman held her stare for a moment and then said simply, 'Yes. That is the nature and the substance.'

Caitlin drew a deep breath before speaking her next words. 'When you have finished your meal, my champion Fintan will escort you to the river. There is nothing more to be said.'

'May Christ have mercy on you, Sister,' declared Seginus insincerely.

'And also on you, Roman,' Caitlin replied, echoing his tone. With that she strode out into the air, making sure to step heavily on the scarlet cloak on her way. Once out of the door she headed for the embankment.

The chill breeze stung her cheeks like a slap. Light rain still pelted. The wind tore at her cloak. But she didn't notice. Her mind was filled with disgust at the arrogance of the Bishop Palladius and at the insults of his messenger.

'Still yourself,' she chided, 'there are further preparations to be made.'

She reached the embankment and passed by the watch-house. The guard had changed and she greeted the new sentry.

'I am going to the stream to wash,' she called, still burning with the Roman insults. 'Tell Fintan I will speak with him at midnight.'

Then, passing through the gate, she carefully made her way down the side of the ramparts. The rain had eased by the time she reached the ditch at the bottom of the hillfort and before long she was standing at the edge of a small stream that fed into the river and then into the lake.

She spent a long while calming herself before raising her hands and head to the sky to embrace the peace of that place. As her eyes scanned the cloud-filled blueness, the words of a poem came to her memory though she was sure that she had never heard them spoken before.

'I am a Salmon in the depths of the lake!' she
   intoned.
'I am the dark-green Leaf of the Holly Bush,
I am the Wolf on the Hunt,
I am the Heartbeat pounding within the Stone,
I am the Black Raven soaring over the Battlefield,
I am the secret walking Shadows of the Evening,
I am the Cloak of the Stars,
I illumine the Night,
I herald the Light.'

As these words passed her lips she felt all the reserves of energy pass from her body. She knelt down by the stream and splashed her face. The shock of the icy cold water brought her to her senses.

'What am I doing out here alone?' she asked herself. She stood to leave but an eerie feeling of impending danger came upon her and she froze in an instant.

Among the bushes on the opposite side of the stream there was a noise and she sensed that she was being observed. 'I am a fool to have come here alone. What if the Roman has his warriors waiting nearby to attack?' Her mind buzzed with possible consequences.

Cursing herself, she slowly, painfully slowly, knelt back down, trying to make her outline as small as she could. The river stones crunched lightly beneath her feet. She heard, or thought she did, a great intake of breath coming from across the stream. Suddenly a huge black shape crashed down the other bank, thundering through the hawthorn bushes and splashing into the water.

Caitlin was caught so unawares that she almost forgot all her training and let out a scream. But years of discipline kept her tongue still and her senses sharp. It took a few seconds for her to realise what had happened.

Standing square in the middle of the moving water, cautiously eyeing her, was a mighty king stag. The stream swirled around his feet as he quietly closed in on Caitlin, his wary eyes always level with hers. Fear and dismay paralysed her. These proud animals, she knew, were unpredictable and often lethal in their dealings with the humankind. He walked up to the water's edge and there stopped just out of her reach. She knew that any move, even a twitch, could jeopardise her life.

His head was bowed forward, his nose just brushing the running water, so that she could see a broken antler and dried blood at his nostrils. He swayed slightly. He was wounded.

Slowly, tenderly, Caitlin put out her hand to him. He let her touch him. She ran her palm over his shoulder. The powerful beast, easily twice her size, groaned softly and contentedly and leaned against her touch. When she withdrew her hand it was covered in blood.

As the stag lapped gently at the icy water, she quickly examined the rest of his body, her fear banished for the time being. Out of his rear flanks two shattered arrow shafts protruded at ugly angles. In a desperate escape from some cruel hunter he had torn much of the flesh on his hindquarters and lost a great deal of blood. It would only be a matter of time before he succumbed to his wounds if he was not given help soon.

Caitlin reached around to touch the jagged splinters of one shaft and the huge animal bellowed in agony, tautened muscles twitching across his body. He held his head high and pushed out the contents of his lungs in a mighty gust, then drew the air back in slowly and with much pain.

'How did this happen to you?' she asked out aloud. 'Who could bring themselves to injure such a magnificent creature?' The stag groaned but gave no answer that she could understand.

Caitlin placed her palm once more on his flank to soothe him and then lay her cheek alongside it speaking lowly to him. The stag relaxed a little, he was calming down at last. Suddenly the animal took in another great breath and pulled away from her looking over his shoulder.

In the bushes on the other side of the stream Caitlin caught the sounds of men talking and then several things happened in quick succession. First she heard a noise like someone blowing their breath violently out between clenched teeth. Then a weight struck her left leg, as if a heavy rock had been thrown at her. She tried to move around to the stag's shoulders but her knee was caught on something and she stumbled.

Then, an instant later, she heard an identical sound, also like a sharp breath, and watched in horror as an arrow pierced the stag's head, entering just above the neck. The terrified animal turned to search Caitlin's face, wild-eyed as the life drained swiftly from him. There they stood looking at each other for a moment until the soul of the beast finally fled his body. The great animal fell forward on his knees, rolled away from Caitlin and died.

With trembling fingers she reached down to where she had felt the impact on her leg. She had feared the worst and her fear was justified.

A hand's breadth below her knee an iron-tipped arrow had pierced the flesh of her leg and passed through the muscle. Now she began to feel the pain of it. The metal point had pushed cleanly out the other side of her limb, mercifully missing the bone. She grasped the tip firmly and pulled the whole missile out along the path it should have followed, wincing with the pain and effort.

From the hawthorn bushes whence the stag had come, she plainly heard voices but could not make out what was being said. Tucking the arrow into her belt, she touched the carcass on the back in parting and limped as quickly as she could up the rocky bank of the stream and into the cover of the woods.

Under the shrubs near the stream she hid for a long time while two men with bows in hand crossed the water, searched for a short while without much conviction, and then set about butchering the stag.

The rain started falling heavily again but Caitlin was close enough to notice one detail about the men. They were foreigners. One wore a cloak exactly like to the one Seginus had, though more tattered, and the other carried a short Roman sword.

When they were finished cutting the choicest flesh from the animal they made a quick inspection of the bank, too quick to see the wounded woman hiding only a stone's throw from them. The larger of the two heaved a sack full of meat over his shoulder and prepared to leave.

'Can't see any sign of her.'

'You bloody idiot, Darach! I told you we'd be seen this close to the fort.'

'Shut up. We got us the meat. So just shut up. Wait'll Seginus sees this. We haven't had fresh venison for weeks. Mark my words, this'll improve his mood.'

'Darach, the only thing that'd cheer him up right now would be if that sack were full of gold. Then it'd be a week in the whorehouses of Eboracum before his face cracked.'

'A month,' corrected Darach. He stopped what he was doing for a moment.

'What was that sound?'

'Where?'

'There, up the bank a little.'

'By Christ, I hope she doesn't make it to the fort or every wild Gaelic warrior in the valley 'll be out for our blood.'

'Look, she's not going to get far. I told you, I hit her in the stomach. She'll bleed to death before she reaches the road.'

'Shouldn't we make sure?'

Caitlin stopped breathing.

'I don't know about you, but I'm taking this back to the camp and then I'm going to saddle up and get ready to meet his lordship at sunrise. I'd rather face a hundred Irish madmen than him if we're late to meet the advance guard.'

'All right ... but I still reckon you're a bloody fool.'

The smaller of the two washed his knife in the water and then followed his companion back across the stream. The whole operation did not take as long as it would for a cloud to pass across the Moon but by the time they had gone, Caitlin had lost a lot of blood and felt very weak. Satisfied that they were not going to return, she made her way slowly and painfully back toward the hillfort.

As she reached the top of the rampart, the agony of her wound became unbearable and she let out a cry of anguish. The guard at the watch-house came running to find the source of the noise. He found her barely conscious, lying in a pool of blood, sobbing uncontrollably.

Seginus was admiring a gold drinking horn as he finished his meal, when the warrior burst through the door of the round-house bearing Caitlin in his arms.

Fintan got up from his seat slowly, not fully understanding what he saw. For a few seconds he said nothing, then he noticed the blood still trickling from the hole in her leg and noticed her torn cloak.

'What happened?' he demanded of the watchman.

'I do not know,' replied the warrior. 'I found her at the top of the ramparts calling out in pain. She passed out on the way here.'

Fintan went to her side and searched her body for other wounds. He was thankful to find none. His hand brushed by the arrow in her belt and he pulled it out to examine it.

'This is not a dart made on these shores. See, it

is not of our style. It is too long and heavy.' He turned angrily to Seginus. 'It is one such as I've heard that your Briton mercenaries use, Roman.'

Seginus glanced up, seemingly uninterested, only the beads of sweat forming on his brow betraying his fear.

'Mmm. Yes, it is similar to those of my people,' he said thinking to himself, 'I will hang those two on the morrow. I told them not to come near this fort!'

The Roman's coldness was too much for Fintan. 'You are here under truce and hospitality!' he raged.

'Are you accusing me of having arranged the ambush of this girl?' replied Seginus. 'Why would I bother to do that? I hardly think she's worth the trouble.'

'You have broken our laws,' cried Fintan. 'You have returned our hospitality with treachery.'

Seginus spun around the room desperately looking for something to defend himself with. 'You would not dare harm me,' he said with more confidence than he felt. 'I am unarmed and alone. Your own laws do not permit you to touch a guest. You would never live it down.'

Fintan let his anger boil, felt his ears ringing with the surging blood of contempt. He held the arrow out before him in both hands and slowly bent each end closer and closer toward the other. The wood screeched as it splintered and snapped. Then Fintan dropped the shattered dart at the Roman's feet.

He turned to the watchman who still cradled Caitlin in his arms. 'Take her up to the warm rooms and wrap that wound,' he ordered, holding back all emotion. Then he faced the other warriors that had assembled in the tower and said, 'He will not be harmed, not so much as bruised. Do you hear?'

The men all nodded, reluctantly agreeing.

Then Fintan turned to Seginus and reached out with lightning speed grabbing the Roman securely by the throat and squeezing firmly. The man's eyes widened in fear and pain.

Fintan held him like that long enough for Seginus to find breathing difficult and then a moment longer. He slowly released his grip and pushed the Roman into the grasp of the closest warrior.

'Strip him!' he ordered.

EIGHT

oetry and music contain the very essence of all things that live,' said Gobann over his shoulder to his young companion. 'And the three Strains of Music are the vital breath of all life.'

'Will *I* learn these three strains?' asked Mawn expectantly, his eyes sparkling with wonder.

'You will,' Gobann confirmed. 'That is one of the many lessons you must master before we can progress with your education.'

'Then we had better start the lessons now,' the boy commented. 'I am ready to begin, if you are.'

Gobann studied Mawn's face for a moment, impressed at his willingness to learn. 'Music has three main modes,' the poet began. 'These modes are the basis for all melodies that are played on the harp or the pipes or which are sung in the style of the Sean Nós.'

'What is the Sean Nós?'

'That is the ancient way of singing that was all the music that our people knew, before they had harps,' Gobann explained. 'All the melodies that you hear come from that old tradition of singing, but only a few people know the ways of the Sean Nós today.'

Gobann realised that he had strayed a little from the lesson. 'The modes that we know today are the Strain of War and of Love, the Strain of Sorrow, and the Strain of Sleep.'

'Why do war and love share a strain of music?' asked Mawn surprised.

The poet was happy that his student had been listening well. 'War and love share a mode because the emotions that are aroused in war and in love are often very similar. Many a bitter war was begun for love, and many a love affair ended in bitter war.'

Mawn nodded, not quite sure what Gobann meant, but he noticed that the poet stared off into the distance when he said those words.

'The Strain of Sorrow is the mode of lamentation,' added Gobann, 'and the Sleep Strain is the mode of soothing music.'

'What about the music of the dance?' queried Mawn. 'Which mode is that in?'

'A dance is usually in the mode of love and war, though it can also be played in the Sorrow Strain or, more rarely, in the Sleep mood. Music is not classified according to the speed at which it is played but rather by which notes make up its fabric. The harp was built specially for the three modes and is the instrument that best expresses all the strains.'

'Is that why I must spend so long at studying it?' asked the boy.

'Aye, lad, twenty summers makes a harper. But one day you will compose a story poem that will be made up of the essence of all the events and people that have gone into your life. You will need to know how to do it properly so that others may remember it and pass it on to their listeners. That is how we keep the spirit of our people alive: through stories to inspire them, music to lull them and poems to fill them with the will to endure hardship.'

Gobann's horse shook the bit in her jaws and

loudly neighed as if in agreement with her master.

'Will people remember my poems?' asked the boy.

'Yes, surely. The gift of poetry is a rare one and poets are highly prized, even amongst the savage folk of Lochlann.'

They rode on in silence after that, the sound of the rain falling softly on the road their only companion. As the day grew darker they stopped by an empty, roofless cottage and set a fire going within its dry earth walls. They unsaddled and brushed the horses and then hobbled them together in the nearby field.

Mawn went to fetch water from the well while Gobann took some dried meat and oat-bread from the packages that Olan had prepared for them and put a small cauldron close to the coals ready to boil. Then he took from his own pack the herbs to make a sleep-tea. When Mawn returned Gobann set the pot to cooking.

His young companion was already drowsy from the journey and even before he had hastily eaten he began to slip into sleep.

'You will stand guard on the fire and the camp tonight,' said Gobann sternly. 'We must each do our fair share from now on. I will wake you for your watch after midnight. Sleep well, Mawn.'

The boy curled up in his cloak beside the wall and, as he drifted off, spoke a few quiet words to himself.

Gobann sat with his harp on his lap listening to the water boil in the cauldron and the breeze calling through the trees. After a long while he began gently to pluck the wires in answer to the sounds of the night. That is how he passed his watch.

Some hours later he woke his apprentice and sat him up.

'It is your duty to watch now until the dawn. Mind that you keep the fire alive and that you wake me if you hear anything on the road.'

Mawn nodded, wrapping the blanket round himself again and leaning against the wall. He was determined to stay awake but try as he might it was only an hour or so before he had fallen once again to sleep.

Some hours later, Gobann stirred to feel heavy rain on his covers and to hear the sound of horses close by. He rose quickly, noticing the fire had gone out. The rain had doused it and there was only a little smoke; Mawn grumbled in his sleep. Gobann decided not to waken him but instead moved swiftly and quietly to where he could get a better view of the road.

Through a short gap in the ruined cottage wall he saw a sight that made his heart race with fear. Not twenty paces from where he huddled there were many horsemen, some carrying spluttering torches to guide their way. They passed steadily by in two columns. This was a full army on the move. The rain became heavier by the minute and Gobann thanked the gods, for it had doused the fire and concealed the site of their camp. He was not yet sure if these troops were friendly.

One horseman suddenly broke off from the column and steered his mount toward the house. The poet ducked his head down behind the windowsill.

'You there! What do you think you're doing?' came a commanding voice.

Gobann prayed that he had not been seen.

'I am taking shelter where it's dry. Can't you see that?' replied the horse-warrior.

'Rejoin the column!' barked the other voice.

'Bugger off! I'm wet and tired. I'll catch you up tomorrow.'

'What's your name?' demanded the voice, now full of threat.

'Leave it off. I'll catch up. Old Dichu's too stupid to notice one missing out of two thousand. He's got more important things to worry about.'

'You'll hang for this,' replied the voice.

'I told you to bugger off. I'm going within these walls to sleep and get dry and I'll find the army tomorrow.' The warrior dismounted and began to unpack his gear.

Gobann watched without a sound. This was much worse than he had at first thought. The whole of the army of Laigin was upon them.

'I told you to rejoin your company,' the voice warned. 'I will not tell you again. If you refuse I will kill you myself.'

'Who do you think you are, ordering me about and threatening me?' demanded the warrior.

'I am Palladius, Bishop of Eirinn,' came the reply, 'and you are a dead man.'

There was a muffled scream. A horse whinnied and then galloped. Gobann was pressed up against the wall, now praying fervently that he would not be found.

'Hang his body from that tree as a warning to deserters,' ordered Palladius. 'And catch his horse, I will need a fresh mount after the battle tomorrow.'

With that the bishop rode on, unaware that one of the chief Druids of Eirinn was hiding a few paces away from him.

Gobann crawled to where Mawn was still sleeping and gently woke the boy. 'We must prepare to leave. But we must do so very quietly, there is great danger to us here.'

Mawn nodded and then started packing his

bundles. Horsemen were still passing by when the
two slipped out of the cottage and down to the
stream where the horses had wandered in their
hobbles. Swiftly Gobann loosed the leather
restraints and tucked them into pockets in his
saddle. Then he took both horses by the bit and led
them down the glen at right angles to the road.
They walked on until dawn and then they finally
rested.

'We cannot stop here long,' said Gobann when
they sat down at last, 'our camping place may have
been discovered and there could be enemy warriors tracking us even now.'

Mawn could only nod; he knew nothing of who
was friend and who foe in this war. He was very
sleepy, unused to being woken in the middle of the
night to march behind his horse.

They ate some oat-bread and drank a little from
a spring then prepared to mount and move on.

'We will not take the road for a while,' said
Gobann, 'it is far too dangerous. We will travel by
the ancient routes, following the streams during the
day and the stars at night. This will be an important lesson for you. It is necessary that every Druid
know the stars. And I must explain to you how this
war came about.'

A broad, well-muscled man walked through the
steady driving rain until he reached the edge of the
sheltering trees. There, under a spreading ancient
oak, he stopped and stood for a short while to look
back upon his encampment.

Then, shaking the drops of water out of his hair,
he slipped a heavy axe from its loop in his wide
leather belt and carefully laid the blade flat

amongst a pile of decaying acorns and tufts of moist grass. When he was sure that the weapon was in a resting place where rain could not reach it, he swiftly removed his short-sword and scabbard from the strap over his shoulder and sat himself down on the rotting leaves that were spread around the base of the tree.

Guthwine was now forty summers old, though he had long since ceased to keep an accurate tally of the passing years. It was a good age for a man of his profession; too old some might have said. There were those among his followers who would have reckoned him a very fortunate man to be so long-lived, but he put his own survival down more to skill than to luck. He had always been a survivor. His body bore bitter testimony to that for it carried the scars of more than a hundred bloody battles, any of which could have proved fatal.

Countless brawls, mutinies and treacheries had also etched deep gouges into the fabric of his soul, reaching to the very heart of him. His spirit had become a mutilated and hideous entity that often times, especially on quiet nights, left his body to wander by itself or roamed his darkest nightmares full of fury, haunting his sleep.

He was a renegade, a mercenary, presently in the employ of Dichu King of Laigin. But he had been born to the people of the Saxon treaty lands of Britain and it was from those folk that he had learned the ways of war.

When still a very young man he swore himself to the trade of a pirate, spending the best years of his life in the service of famous kings or renowned murderers. During his career of raiding and seafaring he had gradually evolved into a living example of the main tenet of his people, which was 'Ever work and war until the world's renewing'.

To him that little saying might as well have been a riddle: the riddle of his existence.

Before great conflicts, faced with the prospect of a violent death, he always found himself coming closer to finding an answer to the questions that plagued him about his life and closer to confronting the beast that lived inside him. It was at these times that his memory would play tricks on him. Ghosts would return from the mists of battlefields long forgotten to torment him, prying open the gashes in his spirit, laying bare the grief of his guilt and his fear of the consequences of a life of murder and chaos.

'Only blood and murder can wash me of the past. Only death can quench my agony,' he resolved. 'And if it is not to be my own death,' he thought, though he had sought that actively enough, 'then I will bring death to others. I am the servant of the Raven of Death.'

Hannarr, his deputy, approached the oak tree cautiously from the direction of the camp. The golden-haired warrior knew his battle-lord well enough to be especially respectful around him at moments such as this.

Discerning the other man's presence nearby, Guthwine instinctively reached for his one true friend, his axe. 'You are the only one I trust, Frarod,' he muttered to himself as he lay back resting against the ancient tree.

Sensing the unrest in the soul of his lord, Hannarr waited patiently at a diplomatic distance, leaning against a young sapling.

'Battle, raiding, fear, fire, the open sea; all of these have been good, solid, reliable life companions to me,' thought Guthwine. 'They are real; they can be touched. Each has a place and a purpose in the world. Each has an easily understood meaning behind it. They are physical proof of the mortality of all things. But this journey to the Hibernian lands has brought me face to face with many things that are impossible to understand. From the moment we beached our ships in the sandy river mouth, strange unexplained omens have haunted this company. The ancestors had a special word for these unusual happenings. They would have called it "weird".'

'Weird.' He formed the word and spoke it, listening to the unfamiliar sound it made as it passed his lips.

It was a particular incident, playing still over in his mind, that bothered him most, for it had happened earlier that very day and had nearly cost him his life.

His company were on their way south on the orders of their employer, the King of the Laigin. Their duty: to pass over the land, wreak havoc and to bring the country people into submission. They were never lazy in the performance of their craft. At a certain village along the way, they found the plunder particularly to their liking: plenty of livestock and healthy young womenfolk. It was just another settlement of defenceless farmers like so many others, but as Guthwine recalled now all of what had happened there, the memory made the hairs on the back of his neck stand on end.

When they arrived the men of his party had set to their task with energy and enthusiasm, spreading havoc and disaster through the little village. Then, unexpectedly, in the midst of the joyous slaughter and easy pickings, a great black Raven plunged down out of the heavens to stand defiantly in the path of his advancing war party.

'The Raven is my battle totem,' he reminded himself, 'but was this one a spirit of vengeance come to take my soul to the halls of waiting? Or a warning from the guardians of this land?'

Whatever it was, the sudden appearance of the unearthly creature had affected his troops badly. They had routed at the very sight of it. Seeing the Raven of Darkness defying their swords and axes, they panicked and a handful of the most superstitious warriors had fled for their lives. Guthwine recalled vainly shouting after them and then turning defiantly to stand his ground before the beast. However, it was not his time for the bird flew on to pick at the cold eyes of another.

What happened immediately after was still largely a blur to him. In the middle of all the confusion a boy, just a country lad, ran screaming into the midst of Guthwine's bodyguard. He struck Gunnar Grunbrand, the senior man of the guard, with the upward thrust of a red-hot iron knife, dispatching the old warrior swiftly to sit among his ancestors. In the melee that followed, the boy spun round swiftly several times managing to inflict a wide and painful gash in Guthwine's shield arm before strong hands were laid on him and he was restrained.

The incident had left the thegn unusually shaken and jittery. This sort of thing rarely ever happened to him. It was uncommon for his bodyguard to be so distracted that they failed so completely in their duty.

In his shock he found himself merciful to the lad. He ordered that his attacker be tied to the back of the baggage cart until a justifiably painful end could be found for him. Then, without thought for further plunder and wishing only to be gone swiftly from the place, Guthwine directed that the village be torched.

As he sat now amongst the grasses under the oak tree, Thegn Guthwine ran his sword hand across the jagged gash in the flesh of his other arm. Then, breathing deeply to banish all troubling thoughts, he looked across at Hannarr and nodded. The younger man acknowledged the signal, bounding over the fallen branches to reach his lord.

'Hannarr Ettenson, what news of the deserters?' bellowed the thegn.

'There were ten only, my lord,' replied the deputy.

'Do you have them?'

'Aye, lord, we have them, though they put up a fight at first. What would you have us do with them?'

'Take one, cut out his stomach and hang him from this tree for all to see. And do it before sundown. I want the others to see the way I reward cowardice. You may release the remainder with a warning and a slash on the lower shield arm. I would like them to bear the same wound as I do for a while. I think they will not run from the affray next time.'

'And what will become of the boy?' enquired Hannarr.

Guthwine's eyes flashed almost imperceptibly from left to right, holding just a hint of fear. 'I have not decided. Perhaps I will hand him over to the bishop. He will certainly know how to deal with the lad.'

'Lord,' ventured Hannarr, broaching the subject cautiously, 'when will we be moving on to the stronghold Dichu spoke of?'

'Tomorrow at noon we are to meet the Bishop Palladius and his troops at a stream half a day's march south. The men should be ready to move at first light. I am assured by the bishop's messengers that there is a great deal of plunder to be had. You may spread the word to the warriors if you wish.'

'Lord, we have seen precious little of the gold and silver we were promised.'

Guthwine cut him off. 'I know it too well. If the situation does not improve on the morrow we will leave the service of our good bishop and do a little warring of our own.'

Hannarr gave a deep throaty laugh and spat into the grass. 'About bloody time too!' he said enthusiastically.

'Bed the men down after the execution and give them plenty to drink. I want them to sleep well tonight. If all goes in our favour we will have busy blades around noon tomorrow.'

'Aye, lord,' answered Hannarr. Then he turned round and headed back for the camp barking orders to the troops as he did so.

Guthwine remained under the tree, resting his weary mind until they brought before him the unfortunate deserter who was to be strung up among the branches. For the first time in many years the thegn did not have the desire to watch a killing. He left the gathered crowd of silent witnesses and went off to find where his horse was grazing.

When the execution was done and everyone had returned to their cooking fires, Guthwine sent for the boy to be brought to him.

'I must deal with this situation swiftly and well,' he told himself. 'If Streng or the others get a whiff of weakness from me, I'll be hanging on that tree like the other crow meat. I must punish the lad, no doubt of that, yet I dare not offend the gods of this land.'

Suspecting that there was a link between the young lad's wild attack and the appearance of the Raven, Guthwine could not but feel that there was some other force at work here, a force that he could not possibly understand.

Within the hour the boy was dragged before him kicking and screaming. Guthwine sat on a split log by the bonfire, his cloak draped about his shoulders and his axe, Frarod, across his knee.

Hannarr, Streng and the bowman Andvari, who knew the language of the Gaelic people, escorted the boy to their leader. Guthwine greeted the warriors all as friends and offered the three of them places by the fire. As was the custom he ignored their prisoner.

Streng followed the boy, firmly grasping strong ropes that bound his hands behind his back. As an added precaution the prisoner's wrists were shackled in iron, with about a shoulder's breadth of chain between them. This left just enough movement in the shackles for him to be able to raise his arms over his head and around to the front of his body so that he could be tied to the cart and walk behind it when they travelled. The chains at his feet allowed him to walk but only in short steps.

Guthwine sat back and let the conversation between his warriors flow, confident that the prisoner could not understand what was being said. This gave the thegn an opportunity to spend a good while observing the boy. He noticed that his young attacker was in a much worse state than when Guthwine had last seen him. His face was filthy and his fair hair matted with blood.

'My bodyguards are often overenthusiastic in carrying out their duties,' he noted with a smile. The lad returned his captor's glance with a gaze full of proud defiance. This determined glare made Guthwine more than a little uncomfortable.

Eventually the war-lord spoke. 'What is your name?' he demanded. Andvari passed on the question.

There was no reply, just hard steel-blue eyes staring full of hate.

'What is your occupation?'

The boy stood still as any stone, moving not so much as a muscle.

'Are you sure that he understands your rusty Gaelic?' enquired Guthwine.

'He understood me right enough when I asked him if he wanted anything to eat, my lord,' replied Andvari the interpreter.

'Tell me, boy, do you know the name of the garrison town a half a day's march from here?'

Again the question met with a cold silence.

Guthwine resolved to try and reason with his captive. 'Lad, all your clan are dead. All but you. You alone remain and you are my prisoner. It is a bloody miracle that you are not rotting in the same ditch as your family. Only your outstanding bravery saved you from that fate. We respect such courage among our people.' He waited as his words were passed on to the captive.

'So I promise that if you tell us about yourself, no harm will come to you. I may even adopt you into our large clan.' He made a sweep of his arm indicating the encampment.

At first Beoga, son of Midhna the blacksmith, listened passively to the red-bearded man who sat before him. But as more of what the thegn said was translated, anger at losing his family and seeing the cruel murder of his kinfolk surfaced and overflowed. He had not yet allowed full expression to his grief, but dreadful memories were now crowding in on him, suffocating him, and he could no longer hold the violent hate inside him.

In his mind he clearly saw Olan, his mother, slumped and bleeding in the doorway of their burning house. He heard the voice of Scéolan calling frantically for his wife and later, as he ran between the flaming buildings, he stumbled across the old weaver's corpse hacked to pieces in the courtyard. He was haunted by the sight of his brother Cen and his father battling the raiders with the only weapons they had, farming tools. They held the savages at the door to the forge for a long while, long enough for Beoga to escape through the fuel room. He picked up a red-hot iron in his leather-gloved hand and raced outside seeking a place to hide. He heard in his ears once again the dull echoes that were the dying screams of his father and of his brother.

A wave of disgust washed over Beoga. Unable to hold back any longer the boy spat an untranslatable obscenity that he had often heard his father use, then he swung round to kick at Streng, who stood behind him, as forcefully as he could.

He missed.

'This one would take on the Giants of the North if one of them were fool enough to catch him and try to keep him a prisoner!' laughed Streng showing his blackened teeth. The stench of his foul breath made Beoga gag.

The others all joined in the joke and even Guthwine smiled, relieved to feel the tension easing. Streng began coughing in his mirth and took a hand from the ropes around Beoga's hands, wiping the tears of laughter from his eyes. With heart beating in his throat, Beoga felt the grip loosen.

Streng made another derogatory comment about the lad and loosed his hold a little more. Anxious to contribute to the conversation Andvari added a line from an old drinking song that was particularly apt to the situation and laughed raucously at his own wit. Streng turned to him in appreciation of the jest, struggling to come up with an equally humorous reply.

In the that instant Beoga struck. With a sudden jerk and a chilling vengeful cry, his hands were free of the ropes that had restrained his movement, though they were still bound together by heavy metal chains. Lifting his arms over his head, he spun round and with the weight of the iron shackles brought his fists down on the man behind him.

Streng, stunned, fell backwards, toppling onto the grass. Beoga lifted his foot as high as he could and with all his force kicked hard at the man's exposed groin. The blow connected and Streng howled in agony.

Satisfied that the most dangerous looking warrior present had been dealt with, Beoga turned his attention to Guthwine. Knocking Andvari off balance, he threw himself headlong at the seated warrior. As he dived forward he slashed the chains mercilessly across the thegn's face and grasped the handle of the axe that lay across the war-leader's knee.

Despite his bound hands, he managed to grab the weapon and swing it high above his head, as he might have done the forge-hammer when he was tempering the iron. The instrument of war was very well balanced and even his untutored hands held the axe in a deadly grip.

Frarod sat high in the air, her spirit soaring, for she was about to deal a death blow, and for this she was made. She did not care that it would be her master that she struck down. The blade whistled lightly through the air as it fell, guided by inexperienced hands toward the target. But Beoga was no Saxon blade-warrior.

Guthwine anticipated the arc of the weapon's descent and rolled backwards out of its range as it came down. It was an old trick but it had saved his life many times.

Hannarr had been waiting for this move. Before the axe was halfway through its downward journey he bumped Beoga's shoulder hard, knocking the weapon out of his hands. It travelled on, striking the Earth a mere body's breadth from Guthwine's head. The boy lost his footing and Hannarr tackled him to the ground, knocking the wind out of him.

Guthwine quickly picked himself up, bellowing heart-felt curses at the boy, and then he laid in with his boot for good measure.

'Bind him well!' he yelled at his men. 'Tomorrow we give him over to the bishop.' Then he turned to Streng who still clutched at his groin and lay in the grass in pain. 'And as for you, get out of my sight, you bloody idiot. Twice you have let a mere farm lad make a mockery of my guard. I've seen enough of your foolery to last the rest of my stay in this country. And mind I don't catch sight of you on the battlefield tomorrow. I might forget who I am meant to be slaying!'

Streng rose painfully, still surprised by the prisoner's dexterity, and dragged Beoga by the feet back to the baggage cart. Andvari followed quietly behind him, thankful that Guthwine had not singled him out for any attention. Only Hannarr stayed with his Lord.

'Thegn Eikenskald?' he asked tentatively when the others were gone. 'Have you any other orders?'

'None,' came the abrupt reply. 'Thank you for once again saving my life. The debt is certainly building between us.'

'Lord, be careful. Tomorrow on the field it could become very dangerous for you. Some of the men are toying with the idea of taking a new leader.'

'Will you stand close by me in the battle, then, my friend?' asked Guthwine.

'As always I will allow no blade but mine to come near you. I promise.'

Streng and the bowman Andvari took Beoga and brutally beat the boy into unconsciousness. When they were done, they tied him to the back of the cart.

As they wiped the sweat from their faces, Andvari produced a flagon of ale from his belt-hook and handed it to the other warrior. The two friends drank deeply together. They spoke only in glances. Not a word passed between them; only the ale parted their lips. When the drink was gone they left each other silently to seek opposite ends of the camp.

Streng was full of the nervous energy that preceded armed conflict and he made no secret of it to those around him. When he returned to his campfire he offered to take on some of the young warriors at wrestling and sword-play. Like a lion cub rehearsing for its first kill, he jumped about and yelled and provoked his mercenary siblings. But the morrow's battle was to be by no estimate his first kill.

He, like Guthwine, had lived a life devoted to the gods of war. He belonged entirely to the ritual contest of sinew against sinew. His very name bespoke that lifelong vocation for it meant, simply, strength.

Among his contemporaries, for whom a valiant death was the goal of them all, Streng was a man whose reputation for reckless valour had already become legendary. He had fought in wars against

Angles, Jutes, Danes and Franks and had sailed south to battle Turks and Africans, until the day he was taken captive by Northmen. He sailed with them as an oar-slave to the land of the Kazkhs and then to the Lands of Ice. On a night when the Northmen were all drunk he slit the oar-master's throat and escaped to join Guthwine in the Saxon treaty lands of Britain.

Now his life was about to take a new twist. As arranged, he slipped out of the camp at sundown to meet secretly with his brother-in-law Draupnir and Andvari.

'I have spent the best part of the day organising it,' reported Draupnir. 'During the battle five men loyal to you will surround Guthwine. In the press of the fight they should be able to push their way through the bodyguards. While they deal with the thegn the rest of us will butcher his troop of bodyguards.'

'Then we elect Streng Thorverson to be our new war-thegn, and we start some real fighting,' added Andvari.

'Do you reckon his bodyguards will be any problem?' Streng asked Draupnir.

'I am one of them so that leaves only six to deal with. I should be able to dispatch at least two, and I'm sure to get a clear stab at Guthwine, aye, that's for certain,' he assured his new leader. 'I swear I'll be holding the axe that parts the head from those old shoulders.'

'Good, good,' rejoined Streng, his rotten teeth showing through wind-cracked lips. But he thought to himself, 'I can't wait to see old Draupnir's face when I pronounce him guilty of treason and kneel him down to face the block! Then it'll be my axe that'll do some head-parting.' Streng's smile broadened, stretching the weathered skin on his face. 'A traitor once can easy turn traitor again, and besides,' he laughed to himself, 'I never could abide cold-blooded murderers.'

The others echoed his laughter, though they didn't guess he was laughing at them. The three parted company then to enter the camp from different directions so that suspicions would not be aroused. As arranged they each straightaway went to their sleeping places and lay down to sleep.

Guthwine walked a circuit of the fires wishing his men well for the morrow and then he listened to a few songs of their homeland before he went to slumber.

All was quiet in the camp of the Saxons until long after the darkest hour. Without warning a commotion broke out some distance from the warleader's sleeping place. Guthwine stirred from his bed a little dazed and rose reluctantly to seek the cause of the disturbance.

He could clearly hear the enthusiastic laughter of many men almost drowning out one man's panicked wailing.

'I want the warriors ·to rest well,' he thought, furious that his orders had been ignored. 'How can they fight well without enough sleep?' He strode purposefully toward the source of the noise.

When he got close to the fracas he gave vent to his frustration and bellowed out at a group of young men gathered around a man mounted on a war horse, 'What's all this bloody noise about?'

No-one answered him; no-one even noticed him at first. They were busy prodding the horse's rump and forcing it to rear up in the confined space.

Guthwine punched several of his men out of the

way and grabbed the horse by the bridle. He yelled for silence and the startled men quickly obeyed.

When the horse had settled, Guthwine noticed that the fellow on its back was naked and had been tied to the animal in a most painful manner, his arms stretched around the creature's neck.

'What in the name of the God of Thunder are you lot doing?' he raged.

All remained quiet, except for a few who could not contain their chuckles. The horseman continued screaming.

'Are you lot deaf?' stormed Guthwine at the assembly. 'I said what the bloody hell is going on?'

No-one dared answer. The horseman was still crying out.

Guthwine, losing his patience completely, turned to the naked rider and grabbed him by the hair shouting at him with all his voice, 'I thought I told you to shut up!'

In that instant he recognised Seginus Gallus the envoy of Bishop Palladius.

It took a few seconds for the thegn to appreciate fully what he saw and then a few more before he could think what action should be taken.

'Get him off that nag and bring him to my tent,' Guthwine ordered in a subdued tone. 'He is my honoured guest.' Then he went to find some strong drink and some clothes for the Roman.

NINE

n the Stronghold of Rathowen, Caitlin was cursing her misfortune. The wound to her leg was not too serious but it would surely restrict her activities during the coming weeks. The bleeding had taken hours to slow and eventually the knee had to be tightly bound to stem the flow. But far worse than this was the certainty that she would not be able to take part in the coming battle as had been planned.

'Our victory relies on everyone being able to contribute to the defence. The warriors must be able to see their chieftain leading them,' she thought to herself.

Fintan was naturally very concerned for her and stayed at her bedside throughout the night, only leaving an hour before the dawn to walk the defences.

He returned shortly after daylight had begun to brighten the land. 'Are you awake?' he asked softly.

'I am,' Caitlin replied. 'Come and help me. I must go to the roof and greet the sun.'

'A place has been set for you there where you may watch and direct any resistance if the enemy manages to breach the ramparts,' the warrior reported, lifting her tenderly out of bed. His cloak brushed against her and she recognised it as the one that Seginus had carried.

'That was a handsome gift!' she exclaimed.

'I took it from him,' said Fintan coldly. 'And all else he owned or wore, save his horse.'

'You did what? Why?'

'He had insulted you and arranged that you be murdered. By his actions he asked for no less.'

'Do you know for certain that is what he planned?' she countered.

'Well, no,' Fintan admitted reluctantly, 'but you can't deny he deserved worse than he got.'

'Aye, but were you the one who should have punished him? For all we know, it may have been hunters who did this to me or it may have been renegades, but whoever it was, I am alive and it is my part to seek recompense for this injury, not yours. You have overstepped your duties. Do not presume to punish a stranger in my hall again!' she rebuked him. 'Now fetch me the piper. I will play a lament on the harp and then I will have him blow a call to arms.' She grabbed her own cloak and stood defiantly but also unsteadily.

'Let me help you to the roof,' Fintan appealed.

'Do as I bid!' she snapped. 'I am well enough to walk and I am not dead yet!'

Fintan bowed low and left the room with a flourish of the long scarlet cloak. Caitlin grabbed her staff and hobbled to the door. With much painful toil and many rest stops she dragged herself up to the roof. Then for a long while she stood catching her breath, the staff firmly in front of her supporting her. Her harp was already waiting for her, set on its flat back beside a chair.

She readied herself to play as the piper filled his war-pipes with breath and began to tune his droning instrument. Though he stood on the furthest part of the hillfort the odd notes of his tuning

drifted up to Caitlin on the tower and they seemed
to dance delicately around her.

'I am the Eye of the Heavens,' she chanted,
'I am the Spark that ignites
The hearth-fire of the Mind,
I am the Sweet Kiss of the Honey-Mead,
I am the Eagle soaring in the Clouds,
I am the Flame of Love that burns in the Breast,
I am the Breath of the Dragon,
I am the Sun on the Earth,
The Bringer of Light.'

When the piper was satisfied that his war-pipes
were in tune, the strange groans of the instrument
faded for a moment and died in the distance. This
was Caitlin's cue to take up her harp. She sat and
found that it was almost ready to play and needed
only a slight adjustment to the wires so that they
would sound sweet. Then, taking a deep breath,
she touched the strings and brought forth an
ancient, haunting melody. It was a tune set in the
War Strain, an air that was composed to stir the
hearts of warriors and inspire them to the task
ahead. It was slow, but it touched them all deeply
and every soldier within earshot froze at his post
and lowered his gaze to the ground.

This was the most moving piece she knew; one
of the many harp tunes that had been taught to the
Gaelic people by the musicians of the Tuatha-De-
Danaan. For a moment Caitlin imagined many
small-bodied folk dancing gracefully around her,
though she knew they rarely took on that dimin-
utive form. Before she knew it, the heart-rending
melody had spent itself and she let the last note
hang on the breeze as if it were part of the air all
around.

The piper was listening carefully, waiting for the ringing of the harp to fade before he struck up another war strain. A lively spirit suddenly filled every breast and the gathered warriors began to walk with a spring in their step.

'It can not be hoped for,' thought Caitlin sadly, 'that any of us will be alive at sundown.' Her scouts had reported a enemy force gathered that outnumbered her garrison five to one.

Then she was sorry for her outburst of anger at Fintan. 'I have been too hard on him. He only did what he did for the love of me. I must make amends while I still have the chance.'

She took up her harp once more and sat then after the piper had gone to his sentry post, strumming at it softly, composing a melody. She ate a little bread when it was brought to her an hour later and then she lay down to rest, still on the rooftop, having secured her guard's promise that she would be woken at the first sign of the enemy.

'Those bloody heathen,' sneered Seginus as he sprawled in Guthwine's tent, having drunk his fill. 'The bastards took everything I had and tied me up like a pig. I've been on that old nag half the night!'

Guthwine's face was expressionless as he chewed a piece of dried meat.

'There's a woman in charge of the garrison! A bloody woman! But she's out of the way for the moment.' Then Seginus remembered his two body-guards. 'When I get my hands on them I'll kill those two stupid dogs,' he snarled. 'This is all their fault.'

Guthwine did not understand all that was being

said so he leaned back against his shield and fell to observing the man sitting opposite. 'He has the air of a warrior but he is so soft and weak. He allows too many of his true feelings to surface,' thought the thegn.

'We will avenge your misfortune soon enough, Cousin,' declared Guthwine. 'Have no fear of that.'

'I paid dearly for that helm, and the cloak was my father's. That snivelling bastard will pay with his life for this insult!' hissed the Roman.

'You and I should slumber now for it is not long until the dawn and we must be ready to march,' Guthwine informed his guest. 'But before we take rest I must ask you something about the defences at the stronghold. Was there any point in the ditches where you think they had left a weak spot?'

'There were sharpened stakes all along the perimeter except for a stretch about six cart-lengths wide that had not been finished. It is quite close to the round central fort, but on the opposite side from where Dichu intends to attack.'

'Very well,' said the thegn, 'tomorrow I suggest that the two of us scout together and make our plans before Dichu and the bishop have arrived. We may be able to find a way of ending the battle quickly and without a siege.'

Seginus went to his rest then for a short while, but Guthwine did not even dare to shut his eyes. His thoughts were full of apprehension at the many ill omens he had been given. As the Roman slept, Thegn Guthwine sensed someone approach the flap of his tent and stand outside it in silence for what seemed an age. It was as though he had expected this visitor and had waited his sleep for his coming. He stared at the shadow cast on the cloth and slowed his own breathing to try and hear any noise or movement.

Eventually the canvas was pulled slowly aside and a tall narrow-bodied form in long flowing garments walked into the middle of the shelter. The face was shrouded; the hands folded deep in the clothes.

'Thegn Guthwine Eikenskald,' sighed the figure and then it melted into the darkness.

'At last,' he thought, 'the messenger I have long awaited.' He knew that in a few hours he would face battle for the last time. He was honoured and overjoyed to be assured of meeting his death on the field of war. That meant he would certainly go to dwell with his ancestors. Satisfied, he calmly took out his sharpening stone and worked on his axe-blade until the watchman came to rouse him.

A little after sunrise the company of Saxons set off. Seginus slept in the saddle. Guthwine walked most of the way, leading his mount. Draupnir stayed close to his lord and Hannarr kept a sharp eye on him, ever ready to strike if his worst suspicions came to be true.

The mercenaries moved swiftly over the land, accustomed as they were to forced marches and hard living. The journey to Rathowen was little more than a stroll to most of them and it was completed in only a few short hours.

Guthwine herded the company around behind the hills near the hillfort until they reached a position where they were close to the breach in the wall yet still concealed from the direct gaze of the defenders.

When Seginus had dismounted, washed and prepared his war gear, Hannarr gave him some leather armour, a broad cow-hide belt and a notched axe. Then they shared some bread together.

'Is this the place where the wall is weakest?' asked the Saxon.

'It is.'

'And the tower is full of gold?'

'I saw some,' Seginus lied. 'Yes, and I'm sure there's more in the cellars.' He noticed the cruel gleam in Hannarr's eyes when he spoke of gold. The Roman decided it was best to string the foreigner along a bit. 'But it's nothing compared to the storehouses in the south, in Munster.'

'Really?' replied Hannarr. 'You have seen them?'

'There are riches there beyond your imagination. When this battle is over I'll take you there.'

'Yes, you must. Together we will plunder them all,' leered the Saxon.

'Let us live through this battle first,' countered Seginus.

'If you live,' began Hannarr, 'will you promise to show me the storehouses of the south?'

'Of course,' replied Seginus, realising that he had got himself in a little too deep. 'I'll take you to the most valuable treasure in the world.'

'What's that?' hissed Hannarr.

To his great relief, before Seginus had to invent any more tales, Guthwine rode up to them and ordered them to mount. 'Come, we will ride to scout the enemy!' he called and both men rushed to obey him.

Caitlin had rested about two hours when Fintan came to the roof to make his report to her.

'We have seen three warriors riding war horses on the high side of the ramparts.'

'On the high side?' she repeated. 'Are you sure?' He nodded.

'Then it is as we expected. Is there a wide enough

gap to let them through?' she asked nervously.

'Oh yes!' answered Fintan. 'Wide enough to let many through.'

'Good. Are they gone yet?'

'No lady, they are still riding along the ridge.'

'Let me see!'

Fintan helped her over to the wall and there she could plainly discern three riders dressed in greys and browns. They were not moving much, but one of them pointed along the ridge in a broad sweeping movement of his arms.

'I am worried that we are making a terrible mistake in trying to defend this place,' declared Caitlin. 'And that the trap we have set will cost us much more than it is worth.'

'I am sure that we are not very wise,' agreed Fintan, 'but our trick will split their force and inflict a slaughter on their army that they won't be expecting. That may mean we will live a little longer. Now also we know for certain that they are coming today and that has put many of our warriors at ease.'

'Do you intend to wear the Roman cloak into battle?' asked Caitlin, changing the subject.

'I do.'

'That will make you quite a target!' she joked.

'I hope so,' said Fintan smiling, 'I would dearly like to meet again the man who gave this to me. And if it be in the midst of battle, so much the better.'

'Be careful,' she said, and was surprised at herself.

'I will,' he assured her. 'I intend to live until at least tomorrow.' His hand sought out hers and they stood together for a long time like that, looking out over the fields without speaking.

'The gap is wide,' noted Hannarr. 'That is a pleasant surprise. It will make our task much easier.'

'They have closed it since I saw it last, I think,' stated Seginus unsure, 'but not much.'

'It is too obvious,' remarked Guthwine. 'It could well be a trap. We should ride closer and see if we are challenged.' He looked at Hannarr and his deputy nodded agreement.

'Are you mad?' shouted Seginus. 'Their bowmen will cut you down in moments! And if not you will give them a clue to our plan.' He placed his own horse between Guthwine and the fort. 'No-one has noticed us. Let us keep it that way!'

Guthwine grimaced and for a moment thought of spurring his horse past the Roman, but in the end he hesitated.

'This could be the only chance we have!' begged Seginus.

The thegn snarled something in his own guttural tongue, then, relenting, he turned his mount around to head back to the ranks of his waiting warriors.

'What did he say?' Seginus asked Hannarr.

'He said, "Thank the Gods there are no cowards where I am going",' Hannarr explained simply. Then he too turned his steed round to follow his master.

'But what did he mean?' shouted Seginus.

As he reached the top of the ridge Hannarr called back to the monk, 'Valhalla!' and disappeared down the other side.

Involuntarily Seginus crossed himself and said an 'Ave'.

Guthwine and the Roman set off soon after with a small group of guards to make their meeting with Dichu and Palladius at noon. After a short hard ride they found the army of Laigin waiting at a place where a stream flowed into the river that fed the loch. A hundred footmen from the south were also gathered there and Isernus sat upon a black stallion at their head.

'Well met, my lord,' called Seginus to the bishop.

'You are late,' Palladius stated coolly, not looking up from his books.

'I have the Saxons gathered on the other side of the ridge, lord,' reported the monk.

'Where did you say?' roared the bishop, standing and knocking over his chair. His eyes were full of the green fire that told Seginus he was in trouble. 'They cannot possibly reach here in time! You were told to meet us here in force!' His face went deep red and he spat on the ground.

'Lord, we have discovered a gap in the defences, but it is on the opposite side of the fort. Thegn Guthwine and I are of the opinion that we may be able to breach the ramparts there and enter the defences without encountering much resistance.'

'So one of my subordinates is taking counsel from a heathen savage now, is he?' shrieked Palladius. 'Guthwine is a mercenary, my boy. He is not paid to think, he is paid to take orders and to wield his sword. How soon can you get your troops over here?'

'An hour, at least, on the march.'

'By the blessed wounds of Christ!' shouted the bishop. 'Dear boy, you may well have cost us this battle single-handedly. If we are to have any chance of success we must concentrate all our forces in a single assault.'

'I am not going to risk my troops in such an exercise,' stated Dichu. He held a knife in his hand and was dragging it across the table before him, scratching the surface. He got to his feet in a measured move that showed, despite his age, he still

171

had the grace and control of a fit warrior. 'How do we know we can trust your Saxons?' The king cast a suspicious glance at Guthwine.

'I am sure the plan will work,' enthused Seginus. 'They have left a huge section of their earthworks unguarded, assuming that we will attack from the front. If we approach them from two sides we will have the advantage of surprise and they will be forced to split their defence. They do not have a chance of winning the battle on two fronts. They will quickly buckle under such an assault.'

'There is no honour in sneaking in behind one's enemy,' King Dichu gruffly replied. 'It will only lead to disaster.'

'It is not a case of honour, dear king,' interjected Palladius with a mildly sarcastic tone. 'This plan of his simply has no hope of success.'

'It is a wonder to me that you Romans ever conquered as much of the world as you did,' laughed Dichu, calmly running his fingers through his moustache. 'While you debate the possibilities, time is passing. If we are to join battle today, it must be soon or not at all.'

The bishop was obviously distressed, but he soon enough realised that there was little or nothing he could do. 'I will lose many warriors climbing that rampart in front,' he pointed directly across the fields, 'unless you can assure me that your Saxons will be within the walls before we attack.'

'I am confident that we can do that easily,' Seginus lied. 'The heathen will not be expecting an attack from that quarter.'

'Very well, I do not see that we have much choice now. I am sure the Emperor Valentian is relieved that you did not remain any longer in his service. Between your strategies and the reliability of the Saxons, the Empire would be all but lost! Tell those savages you are riding with that they must restrain their natural instincts. No earthworks or buildings are to be torched. We will need this place as a last line of defence when Leoghaire arrives with his army.'

'The battle will surely be lost,' Dichu commented matter-of-factly, 'if you follow this dishonourable path.'

'Do you have aspirations to become High-King of this island or not?' sniped Palladius.

'I do but if it will cost me my honour, I am loath to strive for it.'

'Trust me, my king,' said the bishop. 'God is with you today. There is no greater honour.'

'Lord, there is one more thing,' began Seginus, but Palladius had already turned away and added, without looking at the younger man, 'Are you still here?'

'The Saxons have a tribute for you. Guthwine would also pass into your keeping an Irish lad who had been sent to assassinate him. The Lord of the Saxons presents the prisoner to you as a gift of fealty. '

'Thank the Lord Guthwine,' replied Palladius, dismissing the gesture. 'We will treat this captive as an example to all heathens who do not submit to the will of Rome. There is nothing more to be said. Now ride as fast as your horses will carry you and may God go with you!'

'Yes, lord!' Seginus raised his hand to the bishop in the old Roman Imperial sign.

'I am not a centurion, boy, so do not salute me as one,' snorted Palladius, 'and get yourself some decent clothes. Those filthy Saxon rags do not suit a man of God!' With that he turned away from Seginus Gallus and returned to his books and his discussions with Dichu.

The monk and his Saxon escort mounted and rode immediately back toward the other side of the defences where their own troops were waiting. They took a path along the very top of the ridge that swept in a semicircular arc behind the fort. From that point they could clearly see the army of the King of Laigin forming ranks up in the fields in front of the defences.

As Guthwine and Seginus reached their warriors, Hannarr was preparing to set the men in their battle lines. They all quickly dismounted for it was the Saxon way to fight on foot. Seginus took his place beside Hannarr and they waited for the order to advance. It was then that he noticed small fires had been lit at intervals among the warriors and some of the Saxons were dipping arrowheads into the flames. Seginus could clearly see that their plan was to shoot them, flaming, into the hillfort to spread havoc as they advanced.

'Palladius ordered that no buildings be set afire,' Seginus protested.

'Palladius will not be among the first warriors over the rampart,' answered Hannarr laughing. 'And anyway, it's just a piece of harmless fun. You fret too much, Roman.'

Guthwine lifted Frarod high in the air. This was the signal. A great blood curdling yell rose from the three hundred and fifty warriors who were the private army of Guthwine Eikenskald. Then, walking slowly, they came up over the brow of the ridge and stood for a few moments looking down at the defences on the other side. Thegn Guthwine swung his axe around in a wide arc and another bloody scream echoed forth from the Saxon raiders. Then, waiting not a moment longer, they ran recklessly down the slope, throwing themselves headlong at the hillfort.

Hannarr and Draupnir both struggled to keep pace with their war-leader. He was still a strong and fit man, despite his advanced years. Guthwine discarded his shield halfway down the hill and sprinted faster than any of his men, his axe sweeping through the air above his head.

An unusual elation spread along the line of bolting warriors as they realised there was absolutely no response coming from the fortress defenders. Seginus could not believe their luck. Not even a challenge was raised at them. He could sense victory on the wind. He felt for a minute that he was invincible, that the battle would be theirs. The gap was wide in the rampart and every warrior scrambled up the ditch easily to enter the defences.

Across the field at the other side of the fort, Dichu's warriors were advancing slowly between the closely-arranged stakes which had been set to hamper their progress. A rain of arrows fell upon the troops of Laigin and many fell, but they were steadily weaving their way through the obstacles. Soon they would be able to start climbing the ditch on their side.

Seginus climbed onto the flat ground at the top of the rampart, just behind Draupnir and the rest of the bodyguard. He drew the axe from his belt but he could not see any opponents who would fight him.

Directly in front of the Saxons lay the forward defences of the fort. The only enemy warriors in sight had their backs to Guthwine and faced Dichu's army. Seginus could clearly make out the shapes of archers on the ramparts facing away from him.

The Saxon marauders were going mad with joy. Some of them had already reached the foot of the stone tower which was meant to be the last line of defence for the garrison. The great oak door was bolted so a few of them began hacking at it with their axes. A few more put torches to the store-houses and the fire quickly took hold, spreading with alarming speed toward the tower.

Guthwine ran around the main building and had almost completed a circuit when a movement on the top of the tower caught his eye. He walked back a few paces to get a better view.

A woman was moving along the flat roof watch-ing his troops intently. As he observed her, she raised her arms above her head and gave a wild screeching yell. She reached down then and picked up a horn, blowing a loud long note.

The thegn felt his guts turn in horror. 'It is a trap!' he bellowed. 'It's a bloody trap!'

Hannarr ran to him as the troops began to realise what had happened and to turn back in confusion. 'They've put a long row of wooden fence posts across the gap behind us,' he reported, 'and now they're cutting us off.'

'Where did those bloody bowmen come from?' shouted Guthwine.

Enemy troops were pouring out of the surround-ing buildings. Within seconds the first heavy rain of arrows plummeted down amongst the Saxons and many fell. There was total panic. Some of Guthwine's troops tried to make for the other wall but a phalanx of spearmen five deep appeared as if from nowhere to block their way.

The thegn's bodyguard closed around him and prepared to cut their way out to safety. Seginus did not see the woman on the battlement nor did he notice the archers appearing to enclose the Saxons from behind. But he heard the blast of the horn and that was enough for him to know that he had made a terrible mistake. He sought out Guthwine among the frantic warriors but he could not see him anywhere.

He caught a glimpse of a familiar face close by and tried to get closer to the man through the throng. 'Streng!' he shouted frantically. But Streng could not or would not hear him.

'Lift me up on your shoulders,' Guthwine yelled to Draupnir. 'I want the men to see and hear me.' The man looked about him for a few seconds, unsure, then moved to do as his lord commanded. He was bending over to take the weight of the thegn when an arrow fell from above and struck him in the back of the neck. Draupnir stumbled forward and was trampled in the crush. Another of the bodyguard rushed to replace the dead man and soon Guthwine was raised above the heads of his troops.

'Retreat! Go back the way we came!' he ordered. 'Push your way out!'

The Saxons cheered at seeing their lord and pressed against the men in front to rush the archers. All of a sudden about twenty of the Saxon warriors broke ranks and rushed at the archers who blocked their exit. More than half of that twenty fell to Irish arrows but the bowmen were forced to fall back slightly and this encouraged the rest of Guthwine's troops to charge through the ranks.

Within moments the archers' line had collapsed and most of them were running for safety. Guthwine could see this from where he sat atop the shoulders of a young warrior and he gave a shout of joy, dropping as he so did down to the ground. As his feet touched the Earth he felt a sharp pain in his abdomen, as if someone had punched him hard in the stomach and he was heavily winded.

His bodyguard closed round him again and propped him up, but the world was spinning violently around Guthwine. He felt sick and he could no longer feel his legs. His eyesight was blurring. He reached down to feel the spot where the pain in his gut was most intense. His tunic was torn beneath his leather jerkin and his hand was sticky and wet. When he brought it up to his face, his worst fear was confirmed. His fingers were covered in rich, bright blood.

At that moment the men in front of him broke out and ran down the ditch. The press was not so close now and Guthwine found he could hardly stand up. He clenched his hands to the fire in his stomach and he staggered at the very top of the ditch he had climbed so swiftly only a short while before.

Coming to earth hard on his knees he immediately strove to regain his feet, but the energy was draining fast from him. Stunned, he could only watch his fleeing warriors swiftly pass him by.

In their midst he recognised the ghostly figure who had been his visitor the night before striding purposefully toward him between the ranks of panic-stricken men. The figure walked directly up to him and stopped just out of the war-leader's reach.

Guthwine yearned to see the face under the flowing cloths. With the last measure of his strength he looked down at the place where his hands struggled to hold in his guts and then he raised his head once more to look his doom-bringer in the face. Men were still jumping over the edge of the ditch all around him. None seemed to notice the strange figure.

As he stared defiantly at the phantom, a strange thing happened. It transformed, melting into another shape, until before him there appeared the face of Hannarr.

Guthwine gasped painfully, but was deeply relieved that his friend had come to rescue him yet again. He tried to speak to praise the loyalty of his deputy but found he could only retch dryly.

Hannarr knelt beside his lord reaching round to support his back. He lay the man down and made him comfortable. The thegn took his companion by the hand and held it tight in a silent entreaty.

In the next moment a glint of steel caught Guthwine's eye. There was nothing he could do. Hannarr coldly plunged a dagger through battle hardened ribs and deep into the vital organs of Thegn Eikenskald.

'Now that I am thegn things will change for the better,' Hannarr said, still smiling at the dying man before him.

The last thing that Guthwine saw was that smile on the face of his best friend, and then he closed his eyes and went to feast amongst the hosts of his forebears.

From her vantage point on the top of the tower Caitlin had seen Guthwine's men clambering up the side of the embankment and spilling into the middle of the defences. There were many more than she had expected and they were not the levies from Laigin that they had all hoped would spearhead the attack. These warriors were hardened mercenaries. And, worse by far, they were Saxons.

She had crouched out of sight, only seldom snatching a glance at their progress in case any of them saw her and worked out that they were about to take the bait of a deadly trap. She had held off her signal as long as she dared, but when she noticed the bowmen of her garrison already blocking the gap in the rampart with long rows of stakes she decided the time was right.

A hundred spearmen had poured out of buildings and hiding places around the courtyard in front of the Saxons to block their advance. At the enemy's rear another one hundred and fifty bowmen took up positions and prepared to let loose their arrows into the crush of the foreigners.

With shaking hands Caitlin had raised the horn to her lips and blown a blast such as she never had before. The note rose in intensity and cut through the air like a cracking whip. As the sound faded the whole hillfort was engulfed in silence; all the strangers' eyes had seemed focused on her. All but the eyes of one tall and powerful man whose gaze had been toward the rampart. She heard him yell something in his strange language and then the first volley of arrows flew from their bow-strings to land on the unready attackers below.

Curses rose around the tower and she heard the sound of heavy blows pounding on the oaken door. But within a few moments the enemy had given up hacking at it with their axes and had begun to flee.

Neither she nor Fintan nor any of the veterans who defended the fort had expected the invaders to turn so quickly and that was nearly the ruin of their plan, for the bowmen stationed at the top of the rampart, seeing the enemy charging back toward them, let fly only one more shaft-fall before they bolted for cover.

Fintan had led the spearmen forward to close the gap and take advantage of the disorder amongst the Saxons but the army of Guthwine had been too fast for them and Fintan's men were left to deal only with wounded raiders.

The whole incursion had lasted only a few short minutes, but as the last Saxon leapt over the battlement, seventy of his comrades were left lying all about the courtyard at the foot of the tower like as many slaughtered sheep in pools of their own blood.

Fintan's spearmen advanced right up to the brink of the embankment where they formed a line, pushing a few bodies over the edge, while the bowmen retrieved the stakes that had been scattered in the enemy retreat and reset them. Then barricades were hastily erected by every spare pair of hands and the wall secured.

Satisfied that the defence was now in order, Fintan led seventy of his spearmen on to the forward defences, toward which Dichu's troops were now advancing, leaving the rest of his men to hold the barricade.

'Thank the gods!' cried Caitlin. She could clearly see the mercenaries regrouping at the bottom of the rampart but she knew they would think twice before advancing up that slope again.

'Was anyone injured?' she yelled down to Fintan as he passed by at the bottom of the tower with his troops.

He shook his head in amazement, thinking to himself, 'Not yet anyway.'

They had successfully tricked the foreigners into losing many of their own men and they themselves had suffered no loss. Dichu's army, however, would be another matter.

Two horns then sounded, shrill and high, across the battlefield but these were the trumpets of Laigin.

Fintan and his soldiers reached the forward embankment and stood in long rows three deep, waiting for the next assault. The young warrior climbed on the edge of the parapet and Caitlin saw the red cloak flowing in the wind behind him and the plumed Roman helm on his head.

He turned slowly to face her and tore the helm from his head, throwing it down so that she could almost make out the details of his face. Their gazes locked, one lover to another, and then without warning he drew his sword above his head and roared something at his troops.

The words never reached Caitlin, they were drowned in the frenzied cheers of the other warriors. In a moment he had leapt over the rampart and out of her sight, followed by most of his soldiers.

'May the Morrigú bless you and protect you,' she prayed, already feeling a sense of great loss. She realised sadly that she had not apologised for her harsh words to him that morning.

Out of Irish bowshot the Saxons gathered to regroup on the grass at the bottom of the great ditch below the fort. Seginus lay on his back for a long time catching his breath.

'You are a born coward,' he told himself. Instantly he realised that it was his father's voice that spoke to him, and he was filled with anger at the old man.

He closed his eyes to shut out the pain in his side caused by the strenuous run, and tried desperately to control his breathing. When he finally looked about him he saw that the number of warriors in the party was significantly reduced. He sought out Guthwine's familiar form but could not find the war-leader anywhere.

After a while he recovered enough to call out for the thegn. He was answered by the appearance of the great axe Frarod landing heavily on the turf by his side. He strained to make out the face of the man who had been holding it, but the sun was behind the warrior and he could not see him clearly.

'Guthwine?' he said. 'What happened? Are you all right?'

'Thegn Eikenskald is fallen,' came Hannarr's answer, cold as death itself. 'I am thegn now.'

The Roman stood quickly and tried to gather his thoughts. 'We must return to the fight,' he urged. 'Dichu is relying on us.'

'And so we will,' answered Hannarr. 'Our lord must be avenged!'

Some of the Saxons gave a shrill cry and would have climbed straight back up the rampart had Hannarr not restrained them. 'We will go in by the front door this time, not skulk around the back like petty thieves!'

Once again he was greeted with enthusiastic cheers and the mercenaries picked themselves up off the ground to make the move around to the other side of the hillfort where the battle was by now being waged in earnest. For men who had been sprawled about exhausted only moments before, they moved very swiftly, and it was all Seginus could do to keep up with them. They set a cracking pace around the rampart, following the course of the great ditch until they could see the two armies on the field before them.

In the middle distance Seginus caught a flash of scarlet on the field amidst the greys and browns of the common warriors' clothing. He recognised his father's cloak immediately. All the frustration and embarrassment of the last few days flooded through him and his blood began to boil. One thought possessed him: revenge. Retribution for the humiliation he had suffered at the hands of the Irish woman's servant and reprisal for the death of his comrade Guthwine.

The Saxons were a mere thirty steps from the Irishmen when Fintan turned to see them rushing at his beleaguered warriors, as frightening and unstoppable as a tidal wave about to wash a coastal town into oblivion. Defenders all along the line noticed the Saxons joining battle and their resolve grew grim.

'Fall back!' cried Fintan. 'Fall back to the ramparts!'

The Irishmen did not heed him but fought on until there was no choice left to them but to retreat. Now outnumbered at least three to one, Fintan and his spearmen began a rearguard action, slashing with their spearpoints and broad-bladed swords to keep the enemy at bay.

Seginus ignored the expertly wielded weapons of the Irish. All his focus was on retrieving the cloak that his father had been awarded by the Emperor, the mark of a centurion. He felt his strength grow beyond the physical proportion of his body. He was full of hate and of fury. He saw in the crowd a man that he could blame for the murder of his brother, for the ill-fortune of this whole expedition; a man who personified all that was evil about this land; and that man was Fintan, warrior of Munster.

From her vantage point Caitlin could see all that transpired and she screamed to her lover in a vain attempt to warn him of the Roman's approach. Now she watched the spearmen falling back and only caught glimpses of the Roman cloak through the crowded conflict on the field.

Seginus pressed his way toward the object of his anger, throwing his axe wildly about him striking down any of the retreating enemy who fell within the sweep of it as he went. At last he faced Fintan eye to eye and saw his hatred reflected in the Irishman's face. Saxon and Hibernian alike cleared a path for the two such was the ferocity of their meeting.

Blow after blow they dealt each other, deftly parrying or blocking with a twist of the blade or thrust of the shield-arm. The spearmen of Fintan's guard were shortly separated from their leader and though they fought hard to reach him again they were eventually forced beyond hope of aiding him. He did not notice.

'Now, Roman, let me teach you something of Gaelic hospitality!' he challenged defiantly. Then he struck such a heavy stroke with his sword on the shield of Seginus that the other man fell backwards into the horde of Saxons. But the Roman quickly rose before the Irishman could deal the death blow.

'You bloody heathen!' countered the warrior-monk. 'I will give you a lesson in how to bow to the Cross!' He feigned a stroke to the Irishman's left side but redirected it at the last possible moment, as his father had taught him to do, and the flat of the iron blade connected with Fintan's skull.

By now the greater number of the spearmen and others who had charged over the battlement had managed to climb back over the rampart and were preparing for the imminent assault on their stronghold.

Caitlin saw that Fintan was not with them and she scanned the field searching for his form, frantic at his absence. It took her a few moments to focus on the spot where she had last seen him. A man was waving the scarlet cloak above his head and screaming something ecstatically. Although his voice was not strong enough to pass the distance between them, Caitlin's instincts told her plainly that the man was Seginus.

From the rear of Dichu's army a horn blasted out in a low-pitched groan which rose to a shrill cry. The troops of Laigin shouldered their weapons and started to withdraw to their lines, leaving the dead and wounded of both sides scattered about the field. For a few minutes the Saxons standing around their new thegn hesitated and then they too pulled back seeing that they could not hope to gain the hillfort alone.

They carried with them, unconscious, an Irish prisoner of noble birth, and though Caitlin could not see him, her spirit told her that Fintan still drew the breath of life.

TEN

s soon as he realised that the battle was degenerating into a confused brawl, Dichu recalled his army in order to regroup it into an effectual fighting force. The chaos of battle had left many of the warriors milling about unable to have any real impact on the outcome and Dichu was an experienced enough warrior to know that such a disorganised offensive would bear no fruit, no matter what the odds in its favour were.

But the night came on quickly after the withdrawal, the hasty preparations for a final assault, the evaluation of the hillfort's defences and the treatment of the walking wounded, and so the king put off ordering another advance until the next day.

As the evening turned cool the chieftains of Laigin met in Dichu's camp to assess the day's work and to plan the morrow's strategies. Palladius was there, as was Isernus. Seginus, wearing proudly now his father's Imperial cloak, stood beside Hannarr and Streng the new thegn's chosen deputy.

'Our losses were not as great as expected,' stated the King of Laigin.

'We should have pushed on to gain the heights while we had the heathen on the run,' asserted Palladius. 'The Irish all fight as if they fear to harm their enemy.'

'We will do as well tomorrow with our troops fresh and reinforcements come from my eastern provinces,' sighed Dichu. He had been assaulted all afternoon by the bishop's entreaties to continue the attack. As was the nature of the churchman his pleas had soon turned to angry outbursts and then degenerated into sharp sarcastic, if misguided, observations.

'The enemy may also be reinforced by the morrow and we cannot afford a long siege. The odds could well be more in their favour as the sun rises. This is not a child's game we play at, Dichu, this is a war. There can be no place for your weak Irish sentiments here if we mean to win.'

'And what of honour?' demanded Dichu.

'Honour! All you bloody barbarians talk of is honour! What honour can there be in defeat? What good are your foolish laws of behaviour if they lose us our very lives?' sneered the bishop. 'All this talk of honour is a thin disguise for cowardice. I would be better served by an army of feeble-minded children than the so-called pride of the Kingdom of Laigin!'

Dichu was tiring of this war. There had been too much senseless killing. It sickened him to see innocent folk suffer torture merely because they had a different opinion to their captor. 'Death in battle is one thing, but this man would see all who oppose him put to the sword,' thought the king. Besides which, the road to the high-kingship was not proving to be as safe a path as Palladius had promised.

'If the Roman way is to slaughter many for the sake of a few footsteps worth of ground, then is it also the way Christ would have fought?' asked Dichu.

'How dare you quote the life of the Christ to me!'

stormed Palladius, 'A few short years ago you knew nothing of the civilised world; you lived as a savage, worse than an animal with your hideous little stone idols and your quaint tales of heroes. Irish heroes only exist in the stories they tell their brats; they are a spineless race lacking in resolve and hiding timidly behind petty rules which have grown down the centuries to mirror the faint-hearted nature of their kings.'

Dichu sat still on his oak chair and quietly said, 'You are wrong, Roman. Our people and our ways will endure beyond the chanting of your priests and the murderous ways of any invader. You and I may think that we can bring others to the Cross, or subdue the land at our whim, but the Gaelic folk do not bend easily to the will of those who would use brute force to win them over. We may gain this hillfort but your mission was doomed the moment you took a sword in your hand and claimed to be the righteous servant of the Prince of Peace.'

'Are the Irish also traitors?' mocked Palladius. 'Or are you simply seeking an excuse to return to the safety of your hearth?'

'I am a man of honour,' Dichu maintained. 'I have promised my sword arm to your cause and so you shall have it. Whether you had proven to be the Devil himself, still I would be bound to do as you bid; aye, even to slay the innocent or to fall to death in battle for the sake of your imprudent Roman whim. But you are wearing the patience of your allies. Beware that you do not wake at dawn to find you must continue the campaign with only that piss-weak psalm singer to do the work for you!' With this last comment the king indicated Seginus. 'God help you if you should ever inherit an army of their like!'

Seginus said nothing, offering no sign that he

had heard the king's remark. He knew well enough to stay out of any private dispute between the two men. It was not their first. They had argued many times. Palladius was an arrogant man and Dichu was proud. To Seginus there was no question of which of the two of them was ultimately right. Roman ways were the ways of the civilised world. All else was barbarian and evil, inspired by Satan.

While he was reflecting on these thoughts the conversation finally turned to the important matter of the plans for the morning assault.

'We outnumber the defenders,' said Dichu, 'therefore a direct advance on their positions is the best way to defeat them.'

Hannarr whispered into the ear of Seginus, 'Tell them we want to be avenged for the death of our lord. We will lead the assault.'

'Lord Bishop,' began Seginus, painfully aware of his interruption, 'Thegn Hannarr offers his troops as the forward guard in the attack.'

'The Saxons do not shirk their duty,' observed Palladius, his words well-aimed and full of contempt for the Irish. This did not mean, Seginus knew, that the bishop had forgiven him for the failed Saxon attack. 'Very well, tell him he shall lead the charge,' declared Palladius, 'and that I will grant five hundred gold crowns to the man who stands first in the enemy stronghold.'

Seginus passed on the offer to Hannarr, and listened intently to the reply. 'The thegn asks only that after the battle his men receive the body of Guthwine which lies now abandoned in the Irish camp, and that the old thegn be paid the honour he is due for the heroic life he led.'

'And so he shall, for he was loyal unto death to the cause of the Cross,' stated the bishop. 'If not to the sentiment of the church's teaching,' he thought to himself.

'It is settled then,' announced Dichu, eager to end the meeting. 'Tomorrow we storm the hillfort in force, the Saxons leading the attack.'

'And may God bless our endeavour,' added the bishop.

The assembled warriors and monks then went to their own fires and Palladius called Isernus and Seginus to him.

'I expect that you will both be in the thick of the fighting tomorrow. I should not have to say that,' he added. 'It is most important that we give our Irish allies a good example to follow. When they see your valour it will inspire them to greater feats. Fear not for the Spirit goes with you, and should you fall, surely you will plummet into the arms of Christ and be held there close to his bosom forever.' He crossed himself and the two monks instinctively followed his lead.

'I will go now to look to my footmen,' said Isernus. 'God go with you.' There was a finality in that farewell that struck Seginus, and for a moment he felt that it might well be the last time he saw his brother. Isernus disappeared from view making his way between the trees at the bottom of the glen toward the stream.

'Walk with me, Seginus,' ordered the bishop coldly.

The monk did as he was told.

'You committed a serious error of judgement in trusting the Saxons this morning,' said Palladius.

'Yes, my lord.'

'Nevertheless, I am willing to forgive you.'

'Thank you, your grace,' answered Seginus.

'When this is all ended there will be a need of another bishop in the land,' began Palladius, 'subordinate to me of course. Should we be victorious tomorrow I think that you may well have the makings of such rank. What do you say?'

'I would be honoured, my lord,' stammered Seginus. This was totally unexpected.

'You will need to prove yourself to me. A bishop must be cunning and able to deal with any situation that arises. For example, how do you suggest we gain the advantage on the field tomorrow?'

Seginus could not believe his luck. He had intended to ask a favour of Palladius but now he could present his plan as one that could win them the siege.

'The Irish are superstitious, even the most Christianed among them,' he began.

'Yes, my boy, what have you in mind?'

'I hold as a prisoner their war-leader.'

'Well done!' gasped the bishop.

'If we were to arrange a display that showed the ineffectiveness of their heathen ways, I think that the garrison might well capitulate.'

'I will leave the details to you,' declared Palladius. 'I am sure you are more than capable of executing a fine demonstration.' He placed an emphasis on the word 'executing' which made it clear what he wished.

'I will see to it, my lord.'

'I am beginning to think that I have made a good choice of man for the Bishopric of Munster. But I have one more task for you.'

'I am your servant, lord.'

'Word has come to me that the heathen in the south worship a tree, said to afford eternal life to those who eat of its fruit.'

'I have heard many tales of it, my lord,' answered Seginus. 'Even that when Christ visited these shores he himself ate of the berries.'

'Don't talk rubbish, boy! The King of Munster relies on that tree as a symbol of his power. It is the place where oaths are made and it is the embodiment of his authority. You will ride forth after the victory tomorrow and destroy it, banish the demon from it and erect a chapel in its place. Do you understand?'

'Where will I find this tree?'

'You have passed it many times travelling to the monastery in the south. It is the tree at the Cashel crossroads.'

'The great rowan tree?' asked Seginus, astounded.

'The very one, my boy. Now I must bless you and bid you good night. Tomorrow we ride in triumph.' Without another word, Palladius Bishop of Eirinn went to his tent to pray alone in the darkness for victory.

Seginus overjoyed at his new standing with his master sought out the camp carpenter to build two large crosses before dawn. He tried not to think about how he would complete his other task.

Not far from the place where Seginus' two servants had stood to shoot their arrows at the king stag only the night before, Gobann and Mawn set their small fire and settled down to rest.

'We are not far now from the hillfort, but we will rest here tonight,' decided Gobann. 'It is better that we arrive in the light of day in a place where war is present. It may save us both an arrow shaft in the flesh.'

Gobann knew this place well. A few short minutes further would have brought them to the ramparts of Rathowen. 'It will not harm us to wait and see how things are. We are several days late and much may have happened,' he told himself. 'I smell the death of many men on the breeze.'

They had tethered their horses an hour after noon at a well and journeyed the rest of the way on foot. There was now little food in their packs; most of it they left with their bundles near the horses. Gobann bore his harp on his shoulder most of the afternoon, though Mawn insisted on carrying it for at least a short while. Now he was exhausted and Gobann realised that he would have to watch the night alone as the boy slept.

They had spoken little to each other since the last night; Gobann knew this was often the way when a child was taken to the Druid groves. The great upheaval to their individual lives was so overwhelming that a child often took cover in his or her own world for a time.

The sky was dark again for though the day had been sunny and warm, clouds again were gathering and the light of the Moon was not strong enough to penetrate them.

Gobann did not find it difficult to stay awake. He was only too aware of the danger that they faced. If Palladius and his army were following the same road as he and Mawn, there was only one place that they could be headed for.

Rathowen.

'Indeed they are probably already here,' he cautioned himself, and once or twice thought of putting the fire out so not to attract any unwanted attention. 'But it is better we stay warm,' he decided.

Throughout the night he heard distant voices raised in song and, later, hammering from a place not far off in the glen. This put him on edge until he remembered that drunken warriors rarely set sentries and those who have tasks to complete in the middle of the night do not venture far from their work.

Then all was quiet for a long while with only the murmur of the stream and the wind in the branches to fill the emptiness. It was so still that Gobann nodded off for a moment, but just a moment, no more. When he realised what he had done he forced himself to stand to push the blood through his veins.

In the next second he was lying flat upon the ground once more. He had distinctly heard the sound of plodding hoof-beats.

He dragged his blanket over the smouldering fire and lay low. A horse neighed close by. Gobann strained to look through the trees toward the stream. He could just make out two horsemen watering their mounts.

'All the horses were to be sent away from Rathowen,' he thought. 'These then are the enemy.'

A noise behind him in the thicket caught his attention. It was not a loud crash but it was as if some large animal had stumbled in the darkness. Then a huge figure loomed out of the night. It was a mounted warrior.

The man sat perfectly still, his face towards Gobann, but the poet could not tell if the warrior had seen him. Suddenly the man dismounted and drew his sword.

'Who are you and what is your business here?' the warrior whispered in the dialect of the Kingdom of Munster.

Caitlin slept a while that night, but she did not rest. All her thoughts were of the fate of Fintan. A scouting party had been unable to locate his body or his weapons.

'All these years that I have known him and only now when it seems he is lost do I realise how much he means to me,' she berated herself. 'We could have been betrothed months ago, but I would not have any of it. Now he is gone.'

Her leg wound was throbbing but halfway through the night she rose to help attend to the injured in the hope that the work would drive her sorrow and her fears away.

There was much to be done in the makeshift hospice. Men with deep sword cuts and appalling gashes, the like of which she had never seen, lay on the straw groaning or screaming or in the silent acceptance that ushers in death. The healing herbs that she had collected were not enough to help many of them and in the dark hours before sunrise fifteen young men had passed from the world, some in agony, some mercifully unaware of their wounds.

One fellow Caitlin recognised as belonging to the company of Fintan's spearmen. His left leg was broken and his right was split below the knee to his foot. She suspected that he had broken ribs also and he had a high fever. She spent several hours dressing his wounds and giving him water and a herbal infusion, but despite these efforts, he slipped away without having said a word of farewell to anyone.

'I feel like I did when the stag came upon me,' she thought. 'Totally useless! What sort of weapons do they have that can cause such injuries?'

Finally she sat on a stool and cried for all the horror she saw about her and the realisation that her lover had probably fared no better than many of his comrades.

Just after dawn a man who had fought beside Fintan came to her with a message.

'I fear he has been taken alive,' he confided.

'Alive!' she sighed; the word was sweet and full of hope.

'Come, lady,' he said full of sorrow, 'there is a terrible thing to see, and you must look on it with your own eyes for no words I can speak will convince you of the truth of it.'

Caitlin was puzzled by his speech but she let him lead her to the ramparts where she stood close to him, leaning on him a little to support her wounded leg. The morning was clear and the air very warm, which was unusual for the time of year. She looked out over the field where the battle had raged the day before and still there were lifeless forms strewn on the grass where they had fallen. But her sight was drawn to a spot in the distant field. There, in full view of the hillfort and its defenders, the men of Laigin were raising a pair of heavy wooden crosses.

The two groups of warriors struggled to hoist their burdens as if it were a contest to see which team could set their timber monument in place before the other. Lines were belayed around the nearest trees and attached to pulleys, and the men heaved slowly as the ropes cried out with the strain.

'I do not understand why they are raising two crosses, surely one is enough as a symbol to their followers,' Caitlin mused. 'And how is it that such lightly made timberwork can seem so heavy?'

Then the crosses were twisted around in their mooring holes and she nearly collapsed with the shock of what she saw.

Long red trails ran down both structures and on each cross hung a naked bleeding man.

The first one was a boy no more than eighteen summers, but the other had long chestnut brown hair and the build of a warrior, and he was older and his feet reached closer to the ground.

She thought, as she had many times during the night, of the fine brown strands of Fintan's hair and the sparkle in his eye when he teased her; of how they had stood hand in hand at sunrise the previous morning lost in each other's presence; and how, though they had not used words, their souls had spoken each to the other. His laugh, his anger, his boyish ways, his pride, his tenderness; all came to her mind as she sank to her knees with her head in her hands.

The spearman standing behind her caught her as her knees began to buckle but she fought him off, letting her sorrow fill the very air around her.

In the field where the execution was taking place, the gathered warriors were distracted from their task. Across the distance from the hillfort the shrill cry of a woman's voice pierced the morning. It hung on the breeze eerily and more than one man crossed himself and said an 'Ave'.

Caitlin's keening echoed in the glen. The waters of the loch and the hills in the distance repeated her cry. 'Ni'haah.' Then she succumbed to her anguish and fainted.

Unrest spread quickly through Dichu's troops. Few had ever heard the fabled cry of a ban-sidhe, a woman of the dark Faeries, but this was close to how they all imagined it would sound. Some men had mounted their horses and left as soon as the call reached their ears. Others waited, as afraid of the vengeance of Palladius as they were of any spirit.

'What is she howling about,' asked the bishop, 'that it is having such a profound affect on the warriors?'

'She is simply saying, "No",' replied Dichu. 'But it is not what she says, it is the way she says it. The cry of a ban-sidhe is heard before the death of a king or a chieftain or one who is related by blood to the old people, the Danaans. Her voice is the call of a Faery woman. In her pain she is cursing us.'

'Sorceress!' spat Seginus. 'They always resort to their evil magic at the last these Druids!'

'Druids?' repeated Dichu. 'What Druids do they have among them?'

'The woman who claimed to be their chieftain,' answered Seginus.

'You never mentioned that she was a Druid!'

'She is only a woman,' chided the monk. 'Why have you gone so pale?'

'This war is over,' answered the king. 'We will suffer many desertions today and at the end of it I may well be lying beside the Chieftain of the Saxons on the funeral pyre.'

'You Irish are pagan through and through,' taunted Palladius in disgust. 'Even those among you who take up the mantle of civilisation cannot bear it for long and soon return to your heathen ways. Prepare your army, King of Laigin, for in one hour's time we ride into battle and God and Christ will ride with us!'

The bishop strode off to don his mail-coat and leather jerkin and once more offer prayers for the conflict to come.

Seginus stayed for a long time looking on the limp form of his enemy and smiling broadly with the satisfaction of a debt well paid. Just as he was about to leave, he came close to where the Irishman hung. He thought of Linus who died on their first night in Eirinn and he said in a low voice in Latin, 'Thou art avenged, Brother.' Then he turned and went to make his own preparations.

Mawn did not relax at all throughout the night after they were challenged by the guardsman. The boy had been given a comfortable enough place to sleep but his rest was disturbed by thoughts of home. It was now two full days since he had crossed the ford at the Valley of Dobharcú, yet he had a strong premonition that he would soon see someone from that place again.

Connor, one of King Leoghaire's personal body-guard and the man who had found Gobann and the boy where they were camped above the stream, had been assigned by Leoghaire as Mawn's protector. The lad could hear the man shuffling about outside all through the night as he stood sentinel. Gobann had not returned at all to the tent—his duties lay in attending the war council with the High-King.

A long while after Gobann had gone, when the only sounds were Connor's occasional coughs, Mawn experienced one of his visions. He saw a clear image of his father seated at the Brandubh board, laughing at some joke. The scene planted itself in his mind and he could not banish it, so he began to explore the vision in his head.

The first thing that he noticed was that there were many other people in the room in which his father sat. They seemed to be watching intently the progress of the board game as it unfolded before them. Most of the people were unfamiliar to him.

In the centre of the crowd, on a low table, was the seven-squared game-cloth and all the carved black pieces that stood at its edge.

In the days since they had left the valley he had been unable to banish the image of the playing board from his mind. He was fascinated by it, yet also a little afraid to ask his teacher to explain it fully to him. He understood the rules and the strategies well enough—he had played the game since he was a small child—but he was starting to realise that there was something more to it, something hidden beneath the surface in the movements of the beautifully crafted figures, and he longed to know what it was.

Before sleeping this night, he thought and thought on what he had seen, trying to come to some conclusion. The mysterious game-square was the last thing in his thoughts before he finally nodded off. His rest thereafter was crammed with dreams in which armies of Ravens and Kings battled fiercely on gaming boards so vast that they covered the hills and streams and lochs and mountains and the great black birds swarmed together in squawking flocks to assemble in a withered tree for their tribal meeting.

But as is the way with such sleep visions locked safe within the armour of the mind, when morning came he remembered no detail of the dream, only a faint memory.

He woke to the sound of many horses being saddled and the clanking of harness and chain mail as the mounted warriors of Munster made final preparations for bloody conflict.

'I will make a poem about this war one day,' he promised himself as he took in the many noises around him.

Everywhere in the camp the fighting men of the

High-King were donning their war gear and checking the tools of their trade.

Outside the little tent that Mawn had spent the night in, his guard still stood.

'Connor!' Mawn called to him. 'Connor, are the soldiers leaving now?'

The man stuck his head of chestnut brown hair through the entrance. 'Aye, lad, they will soon go to war. Have you slept well?'

'Yes, Connor, I have. But you promised to wake me when the battle started.'

'It'll be a while yet before we face the enemy, and my king ordered that you be kept safe, so you'll be not getting too close to it.'

'Oh but Connor, you promised!' cried Mawn, deeply disappointed.

'It is more than my life's worth to let you go wandering around a battlefield when the two most powerful kings in Eirinn have charged me to hold you far from the fighting.'

'Can we not go to a safe place where I can see it?' he pleaded. 'How can I compose a poem about the brave deeds of the warriors if I can't see the battle?'

'You will hear soon enough about the fight from those who are brought in wounded,' replied the sentry.

'But I will know better if I can see for myself,' appealed the boy.

Another voice interrupted the guard before he had the chance to repeat his refusal. 'Mawn, are you awake then?'

It was the poet.

'Gobann. Tell him to let me see the fight,' sulked Mawn.

'You may be permitted to see it,' answered Gobann, 'but only so that you will always be sickened by war and never enamoured of it. First we

202

must do the bidding of the High-King and the High-Druid, and then there are other errands to be run before we have any leisure to view the fight. Have you forgotten that you are training now to be a poet? A poet may not always go where he wishes. Are you dressed?'

'I am, master.'

'Then come, there is much to be done this morning and you and I have our duties to perform.'

Gobann took the boy by the hand and they walked through the camp weaving a path around all the gear and horses and smouldering campfires. Connor followed close behind with drawn sword.

They had not gone fifty paces when they passed a gap in a whitethorn hedge. There, Mawn noticed, across the open ground, about another four hundred paces away, a sight that he had never before seen. Two trees without leaf or branch, and with smooth straight boughs that looked man-made, stood alone on the plain, each growing unnaturally out of a small rocky cairn. This was so strange a thing that Mawn stopped to study hard what he saw, for he had never heard of anything like it.

Gobann waited a little further on for him and after a few moments answered the question that he knew was in the boy's head. 'They are death trees,' he stated without any emotion. 'The Romans use them to murder those people whom they consider criminals.'

He hesitated a little longer, unsure if he should go on, but then decided it was better that the boy be given as much information as possible. 'The Romans hang the unfortunate man or woman on the tree and leave them there to die, sometimes driving long nails into the victim's wrists and then on into the wood so they are gradually weakened by the loss of blood. To stop the flesh tearing away with the weight of the body they also tie the poor souls in place with strong ropes.'

'Why do they nail them?' gasped Mawn in terror.

'It makes the job of rescuing the prisoner almost impossible, for even if they are freed they will usually die from the shock of their injuries. It is a long and slow death and there is much pain.'

'How do we kill our criminals?' asked the boy.

Gobann was a little taken aback. He had not expected this question. 'We do not usually kill them. We exile them. In many ways that is a worse fate. An outlaw is no longer entitled to the rights and honours due to everyone else in his clan. No-one may acknowledge him: he becomes invisible. He has no honour price, that is to say he is no value to his community, and he may never claim recompense for mistreatment from his neighbours. Such a punishment may have a time limit but if a criminal is exiled beyond the ninth wave then he may never set foot in Eirinn again. To do so would put his family's honour in jeopardy also.'

'I am glad we do not murder criminals,' said Mawn, relieved.

'It is not right that anyone should kill another man or woman unless in open warfare and even then I think it is against the nature of the universe. I know of many pure souls who have died before their time, yet who deserve to have lived long and happy lives; but it is beyond the powers of even the Druid Council of the Danu to give it back to them, so if we cannot grant them life, what right have any of us to decide who deserves to die, no matter what their crime?'

Mawn listened and nodded his head. 'Where are

they now, the two who were hung up on the trees?' he asked.

'They are near to death and we must now visit them. It falls to me to play for them the Sleep Strain.' Then Gobann realised that it was easy to speak to this boy as if he were an adult, which was a sign that he would be a good student.

'Come along, Mawn, we must hurry if we are to reach them before they leave the world. They should hear the harp sing the lament for them before they go.'

The boy caught up with his teacher and they continued across the encampment at a slightly faster pace. Gobann stopped off at a heavily guarded tent to collect his harp and a flask of mead. Mawn waited outside trying to catch a glimpse of the interior through the flaps, but he could see nothing. Connor was quiet and had sheathed his sword again and managed to find himself some water and a little bread which he shared with the boy.

A troop of warriors rode by and Connor called to them. They returned his greeting but rode quickly on. 'The battle has begun,' he muttered to himself when they had gone.

When the poet emerged from the tent he had the familiar otter-skin bag over his left shoulder and he wore his silver sun-wheel over the top of his tunic.

'Let us go then,' he stated. 'I have heard news that the fight is already upon us so we will go to the healing place to lend a hand. I am sorry, Mawn, but you will have to wait yet to see your first war-fight.'

Mawn was deeply disappointed but as they walked on he could not resist another question. 'How did the two who were hung on the death trees come to be rescued?'

'A party of our scouts ranged in among the guardsmen of Dichu,' replied the poet. 'That would have been an hour or so after the dawn. They managed to drive the enemy off for long enough to pluck the two down to safety. Then foot soldiers of our army brought them to the camp. The healers of Munster and Midhe are with them now, easing them through their pain.'

'One day,' decided Mawn, 'folk will call on me to play for them, not only at their deaths but at their births and their feasts. One day people will look on me to do this duty.' And he was proud to be Gobann's pupil.

eLeveN

aitlin spent a long while after her collapse in a numb state that bordered on unconsciousness. Her warriors had lain her to rest on a straw pallet in the tower to recover, realising that she would be unable to join them in battle. Her wound had been bleeding through the bandages and she was exhausted, so a guard was placed on her room and one of her veteran fighters took charge of the defence.

Her fitful rest was ended by the sound of her piper calling the fort to arms. She felt the injury burning still and her whole body ached, but once she had opened her eyes she found she could not rest again because of the pain.

Unable to sleep but unwilling to rise, she lay looking at the ceiling and trying to banish from her mind all that she had seen during the previous day. Eventually she resolved to face whatever was to come. She rallied herself and tried to get up, knowing that she should be out on the ramparts; but it took all of her energy to raise herself and she was still weighted down by an overwhelming grief.

In her mind her duty as chieftain was clear. 'You must go to the walls and stand with your tribespeople,' she told herself. 'This is the reason you were born: to lead them in time of need.' With these words echoing through her being she grabbed a stout blackthorn stick and slowly descended the spiral tower steps with her guard following.

Out on the defences the warriors were stern-faced and resolute. They all knew too well that they could not stand long against the combined army of Laigin and the Saxons. Many were making prepa-rations to leave the world, saying farewells to friends and giving parting gifts.

The enemy had crossed the fields and by the time Caitlin was up on the wall they were already advanced to the forward lines of defence at the bottom of the great ditch. The Irish war-riors, many exhausted from long watches through the night, took to their posts in earnest when they saw their chieftain appear. The piper played on and every man and woman in Rathowen listened intently.

Caitlin looked down on the enemy soldiers knowing that in a few short minutes the first of them would climb the battlements and bring death to many of her warriors. She drew her own sword, the blade that had been her mother's and her grandmother's, a blade that she herself had never before needed to wield. Her legs began to feel weak and she knew that it was not just her wound that was the cause.

As the army of Laigin came closer to the battle-ments and she could make out details of armour and apparel and the colour of each man's hair, her blood began to pump loudly in her ears and her breathing became shallow. She gripped her sword tightly through sweating palms with all her remaining strength.

A few arrows flew into the hillfort from the enemy side and struck impotently at walls or fell on the stone paved courtyard with a clatter. She realised that she was closer to death now than she had ever been. The words of an old invocation came to her mind and she ran it over again and again in an effort to calm herself.

'Fire of the heart,' it ran,
'Water of life-blood,
Air of the senses,
Earth of the bone,
Be with us,
Comfort us,
Do our bidding,
Be our strength,
Help us in our work,
Guide us in our dreams,
Keep us safe in time of danger.'

She repeated the last line three times and closed her eyes. Suddenly an arrow pounded against the dry-stone beside her and in the next instant the first Saxon reached the lip of the rampart. An old grey-bearded Irish warrior stepped forward and brought his sword down on the man's head before he had lifted himself over the wall far enough to face his foes. The helmet shattered and blood gushed out of the crushed skull and the Saxon fell back on top of his comrades.

When the foreigners saw the first of their men slain they started up a blood curdling war chant that chilled Caitlin to the core. It was the same sound they made when they rowed their oars together, rhythmically cutting through the sea. The words meant nothing to any of the Irish; indeed even if any of them understood their language, they would have had a hard time interpreting any meaning in the strange sounds. Caitlin understood only that it was a song of threat.

'Ho O Ro Ho,' they sang slow, deep and menacing.

Seeing them at close quarters, Caitlin realised that they were not just foreign, but they seemed to be of another world. Their skin was dark from the scorching of the sun, their clothes dirty and poorly made, and they adorned themselves with trinkets of gold, silver, leather and bone.

'If their bodies were not so well proportioned,' she thought, 'they could be mistaken for the evil Fomorian folk of the legends, who were disfigured and gruesome.'

Now Saxons were climbing up all along the top of the wall, but none had lived long enough to get within the defences. Wherever one foreigner climbed up, three Irishmen met him, and three could easily strike down one who was clawing a handhold with one hand and balancing an axe in the other.

But the numbers thronging at the bank soon increased and, here and there, a Saxon managed to knock down one of his opponents, so it was not long before one lone enemy warrior gained a foothold in the fort. Wherever one Saxon fell, four more replaced him; nothing seemed to deter them.

Caitlin knew that the forward defences could not long survive this kind of onslaught. At the same time she could see no use in retreating to the tower and enduring a siege. In the distance two crosses bore witness to the fate awaiting all those who were not killed cleanly in battle.

Hannarr made it to the top of the ridge in time to see Streng hack down three Irish swordsmen in as many sweeps of his axe. Not for the first time the new thegn was glad to be with Streng and not opposed to him. Hannarr sang the war song and Streng happily answered him, allowing the joy of battle to take him.

Directly behind the Saxons came the army of Dichu, pushing the living forward and treading on the dead until they no longer held a recognisable human shape.

Stopping his song for a moment, Hannarr strained to look back over the ground they had traversed. He saw that all the troops loyal to Palladius were now either on the slopes of the rampart or within the hillfort itself. Then he raised the axe Frarod and plunged into the affray in earnest.

Steel clashed heavily against steel, echoing all along the battlements. Screams, prayers, entreaties, curses, all mingled with the smell of sweat, blood and urine, and the awful stench of bile from many sword-slashed guts. There was laughter, too, the wild laughter of a madman losing control of himself in blood-lust.

It was Streng.

The man danced chaotically about, taunting his enemies, his arms dripping red gore to the elbows, his dirty teeth showing clear against his grimy face. Caitlin noticed him almost the moment that he had entered the fort for the sight of him was a dreadful thing to her. He was a demon sprung from her worst nightmares: eyes rolling violently in his head, mouth foaming.

She was suddenly seized with a desire to destroy this foul creature. Some instinct told her that if she did not kill him, here and now, there would come a day when he would step out of her darkest dreams to terrorise her again. If she allowed him to live she sensed that their destinies would be bound closely together.

She grabbed a bow from under the body of a dead archer who lay by her side and took up an arrow, holding it taut against the gut-string. Her target was a mere twenty paces away but she took her time, aiming, drawing the gut back to her face so that it dug into her cheek. She breathed in slowly, and then out more slowly still. When the last morsel of air had passed her lips she let the missile fly. The gut-string thudded painfully against her wrist as the arrow sped off on its mission.

In less time than it takes for lightning to strike, the arrow-shaft found its mark, sinking deep into the neck of its chosen victim, hitting him just above the collarbone and below the Adam's apple.

Streng tried to scream but the air would not pass through his windpipe: it was blocked by the arrow and the sudden flow of blood. He desperately grasped the shaft in both hands and with a massive effort tore it from his body, ripping open the flesh of his neck with the barbs. He fell to his knees in shock, still holding the arrow tightly, staring at it wide-eyed.

Then Caitlin heard a sound that would linger in her memory for the rest of her life. It was the noise of war-pipes. It was not her own piper for she had seen him fall; this was the sound of many pipes all playing in unison.

'I did not know that Dichu had such musicians in his army,' she thought. Then she realised her mistake.

A great commotion broke out at the rearguard of the enemy warriors. Horses were screaming and neighing; swords were clashing with shields; the Saxons were looking nervously over their shoulders.

Caitlin struggled to make her way as close as she could to the edge of the rampart and when she could look out over the edge she saw to her ever-lasting joy the banners of the King of Munster and

the High-King of Eirinn flying free amidst a great
company of horsemen.

The Prince of Cashel and Chieftain of the southern
Eoghanacht clans, the red-haired Murrough,
spurred his horse forward toward the sloping rise
of the embankment. Though his warriors had
marched through the night to reach Rathowen and
had rested only a few hours, they eagerly took up
the call of the war-pipes and at once threw themselves enthusiastically into the fight.

Wailing over the din of battle like a chorus of
wild ban-sidhe, the screaming reeds of the pipes
filled the army of Dichu with fear and dread. Only
the Eoghanacht had such a company of musicians
and they were believed by all to be the magical
source of that clan's power and invincibility in
battle.

Many of the Laigin men did not wait to engage
this force; there seemed no point. Without hearing
the cries of their officers and chieftains, the soldiers
of Laigin fled in disarray from their enemy like a
wave of the sea retreating from the shore when it
has crashed heavily down upon the beach.

Many more of them, still reeling from the previous day's battle and hearing the fearful skirling,
did not bother to flee but simply laid down their
arms before the footsoldiers and horsemen of
Munster and begged for mercy. Morann, Prince
Eoghan, granted it quickly but ordered all who surrendered to leave the field immediately.

A few others in the army of Dichu saw their
chance to escape the mistreatment of Palladius and
the meagre rations that they had suffered since the
campaign began. They threw in their lot with the

army of the High-King. Within a short twenty minutes the fortunes of battle turned disastrously against the King of Laigin.

Dichu watched helpless as many of his finest footmen fled; his few remaining warriors he observed succumbing to a state of total confusion. Then he saw the assault on Rathowen crumble like a wall of sand in the wind. Only the company of Saxons and a very small number of his own troops had actually managed to force their way inside the ramparts of the hillfort, and even they were rapidly being surrounded by the foot soldiers of the High-King.

When he realised that the tides had turned against him, Dichu searched about him in panic for a clear path of flight, but it was obvious that he was firmly trapped in the midst of the havoc of his own bewildered army, only halfway up the rampart slope. Like a defeated King of the Brandubh, he was blocked in on all sides by blood hungry enemies. There was to be no escape for him.

Dichu was not so stubborn a man that he could fail to catch the smell of defeat in the air around him and certain death if he chose to continue the struggle. 'If I give ground now I will live to bring my fight to Teamhair again one day,' he decided. 'Better that than an arrow in the chest, a muddy unmarked grave and an end to my plans.'

'Give me the banner of Laigin!' he shouted at his standard-bearer. 'I will call this useless struggle to an end.' Taking the symbol of his clan and raising it high in the air, he proclaimed his orders to his men. 'Enough! We will spill no more of our own people's blood for the sake of the foreigners. Lay your weapons aside and yield to the High-King!'

The few hundreds of his loyal clansmen who had

not already done so hastened eagerly to obey him, throwing down their weapons and banners that bore the cross and the seal of the Bishop of Eirinn.

Then Dichu commanded the trumpeters to blow the signal of withdrawal and soon even those warriors who were out of earshot of their lord's command passed the word of his wishes along the line to their comrades.

On the battlements Caitlin stood her ground almost completely engulfed in the midst of a tight formation of Saxons. A bitter hand-to-hand fight raged on between the strangers and the despairing men of her own garrison. Space on the top of the battlement was so tight, and the numbers of combatants so great, that elaborate sword wielding had degenerated in places to an all-in brawl.

She didn't hear Dichu's trumpet call through the din of the fray—she was too busy fending off the strokes of her attackers—but Caitlin felt a thrill deep inside her that told her that all would be well and it filled her with new hope.

Even while she was beginning to regain some confidence, two large Laigin guardsmen continued to hold her at bay with their broad blades. Gradually, pace by pace, she lost ground to them, taking blow after battering blow, falling back each time to safety just out of the reach of their sword-arms.

Even the sense that victory was within grasp could not help her defer the steady pounding of their iron weapons on her light armour. In a frantic bid for survival she concentrated every ounce of energy on holding her shield high above her head. But the unsteadiness of her feet and the shallowness of her breathing told her plainly that she was weakening under the savage hammering they dealt her.

Eventually her footing slipped in the dust and

suddenly the taller of the two men raised his arm in the air and smashed his blade down onto her shield. She felt the timbers warp slightly with the stroke. This was as much as she could take and her legs could hold her no longer. Her knees buckled forward and she landed on them in the dirt. With all her will she desperately raised her shield and huddled beneath it, in wait for the blow that she knew would soon strike her senseless or dead.

It never came.

When after a time there was no final stroke, she peered out from behind the oak-boards of her shield to see her enemies all around kneeling in submission, begging for mercy, their weapons reversed. The order to surrender had finally reached those in the forefront of the army of Laigin.

In disbelief and utter exhaustion Caitlin made to stand but she stumbled and fell forward unconscious across her upturned shield. That is where they later found her, unharmed but unable to move.

Gobann, Mawn and Connor hastened to reach the healing ground and it was not long before they spotted a thin streak of grey smoke rising in the still air. A little further, just beyond a small cluster of birch trees, they found a tent of plain undyed cloth and near to it a fire over which was hung a large cauldron of water, bubbling and splashing little drops into the coals beneath.

Mawn saw the smoke of many other fires that were just over the next rise and realised that the enemy camp must have been very close to the camp of the High-King.

Gobann was well aware of this but he was confused as to why no scouts from either side had made contact during the night. 'Perhaps they simply did not expect us to come upon them so soon,' decided the poet.

From within the shelter there came a low moaning sound as of an animal in great pain. Mawn had heard the cows make such noises as they were giving birth, but this voice was human and it was haunting, like an old slow song carried on the wind over the hills. There was a quality about it; something like the wailing of a baby crying to be fed. It was the voice of a dying man.

As they got closer to the fire and the tent they were challenged by a guard who sternly demanded to know their business. Gobann had only to show his harp case for the three to be allowed to pass.

The tent was a huge sheet of flax cloth stretched between two trees and high enough that a horseman could have sat upon his steed and his hair would have just brushed the ceiling of the shelter. Beneath its folds were nearly twenty beds of straw made ready on the ground. Of all the beds only two were occupied. Beside each stood an armed guardsman and at a table near to them two old healing men huddled deep in conversation. Beside the two healers, holding a bowl of water in both her hands, was a young girl.

Mawn noticed her at once and smiled at her. She returned his gaze and he saw immediately that her eyes were full of tears. She turned away from him quickly and bowed her head. Her hair, he noticed, was of the same blue-black sheen as the poet's.

'Gobann, we have been waiting for you,' said the nearer of the two healers turning abruptly.

'I have brought the boy as you instructed me to do,' replied Gobann with great formality.

'You have come not a moment too soon,' added the healer. 'Thank the gods you are both safe.' The old man approached Mawn and raised his hand in blessing.

'Welcome, Wanderer,' he said. 'I am called Cathach, I am counsellor to the Kingdom of Munster. This is my good friend and fellow counsellor, Lorgan the Sorn.'

The other man, already stooped by age, bowed a little more and nodded to Mawn respectfully.

'And this is my granddaughter Sianan,' Cathach indicated. The girl had dried her eyes but they were still red from weeping. She touched her hand to her forehead in a greeting and then turned away before Mawn could return the gesture.

Cathach grasped the poet in a friendly embrace and his old eyes reflected relief and joy at the meeting. As they broke apart, a trumpet sounded in the far distance. Everyone stopped talking and listened for a brief while but none could be sure if it was an enemy call or one of their own.

'You must strike up the harp now, Gobann, for they are passing quickly,' Lorgan said, breaking the silence. 'They have suffered much and need the comfort of the harp song if they are to travel on peacefully and find their way home. And we will soon be busy enough tending others.'

'Alas, I think it is too late for the young one,' remarked Cathach. 'He has lapsed into the death sleep and will be away on his voyage very soon.'

'At least he is no longer in pain,' rejoined Lorgan. 'In all my years of witnessing the trials and tortures of war in other lands, I never saw such a barbaric thing done by one human to another. Sad that my eyes beheld it here in Eirinn.'

'Truly do the Christians talk of the evil that walks in the world, but often it seems evil treads closely in their shadow,' added Cathach.

'Not all Christians follow the Roman way.' The voice came from the entrance to the tent where a small dark-skinned man was waiting. His robes were of the whitest Mawn had ever seen and contrasted sharply against the man's complexion. Mawn also noticed he wore a sun-wheel that was almost exactly like Gobann's.

'True enough there are none like the Romans. Come in, Brother, and join us,' said Cathach. 'We will be needing your skills soon.'

The man, young though he was, carried a staff and walked slowly as if he were mindful of his every step.

'Mawn, this is Origen of Karnak, he is a brother to us all and a great healer.'

The man touched his forehead lightly with the very tips of his fingers in salute to the boy. 'I have been told of your coming,' said the man. His speech was a little strange to Mawn's ears but the boy understood it well enough.

'Origen is an expert in the making of incense, perfumes and healing liquors,' added Lorgan. 'In this art he is highly valued by his people.'

'Are you not from the Isle of Eirinn, Origen?' asked Mawn and then remembered that it was impolite to ask questions of strangers. He felt himself blushing.

'No, my son, I come from a country in the south, where the wasteland begins.'

Mawn wanted to ask what the wasteland was but Cathach spoke first.

'We must be silent now for the poet to perform his duty. Please, Origen, join us. You know that you are always welcome.'

Once again the stranger touched his forehead and then sat down cross-legged on the ground.

Gobann had already untied the knots on the

harp cover and was setting the harp on his knee to tune the fine brass wires. He placed himself in harp on his knee to tune the fine brass wires. He placed himself in between the two beds where the victims lay and made the necessary adjustments to his instrument as quickly as he could.

Hearing the tuning of the wires, one of the men tried to raise himself on his elbow. His long brown hair fell lank and sweat-soaked about his face and his eyes were already dull and lifeless, but he searched, unseeing, around the room.

'Caitlin? Is that you?' he called feebly. 'Cait, are you there?'

He was so weak that this expense of energy caused his head to drop forward and he began to fall back onto the makeshift pillow. With surprising swiftness Lorgan raced forward, caught him and lowered him gently back down upon the bed.

Fintan opened his mouth again as he relaxed but no sound came out, only the heavy rasping of the death rattle.

'He has been calling for her since he was brought in,' Cathach stated. 'I sent a messenger to Murrough to beg him to bring her here before the fellow passes away but I fear that he will soon be gone.'

Then Gobann moved his long fingers to gently strike the brass wires and Mawn thought that he had never heard any sound so pure, so beautiful, like the rippling waters of the brook as it passed over the rocks or the gentle plip-plop of fishes catching flies in the pond.

'Is this the Sorrow Strain?' he wondered. 'It makes me think of summer, of warm breezes and the smell of fresh hay.' And then thoughts of his family came to him and the tears began to well up in his eyes, but he held them back for he did not want to let Sianan see him cry. She was the first person close to his own age that he had ever met outside of the valley of Dobharcú and he had a sense that they would be friends. He did not want her to see him crying for homesickness at their first meeting.

The other poor soul who lay unconscious and close to death let out a moan and his eyes opened for a moment. Mawn had an overwhelming feeling that of all the people in the tent, the fellow was calling to him and so he went boldly to stand by his side.

The face was horribly disfigured. It had been burned severely with hot irons and beaten until it was only a bruised mash of flesh, no longer resembling a face at all. This was shocking enough for Mawn as he had never witnessed such injuries, but the worst shock of all was that he immediately recognised his elder brother, Beoga.

Mawn's eyes instantly clouded with tears that ran down his face and over his chin to drop onto the deep green cloak his mother had made him. All the emotions he had ever felt, all the joy, all the fear, all the love, all the laughter, all the anger, all the hope, coursed through his body in a matter of seconds. He grabbed at the edge of the bed to support himself and muttered a few unintelligible words before sinking to his knees at his brother's side.

Still he was aware of his teacher's scrutiny and of Sianan who had been weeping when he met her, and so he controlled his emotions as best he could. Always introspective, he became more so, withdrawing into a world of his own where he could escape pain. But for the first time in his life he found that withdrawing from the real world could not alleviate the sadness that he felt.

Sadness that he had never come to know his brother very well and that now it was too late. Sadness for the pain Beoga had suffered. Sadness that came of guilt for his mother's favourite. Sadness, in looking on this pathetic broken form, that his elder brother was in reality a stranger to him.

Mawn's attention was drawn to his brother's hands. One of them was torn to shreds by the beatings he had received, the other hand was fairly clean, but both his wrists had puncture wounds about the size of a small clover leaf.

From the corner of his eye Gobann observed his young student carefully, but he had no idea of who the fellow was that Mawn knelt beside.

Without a show of fear the boy tenderly reached out and took Beoga by the hand that was least damaged, and stroked the fingers with infinite care.

He whispered into his brother's ear, 'If I only I had known that this would happen to you I may have been able to prevent it. If I had not left home perhaps I could have done something to save you suffering this terrible agony.' But Mawn's sadness soon gave way to anger. 'I promise you that I will find the one who did this to you.'

In the very next moment Gobann began a tune, composing a melody as he went. The harp call filled the air. All within earshot were captive to it. Even Cathach and Lorgan, who had listened many times to the playing of Gobann, found themselves sinking to the ground on their knees, closing out the world, saving all their senses for the wondrous voice of the music-loom.

Sianan, the girl with the jet-black hair, sobbed a little and then she too closed her eyes. For those within its reach, nothing existed beyond the sounding of that harp. Each was enraptured by the chiming reverberation of its wires.

'If these sounds could be made of any solid form,' thought Cathach, 'they would be of the purest gold and the clearest crystal. There is no harper alive in Eirinn who can match the skill of Gobann and there is no harp as exquisite as the one he carries.'

Through the chiming music Sianan found it easy to imagine the souls of those two tortured bodies slowly rising from the straw to dance around the room with smooth peaceful grace. It seemed that she could sense a gathering of many spirits from the beyond crowding the little tent; some murmuring incoherent phrases, others lifting their voices as one with the graceful music.

Sianan did not feel frightened at these ghostly presences; her instincts told her that she was perfectly safe. She repeated to herself the words that her grandfather had spoken to her many times concerning the passing of a soul. 'We change the form of our bodies through the ages as often as we change our clothes in this short life. Death is the beginning of a new journey and who knows what shape we will wear next?' Sianan's eyes remained shut for she was afraid that if she opened them the spell would be broken, nevertheless she felt compelled to sneak a glimpse of Gobann's harp. When she parted her eyelids she was looking directly at Mawn.

From the bedside where he knelt, the boy looked up at her sharply as if he had heard her thoughts. His eyes were red with weeping and his gaze was cold. She snapped her eyes shut again so as not to have to witness the pain that she saw reflected in his face.

Mawn knew that she had noticed him and he determined never to show this pain to anyone for it was a private thing that he did not wish to share and he knew from all that Gobann had told him that a Druid was expected to bear suffering in silence.

All across the battlefront the Laigin warriors were bowing to the forces of Munster. It was not the nature of the Saxons, however, to succumb so easily. They fought on savagely, beating back the defenders of Rathowen, step by step.

A few of Streng's companions lifted their wounded comrade up and carried him away to shelter at the side of the ditch. From there they made their escape over the stream toward the loch, unnoticed in the great confusion of the retreat.

All of them were aware of the likely fate of foreign mercenaries at the hands of the High-King. Death. As they were foreigners there were no clan ties to protect them. So, hacking a path through the ranks of their former allies, two dozen of them cut their way out of the defences and made off, scattering in many different directions. These, and a few others, were the only Saxons to escape with their lives.

No-one in Caitlin's garrison had the strength or the will left to pursue the foreign raiders. The warriors of Munster and Teamhair also let them go; Morann being unwilling to leave the field in case Dichu lived up to his well-earned reputation for treachery. For all his talk of honour, he was, after all, a practical man who might well take advantage of any favourable situation.

It was late in the afternoon before Morann the War-Prince of Munster felt that the situation was safe enough to send troops to hunt the Saxons down, and by that time they had regrouped and were already planning their next enterprise.

At the same time as his mercenaries were making good their escape, Dichu was riding directly toward the banners of the High-King, his guardsmen desperately trying to pace their mounts with his. The pipers of Eoghan struck up the march of their clan as the enemy troop approached and twenty horsemen of Leoghaire's household met and surrounded the defeated king. In submission to the victors, Dichu threw the banner of his kingdom and his clan in the dust at the feet of his foemen's horses.

Murrough, stationed among the warriors of Teamhair, dismounted and took up the flowing red cloth, in turn handing it to the High-King who held it aloft for all his followers to see before passing it to Murrough's father, Eoghan Eoghanacht, the King of Munster.

Then Leoghaire the High-King of Eirinn spoke to Dichu for all to hear. 'Traitor to your people and the peace of this land,' he exclaimed, and all the warriors on both sides were silenced by the fire in his words, 'throw down your sword and give over your liberty.'

Never letting his eyes drop from Leoghaire, not even for a second, Dichu slowly unbound the belt at his waist and let the weapon drop to the ground with a clatter. Disarmed, the King of Laigin was set upon by Eoghan's men, bound with strong ropes and led away to wait until his crimes could be fully judged. His guardsmen were made to lie face down in the dust without their weapons or their dignity and their horses were then led over the field to the High-King's enclosure.

Within a short time of their king's surrender, those warriors of Laigin who had not managed to flee were assembled in a large group. Their swords, shields, bows, axes, helms and armour were heaped in a mound before the tent of the High-King. And there they awaited their fate, many painfully aware that they had broken the custom and laws of the land and that Leoghaire would be justified in repaying their ruthless behaviour in kind.

Both King Eoghan of Munster and Leoghaire the High-King of Eirinn were wise enough to know that no crime committed in the name of Dichu or Palladius, or any god for that matter, would be justification for these simple men-at-arms forfeiting their lives. And they both realised that the repercussions of such an action could haunt the reign of a high-king for many years.

'I am no tyrant,' stated Leoghaire to those of his chieftains who insisted on the mass execution of the Laigin warriors. 'Will we so readily adopt the customs of the Romans? There has been enough killing of kindred by kindred today. There will be no more. We will let them go home if they make a solemn promise never to rise up again. It is their masters I seek to punish.'

Then he stormed away from the gathered chiefs to address the Laigin men. 'You who are the warriors of the Eastern kingdom,' he proclaimed to them, 'will receive the mercy of Teamhair on oath that you will never again bear arms in a fight against Munster or the High-Kingship of Eirinn. Some of you have committed deeds that are unforgivable and that will follow you the rest of your days. But I am as guilty as any of you. I once also believed the words of the foreigners. It was my lack of vigilance that brought about this terrible war and so I find I cannot punish you for falling into a similar trap.'

Almost to a man the forces of Laigin gratefully agreed to the terms and knelt to swear their promise before the kings. Those few die-hard supporters of Palladius who refused to make an oath were held in keeping to be exiled forever from Eirinn.

As soon as the fighting had ceased and a surrender effected, a frantic search was begun among the many prisoners for Palladius, Seginus and Isernus, but they were not found in the ranks of captured warriors.

Morann gathered a troop of his mounted men and set out to scour the fields and farms around about. Everyone in Leoghaire's camp feared the worst: that the Christians had escaped amongst the fleeing Saxons.

While his elder brother led the hunt for the Roman priests, Murrough made his way to the stronghold of Rathowen, hoping to lend a hand wherever he could. On the way a messenger from Cathach delivered the old Druid's request that Murrough fetch Caitlin to the tent as soon as she could be found. The prince guessed that the man who had been calling out for her was her lover or perhaps even her husband.

The road had been cleared of its barricades and so the prince led his troop of guardsmen unhindered along the path through the main gates past the watch-post. The scene that presented itself to him as he entered the compound brought him almost to tears. Many warriors of the garrison lay where they had fallen; almost half of Caitlin's troops were wounded or dead, the rest lay sprawled still exhausted at their posts even after the passing of more than an hour.

The fight had gone heavily against the defenders soon after the enemy had climbed the forward ramparts, and those who still breathed were sapped of all vitality and numbed by the whole experience.

Over at the foot of the tower Murrough noticed a young woman ordering the treatment of the wounded and organising the distribution of water. Her cloak and breeches were torn and she supported herself with a blackthorn stick.

As Murrough got closer to her he saw that her face and arms were smeared with soot from having to fight fires that the enemy had started, and her voice was hoarse from shouting. But she was a figure of authority and strength in this chaos, so the Prince of Cashel guessed she was the chieftain he was seeking. He rode directly up to her and leapt from his horse.

'Are you Caitlin the daughter of the house of Úaine?' he asked directly.

'I am she,' Caitlin answered bluntly, returning to her task. 'Are you come from the High-King?'

'Yes,' he replied. 'Leoghaire begs that you come with me to tell him what you need for the comfort of your warriors and your people.'

Caitlin sighed deeply. 'It is too late for many. We need Druids skilled in the healing arts and we must have clean water. Could he send us that if nothing else?' She was still slightly dazed and found that, though she knew there was much they were in need of, she could not concentrate well enough to list it all.

'I think that fresh water is the main thing,' she sighed finally. She was deathly pale, feeling hopelessly daunted by the destruction around her, and she seemed to Murrough to be very near to breaking point.

There was something about her that touched the prince deeply; whether it was the contrast between her control over the situation and the tattered state of her clothes, or whether it was the strong spirit that seemed to stand taller than the exhausted body it inhabited, he did not know. Watching her sway slightly as she spoke he also knew that she had pushed herself too far.

'I think that you should rest,' Murrough ventured.

Caitlin stopped what she was doing and turned slowly to face him. 'How dare you speak to me like that!' she flared.

What she said next was through clenched teeth that barely contained the force of her indignation. All the pent-up anger and frustration of the last few days spilled out from her. 'I have fought today alongside the bravest warriors of my clan and I have seen the best of them slain.'

She gestured at Murrough and his guardsmen. 'Look at you! Why, you don't even have dust on your cloak from your journey! Go back to your lord the High-King and report what you have seen and leave me to attend to the business of comforting the fallen. And make sure you pass on my message swiftly or you'll pay with my fury.'

The prince stood his ground and examined her dark-ringed eyes. 'She is proud,' he thought, 'but she will surely kill herself if she does not allow herself time to recover.'

'All I said was that I think you are in need of some healing yourself,' he repeated calmly. 'I have been asked to bring you to the place of healing.'

'Get out of my sight!' she shouted. 'I am not in the habit of taking orders from men who are conveniently absent from the field in time of need.'

'I was in the midst of the fight, lady,' Murrough

began, a little offended that she should accuse him of cowardice.

'Hiding with the other heralds in the shadow of Leoghaire's war mare!' she snapped.

'Lady, I was with the High-King and I had no choice but to stay there at his side, that was my appointed duty. But I was also among the warriors who rode up the embankment to your aid.'

'Enough boasting!' she replied. 'Deliver my words to Leoghaire and make haste before these men who are twice your worth suffer any more than they have to!'

Murrough had seen enough fighting for one day and was in no mood for a war of words. He climbed back on his horse and turned to his guardsmen. 'Stay here and do as the lady bids,' he ordered gruffly. 'Anything she asks, it is your duty to deliver.' Then he turned his mount around and galloped over the rampart toward the stream.

Caitlin realised, too late, that Murrough was at least a chieftain and that she had been far too severe with him, but she shrugged the incident off quickly and called to his soldiers to help carry the wounded into the tower.

And it was only after he was long gone that she realised that he might have had some news of Fintan.

The Prince of Cashel did not immediately return to the High-King or to Cathach. He rode down to the stream where the pack animals were being watered, then he sent a message to his father's retinue. He followed the little watercourse until he could see the loch in the distance. There he dismounted and lay on a grassy hillock, staring into the distance. He was a warrior, true enough, but he had seen precious little real warfare during his life and he now was experiencing the first shocks of witnessing a large-scale battle.

When the horror of the bloody slaughter began to subside a little, he found that all he could think of was Caitlin. 'She is as beautiful and as strong and as fiery as they say,' he thought, 'and she has the demeanour of a queen. She is the sort of person with whom I could share my burdens and she has the will to carry on through any difficulty. It would be very easy to love her.' Then he suddenly remembered the message he was supposed to have passed on to her. 'How could I forget that?' he rebuked himself. He was not to know that he was suffering from the battle weariness that can strike at a warrior's memory.

And then his inner voice spoke and reprimanded him in harsher tones. 'You did not tell her because you fear that she will hold it against you, the bearer of such bad tidings, forever more.'

He got up off the grass then and quickly mounted his horse, realising that it was his duty to bring her the news of Fintan and escort her to his side.

This decided, he spurred his mount on as fast as it would carry him straight back to the fort of Rathowen.

TWELVE

annarr was not merely a tried warrior and a moderately successful brigand. In his marauding career he had also come to learn a considerable amount about classical battle tactics. Nevertheless, it did not take a trained centurion to see early on in the conflict that the fight was going badly.

The thegn had taken note of the positions of all the troops on the field, carefully projecting their lines of advance, nervously aware that his own warriors were in a very dangerous position. When the soldiers of Dichu had dropped their weapons and Hannarr had plainly seen that the enemy had almost surrounded the ramparts to prevent the Saxons escaping, he decided not to risk trying to cut his way out. He proudly thought to make a stand.

A small band of his men had stayed with him but they were soon overwhelmed and as the situation had worsened, Hannarr had cleverly feigned death and sought a safe place to conceal himself.

He had not been in the mood to run again that day. 'I am sure there is something to be gained by biding my time, some trinket or some snippet of information will present itself to me,' he thought, unwilling to admit to himself how fearful he really was for his own safety. He also remembered that Seginus had mentioned a great store of gold within the tower and that encouraged his curiosity a little.

It was not until his mercenaries had all left the ramparts that he woke up to his mistake and he cursed his stupidity at not realising that his men would not return at all for him, or that they might have given him up for dead. 'Not that Streng would rush to my assistance anyway,' he thought bitterly.

So it was that he was huddled in a corner of the earthworks facing the gatepost when Murrough rode up to the tower a second time and rushed inside. 'That man is one of their chieftains,' he realised, 'and I could have reached out just now to touch him!'

Slowly Hannarr searched with his fingers for his sword-hilt. 'This battle is truly lost,' he told himself, and weighed up his chances of striking the chieftain a death blow as the fellow emerged from the tower.

At that moment Murrough came out of the door again with a large bag slung over his shoulder. He called to his men to fetch another horse and then he prepared to ride off.

For an instant it seemed to Hannarr that the prince was looking directly at him. The Saxon half-closed his eyes and relaxed every muscle in his body. He breathed slowly. An instinct told him that he should not strike out at this man, that he would achieve nothing by killing him. Hannarr shut his eyes tightly and did not look at Murrough any more.

When a few more moments had passed two horses galloped off but the Saxon never saw who the other rider was. Seeing that there were many warriors moving about, he realised that escape from the hillfort would be very difficult for him without serious risk to his life.

233

'After nightfall I will make my way out,' he decided, propping himself against a wall to wait.

How long she sat in the healer's tent and listened to the wondrous music, Sianan never really knew, for time passed there as she had often imagined it might in the Faery country. Listening to the notes falling from the music-loom she remembered all the tales she had ever heard of that magical realm where a single day could be equal to the passing of a hundred years in the land of Eirinn.

It must have been after a long while before she noticed that her feet were numb under her and her legs ached. Still she did not want to move lest the tiniest rustle of her clothes break the spell.

Her thoughts were dragged away, though, from her own discomfort and into the world of the spirit. The souls of the two men had deserted their battered bodies and were free. She knew that Gobann was imparting to them a great gift and that they could now find their way home. She was acutely aware of the quiet that had descended in the healing place and of the overwhelming peace that beckoned her to lay down on the ground and sleep. She could not help but wonder, if she did so, whether she would ever wake again or if she would open her eyes to find that a century had passed and everyone around her was long gone. A cold shiver travelled through her, telling her that she had glimpsed something of the future. Sianan concentrated all her will on the sound of the poet's tune, forcing herself to banish any thoughts of what might one day come to pass.

She had only just brought her mind back to focus on his playing when the harp call suddenly increased in intensity, as if another harper had struck up the tune beside Gobann, complementing the music, adding to it. This new harp had a distinct tone, completely different but just as beautiful, just as delicate, as the harp Gobann played.

'A Faery harper has come to play also,' Sianan thought excitedly and she fought the impulse to look upon the otherworldly musician in case the creature vanished and with him the Faery music. In the end she made herself content to only listen.

From somewhere nearby a woman's voice rose in a chant. When the chant died off, the same voice rose with the words of a beautiful song. Sianan thought that she had never heard tones so sweet or so sad.

'Oh soul of radiance,' it began, 'friend to the stars
    that fill the dark sky,
Who came from the kingdoms of the spirit,
I call to you: come to me;
Hold me close once more before parting
And I will sing this song to your soul
For to lift your heart and keep you from fear;
There is no danger, your voyage takes you now
    over calm seas;
I will lend you a lighted lantern to steer you,
To be a guide for you,
To show you the way onward
To your next port of call.'

No force on Earth could hold Sianan's eyes shut any longer. As her eyelids parted to let in the light, she discerned before her a woman dressed in dirty rags, yet holding a harp that looked much like Gobann's. Murrough, the Prince of Cashel, stood beside her and though they did not touch, it seemed she leaned against him slightly.

Then suddenly the spell was shattered. As softly as the music had begun, it ceased and Sianan realised that the tent was full of wounded warriors: every bed was occupied and the spaces between were also being filled. There was mayhem and the moaning of many wounded. Where there was provision for twenty, a hundred warriors were now crammed. Men were crying in pain and anguish; others were silent and did not move. All of the straw beds were splattered with blood.

The woman, the sad singer, got to her feet and passed her harp to Murrough, who cradled it in his arms as if it were a child. Then, leaning on a walking stick, the harper hobbled over to where the young brown-haired warrior lay. She placed her right palm over his face and slowly drew her hand down across it, closing the eyes forever.

As she did so she pronounced, so softly that Sianan had to strain her ears to hear it all, 'Your soul is free, my friend. Let it rise from your broken body, and may the ancient ones who watch over us escort you to the place and time of your new birth. May the eternal circle grant that we may cross paths again. Farewell.'

Gobann came to stand beside her, and Cathach also, to perform the final ritual of soul-parting.

'The three slender things that keep us alive,' he began, 'the slender stream of milk from the cow's udder,' and he poured some milk into the dead mouth, 'the slender stalk of corn,' and he placed a dried kernel under the cold tongue, 'and the slender thread spun by a skilled woman,' and he drew the covers up over the shoulders of the corpse, 'go with you now to your new beginning.'

Gobann came and took Mawn's hand and Sianan found herself moving to stand beside the poet. Origen approached the woman harper and gently touched her shoulder. She turned to face him with a tearful face and, leaning heavily on his arm, she left the tent. Murrough followed, still carrying her harp.

That was the first time that Sianan saw Caitlin Ni Úaine.

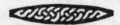

In a wood three Roman miles south of Rathowen, Seginus lay curled in his cloak and covered in leaves and brush. The trees grew close together in this part of the wood and a horse would not pass easily between them, so he felt secure that the enemy would not search too carefully here.

'I was lucky to get away with my life,' he reminded himself over and over.

He was still shaking from the thrill of the fight, and the flight, and something deep inside of him was crying in outrage. It was calling him coward.

It was the voice of his father.

A horseman rode by in the distance and Seginus quieted his breathing so that he could hear how close the enemy passed by.

The cool air was unusually still, the breeze was no longer rising from the loch and in a few hours the land would be in darkness.

Seginus resolved to try to sleep so that he would be rested enough to continue his escape under the cover of night. But whether it was the excitement of having come from a great battle or fear for his life if he was caught, he could not keep his eyes shut for very long.

His mind drifted this way and that and he began to reflect on his past. He was born the son of a famous and gallant Roman officer, a veteran of the wars in Africa and the campaigns against the

237

Eastern Christians. His grandsire was the great tactician Ephesus Alexander, who had been converted to the Cross in the time of the Councils of the Faith at Nicea, over a hundred years before. His lineage was respected and admired; a famous book of the time had been written about the exploits of his ancestors and was required reading for all of humble background who aspired to high office.

Somehow, however, Seginus had never lived up to the grand expectations of his father and family. Throughout his teenage years, he flirted with the idea of a military career and even accompanied his father on expeditions to the lands of the Allemagnie. It was there that he met Saxons, and it was amongst them that Seginus learned his first real lessons in life. He was not long in their company before Roman ways began to seem soft and unsatisfying compared to the reckless and lusty culture of the Allemagni, which was their Latin name. Nor were the Saxons a people to be dominated easily. Not like the Celts.

'Celts,' thought Seginus with contempt. 'I have never felt anything but disgust for Celts. My earliest memories are of watching Father's Gaulish slaves beaten and wondering why they never revolted or struck back at their masters. They are a conquered people with nothing to contribute to the civilised world.' As usual he chose to forget that he was half-Celtic himself, for his mother was of the continental race, a Gaulish princess.

Seginus did not take well or happily to the military profession and consequently his days in the legion were numbered. Though his father was well known in the army and his family name respected, his mixed blood made it difficult for a commander to maintain discipline among the veterans of the Imperial army and as a result Seginus never really enjoyed the life of a Roman officer. It was to be the way of the Cross that finally engulfed his passion and not the way of the sword.

When his father died, Seginus, at seventeen still little more than a boy by Roman standards and already with a failed military career to live down, was sent, with his younger brother in tow, to the monastery of Saint Eli in the west of Gaul.

In the monastery his existence had taken on a whole new meaning. He threw himself into the service of his abbot and of the Holy Mother Church. In the long vigils of his novitiate he discovered that he had a talent for reading and memorising the chants of the Mass.

Now that he thought about it he could remember clearly the first time he heard about the heretics in the land of the Franks and their outrageous version of Christ's teaching. He knew, not long after, that he was called to minister to the heathen and he naturally shared the view of many of his fellow clergy that the Devil was afoot in the world and no less so even amongst the Holy Orders. This was no more evident to Seginus than in the behaviour of his half-brother Linus.

The boy had always been what might be considered licentious even by Roman standards, but once within the confines of the monastery he grew to be what any abbot would consider evilly perverted. Seginus saw it as his duty to protect his half-brother from the corrupting influences of some of the older monks. But he could not watch the boy all day long and Linus began to gain for himself a reputation that should not perhaps have attached itself to a man of God. Seginus also put it down to the fact that Linus was born of a brief affair that his mother had indulged in during one

239

of his father's long absences.

'It was his mother's slave blood that brought that behaviour out,' thought Seginus. 'There were enough women around the monastery. Why didn't he get himself one of them and be satisfied? Christ knows, I had a few. They were always there for the taking.'

It was partly to save a scandal and partly in search of adventure that Seginus volunteered himself and his brother for the mission to Eirinn. 'I still cannot believe that he is dead,' he muttered to himself. 'And now our bishop is a prisoner and will surely be put to the sword also.'

'God curse these heathens!' he cried into his cloak. 'Give me a sign, God. What am I to do? I cannot carry on without my Lord Palladius.'

There was no answer. The woods were silent and unmoved by his plea.

Streng and the other survivors of the Saxon war party gathered on the southern edge of the loch at nightfall. Their numbers were greatly reduced and they were all spent, but Streng judged that they were finally beyond reach of any threat from the army of Munster.

The bleeding in Streng's neck had been stemmed but he was unable to speak in other than a hoarse empty wheeze, which was a shadow of what his booming voice had been.

Despite his injury, and the misfortune that had befallen the company, Streng noted with some satisfaction that Hannarr was not among the survivors at the agreed meeting place.

'He has fallen to the enemy or run off like the coward that he always was,' resolved Streng, though he only half believed it were true. 'Now I will take command of this war raid and we'll do some real fighting.'

He refused to admit that he was still very weak or to see that there were only twenty-seven raiders gathered around him, and they not the best of the warriors who had sailed from Eboracum six months before.

For the first time in his life, Streng considered taking the easy way out: heading for the ships where they were moored in the south and leaving Eirinn to the Irish. But the possibility no sooner crossed his mind than he dismissed it with a dry laugh.

'When I go home it will be with arms full of gold,' he decided, 'or not at all.' Then he lay back on the furs that had been set out for him and rested, his hand on the hilt of his sword.

Mawn spent the rest of the afternoon assisting Origen. He worked tirelessly, obeying the orders of the healer and helping to administer some of the liquors that the man carried. Origen encouraged him to look on the wounded with compassion and with admiration for what they had achieved.

The shock of seeing his brother broken and savaged after hanging on the death tree was so profound that he had said not a word to anyone about it. He assumed that Gobann had recognised Beoga and would at some point offer words of comfort, but the poet was busy in council with the kings and chieftains and had not been back to the tent for some hours.

By the closing of the day Mawn was tired and he was missing Gobann's company. 'They have forgotten me,' he said to himself and the tears began to rise again but he stubbornly fought them back. 'Gobann told me that I would have to learn to put my own feelings aside,' he rebuked himself.

The full force of what had happened only really hit him later when he had time to himself to think and question what had become of the rest of his family if Beoga had been captured by the Romans.' The answer thrust itself at him from every direction. Mawn only had to cast his eyes around the place of healing and gaze on the ugly wounds that many of the warriors bore to begin to realise that he would never see his mother or father or any of his clan again.

All that had happened to him in the last few days, coupled with the realisation that he had likely lost his family forever, suddenly fell upon him like a great weight and he knew he must leave the healing place for a while. When he thought the healers were too busy to notice him, he left and went in search of a place to be alone.

As he walked he came across a woman wailing over her dead husband, trying to drag the corpse to some place where it would not be trampled by the many horses on the field. Mawn helped her with the body and then sat with her while she wept. He wept also, long and bitterly for all that was changing, for all that he had lost and for fear of the future.

He left the woman cursing the one who had killed her husband and her words remained in his head when he returned to help Origen once more. He formed a curse in his head aimed at the one who had murdered his brother but he did not speak it for he knew that any curse could return to haunt him seven times over.

He managed to gain control of his thoughts and

his emotions, however, and resume the work of assisting with the wounded. The ability to work harder and longer hours when a crisis demanded it was a skill he had learned from his father.

In the early evening, Murrough's guardsmen brought thirty more wounded soldiers into the compound and Lorgan arranged places for them around the fire, for there was no more room under the tent. Then the old man called all the healers together for their evening meal.

'It is early yet to be eating but we need our strength if we are to tend the dying through the night,' he said. 'Each of you may rest one hour and then return here to help again.' He went then to supervise Sianan who was handing out bowls of meat broth.

Origen had been carefully observing Mawn while he worked with the healers. He followed the boy when he got his bowl and then sat down beside him to wait patiently for him to finish his meal.

'You have worked very hard, young one. Thank you for your help,' he said eventually.

'I am very tired,' replied Mawn with a mouth full of food.

'My people have a saying: weariness of the limbs after hard work is better than weariness of the spirit. Weariness of the limbs lasts only for an hour; weariness of the spirit lasts forever.'

Mawn noticed that Origen had no food with him. 'Aren't you going to eat?' he asked.

'I do not eat of the flesh of animals. It is against our beliefs to harm our fellow beings in any way.'

'Aren't you a Christian?' queried the boy in obvious confusion.

'I am a Christian,' said Origen, laughing a little, 'but I am not a Roman. My people have a different way of looking at the world than the Roman Christians.'

'I am glad,' said Mawn, 'because I would not wish to hate you as I do them. You seem kind.'

The stranger noted the bitterness in the boy's voice. 'The young fellow you comforted this afternoon,' began Origen, and he saw Mawn wince slightly, 'did you know him?'

Connor, who was still hovering nearby on guard, pricked up his ears. Mawn turned his head to answer, wanting to empty his heavy heart to the stranger, but before he had a chance to speak, Sianan approached with some bread for the foreigner and suddenly Mawn no longer felt like talking.

Origen gratefully accepted the bread and then said to Sianan, 'Mawn has worked very hard with me today, but tonight you must take care of him. He is alone in the camp except for Gobann. You and he will be good friends, I am sure. Make certain that you both rest. I have a feeling that tomorrow you will be required to witness the trial of Palladius and you will be expected to be wide awake for it as one day you will be asked to repeat the story of it. After the Roman's trial I believe you are both to be brought before the High-King.'

Mawn's eyes widened. 'The High-King!' he exclaimed. 'Me?'

Origen rose from his place, laughing under his breath, his dark eyes full of mischief. He reached into his tunic and brought out a small leather bottle and handed it to Mawn. 'Take this bottle as a gift. You must only sip a tiny amount of this liquor for although it will help you to sleep and it will ease your pain, it is dangerous to drink too much of it. I would like you to regard it as a payment for your hard work today. Keep it safe for one day you may stand in real need of it.'

244

Then Origen touched his forehead with the tips of his fingers as was his custom and returned to his duties. Mawn watched him go and wished that the stranger could have stayed a little longer to talk with him.

'His people call it the water of life,' said Sianan.

'What?' answered Mawn, shaken from his own thoughts.

'The liquor that he was giving to the wounded today. His people call it the water of life.'

'Where is Gobann?' said Mawn aware that he was not changing the subject as politely as he might have done.

'He is with the kings I expect,' replied Sianan. 'He won't be back tonight. You are in the care of Lorgan the Sorn and myself for a while.'

'Oh,' said Mawn disappointed. 'Where can I go to get some sleep? I am very tired.'

Sianan saw that he was about to collapse from exhaustion so she took him by the hand and led him to Cathach's tent.

The sun was long gone behind the rim of the Earth and darkness had covered the land when Seginus woke. He did not know how long he had lain there among the moist leaves but he was suddenly aware of how cold and hungry he was.

He stretched a cramped leg and the noise of his body moving in the rustling underbrush made him catch his breath. He had an eerie feeling that there was someone nearby.

Very near.

He slowed his breathing and listened to the sounds of the night. Somewhere in the trees there were two owls calling to one another and not far from where Seginus lay a small animal was scratching around between fallen branches. All else was silent.

He decided to get up slowly and try to ease some life back into his sore limbs. The pain in his right leg was almost unbearable and as he tried to rise, the cramp became worse, making the muscle twitch involuntarily. He writhed in agony and bit his tongue. Rolling over onto his stomach, he pushed his body up with his forearms. In a moment his head emerged from beneath the pile of bracken and he looked carefully about.

Directly in front of him, not five paces away, a badger was nibbling on a tasty morsel. The animal froze and stared at Seginus with two small bright eyes. Intuitively the Roman mirrored the little creature's stance. Seginus blinked and in that instant the badger dropped his dinner and vanished back into the woods.

The warrior-monk relaxed and laughed with relief. 'I am safe,' he assured himself. 'Safe.'

He stood up and stretched his muscles, realising that the damp ground had badly affected his right leg. As he stretched the limb and manipulated the knee he discovered that it was badly swollen and the joint almost frozen from an injury. Then he recalled receiving a blow to the leg from the flat of a blade during the fight and realised that there might have been more damage done than he had first thought.

He began to search about for a stout stick with which to support himself but the darkness hampered him and he wasted a long while stumbling around trying to get his bearings. By the time he finally found a branch strong enough for the job, he had completely lost his sense of direction and was forced to make a guess at which way led to safety.

He set off cursing his stupidity but not realising that he was still very bewildered by all that had happened to him. Blundering through the gaps in the trees, he reached in a matter of minutes a narrow path that served as the road to the loch from Rathowen. He took a while to crouch in the bushes at the roadside and decide which way would lead to safety. His view was blocked by trees in both directions and his knee was now extremely painful from treading the uneven ground in the wood.

He was just about to rise again when he heard hoof-beats once more pounding down the track toward him. Without hesitation he spread himself flat on the ground and lay still, hardly daring to breathe.

The horseman thundered past, on some vital errand no doubt, without noticing the fugitive hiding in the bushes.

As Seginus struggled to get up, he decided that it was far too dangerous to travel by the road, but neither could he travel over the rough ground of the woods for his knee was far too painful. In desperation he lay back down on his stomach on the damp earth and spread his body out in the shape of the cross, as he had many times when in penance before the altar. And just as he had done on so many occasions at the monastery at Saint Eli, he spoke his prayer out loud.

'Merciful Father, hear the prayer of your servant Seginus Gallus. All your plans are in wreck, and so many of your servants are at this moment facing death in heathen hands. In this hour of my great need I beg you to show to me your mercy. Let me live that I may come again to Rome and tell the world of the barbarity of these people and the martyrdom of Palladius. I beseech thee, O

Lord, deliver me from danger into the hands of friends!'

At that moment Seginus felt a rough grasp on the back of his collar and he was dragged up onto his elbows.

'Shut up, you stupid Roman, or you will get us both killed!'

It was Hannarr.

ThIRTEEN

aitlin never returned to the Dun of
Rathowen. Not that day nor ever
again. In the minutes after she had
bid farewell to Fintan she made the
decision to give over all the responsibilities of chieftainship to her father's family and
thus to her younger brother who was in Armorica
in the Gaulish provinces training as a warrior.

Like so many others who had been on the field
of the battle, she had been deeply affected by the
fighting at the ramparts of the defences. It had been
the first taste of real warfare she had ever experienced and she was not keen to see such bloody
slaughter again.

In her heart she knew it wasn't just fear for her
own life that had changed her, nor was it witnessing the great suffering of the wounded, though that
certainly clawed at her in another way. Neither was
it the cruel death of Fintan or of so many of her
friends that unsettled her. What had made her
walk away from her chieftainship was the realisation that, despite all her training in the Druid mysteries, she had failed to heed the most obvious of
signs.

She knew now that nothing had been more
certain to her than that Fintan would die in battle
that day. She had known that very morning when
he stood beside her watching the sun light the land.
She had known when he leapt over the rampart

and disappeared from sight. 'Why did I not do something? Why did I not warn him? How could I sit back and just let it happen?' her spirit screamed over and over.

In the end she forced the sadness, the fear, the anger and the dread into a corner of her mind where she could not hear them cry out to her any more. But once locked firmly away those emotions stayed locked away. When finally she had stood beside Fintan's cold body, she could not summon any of the emotions that she knew should be within her grasp. She could not give in to her true self; she could not scream out; she could not mourn him. Though her soul longed to, she could not even shed a single tear. If she had known that almost everyone that day had suffered more or less the same guilt and soul-numbness, perhaps she would not have been so hard on herself.

When her lover had passed away and Gobann and Murrough had left the tent, Origen had led Caitlin to the stream to pass his blessings on to Fintan in the manner of his people. She followed him like a young goat strayed from its elders and when they got to the edge of the stream she threw herself into the running water and held herself under until her breath was gone, punishing herself, forcing herself to feel something.

When she could resist the urge to breathe no longer, she lifted her head up into the warm sunshine from the murky blueness of the brook, sucked the air in deeply and looked upstream. Little rivulets of water flowed across her eyes and her face. The freshening wetness caught her hair and spread over the contours of her body as the water rushed on its journey to rejoin the stream.

For a moment or two her vision was blurred by

the water clinging to her eyelids but then she discerned, just upstream, a large brown-clad shape
squatting in the cold swirling rill. She wiped her
hands across her eyes to clear them and the shape
became more recognisable. An old woman was
bent over in the midst of the flow, scrubbing a
blood-stained shirt. The hag raised her face to meet
Caitlin's gaze. She was toothless and bald and her
frame was hideously skeletal.

'Danaan.'

Caitlin wiped the water frantically from her eyes
again and when she focused once more she saw
only the lifeless body of the red stag, half-kneeling,
half-lying in the middle of the current where it had
been cut down by the huntsmen's arrows. A small
magpie perched in its antlers and insects swarmed
around the carcass.

'The circle is coming to its round once more,' she
said aloud, though she was sure that the words
were not hers.

The stag's coming had been an omen of what
was to be and it was only now that she realised it.
Her powerlessness in preventing its death was a
portent of the events that took Fintan away from
her. As she knelt in the middle of the stream she
began to perceive also that the stag had offered up
its life so that she would live.

'In the same way perhaps, Fintan sacrificed his
life,' she thought.

For a long while she had sat on her knees in the
stream, staring at the dead beast and quietly giving
her thanks. When Origen had finished his ablutions
and blessings, he came and helped her to stand and
then he took her to a tent where she could rest.
Before leaving he convinced her to drink a portion
of one of his liquors to make her sleep.

The liquid burned her throat, not in the way of

the Gaelic people's mead that warmed the body, instead this really burned. She could feel it running into her stomach, setting it on fire and she coughed out the fumes of it. But in half an hour she was fast asleep.

In the tent where Eoghan Eoghanacht was quartered, his eldest son, Morann the Prince of Eoghan and heir to Munster was deciding on the changes he would make in his life.

As always, these days, he passed the night on a pallet set at the opening to his father's tent. Eoghan was now past seventy summers. The old king's days were spent in arthritic agony; his once nimble fingers, which had helped his wife at the spinning and at the loom, now were unable even to grasp the handle of his walking stick firmly. For some years his slumber had been fitful and interrupted and rarely did he pass the hours of darkness without some disturbance. So it was that Morann often guarded his father's sleeping rooms, aware that it was his duty as the eldest, but also in the sincere hope that someone would do that service for him one day in the autumn of his life. There was nothing he feared more than a lonely death.

Morann was the logical successor to his father, though he would still have to be presented to the free-people of Munster and then duly elected. But he was popular with the chieftains and the country folk and over the last two years he had gradually taken on more and more of the responsibilities of the actual ruling of Munster, until his father had become no more than a figure head. However an outsider would never have guessed that this was so, for Morann was careful not to take credit for any of his own work, but always saved his praise for the king.

This night neither man could rest soundly. They both lay on their pallets of straw, silent and brooding, the weight of kingship shared somewhat between them but no less a burden to both.

'Are you awake, Father?' Morann whispered.

'I am,' came the quick reply. Eoghan raised his head to search the darkness for his son's face. Morann and his brother were so alike that even their sire sometimes confused the two; but that was perhaps also the legacy of advancing age.

'I have decided that I will not put myself forward for the kingship, Father.'

There was silence for a few minutes as Eoghan struggled to sit upright. He patted his trimmed grey beard. 'Once again you have shown that you have wisdom beyond your years,' began the old man. 'If only I had been able to make that decision for myself when I was young, but your grandsire would have had me fed to the dogs if I had so much as considered it!'

He laughed and so did his son, who only dimly remembered Eoghan's father, but he recalled enough to know that the old man would have probably done a lot worse if Eoghan had refused the crown and the colours of the kingdom.

'What then will you do?' asked Eoghan, no trace of sadness or regret in his voice.

'I will go to Armorica to study at the College of Druids. I wish to become a law-keeper, and in time a Brehon,' he replied.

'That is a good ambition, my son,' began Eoghan, showing none of his real disappointment, 'but a judge's life can be as cruel as a king's.'

'A judge does not look back on his handiwork at the end of the day and count his success in the number of fallen foemen that lie at his feet.'

There was a sadness in the prince's voice that his father had never heard before. 'I can understand that,' thought Eoghan. 'This was the bloodiest fight I ever saw. Aye, and the quickest.'

'What of the kingdom?' returned the old man. 'The people expect you to serve them in some way.'

'I will serve them best by keeping the law. I have no wish to be the one who must enforce it.'

'Nor would you wish to be enslaved by the law as a king is,' added Eoghan. 'Thank you for your honesty, my son. I have long suspected that this day was coming and would not think to keep you as Lord at Cashel against your will. You and your brother were made in the same mould, but he has more the temperament for ruling. He will carry on the chieftainship of the clan and perhaps, one day, the kingship.'

With that, Eoghan Eoghanacht sighed heavily, rolled over and wished his son good night. He thought back on his own youth when he had fought beside the famous High-King who was called Niall of the Nine Hostages and how they had carved their names into the songs of their generation. 'Those were real battles,' he reminisced, 'not a bloody brawl like I saw today. In those days we sent out champions to do the fighting and few warriors were ever actually killed. The worst that happened was that their pride was bruised, but that was usually enough to settle an argument. There are many widows in Eirinn today and I am ashamed to have been a party to their husbands' deaths.'

By the entrance to the royal tent, his son lay looking out into the night and thinking about the king's words. 'It is true,' Morann told himself, 'Murrough and I are cast from the same die, but he will be a better king. I spend too many hours debating with myself the best and fairest course of action, and in the end there is no time left for deeds. He simply decides on a stand and then takes it. He makes mistakes often, but he learns well by them. He is a warrior. I was not made for that path. I don't have the stomach for it. Tomorrow I will speak with him. Tomorrow.'

Three hours after dawn the next day, the gathering of the councils was announced throughout the camp. The inner council of the High-King was first to assemble. As was the custom the meeting was chaired by Leoghaire himself, and present were King Eoghan, his adviser Cathach, Gobann, and Lorgan who was the High-King's counsellor.

It was a very informal gathering. Sessions of the inner council always were. It was one of Leoghaire's preferences that they all deal with each other as friends whenever possible. This Árd-Righ, as the High-King was known in the Gaelic tongue, did not believe in making any decisions without advice and for that he was reliant on the most experienced people in the land. Seeking many viewpoints made a great deal of sense to him and formal structures, he felt, bred deceit and intrigue.

Leoghaire's tent was not particularly grand, in fact it was the tent of a soldier: practical but roomy enough to hold a number of delegates or petitioners. Comfortable living quarters had never been a great priority for Leoghaire, but he was well known for the generosity of his table.

As the council members arrived to take their places, the Árd-Righ himself met each one at the entrance to the tent and handed him the ceremonial cup of welcome, the cuaich. This was really not a cup at all but a bowl that four cups would not have completely filled. Two ornate handles on either side, fashioned to resemble lions, merged with silver spirals and zigzagging lines. The base of it was set with crystals and with rare green Glascloch stones. As the mead was passed to each new arrival, a little more was drained from the cuaich until, when the liquid was finally gone, the finest design of all was exposed in the bottom of the vessel. A breath-taking triple spiral of gold, silver and brass wound its intricate way into the middle of the cuaich where, as the eye followed, it transformed in its central twist into the heads of three women. Some said they represented the ancient Danaan Queens of Eirinn; others said they were the three aspects of the Morrigú: the mysterious goddess of birth and death who was maiden, mother and the wise old woman all in one. Everyone agreed that they were exquisite.

The passing of the cuaich was a ceremony as old as the concept of kingship itself. It cleared the air between all parties as much as humanly possible for it reminded all who partook of it that their fates were entwined as intricately as the three spirals and the shared mead they sipped.

When everyone was seated, the cuaich was placed on a stand that Leoghaire had specially commissioned, its gorgeous design in full view. Then the real business of the meeting commenced.

The High-King asked for silence and then went straight to the matter in hand. 'Dichu is an opportunist,' he stated. 'He has clearly taken advantage of the coming of Palladius to further his own ambitions. I doubt that he would have dared lift a finger against me if the Roman had not filled his head full of ambition for the High Kingship.'

'Are you suggesting that we be lenient with him?' muttered Lorgan, taken aback.

'Quite the opposite,' affirmed the Leoghaire. 'I am proposing that we consider revoking his kingship, redistributing his lands and banishing him and his clan up to the third generation.'

'The British lands of the King of the Dal Araidhe might be a good destination for him and his people,' suggested Gobann. 'North Britain is largely uninhabited, I believe, and the Dal Araidhe are always searching for able Gaelic warriors to serve them. Dichu might even get a chance to promote himself as a candidate for the kingship in that land.'

'That is a very good plan. If he's plotting for the headship of North Britain,' stated Cathach, 'he'll be too busy to interfere with our work again. There is no love lost between any of us and the Dal Riadans since they sailed off for Alba, so there will be no risk of offending them.'

'What of Palladius?' asked Lorgan. 'He is a foreigner who has broken the sacred law of our people and murdered many. If we allow him his life and that of his black robed lackeys, it will send a message to every evangeliser from here to Alexandria that they are free to commit whatever crime takes their fancy all in the name of Rome and without fear of retribution.'

'If we execute him, his people and his followers will pronounce him a martyr. He will be all but worshipped as a saint,' countered Gobann. 'In which case he could certainly prove to be more of a threat to our plans as a corpse than he would if we let him live.'

Leoghaire leaned over from his seat and plucked a stalk of grass from the ground. He put the white root of it in his mouth and chewed thoughtfully. It was cool and moist from having been sheltered by the tent.

'I cannot allow you to forget the manner in which those two poor men died, nailed by their hands and feet,' declared Cathach, speaking slowly to emphasise the seriousness of the crime. 'Anyone who can order such an act to be committed, let alone to think of doing it in the first place, has, in my opinion, forfeited his right to enjoy any liberty. And there is still the question of the many others who were slaughtered by his servants and allies. '

'Would you really consider putting the man to death?' exclaimed Gobann horrified.

'My son,' exclaimed Cathach, his cheeks flushed with anger, 'if you had not left Dobharcú when you did, you yourself would have been one of his victims.'

'What do you mean?' queried the poet.

'The good bishop's mercenaries arrived there not long after you left. They levelled the place and murdered everyone, every living soul: humans, horses, cows, fowl, pigs. Then they set the whole place afire.'

Gobann's face drained of its colour. 'When did you hear this?' he gasped.

'This morning a messenger that Fintan had sent to the valley to seek you returned. He brought a broken axe-haft that he found among the ruins. It was undoubtedly of Saxon make for it had their crude letters carved into it. In the whole of the valley he found no-one who remained living and no building that remained standing.'

'I would have stayed there if I could,' thought Gobann sadly. 'It was so peaceful and the people were generous and caring. It reminded me of home.' Then Midhna's face flashed before his mind and he wondered about the night of his terrible vision. 'Was the Faidh sent to warn me of my own death or the rape of Midhna's village? Or both?'

'Has Mawn been told?' was all he could manage to say.

'No, Poet,' answered Cathach, the sympathy showing in his voice. 'The decision is yours to tell him, or not, as you see fit.'

'It seems to me,' announced Leoghaire, 'that the Roman should be punished as severely as the law allows. Only that way will others be put off the same kind of action. But I fear that an execution would create a precedent for future rulers to follow. His crimes are of the most evil nature but death has never been considered a suitable penalty for any crime, however heinous. Yet I cannot see any other way, though I wish I could.' He dropped his eyes to the ground for a moment. 'I will certainly banish all the other Romans,' he concluded.

'They will come again to this land whether you pass a law against it or no,' stated Cathach. 'For now there may be one or two of their kind from whom we could learn something of their ways. The more we know of them, the readier we will be when they start crossing the sea in their hundreds.'

'They are all dyed with the same berries,' added Lorgan, bitterly. 'Origen has told me of their methods. If you think these monks were brutal, it is nothing compared to how the Roman-trained professional soldiers behave. If we execute one insignificant Christian priest,' he reasoned, 'the Roman church might choose not to notice, but a bishop put to death and half a dozen of his servants cast out on the sea might encourage the Pope to embark on military reprisals. There is no telling what might happen if they come with warriors.'

'Clearly there is much to be considered,' sighed

Leoghaire heavily, the weight of his office visibly bearing down upon him. 'I wish that we had one of the Romans that we could speak with. I might judge the situation better if I could look on one of these men who are the cause of our discomfort. Has the bishop been found?'

'Not yet, I fear,' answered Gobann.

At that, Eoghan, who had been brooding silently, remembered that he had other news for the High-King. 'A patrol of my horsemen brought in a Roman monk a few days ago. He claimed to have a message for the High-King. He spoke our language very well and I was impressed with him but I decided to wait until the fighting was resolved before doing anything with him.'

'Who is he?' asked Cathach.

'He said his name is Declan.'

'That is a Gaelic name,' said the High-King. 'I will speak with him immediately. Send for him.' Then Leoghaire sighed deeply once again, wiping his brow and dropping the stalk of grass from his hand. 'Until he arrives we will break from our meeting. I have much to consider.'

Declan Abbot of Ardmór was duly summoned to attend Leoghaire's tent and he arrived a short while later. Only Lorgan, Eoghan and the High-King spoke with the man; the other counsellors were obliged to wait outside. So it was that only the two kings and the old Druid judge ever knew precisely what was discussed with him.

To keep busy while the man was being questioned, Gobann went to find Mawn to break to him the terrible news of the burning of Dobharcú and to summon him and Sianan to the Council.

He found the two of them seated together in the sunshine near the cooking fire at the tent of healing. They were both thoroughly engrossed in a game of the Brandubh.

'You jumped your High-King over one of my pieces!' Sianan suddenly accused her playmate.

'I did not!' returned Mawn, sounding guilty.

'Yes you did,' she protested. 'I had all the white kings surrounded and there was no way for any of them to break out.'

'You must have left a gap,' Mawn offered feebly.

'I did not leave a gap!'

'You must have.'

'You cannot stand to be beaten by me, can you?' teased Sianan.

'My father was the best player in the valley!' declared Mawn.

'I am sure he was, but you'll need a lot more practice if you think you can trick me so easily. I was playing this game with Druids at court when you were still toddling about chasing goats to their pens.'

'And who taught you to play so well?' demanded Mawn. 'Your father must have been a champion.'

Sianan dropped her gaze to the ground and clenched one of the Ravens tightly in her fingers. 'I never met my father,' she mumbled almost inaudibly. 'He was a poet who went away with the Danaans and did not return.'

Mawn instantly regretted his words. He could feel a great sadness in Sianan and it mirrored his own for the loss of his brother and his whole family, but again he fought back the tears and the anger. His body shuddered with the effort of suppressing such emotions and his thoughts became scattered. Finally he managed to calm down, reminding himself that this was not the manner in which a Druid should behave.

He focused all his attention back on the game and grasped the piece that had been under contention. Carefully he placed it back within the closing circle of the Raven pieces. 'You are right, Sianan,' Mawn admitted. 'I'm sorry. It was not right of me to cheat. My father always told me it is far better to learn well your craft and win the praise of others fairly than to pretend to be something you are not.'

Gobann was once more impressed with his new student, and as he got closer the poet recited a verse from the *Senchas Mor*, *The Great Storehouse*, as it was called, which was the word of the law. *The Storehouse* was memorised, word for word, by every Druid.

' "Purity of your hand, gifted and without wounding. Purity of your mouth without resort to poisonous satire. Purity of learning without any stain of deceit. Purity of your guidance to the people of Eirinn." These are the things you must learn to aspire to, my young friends. If you forget all else that I tell you, remember those few words, for they are the goal of every poet.'

Gobann sat down with them for a while at the Brandubh and eventually took over Mawn's troops, showing him a simple strategy that forced the attacking posture of Sianan's Ravens into a defensive one and finally into a retreat.

'The trick is never to allow your opponent the initiative,' Gobann pointed out.

'Will I have a set like this one day?' asked the lad.

'There is no other set like this one for these were made especially for me, but I am sure that you will own a fine one.'

'Who made them?' enquired Sianan, looking

closely at the pitted spiral designs that covered their surface. 'I have never seen such work as this. They are very beautiful.'

'A Druid queen that I knew once had a skill in fashioning clay and carving the bones of the seals that dwell in northern waters.' He paused, long enough for Sianan to realise that she had asked him too much. 'She crafted them,' he finished quietly.

Gobann decided then and there that this set would pass to Mawn when the time came. 'Síla would have liked that,' he told himself. A bitter-sweet memory had stirred in the poet and he decided not to mention anything about the murder of Mawn's kin. He resolved to let the matter lie for a while and to tell him later, when his life was more settled.

'It is time we were going to the Council,' he announced to them. 'Are you ready?'

They gathered all the Brandubh pieces and rolled them into their fine woollen cloth. Then the poet took the two children hand in hand to Leoghaire's tent to meet with all the most important people in the kingdoms.

It was a short walk to the High-King's campfire and they arrived just as Declan was emerging from the tent to be led back to his confinement. Mawn noticed that he was a slightly built man, about the same age as Gobann. His face was very pale, almost pink, and the black robes that he wore accentuated the tone of his skin. The back of his head, the very crown, was shaved in a circle, like a skullcap. The guards led him away in the oppo-site direction but the man looked hard at Gobann and his two charges, turning his head as he was dragged off, trying to keep eye contact.

'We will now go before the High-King of Eirinn,' said Gobann, brushing the dust from their clothes with the palm of his hand. 'Listen carefully to all that is said. One day there will be many who will ask to hear this story from those of us who were here.' He looked both of them squarely in the eye and was convinced they were as ready as time would allow. 'Let us go then.'

Mawn led the way, gingerly pushing aside the tent flap, not knowing what to expect. In a second it was drawn out of his grasp by Lorgan, who stood just within the doorway.

'Greetings to you, lad,' he remarked, 'and to you also, lass.'

Then Murrough, the Prince of Cashel, pushed in beside them through the door and led them to Leoghaire. 'The Wanderers are come, my lord, 'he announced.

'Welcome, my children,' called the High-King looking up from his contemplation. 'I am honoured to meet you.'

The tent flap pulled aside again as Cathach and Caitlin entered, Caitlin leaning heavily on the old Druid's arm.

'We are assembling now to discuss your future,' the High-King continued, nodding almost imperceptibly to the newcomers as they entered. 'Please sit here with me.' He gestured toward two small stools that had been set for the children.

As more of the Great Council arrived the proceedings took on an air of formality that was absent at the assembly of the inner council. Lorgan moved to sit by Leoghaire and Cathach took over the role of admitting people to the tent one by one, touching each one of them with the top of his staff as they passed him. The old man had dressed this day in his finest blue robes topped with a long white cowl that had been a gift from Origen. The headpiece was made of linen from Alexandria and it shone like a jewel against the deep Druid-blue of Cathach's other vestments. His timeworn staff was made of the finest polished blackthorn. Spirals, carved into the timber, coursed around the body of it and were rendered with such uncommon beauty that the staff seemed not to be made by human hands.

Soon the tent was full, bustling with Druids and advisers and warriors finding seats for themselves on the grass or leaning against the support poles of the royal tent. Dutifully both Mawn and Sianan sat quietly on their stools and the conversation buzzed around them. All fell silent, though, when Cathach struck his staff three times against the central tent-tree.

'Silence for the Great Council of the High-King!' he ordered. Then he passed his staff to the King of Munster, who wished to address the assembly first.

'Before we come to the other business,' began the old king, seizing his opportunity, 'I have an announcement to make. My son, Morann, is to stand down as heir to the clan and to the throne of my kingdom.' A murmur passed around the small assembly. 'I would now ask the High-King to approve the handing of his titles and lands to my younger son, Murrough, the Prince of Cashel.'

Morann stood up and his father passed the staff to him. 'I only wish to be free to study so that I may better serve my father's people,' proclaimed Morann.

'You are right to do so,' commented Leoghaire. 'I have no objection to the proposal. I wish you the best in your new profession, Morann. A kingdom can never have too many judges.'

'But it can have too many kings,' quipped Eoghan under his breath, passing a sly knowing wink to the High-King.

'I have one last duty for you to perform, though, as war-leader of Munster,' Leoghaire went on. 'I want you to travel south and along the coast with all speed and gather every warrior and levied foot-soldier that your kingdom can muster, for I fear that we will need to raise an army before the summer is too far advanced.'

'I will leave as soon as my small company are rested and ready to ride on,' Morann assured him.

Cathach took the staff back once more from Morann. 'We will now decide the guardianship of the Wanderlings,' he declared.

'Why are they passing the shepherd's stick between them?' Mawn whispered to Gobann.

'That is the speaking staff,' explained Gobann. 'The one who holds it has the right to speak until handing it over. Only Leoghaire is exempt from the rule for he is the High-King and this is his assembly.'

'It would seem to me that Murrough would be an excellent choice,' commented the Árd-Righ, 'if he only had himself a partner. The children will need the balance of male and female if they are going to follow the path we have planned for them.'

Murrough blushed hotly and the more he became aware of it the more his face reddened. He was twenty-three years of age: too old for a prince of his standing to be unwed or unpromised.

Across the crowd, Caitlin watched him. She had not had a chance to apologise for her behaviour at Rathowen and was very anxious to do so. 'I will never let another chance go by to tell someone how I feel about them or to let them know I am sorry,' she promised herself.

Murrough was given the staff. 'You have given me a great honour,' he began. 'I will care for them as if they were my own.'

'Maybe it is time you had some of your own!' goaded Leoghaire, pressing the point.

Before Murrough could open his mouth to object, Cathach took the staff back from his hands and his right to answer went with it.

'The matter is decided then,' intoned Cathach, as if he was very eager to have it so. 'Let all bear witness to it.' He raised the staff in the air to indicate that he had a further announcement to make. 'While the King of Munster was speaking a messenger came from the captain of his horse-guards,' he said.

Cathach waited for silence. Even Leoghaire sat forward to listen. He had not been made aware of any developments.

'Palladius is captured. He is being brought to you now, my lord.' The tent erupted into spirited conversation and speculation. Cathach leaned the speaking staff against a chair. It would no longer be of any practical use.

Finally Leoghaire spoke up and all the tent hushed to hear him. 'Let us go outside in the open air, I will pass my judgment on him now. I want as many as possible to hear my words.' As the Great Council began to disperse toward the stream he leaned over to Lorgan and whispered, 'Have Dichu brought out before me first, and then the other monk after Palladius. I will deal with them all one at a time.'

Lorgan nodded his old head and, with surprising agility for a man of such advancing years, left to do his master's bidding. The assembly, dismissed, moved quickly on to the natural amphitheatre created by the sides of the stream where the banks met the ditches of Rathowen.

When all were gathered, Mawn and Sianan sat again near to Leoghaire on the side of the hill, as did Cathach, Gobann, Lorgan the Sorn, Eoghan and Murrough. Caitlin found herself a place in amongst the greater assembly beside Origen.

Dichu was dumped on the ground at the bottom of the slope, in the middle of all, his arms bound tightly behind his back. Warriors of Munster and Midhe hovered about him.

'Dichu, who calls himself King of Laigin, stand before the justice of Leoghaire High-King of Eirinn,' called Cathach.

Dichu's arms were so well secured that he could not rise quickly without help, so two soldiers stepped forward to prop him up.

Leoghaire rose from his seat and spoke, conscious of his audience for he had trained as a storyteller when he was younger. 'The charges against you are many,' he began.

'Treaty-breaker, murderer, kin-slayer, traitor, these are but a few. Bringing clan war upon the land was your most grievous crime and there are those in the council who argue that I should have you strangled slowly in front of everyone present here.'

He paused momentarily, waiting for the words to strike at Dichu. To execute a king was unheard of in Eirinn. Beads of sweat formed across Dichu's brow and his body shivered a little, not with fear but with apprehension.

'I order you instead to leave this land forever within the period of three nights with all your kin unto the third generation. Any of your clan who are found here after that time will be put to death. You are banished beyond the distance of the ninth wave from these shores. Any who give you aid or shelter are also judged outlaw and will be banished.'

The shock of the pronouncement passed quickly

over the rebel's face. No king had been banished from Eirinn for over three hundred years. He had certainly not expected Leoghaire to be so severe.

'Loosen his bonds,' continued the High-King, 'and escort him immediately to the eastern sea, but do not let him return to his own hearth on the way and do not let him speak to another soul while he walks the soil of this land.'

The two warriors who flanked the man happily obliged their lord, leading the unhappy man away to his fate. A loud cheer rose from all those present as Dichu disappeared from their view.

'Are you sure he will land in Dal Araidhe and North Britain?' whispered Gobann to Cathach.

'He will,' answered Cathach. 'I have already arranged the boat for him. And he will be set adrift on the current that lands all craft somewhere along the British coast.'

At that moment another figure was hauled out before the people. The crowd abruptly hushed in wonder at the sight of the man, for he was the cause of all this conflict. Without warning, Palladius broke from his escort and proudly marched to the place where Dichu had stood. He was a tall man and the black robe he wore gave him the appearance of a huge crow. His long nose and slight stoop did not lessen the obvious resemblance.

'You are Palladius who calls himself Bishop of Eirinn?' asked Cathach.

'I am,' came the heavily accented reply.

'By what right do you claim that title?' enquired the Druid.

'By right from His Holiness Pope Celestine,' answered Palladius calmly.

'This Celestine you speak of lives over the ocean and is not recognised by the Kingship of Eirinn,' continued Cathach. 'Where does his right to confer titles in this land originate?'

'From God,' Palladius stated simply, 'and the Holy Apostles.'

'From a god that is not worshipped or recognised in Eirinn,' returned the Druid.

'You are a mindless heathen savage. I do not expect your kind to understand and follow the Word of the Gospels.'

Leoghaire, still standing, broke in angrily over the top of the bishop's words. 'You have incited the people of Eirinn to rise in arms against their elected High-King. You are responsible for countless atrocities in the name of your god and your pope, the worst of which saw two men nailed to a cross to die, in the very manner that your own god was said to have been tortured.'

'That was none of my doing and so you may not charge me with it. It was the work of Seginus Gallus,' declared Palladius, reflecting that he wished he *had* thought of it.

Mawn heard the name Seginus Gallus and repeated it to himself to remember it. Caitlin also sat turning the name over in her head, though she could also put a face to that name.

Palladius straightened his back and said, 'Those two heathen got better than they deserved. They experienced, first-hand, the manner of the blessed Passion of Christ.' A sneer of contempt passed across the bishop's face, and he arrogantly began to survey the assembly.

The crowd were as silent as a boulder lying deep in a lake and to Palladius that suddenly made them seem all the more menacing. He faltered for a second, long enough for Leoghaire to see the uncertainty in his enemy and to push home his charge.

'Nevertheless, it was within your power to put a

stop to such barbarity, and under our laws that makes you just as guilty as the man who committed the act. Indeed you need only be found guilty of one murder for this court to pass a sentence.'

'You will not find that I have killed anyone unjustly!' countered Palladius.

'What of the cold-blooded killing of a young Laigin warrior on the way to this battle?' asked Leoghaire. 'His only crime was that he wished to take shelter from the rain.' Unknown to Palladius, Gobann had given Leoghaire a full account of his experiences on the way to Rathowen.

Cathach glanced at the poet, who closed his eyes in acknowledgement.

'That murder was done by your own hand,' continued the High-King. 'One of our people witnessed it.'

The bishop was silent, his eyes filling with fiery rage.

'Is this true?' shouted Leoghaire. Everyone jumped a little at the High-King's outburst, even the Roman.

'I am on a mission from God,' shrieked Palladius, desperately. Then he realised that losing his temper at this time could prove fatal and he instantly changed his tone. 'I am His instrument. You may not judge me,' he stated coolly.

Leoghaire went on unflustered. 'The crimes that you have committed are enough to warrant an unprecedented action by this court. That is your immediate execution, here and now, by the quickest method known and without any honour.'

Palladius stood suddenly taller. He reached under his robe and brought forth his silver crucifix. He had expected this would be the way it would end, indeed he had even prayed for it. Now he would certainly be admitted to the gates of

271

Heaven. He would be remembered for all time as a blessed martyr of the Cross.

The High-King was only baiting the man though. 'But you, it would seem,' he continued, 'have broken even the rulings of your Pope Celestine.'

Palladius looked at him strangely, not sure if he had heard correctly. 'What do you mean?' he countered, a frown across his face.

'Your Pope Celestine forbade you to interfere in the political workings of our kingdom when he sent you as emissary to Eirinn.'

'How could you possibly know what passed between His Holiness and myself,' mocked Palladius, 'except if the Devil himself had told you?'

'One who was there informed us of all that passed between you and your pope,' Leoghaire said.

The bishop looked about him as if he expected to find the evil culprit lurking nearby in the shadows. 'Does the wickedness of your Druidic enchantments spread as far even as Rome?' cried Palladius.

Leoghaire left the Roman to answer that question for himself. 'Thus I find,' concluded the High-King, 'that I am not the only potentate who seeks retribution from you. Nor is it therefore fully within my jurisdiction to sentence you to death. So you will be dispatched to the nearest Roman mission, which happens to be in Britain. I have already sent letters to Rome explaining how you have transgressed against us and the papal rulings. You will be stripped of all possessions and clothing and cast adrift without oars, in a cowhide boat, beyond the nine waves as close to the prevailing currents as possible. If you ever return again to these shores it will be on pain of a long, slow, lonely death. I guarantee that no-one will ever know your fate and your martyrdom will therefore be in vain.'

'You have no right,' spluttered Palladius. 'I am the Pope's legate to this island. You will suffer for this insult!' Leoghaire was unmoved, the crowd still silent. 'I will return with a Roman legion to do the job properly next time! You are a fool to release me!' Palladius added desperately, hoping that they would not risk his release.

'It is only by the pleading of one of your brothers that I did not send you in chains directly to Rome, so still your tongue,' the High-King ordered.

The two men stared at each other for a long moment, neither willing to break eye contact and give in. Then a figure, also dressed in black, rose from the crowd behind Palladius and said in Latin, tinged with a slight Briton accent, 'You have committed sins in the name of the Church that are contrary to the teachings of Christ. Go now, and leave these good people in peace.'

The bishop recognised the voice immediately, though he had not ever expected to hear it again. He turned around slowly to face the man. 'You! You are a coward and you always were. You are not fit to wear the robes of the Holy Mother Church. By the power invested in me as legate of Rome and in the name of God I excommunicate you and all your followers. And if ever we meet again, Declinu, I will make sure you suffer the fiery death of a heretic!'

Declan sat down again in silence.

'Convey him now quickly to the sea,' Leoghaire commanded, ignoring the bishop's latest outburst.

'I curse you with the curses that Christ places on all devils,' spat Palladius. 'I will not rest until all the trees and idols and springs of this land are replaced with monuments to Christ! The Great Tree in the south is already dead, my Saxon warriors have seen to that!' he shouted. 'And they are led by Seginus who is the son of a Roman centurion!'

All in the assembly were deeply shocked. The destruction of the Great Tree was an unthinkable act of barbarism.

'When they have finished burning the bough of that tree they will topple the stone circles of the east!' he lied. 'You are all cursed. But it is on you, Leoghaire, that I lay the mightiest curse of all: if you do not accept the teachings of the Christ and a Christianing into the faith, your kingdom will be a deserted wasteland before your life is half ended.' He would have spat many more maledictions but he was grasped firmly and whisked out of earshot, and his mouth was covered with a soldier's shawl so that his curses became only muffled sounds.

'Is the man Isernus there?' queried Cathach. Isernus, bound, was also led forward.

'You have been vouched for by your companion Declan of Ardmór,' began the High-King. 'and since it seems that you are at least repentant of your part in this war, I release you into the abbot's keeping.' Then he raised his voice. 'Declan step forward.' And the abbot did so.

'You have proven that not all Romans are painted in the same bloody shade as Palladius. Even so I would not have any Roman Christians in the five kingdoms until an emissary has come from Celestine to make amends for the trouble that Palladius has caused. You will stay for the time being under the keeping of Murrough, Prince of Eoghan and Cashel, until comfortable transport can be arranged for you back to Britain.'

Declan bowed, not sure what else to do, or even if he should be grateful. He took a stunned Isernus by the hand and they retreated into the crowd.

'The judgments of this Council are concluded,'

announced Leoghaire. 'We march for Teamhair after the burials of the dead are completed.'

With that the assembly dispersed, warriors to stand watch and to gather their possessions, others to the task of preparing the rites for the departed. Only those that Leoghaire had personally requested to accompany him back to his tent and fireside followed him. There was still a good deal to discuss and resolve.

Within that tent they shared a victory feast, but it was not a very joyous affair. Almost everyone had lost a friend on the battlefield Rathowen and the threat that Palladius had made on the Quicken Tree had soured any celebrations.

It was dark by the time the feast had ended and the inner council were ready to speak with each other again. As Chieftain of Rathowen Caitlin was invited to attend, and Murrough also, now that he was heir to the Eoghanacht.

'The Tree must be preserved at all costs,' confirmed the High-King when they were all present. 'But we do not know the size of the renegade force and we cannot be certain that they will head there directly.' Leoghaire was very sensibly weighing up the chances of the mercenaries doing some spirited raiding elsewhere on their way south.

'Lord,' suggested Murrough, 'my guardsmen could be ready to ride in an hour. It will take us two or three days to reach the Quicken Tree, but the enemy probably do not have horses, since we took all of Dichu's mounts and those of his Saxons, so I am sure we will overtake them.'

'I was counting on your help at Teamhair,' said Leoghaire. 'Many of my subjects were led on by Palladius and there may still be widespread resistance to his exile.' In truth the High-King was concerned that a full-blown rebellion might be about to erupt, and he wanted his best warriors by his side, but he did not want to speak about that fear at the present moment.

'Also there is the matter of who will become King of Laigin once Dichu is gone. I rely on the advice of the lesser kings. If you aspire to that rank, Murrough, you must begin to take on some of the responsibilities.'

'There are no other troops who could make the journey so quickly,' asserted Cathach. 'Murrough's men are the best we have at our disposal. And the Tree is the focal point of the Kingdom of Munster. The loss of it would be a tragedy.'

'And what of the Danaans?' asked Lorgan. 'If the Sidhe-folk see us falter in upholding our treaty promise to protect the Tree, they may withdraw their support of our longer-term plans. The Quicken Bough is essential for many reasons, not the least of which is that we require a goodly stock of its fruit for all of our work to be worthwhile.'

'I have heard much about this tree,' interrupted Leoghaire, 'but I must confess that I have no idea how it may help us by the bearing of its fruit!''

'If the High-King will permit me,' interrupted Gobann, 'I will relate the tale of the Quicken Tree.' Leoghaire nodded and Gobann sat before him, though he addressed all who were present.

'When the Danaans first came to Eirinn in their wanderings they brought with them hazelnuts, apples and sweet rowan berries. These foods sustained them on their journey, though they also collected honey and milked their cows along the way. It happened that when a group of them were travelling through Eirinn shortly after their arrival, a bard, who was entrusted with keeping the rowan berries that they had gathered in their home country, in carelessness dropped one from his pouch. In time a tree grew up from it and became strong.' Gobann took a deep breath before he continued.

'An age later, when the Sons of Mil, who are our forebears, settled in the south, they discovered that this tree had special properties. There were magic virtues in the berries that grew from this tree: first, no sickness or disease would ever take any person who ate them; second, anyone who ate of them would feel more alive than they had ever done and they would be light-hearted and carefree. And two other qualities were discovered later: that an old person who ate them would immediately be young again, and that any girl less than twelve summers who ate them would grow up to become a renowned beauty.' Leoghaire was listening intently.

'The Tuatha-De-Danaan soon realised that the Tree was one of their own sacred boughs and demanded its return to them. But by that time the treaty between our peoples—that our folk would retain all that was above the ground and their folk all that was below—was already agreed. As the Quicken Tree was both above and below the ground, the Sons of Mil promised to protect it as a symbol of the relationship between our two kindred. The berries of it are the source of Danaan immortality and their beauty, but if prepared incorrectly the fruit is deadly, and so our ancestors promised never to make use of the berries without the consent and advice of the Danaan Druids.'

'They have agreed to allow us to collect a limited number of the fruits for our purpose,' added Cathach, 'but they have made us promise that only two of our folk, a male and a female, will ever be permitted to eat the berries.'

'When Murrough goes to the south, he must

gather the fruit, as much as he can, for the Tree
will probably always be under threat,' stated
Lorgan. 'We can only be sure of the success of our
scheme if there is a good supply of the berries.
Murrough will act as an ambassador from the
people of the Gael, but a Druid should also go as
a representative of the Druid Council to the Sidhe-
folk.'

'I will go,' declared Caitlin. 'I will ride with the
Prince of Cashel for he saved my life and those of
my folk who could be saved, and I wish to repay
him that debt.'

'Are you well enough to travel?' asked Gobann,
surprised. 'You have suffered much in the last two
days, and you have not given yourself enough time
to begin to heal.'

'I must go,' she answered him. 'It will do me
good to travel and I have to get away from
Rathowen for a while.' Cathach nodded his consent
and a knowing glance passed between him and the
poet, but it was Lorgan who spoke up to give permission for her to travel.

'None of us may choose the hour or the manner
of our death,' he stated. 'It is left to us, however,
to choose the manner of our healing, so if it is your
wish to go, then the Druid Council will certainly
approve.'

Murrough sat calm-faced and gently nodded his
appreciation to her, careful not to show that he was
overjoyed.

FOURTEEN

eginus and Hannarr trudged on through the night until they reached the meeting point by the loch where Guthwine had arranged for his party to assemble after the battle. They would have moved much faster but for the monk's swollen knee which had ballooned ever larger and almost paralysed him with pain. Hannarr was forced, reluctantly, to lend him a hand and he half-carried him down the last stretch to the water's edge.

But it was certainly not out of a sense of duty to a fellow human being that Hannarr came to the Roman's aid. Duty to others had never been a pressing concern of Hannarr's. It was greed that drove him on.

'Seginus knows the whereabouts of the southern treasure houses,' he thought to himself. 'Until he has led us to them he is of use. After that, I will not need to treat him so well.'

Streng was asleep and all the mercenaries dozing or drunk when the two limped into the Saxon camp just before dawn. No-one challenged them and they quickly found themselves a place at a fire and sat down. When he was sure that Seginus was comfortable and had not passed away on him, Hannarr found a skin of ale and offered the monk a good portion. Then they slept, unnoticed by anyone in the camp.

About three hours later, Seginus woke in the dim light and staggered down to the stream to drink and wash. Then, with the aid of a branch to take the weight off his knee, he hobbled into the bushes to relieve himself.

When he returned not five minutes later, the campsite was echoing with shouts and enthusiastic catcalls and the ominous sound of two swords clashing. Seginus wisely decided to stay out of sight and observe what was happening.

Moments after the Roman had gone off to the forest, Streng had woken and almost tripped over Hannarr in getting up. Hannarr instinctively drew his sword and that had been all the provocation Streng needed.

In the next breath the two men were at each other with deadly intent and the whole camp had stirred to the excitement. A half-dozen or so men cheered Hannarr on; the remainder waited prudently silent for the outcome of the contest.

Streng didn't realise how weak he still was from his wound and when he tried to use his wild rage to intimidate his opponent it did not take long for him to weaken further. Hannarr simply darted around, dodging his blows, until he was convinced there was not much fight left in Streng.

When the wounded man collapsed on the ground in a fit of wheezing, Hannarr overpowered him, holding his hand at Streng's throat.

'You should never lie in wait for a man like that, Hannarr,' Streng strained. 'It will be the death of you one day.'

'It was nearly the death of you!' joked the tall fair-haired warrior, releasing his grip. 'That is the best sport I've had since I feigned dying and faced the Prince of the South as close as this.' He held his palm before his eyes and touched his nose with it.

'You never saw any Irish prince,' scoffed Streng painfully through his damaged voice-box.

'It was just yesterday and had I not been otherwise occupied I would have struck him down on the spot.'

'And where would the likes of you learn to tell the difference between a royal and a piece of rancid pig-meat?' countered Streng.

'I described the man I saw to Seginus, who has seen the prince many times.' Then he suddenly remembered the Roman. 'Where is Seginus?'

'I am here, Hannarr,' came the reply as the monk stepped forward. He had waited until Streng was on the ground before he broke his cover. 'I went to relieve myself.'

'Come, Seginus,' said Hannarr, 'we will talk more now of the great treasure that you spoke to me of before the battle.'

'Treasure?' ventured Seginus, momentarily confused, then he remembered the conversation he had with Hannarr on the embankment before the fight in which Guthwine had fallen. 'Ah yes, the treasure in the South.'

'The most valuable treasure in the world,' Hannarr reminded him, theatrically repeating the phrase for all those present.

The Roman urged himself to think quickly. These men were his only way out of Eirinn for they had ships. Then the kernel of a plan seeded itself in his mind. He knew that he would need some time to work out the finer points, but if he was careful, it might be possible for him to knock two birds out of the sky with the one small stone.

'I will tell you all about that when we are closer to our destination,' he began. 'There is gold in Cashel and silver, more than you could carry, but

281

there is a greater treasure there for him that knows how to find it.'

'Greater treasure than gold!' rasped Streng. 'There is no greater treasure than gold, my friend.' He took an ale-skin and spilled the drink down his chin in his rush to swallow.

'Ah, but there is,' returned the monk. 'What good is all the gold on earth if you only live another forty years to enjoy it?'

Streng and Hannarr looked at each other and then back at Seginus, questioning frowns spreading across their faces.

'What if you could live for another fifty years or a hundred or two hundred? Would you not then have the opportunity to become wealthy beyond your dreams?' Seginus teased. 'Not to mention the further opportunity you would have to enjoy all the pleasures that life has to offer.'

'You are babbling, Roman,' Hannarr laughed. 'You must have shaken your brain when your knee was bumped!'

The monk ignored him. 'I know of a secret place where grows a tree,' Seginus went on, inspired almost to believe the heathen tale he was telling, 'and the fruit of that tree will grant anyone life eternal.'

'Where did you hear of this thing?' demanded Hannarr, the mocking smile dropping from his face, urgency in his voice.

'Palladius told me of it, and an old Druid told him. The Druids say that the evil Danaan people eat the fruit and that it is the source of their magic.'

The Saxons were all silent. None who heard his speech uttered a word but none seriously doubted him. Too many eerie things had happened to them lately for any of them to dismiss the tale out of hand. The mention of otherworldly folk made both

Hannarr and Streng stop to consider that there was something more to the story than any of them could comprehend. Luckily for Seginus, it was in the nature of the Saxon folk to be superstitious and to believe in all things supernatural.

'Shall we make for the treasure houses of Munster or for the sacred Tree of Life?' asked Seginus casually.

'And you can guide us to them both?' asked the thegn.

Seginus nodded. 'To the tree first, though, for it is closer.'

'What do you want in return for guiding us?' queried Hannarr, full of suspicion.

'I wish to travel to Britain or, better still, to Gaul,' he began. 'You, I believe, have the ships that can take me.'

Hannarr smiled a gap-toothed grin. If there was anything he loved more than raiding, it was striking deals. Especially if he could see a way of withholding his part of the agreement. 'You have yourself a bargain,' he declared.

It was midday before the mercenaries gathered their collective wits enough to realise that the longer they dallied by the loch the more likely were Leoghaire's men to come upon them. Hannarr set two of his men building a stretcher for Seginus so that they would not be slowed too much by his injury. The seriously wounded among his own people he dismissed as a liability, but then realised that they could make an excellent diversion.

'You men will wait here at the road for our return,' he told them. 'If you are captured, remember to say that you are the only survivors. We will return in two weeks for you.'

The five men knew full well that they would

283

never see their comrades again, but it was dangerous to argue with a thegn, better to take their chances with the Irish. They were all too weak to care anyway.

Having rid the party of any unwanted burdens, Hannarr was left with nineteen fit warriors, Streng who was weakened but stubborn, and one Roman. It was nightfall before they set out in hopes of covering thirty-five Roman miles a day for two to three days.

As chance would have it they were setting off only hours before Murrough was ready to leave with his troops hoping to intercept them.

After the Council meeting, Caitlin gathered what travelling gear she could muster without having to return to Rathowen and borrowed all else that she needed for the journey south.

Her harp she bundled into its case, which was not otter-skin like Gobann's, for only the most honoured poets carried such an item of craft work; instead her case was of calfskin, made waterproof with the application of many layers of raw fat. This made the covering very greasy but her instrument was always protected from water and any change in temperature. For a harp, drastic weather changes could be lethal. The brass wires exerted immense pressure on the body of the instrument, testing the wood and workmanship to their limits. A sudden cold snap would cause the wires to contract and possibly shatter the joints that held it together. A poorly-made harp might not exist more than a decade or two, the flaws in its material or design causing it literally to explode with stress.

But a well-made harp, such as had been made

for a master musician, would not come into its prime for a hundred years or more. Thus the first owner of a great harp was never considered to be more than a caretaker who nurtured the instrument through its early years, teaching it the tuning, ready to pass it on to another. The next harper in turn would introduce it to the music, so that when the time came in the third generation to pass it on to the poet for whom it was intended, it would be already well played.

A harp of this pedigree could often take three generations to build. The oak timber for its body was lain deep in a peat-bog to age and harden for a hundred years before it was shaped or cut to form the familiar triangular shape. Caitlin's harp was not one such as this. Hers was suitable to the rank that had been foretold for her at birth. It was nevertheless a good instrument, built by the famous blind harper Colm Dhall. Like every harp, hers had a name and a personality: a soul. She treated it as her friend; a friend that spoke in the language of music and that sustained itself not with bread or mead, but with experiences.

She remembered, as she tied the case securely, the night that Colm had presented her with it; how he had whispered its name to her and how she had kept that name secret ever since, only addressing the instrument personally when she knew they were alone together.

'There are some things that one only shares with a lover,' she thought. There was no stab of pain, no guilt, no remorse, but even so, Fintan's face burst upon her memory.

She forced herself to concentrate on Colm and he came back to her mind to nudge out thoughts of Fintan. Colm, who took her harp out to show it the first snowfall so that having witnessed the winter first-hand it could sing of such things with authority; the same Colm who had never himself seen the snow for he had been blind since birth. And yet he could see clearer than anyone she had ever met what the world was really about.

Her gear slung safely, Caitlin heaved the case across her shoulder and, with Murrough's gentle help, mounted the dapple-grey horse she had been given. Her feet found the stirrups and locked into them. The pressure on her arrow wound was less than she had expected and she thanked the gods for it.

'We'll see how it is after twelve hours in the saddle,' she thought with some apprehension.

Gobann came to wish them well and he went first to Caitlin. 'I have something for you,' he said. 'Well, not really for you.' He produced from his pouch a small acorn beautifully wrought in silver. Around it the craftsman had cleverly curled a salmon, a raven and a dog, their tails wrapped about each other linking them in an endless knot.

'It is a gift that I would like you to pass on for me.'

'Who is it for?' asked Caitlin admiring the handiwork and thinking it must be intended for one of the Danaan people.

'I don't know,' answered Gobann in all honesty for he had only brought it out on the spur of the moment, 'but I trust that you will know when the time comes.' He ran his hand over his short crop of dark hair, suddenly realising what a strange request he was making. 'May the Road be good to you,' he said in blessing.

Then he went off to farewell Murrough, leaving Caitlin a little confused as to what exactly he meant by 'You will know when the time comes.' Finally she gave up trying to work the poet out and attached the clasp of the piece to the leather strap round her neck and tucked it under her clothes.

'Fair journey to you,' said the poet to Murrough. Then, lowering his voice a little, he added, 'And make sure you look after her.' He indicated Caitlin. 'I have a feeling that the events of the last few days will catch up with her very soon and that it will fall on you to care for her.'

He leaned in close and added mischievously, mimicking Leoghaire's tone, 'Time you found yourself a partner, my boy.' The two shared the joke, though Murrough's laughter was nervous enough for Gobann to realise he had struck a nerve.

When all was ready the party set off hoping to reach only as far as the southern edge of the loch this night and then ride on in full daylight after resting.

'Ride easy now,' Murrough advised his company of thirty horsemen. 'Tomorrow we will increase the pace; for the time being we only need to get as far as is comfortable in a few hours. The road is fairly well maintained here so we should not strike any difficulty.'

Caitlin's injury was his main consideration. He did not want to put too much strain on her at first, preferring instead to ease her into the journey. 'There is no chance that any stragglers from Dichu's army will reach the Tree before us as long as they are on foot,' he decided. 'And if she is too ill to travel I will send twenty guardsmen ahead and keep the other ten with me and her.'

Only now as they were making their way out of the camp did Murrough question why the Council had allowed Caitlin to come with him, knowing as they did the nature of her grief and her injuries. But the thought was a passing one for he had more pressing worries that demanded his attention.

The clanking of the war-gear, cooking implements and harnesses echoed across the stream and the loch and the sentries in Leoghaire's camp could hear them trudging still when they were far away down by the edge of the woods.

It was not until the last flickering light of a campfire disappeared from her view that Caitlin began to relax. Leaving Rathowen behind her she breathed easier, though years later, she would regret not being present for the burial of the fallen.

Leoghaire watched Murrough and his party for a long time from the edge of the encampment, an old leather cloak about his shoulders so that none of his warriors would recognise him. He found himself wishing that he could melt into the crowd like this more often.

In the five years of his reign he had always been engulfed by people, never having a moment to himself unless he stole it, much as he was doing now. He had always enjoyed the hectic lifestyle of a High-King; that is until the previous day when he had seen Gael killing Gael and hatred in the eyes of his subjects. Now he was beginning to look on the office as a burden.

When he was sure that Murrough's party was gone he called for his herald and sent out orders that the services for the dead were to be held early the next morning. The ceremony was to be as brief as possible—he was suddenly impatient to return to Teamhair. Leoghaire knew well enough that his presence at the seat of kingship would do much to prevent rebellion taking root in the rest of the country.

'The peace has been shattered,' he repeated to himself over and over. 'Morann and Caitlin, the two most talented young chieftains in the kingdoms, are standing down from their duties. Soon there will be more fighting. I have laboured all my life to keep the warring tribes apart and all it takes is one foreigner who lands by chance on our shores to destroy all of that work.'

The full and bitter irony of the situation was not lost on him. 'If the land had not known the peace that I brought, then perhaps there would have been more experienced warriors to fill the ranks of my army. Perhaps there would have been less chance of a real fight if the soldiers in my force were better armed and trained. Perhaps . . . ' He looked into the bright starlit sky, but all he saw were storm clouds gathering.

Preparations at the burial place continued throughout the rest of the dark hours so that the dedication could take place at dawn. All those killed, including the two men slain on the death trees, were lain in a deep pit. As was the tradition, their bodies were covered first with soil, then with rocks, then with what flowers could be found at that the time of year, followed by more leaves, then more soil, and finally a mound of stones from the battlefield to mark the grave. On the summit of the new hill was placed an upright stone and on it cut Ogham signs, the oldest language of the Gaelic people, the mystical letters of power. The inscription literally read, 'Here there lie many of Leoghaire's people.'

Gobann had been asked to compose the words and as with everything that he did, he arranged the letters so that the message could be interpreted on many different levels, each with subtle variants of meaning, all of which were true. So in only ten or twelve signs, much was imparted to those who could understand the secret Ogham about how so many came to be buried in one large grave.

The Saxon corpses were collected also and buried on the far side of Rathowen at the foot of the embankment, below the place where they had been tricked into breaching the battlements. A stone was set for them but no-one knew their tongue well enough to prepare an inscription, so it was not considered appropriate to cut signs for them. Instead their weapons were laid around the base of the mound in a display that many of them would probably have appreciated.

In composing the Ogham, Gobann took a long thoughtful while. It was his first real opportunity to teach his two new students something practical that would aid them in their future life.

Mawn and Sianan, consigned into Gobann's care while Murrough rode off to the south, watched intently as the poet sat before the fire carving the shapes into the soft bark of a branch, until eventually he came up with the combination he thought the most succinct and closest to the truth.

'Ogma gave his people the writing,' remarked Gobann. 'He was of the Danu folk, and they in turn passed the art on to us.'

'Where did he get the letters?' asked Sianan.

'He observed the trees. Each sign is named for a clan of trees.' With the stick that he held, Gobann scratched a sign in the dust at his feet, a long stroke with two short branches jutting out on the right parallel to each other.

'That is the sign for the rowan tree. The two branches at right angles mark it as the Ogham symbol for that family of trees,' he explained. 'All the signs have branches. Some fall to the left, some to the right. Some cross through the centre.'

'The Quicken Tree belongs to the rowan clan of trees,' Mawn added confidently. He had listened very attentively to all that Gobann said in the last few days.

'Yes,' remarked the poet, 'but it is a descendant of trees that come from the lands of the Tuatha-De-Danaan. The rowan tree is the tree of possibilities, the tree of magic and of enchantment.' He looked at them both very seriously. 'The rowan trees are your protectors. You must never forget that.'

This information was central to an understanding of all that the poet wished to teach them later, so he knew that he had to present it clearly.

'Most trees have longer lifespans than humans,' stated Gobann. 'The Quicken Tree has already lived a thousand winters, so it holds a memory within it of all that has happened in that time. To those who know how to listen, the spirit of it may be enticed into telling its tale. When the Quicken Tree one day passes on, as all things must, its soul will probably be reborn as a wise person or a teacher.'

'How is it that the rowan is also Murrough's tree?' asked Mawn.

'It is merely one of the trees that the Eoghanacht swear their oaths to,' replied Gobann. 'But the Quicken Tree is one of a kind. There are no more on this Earth like it. It bears witness to the pact between our people and the Sidhe-folk and is in the keeping of the Kingdom of Munster. The Eoghanacht are sworn to protect it forever.'

He paused to carve a sign in the branch, trying another combination of signs, but was not happy with the result.

'But the Eoghanacht,' he continued, splitting his

concentration between the lesson and his composition, 'consider themselves to be more closely related to a great yew tree and that is where they get their name, for Eoghan is the word in the ancient tongue for the yew clan. The yew lives longer than almost any other tree and there is one in Munster that has already lived twice as many winters as the Quicken. The yew is the tree that we signify as the keeper of tradition and the link with our past and future lives. The yew clan will also be your guardians.'

Seeing that he had their attention, Gobann put the carving aside for a while and began to explain the other signs of the Ogham. He drew the sign for the oak tree and followed that by the sign for hawthorn, holly, blackthorn, elder, birch, willow, alder, ash, hazel, apple, nettles, reed and brambles, explaining each in turn.

'Will Fintan and the boy return as trees?' asked Sianan.

Mawn shot a glance at her when she spoke, but was careful not to reveal any of what he was thinking. His eyes darted between his teacher and the girl as they spoke and he noticed for the first time the same light of compassion in Sianan's eyes that he had so often noticed in the poet's.

'Why do you ask?' returned Gobann.

'They met their death on trees. So I thought maybe they would return as trees.'

'Yes, perhaps they will,' Gobann considered. 'The soul's journey after death is rather more like being cast adrift on the ocean, naked and without oars in a little cowhide curragh. Few people living know how that feels, but I am sure the Bishop of Eirinn would agree that it is a somewhat frightening prospect, not knowing where you will next touch the solid earth. There is no-one alive who can tell what form their souls will take when they return.'

The poet smiled, happy with his analogy, and then returned to the lesson on letters. 'A tree must always be consulted if you wish to use the standing wood for building or any other purpose. None of the Ogham trees may be cut before they are nine winters on the Earth.'

'Why is that?' asked Mawn.

'Two reasons,' answered Gobann. 'First it is to ensure that our land is not denuded of its woodlands, which has happened in other places. Nine years give most trees enough time to become established and have some offspring. It is when all the trees are cut down that a country quickly becomes a wasteland, for the Earth is no longer held down by their roots, and animals that would otherwise dwell in branches burrow in the soil. Eventually the wind just picks the land up in its fingers and carries it away. All that is left is the clay that was too heavy for the breeze to lift and nothing grows in clay.'

Mawn thought of when Origen had told him that he came from the place where the wasteland begins. 'Is that what Origen's land is like?' asked Mawn.

'I have never been to Alexandria, though I am told that it was once a place of gardens and waterways and forests. Now there is only sand and salt water.'

'You said there are two reasons why we should not cut a young tree,' Sianan reminded him.

'Oh yes!' Gobann exclaimed, realising that Mawn had a knack for leading him off the track. 'The second reason is that it is not good to interfere with any of the longer lived creatures on this Earth before they are nine seasons old. This is out of respect for the soul of that creature. You are both nine years old, and you have been chosen at this time because it is an important stage in your life. In fact humans pass through three-yearly progressions, so this is the third stage of your life.'

'How old are you?' Mawn butted in.

Gobann was a little taken aback. 'I am twenty-seven seasons on Earth.'

'That is three times three stages, of three years,' Mawn calculated aloud. He had learned numbers from his father. A blacksmith needed to know such things and as the goats were also Mawn's responsibility he had often needed to tally them, so he was well practised in counting and calculation. 'This is an important time for you also,' the boy stated with confidence.

'Yes, it is a very important time for me,' agreed Gobann. 'I am experiencing a lot of changes in my life.'

'Then we three must all look after each other,' stated Sianan very seriously.

'Yes, we must, 'nodded Gobann, smiling.

FIFTEEN

annarr and the survivors of his raiding party moved quickly across the countryside despite the burden of the injured Roman. The new thegn had taken all of his men into his confidence regarding the goal of this adventure.

'There are enough fruits on the tree for all of us,' he told them. 'Once we have that treasure we'll raid the storehouses of Munster while the High-King is still mourning the dead back at the hillfort. And then we will leave these shores forever!'

His men had cheered heartily at that, but Hannarr was aware that to the majority of them the most appealing section of his speech was the leaving of Eirinn forever part.

They carried Seginus two at a time and changed bearers every hour so that the pace did not slacken. 'The Irish have horses,' Hannarr cursed again and again, for the loss of all their mounts was a great blow to his ambitions. 'If they manage to get a force to the south before we can reach there, we'll be slaughtered.'

After a night of cross-country trekking they struck the north-south road just before dawn. There they rested five hours behind a round hill and all including Seginus slept. They posted no sentries for Hannarr believed it was better that they take their chances with being captured and all get as much rest as possible.

As mid-morning approached he roused them with shouts and curses. He allowed them a little food and they drank from a nearby well. While his men broke camp the thegn made the decision to take the shortest available route south. So the party set off on the next leg of their journey along the road that linked the northern kingdom of Ulster to the southern kingdom of Munster.

They trudged on the remainder of the day and rested a few hours in the noontime, then briefly again after dusk. Hannarr forced them on for a further three hours in the darkness and then he let them sleep again until dawn. As the sun rose he was kicking his warriors awake and screaming abuse until they were ready to depart. Once more they ate little and drank only what was necessary for survival. They covered their fire and left the ground where they had camped in such a way that no-one would guess twenty-two renegades had slept there the night before.

Seginus was astounded at the speed they travelled once they had hit the road. He had never heard of troops, not even Scythian levies in the Imperial service, who could travel so fast and endure so much. All food was strictly rationed to preserve the supply against a disaster; water was not carried but gathered whenever there was a rest and when it was available.

'They have become almost like horses, like pack animals,' thought the monk, appalled. Still, he could not help but admire them. 'If only they were Christians,' he thought, 'the whole world could be brought to the Cross with such soldiers!'

As during the previous day, Seginus was bundled onto his stretcher and strapped in so that he would not tumble out. He alone of the party had a waterbottle; he alone was allowed a little more than the normal ration of bread and dried meat. He was as valuable to Hannarr as the treasure he was leading them to. For now.

The terrain was a little rougher this day than the last. They had come to a stretch of the road that was not maintained well for it was in disputed territory and, though two chieftains claimed the ground, neither was willing to pay for the upkeep of the highway.

Seginus tried to read his little Gospel as he was carried along, but his two bearers bumped him around too much for him to be able to concentrate. He tried to sleep, but the day was warm and as the morning progressed once more to midday he became hot and uncomfortable on the stretcher. His knee was still immobile and whenever they rested he could only walk a little before it would suddenly freeze up without warning and refuse to do his bidding. Five hours of travel without a break left him exhausted and sweating, though he was only lying flat while others did the back-breaking job of carrying him.

He reached round for his leather bottle where it was secured at the side of the stretcher. He carefully released the cork and was just about to swallow a mouthful of springwater when Hannarr ordered the band to stop in their tracks. The thegn put his ear to the ground for a moment and then waved to his men to make quickly for the roadside ditch to hide.

In the panic Seginus lost his hold on the bottle, but its strap caught on the fastening of his cloak which was rolled by his side and so he did not lose it. Within moments all the Saxons were lying spread out on both sides of the road, their faces in the grass.

Seginus listened, but it was a long while before

he was sure that he could hear a horseman approaching from the direction they had come. He checked for the waterbottle to make sure it was secure. His fingers found it and he was reassured. Even a tiny clue like that, left on the road, could have betrayed their presence.

The errand-runner galloped up and on by them with no slackening of pace, but Hannarr let his men lie still for ten minutes just to be sure. Then he stood up and checked the highway.

'Get up, you lazy scum,' he called harshly, 'let's go!'

Without a word the warriors rose from their places and climbed over the ditch onto the road. As Seginus was lifted, the strap of the leather bottle caught on a fallen branch and he heard his precious cloak tear loudly. The branch was rotted and gave way quickly, leaving the bottle trailing on the ground attached only by a flimsy piece of cloak cloth. There it dangled just out of the monk's reach for he was still strapped into his stretcher.

Wasting not a second, the company was off again, their pace slightly faster as if they had rested ten hours not ten minutes. Seginus tried to tell his bearers about the bottle but they were oblivious to him, all their concentration on the bearing of his weight.

With all the jostling and bumping it was not long before Seginus heard the cloak tear again and then the bottle dropping from where it hung. The Roman turned his head as best he could and watched desperately as it rolled along briefly before landing in the grass at the side of the road. He had a premonition that it would not lie undisturbed for long. 'It will never be found,' he tried to reassure himself, but thirty paces on, the red cloth was still clearly visible to him.

With dust-dry throat Seginus lay back and covered his face with a piece of his torn shirt and after a while he finally slept putting his fears aside for a while.

The outlaws travelled on like this for two full days and nights.

Murrough was not at all surprised to find the five wounded Saxons camped by the loch when his company rode down to water their horses. He was, however, surprised to find so few of them.

'The others must have fled,' he decided, and tried to remember how many foreign corpses had been collected from the battlefield.

'Murrough,' called Caitlin, 'I am sure that there are more of them about. It is not possible that all of them were slain or wounded.' She paused as he nodded in assent. 'And where are their leaders? None of the dead but one showed any sign of wealth and certainly none of these fellows is a chief.'

'You are right, Caitlin. But we cannot spare the time to search for them. Nor can we waste guards on this lot and none of us speaks their tongue so we are not likely to get any information from them. We will leave a little food for them and go on at daybreak.'

Caitlin dismounted with difficulty but she did not allow her pain to show to Murrough, thinking that he might send her back if he considered her to be a burden. But Murrough had been watching her carefully and could tell that although she was not letting her pain get the better of her, her wound was troubling her deeply.

'We will take it slow again today and then we will see,' he decided.

They rode from dawn to midday, once again at a comfortable pace, not pushing the horses. They left behind them the five injured Saxons, though Caitlin had a feeling that they should have tried to speak with the foreigners. The opportunity was lost, and only after a long while on the road did she regret it.

By the time they took their second rest stop at the end of the day, Caitlin was beginning to feel very ill. Her fever had risen steadily throughout the afternoon and although she drank much water and shed some clothes, it continued to grow worse. Her leg was now agony and there was a purple swelling around the wound, but somehow she kept her condition a secret until evening. Only then did she let Murrough know what was ailing her and then they hurriedly laid her down by a hastily lit fire to examine the injury.

'Pus,' said Ruari, one of the hardened veterans. 'It's poison that's collecting around the arrow-hole.'

'What can we do about it?' asked the prince, his worst fears fast becoming reality.

Caitlin raised herself from her resting place onto one elbow and said, 'We can do two things, lance the wound and drain the poison or wait for the swelling to burst.'

'But then there's a chance of the blood becoming poisoned,' stated Ruari with authority. 'It is better that we lance it.'

'If you do that I won't be able to travel tomorrow,' Caitlin protested. 'And you cannot afford to waste time waiting for me to heal. I will ride on tomorrow and hope that my condition does not worsen.'

'We may have to do just that,' admitted Murrough. 'The only other alternative is that I send twenty men ahead. The rest of us could catch up later.'

'You must not split your force!' Caitlin cried. 'You have no idea where the remaining Saxons are heading or when you will encounter them. You don't even know if Palladius has more mercenaries at his disposal. It is too much of a risk. I will sleep now and ride again tomorrow.'

Such was her resolve that Murrough shrugged his shoulders and left her to rest. 'I will judge it in the morning,' he told himself. Throughout the night, though, he returned to check on her again and again.

When morning came Caitlin had slept well and the swelling around the wound seemed to have become less fluid and more firm to the touch, which both Ruari and she judged a good sign. Her fever had dropped a little also and she ate some dried meat and bread. From her pouch she retrieved some herbs and boiled an infusion over the fire which, when she had taken it, seemed to brighten her eyes, so the prince resolved to allow her to ride on, though it was against his better judgement.

'Gobann,' enquired Mawn, 'do Druids ever marry?'

'Of course they do,' came the reply. The poet was beginning to get used to the boy's unsettling questions.

The burial rituals had just been concluded. It had been a very brief affair and they were now waiting to break camp in preparation for the journey to Teamhair. Their horses were retrieved for them and were saddled waiting near where the tents had stood. Sianan brought her pony over to join them for she intended to ride alongside Gobann and Mawn.

'Why did you never marry?' asked the boy.

'A Druid is not required to take a partner for life, but is not prevented from doing so either,' Gobann explained.

'But why did you never choose a partner?' the lad persisted.

'I did once have someone who was my partner,' admitted Gobann, 'but a long time ago she left to travel in Britain and to study.'

'Have you heard from her?'

'I have heard about her,' said Gobann. 'She is one of the Druids who travels among the tribes of the Cruitne.'

'The Cruitne are the savages who live in the north of Britain,' Sianan piped up. 'I have heard my grandfather speak of them. They paint the whole of their bodies in blue and they roast Gaelic people alive and then they eat them!' Her eyes rolled dramatically.

'They do paint themselves blue,' said Gobann smiling, 'and the Romans call them "picti" in their tongue, which means "the painted ones". But they do not eat Gaelic folk, or else I would have been breakfast on more than one occasion.'

The children's eyes lit up in wonder.

'You lived with the savages?' asked Sianan.

'I stayed a long time with them. The woman who was my partner is one of them.'

'What are they like?' gasped Mawn still unwilling to dismiss the story of cannibalism, and suddenly fascinated with Gobann's past.

'They are darker skinned and shorter than our people and their hair is mostly jet-black and,' Gobann could only see one face now: the face that entered his mind when he addressed the Even-star;

302

the face that took on the form of Niamh or any of the heroines of the stories whenever he told those tales well, 'her eyes were dark and pure like the shimmering moonlight across the lake.' He woke suddenly from his little reminiscence and laughed aloud at himself and Sianan smiled at him.

Connor rode up in that instant. 'It is time to mount,' he called, 'and I am to be your escort once more.'

For a moment while his two companions were both distracted, Mawn noticed again how alike Gobann and Sianan were. Not just in the way they each looked at the world about them, but even in the smallest expressions, and in their laughter, and in the brightness of their eyes.

After her self-administered herbal cure Caitlin seemed to brighten and to travel well. Murrough could see no sign of any sickness in her the rest of the second day. She convinced him that the poison had subsided and that there was no danger, so he concentrated his efforts on getting the party to the Cashel crossroads and the warriors picked up their pace a little.

However, when she woke on the morning of their third day upon the road, Caitlin discovered that her leg was entirely without feeling below the knee. The wound had puffed up again during the night and was a hideous red-purple colour. Where the hole had previously begun to close, the flesh was splitting apart once more from the large quantity of poison just under the skin.

Despite the ugly nature of the wound she never for a moment considered that either her life or the health of her limb was threatened. She resolved to carry on without bringing it to Murrough's attention, knowing that she could otherwise cause him to split his troops and lose any advantage to be had from superior numbers. It was not difficult for her to conceal the injury from the other warriors. She could feel only a slight twinge of pain as she mounted her horse, and otherwise was no less mobile than before.

However, within an hour of their setting out, she realised her mistake. Her face began to flush hotly. The sweat broke out in streams along her brow. Then her hands began to swell so severely that her fingers could no longer close in a fist. Her leg began to throb fiercely. Worst of all she could not keep her mind from wandering and a great thirst burned her throat so that it felt as though she had taken a mouthful of hot sand.

She was turning all of her efforts to staying seated on her horse when out of the corner of her eye she noticed one of Murrough's warriors riding close beside her. She knew that she could surely die if she did not tell him what ailed her, but a part of her was too proud to ask for help.

'If Murrough wastes any more time waiting for me to heal, the Prince of Cashel will lose his Tree,' she argued with herself, 'and then he will no longer be Prince of Cashel.'

Her mount stumbled slightly and she was jolted a little. When the horse had recovered Caitlin moved in her saddle. As she did so she felt a sudden stabbing pain in her left side, so sharp and unexpected that she could not help but let out a stifled gasp. She knew then that her guts were suffering from the poison in her blood-stream and she was coming close to death. Finally relenting, she turned to the warrior who rode beside her to ask his help.

What met her gaze when she faced the man shook her to the very core. The man riding alongside, watching her intently, had a deep festering gash in his forehead; his flesh was grey and his eyes held no light. The Roman cloak around his shoulders was stained with mud and blood and all that remained of his teeth were sharp splinters of yellow bone.

Tufts of his hair had been torn from his scalp and his nose bent obliquely to one side, cleanly broken. She never doubted for a moment that it was a horrible vision of Fintan, come to farewell her or perhaps to take her with him. Delirium began to take hold of her. One part of her was still conscious enough to recognise that. The other part of her only wanted to be with her love and to rest in his arms.

The wraith reached out its bony fingers toward her and she clearly saw a hole through the wrist and the torn muscles all around. Her Druid training told her not to touch hands with a fetch from the dead, for it could take on any guise, even that of a loved one.

But if this was a servant of the dark Faeries, his eyes, though dead, were Fintan's eyes, his expression was Fintan's expression. It was his horse, his armour, his sword, his saddle. 'It is him,' she told herself and she leaned out to embrace her slain lover. 'I will go with him.' Her harp, slung as it was across her shoulder, restricted her movement and so she loosed the strap and it fell with a dull thud onto the grass at the roadside.

At last she was free, but just in the instant that they would have joined hands, the ghost pulled back away from her and in an eerie whisper beckoned her not to come too close. 'Your path lies with the prince,' came her beloved's voice, 'not with me. I am riding on to new lands.' Then he lifted the

305

cloak about him, 'It is a fine cloak, is it not?' he joked. 'But a very good target!'

'It is a fine cloak!' she called to him as his form pulled its ghostly mount up to a sudden standstill.

'I am sorry!' she yelled. He nodded and waved to her as his horse stamped.

Murrough heard her call out though he did not hear exactly what she said. He spurred his war horse to turn back toward the end of the column where she had allowed her mount to straggle. She saw the prince approaching, but her mind was in a spin and she could not focus her eyes properly. She knew she would not be able to compose herself in time to face him and to hide her pain. A part of her wanted him to see her in this state so that he could comfort her, for that was what she craved, but her senses were slipping away as unconsciousness clawed at her.

Her horse, sensing that she was no longer in control, wandered off the edge of the road into the tall grass at the bank, intending to fill his belly.

When her mount stopped she turned around in the saddle to get a last look at where Fintan had called his horse to a halt. As she turned in her seat, her horse bent down to the grass and she lost her balance, falling from the saddle. The awkwardness of the fall caused her to strike the ground so hard that she was almost completely winded and could not call out.

Murrough was at her side in a moment, lifting her head and putting water to her lips. She felt his reassuring hold about her and tried to rouse herself. But all she could see when she opened her eyes was a leather bottle lying on the grass before her. Caught in its carrying strap was a piece of bright red Roman cloth twisted tightly and torn.

'It is a fine cloak!' she muttered and then she closed her eyes.

There was a low hedge of blackthorn bushes that ran along the ditch at the side of the Cashel road. Out of the rising wind, sheltered by these bushes, Murrough laid Caitlin down as gently as he could. He covered her with his cloak and called for more water and for a fire to be lit.

The prince cut the trousers from her leg to better see the wound. It had grown large, much larger than the day before, and it was fit to burst with poison. He had not long lain her down when Caitlin slipped deeper into unconsciousness and her fever rose markedly. Sweat poured relentlessly off her body and violent convulsions of anguish shook her.

Ruari, the veteran, was summoned to lance and cauterise the ugly cause of her distress. 'She is close to death,' he said as he sharpened a spear-point on his whetstone. 'We have left it far too late.'

'We will see,' replied Murrough. 'She is made of tough leather, this one.' To himself he was already adjusting his plans to account for her having to remain still for hours if not days to recover. 'We cannot wait too long here, that is true,' his good sense told him. 'If she can be moved we will go on. If not I will leave a guard for her, and I will make for the Quicken Tree myself.' He reckoned that they only had a half a day's ride to their goal.

When Ruari judged the spear-point sharp enough he called three warriors to hold Caitlin down and plunged the iron tip of the makeshift lance into the coals of the fire. He moved it about in the heat until its jet-black surface had turned bright orange. He grasped it by the shortened wooden shaft and brought the glowing instrument

over to where Caitlin lay. She still tossed about fit-
fully, calling names and curses or mumbling unintelligible phrases.

'Get those bindings ready,' Ruari called to Murrough, then suddenly remembered who he was
talking to. 'We will have to wrap the wound as
soon as the poison gushes out and I have covered
the burns with salve,' he added more respectfully.

With that he ran the edge of the weapon along
the extremity of the swelling. Caitlin regained consciousness for a brief second and screamed at the
top of her lungs. Three battle-hardened warriors
had to force her to be still, yet she managed to kick
her good leg about enough to threaten injury to
anyone straying too close. Then she lapsed into
unconsciousness as the seared flesh leached out the
infected fluid, which flooded over the grass. The
stench was horrible: burning skin mixed with the
vapours of the foul liquid that had collected in her
body.

The rough and ready operation took no more
than a few minutes and when the resulting gash
was cleaned and wrapped, Ruari forced a herbal
decoction down Caitlin's throat and then set about
building a sturdy lean-to shelter around the spot
where she lay.

'She cannot be moved tonight,' he stated, 'or she
will certainly die. But if the fever drops by morning
she may be able to be carried a little way.'

'Very well,' the prince sighed. 'We will wait until
morning and pray that we are not too late to save
the Tree in doing so.'

It was a decision that would later cost him
dearly.

SIXTEEN

n a sandy windswept beach by the mouth of a slow-moving river, a group of twenty warriors, two Druids and all the fisherfolk who dwelt for miles around gathered to witness the enforcement of the High-King's justice.

Palladius, former Bishop of Eirinn, and Dichu, in happier times the King of Laigin, were held in check by a party of royal guards. Dichu was the shorter of the two but of a sturdier build. He had been strong in his youth yet now in the mid-term of his life he was less fit than he would have wished and his hair was sprinkled with silver.

Six fishermen brought two of their retired boats, called curraghs in their tongue, made from basket weave and cowhide and tarred to stop them leaking, and lay them at the water's edge. A larger boat of the same oval design was carried between another half-dozen men. Curraghs were light and perfect for casting nets close to the shore, or swimming cattle across to the nearby islands to fresh pasture. They were fashioned in a style that had been passed down from father to son for many generations along this coast, since even before the Gaelic people had dwelt in Eirinn.

The weathered, smaller boats, kept for making patches and repairs to other curraghs, were in very poor condition. The hide that stretched over their woven reeds was dry and cracked, but the Druids deemed that they would more than likely survive the journey across the Hibernian Sea to Britain. These craft had no rudders to steer them, they were propelled by oars alone which, along with anything else that might be of further use to the fishermen, were removed.

When the curraghs were ready the guards stripped Dichu and bound his hands tightly behind his back, laying him face down in one of the boats. He took their rough treatment with dignity and said nothing. 'I am already dead,' he told himself, for he did not believe that he would ever set foot in Eirinn again.

Palladius covered himself with his hands when they tore the cloaks and undergarments from him and the sandals from his feet. But he did not speak save to mutter a prayer when he saw the tiny curragh that would bear him to Britain. Pride would not permit him to do otherwise. The guards left him only his silver crucifix, for not even the most hardened warriors would willingly separate a man from his god.

Despite this show of respect, there was one among the guards who could not resist a little joke at the bishop's expense. He brought out a small bell made of tin, such as the shepherds and goatherds would tie around the necks of their more wayward animals so as to keep track of them. It was a simple device: a piece of flat metal bent over and welded together along two seams, with a hole in the top for a leather strap and a ball of brass to act as a clanger. The guard put the bell around the prisoner's neck and jangled it about.

'We'll be sure to hear the goats coming next time!' he jibed. All the others fell about laughing, even the Druids had to control their smiles, but the bishop stood proud and wore the bell below his

Cross with all the dignity he could muster.

'They would not grant me the martyrdom of blood,' he assured himself, 'for I am a servant of Christ and they fear the retribution of God. So they have given me the gift of another kind of martyrdom, not red the martyrdom of blood, but white, the martyrdom of exile. I am the first of the White Martyrs of Christ.'

Grim-faced, the bishop was bound hand and foot and his mouth gagged, for his crime was considered the greater and he the more dangerous of the two. He was placed, like Dichu, face down in a curragh. The warriors who were charged with fulfilling the sentence of Leoghaire lifted the two craft into the water where the sea gently lapped against the shore and the fishermen put their larger boat in alongside.

Six strong men then took to the oars and commenced to tow the condemned outlaws out to a point where the colour of their hair could no longer be discerned by those who stood on the beach. This was the barrier of the ninth wave.

It was a long while afterwards, having discharged their duty, that the fishermen wearily returned to their homes. Only then did the warriors finally began their journey back to Teamhair and by that time the exiles were already drifting with the current beyond sight and knowledge of the people of Eirinn.

At about the same time as Caitlin was reaching out with her soul to the ghost of her lover, the first mounted warriors of the High-King of Eirinn were entering the enclosures of Teamhair on their way back from the battle at Rathowen.

Teamhair of the Kings it was called, though it was also Teamhair of the Queens, having been named after the wife of Éremon the first Gaelic King of Eirinn. Queen Teamhair was reputed to be the most beautiful woman in the world and the daughter of a king from the lands in the faraway east. The Sons of the Gael had always been in dialogue with distant lands, for that is where their origins lay.

On the top of the central hill at Teamhair stood the Lia Fál, the Stone of Destiny, the standing rock that Éremon's people had carried on their wanderings ever since earliest times, even taking it with them when they traversed the deserts of the farthest east. In later ages they took it to North Africa and across the straits that the Greeks called the Pillars of Hercules further north into the lands of Iberia.

More than anything this stone represented the right of the Árd-Righ to rule, for no man could hold the High-Kingship unless the spirit of the Lia Fál had spoken out at the candidate's touch. The most famous King of Cathach's time, Niall of the Nine Hostages, had not even had to do that. The Lia Fál had screamed loudly at the very moment he was elected, thus accepting him, sight unseen, as the rightful ruler.

It had shrieked for Leoghaire too, and all the kings of all the generations before, and thus the worthy leader was always known to his or her people. When the Gaels came at last to Eirinn, Teamhair the Queen of Éremon asked that upon her death she be buried under the hill and the stone serve as her memorial, and so the royal enclosure was named after her.

'The Hill of Teamhair,' Gobann explained to Mawn and Sianan as they approached the first rampart, 'is set out just like the Brandubh board. The Árd-Righ has his hall in the centre. Around that on the four quarters—north for Ulster, south for Munster, east for Laigin and west for Connachta—lie the halls of the lesser-kings. Between each of these four halls there are four more: firstly the House of the Hostages where all the young sons of the four kingdoms who are being fostered in Leoghaire's protection live. Then there is the Gríanan of the Single Pillar, the sunny hall where the women of Teamhair gather. The Hall of the Champions is next where the chief warriors of each kingdom reside. Last of all is the place where we will be staying, the house of the Druids which is called the Star of the Poets.'

Mawn was too busy looking about him to take much of this in, but he was listening well enough to see a picture of the Brandubh board in his mind and imagine how Teamhair was arranged

'These nine halls are the main dwelling places in the royal enclosure,' continued Gobann. 'They are just like the nine central squares on the Brandubh. There are seven ramparts that protect the enclosure from attack, just as there are seven squares along each side of the playing board. And around the edge of the enclosure are the houses of the chieftains, one dwelling for each chief of the twelve tribes who live in Eirinn.'

'Just as there are twelve Ravens at the edge of the Brandubh,' added Mawn somewhat distantly.

'Exactly,' commented the poet, satisfied that he had communicated the main part of the lesson. Sianan was bored with all this talk. She had heard it many times for she had grown up in and around Teamhair. Until this day though, she had lived in the Gríanan with the women. She had never visited the house of the Druids.

And for all her privileged upbringing and courtly favours, the young girl had also never been granted the chance to meet her mother. Her earliest memories were of the royal nurses who cared for all the children of the enclosure communally. Cathach, her grandfather, had visited her a great deal when she was younger and her grandmother, Aine, while she was alive, had stayed with her in the Grínan more often than not. Since Aine's death Cathach spent a lot more of his time with his grand-daughter, taking her to Cashel on his many journeys south and filling her head with stories and songs. They had become very close, she and the old man, and she was a little frightened at the prospect of not being able to spend as many of her days with him. Then she realised he would be staying in the house of Druids. 'I will see him every morning.' she thought. 'I just won't be able to travel with him anymore. When we move south I will be like a prisoner in Cashel.'

That prospect did not cheer her very much. The Rock of Cashel was a stony outcrop of a hill, not big enough to be called a mountain, too large to be called a mound. The winds whipped around it day and night and it was far from the sea. Sianan loved the sea.

The poet brought his horse to a standstill at the gates to the inner walls of the royal enclosure and Mawn and Sianan followed his lead. Gobann slid gracefully out of his saddle and onto the ground and began to unbuckle the harness.

'I must wait outside until I am summoned to sit in my place in the Star of Poets,' he explained, 'for I have been undergoing a test these past three months and my teachers must judge my progress before I may take my seat again.'

'What sort of test?' asked Sianan, aware that very

314

few of the Drúi underwent formal testing these days. That was a custom of the most ancient times and was rarely thought necessary during the reign of Leoghaire.

'I was given several géas that I was obliged to follow,' replied Gobann. 'That is, there were some rules I had to respect during my journey.'

He decided it was better to explain this in detail for he knew that they too would one day have géas placed upon them. 'I was not permitted to eat the flesh of animals for one month. I was not allowed to take active part in a war. That one was nearly broken, though no-one expected that there would be a war when the géas were set. I was not permitted to sleep with a woman for one month.'

'That at least was not difficult,' thought the poet. 'There was only ever one I wished to be with and she is far over the sea.'

'I was to spend as many days in solitude as I could arrange,' he continued, 'for soon I will be surrounded by people for the rest of my life and may never have the luxury of loneness again. And finally I was not allowed to sleep under one roof more than two nights.' Gobann raised his eyebrows in admission of his failure. 'That one I did not keep for I stayed in Dobharcú three nights. But it really was not my fault.'

'Will we have to wait long?' asked Mawn.

'They will summon us just after sundown, so it is best that we rest until then.'

'I'll start a fire to keep us warm,' said Sianan, for the days were still cold at beginning and end.

'You should know better than that!' the poet snapped, but he was instantly sorry for the tone of his rebuke. 'The next few days are the festival of Beltinne,' he reminded her more gently, 'and none may light a fire but that the spark has come from the High-King's hall. We will do without for a few hours.'

Mawn sat back against his saddle and dozed. His thoughts wandered and he began to rest. As had happened through the night after they had come to Leoghaire's camp at Rathowen, the images that filled his half-dreams were of the Brandubh. In his mind the Ravens flew over the playing board and began to gather in an old, bare yew tree.

There were only twelve of the dark birds to start with, but soon many more came. He knew some had flown from across the sea, though Mawn had never seen the sea.

Then he got the strangest sensation that told him that the yew tree was not really a tree at all but a collection of people all standing together in the shape of a tree, but the vision was unclear.

Within a short while the yew was full of huge black winged creatures and there was no room left on the branches for any more. Squabbles broke out between birds who were being edged off their perches. Still more Ravens arrived and these, finding no refuge in the tree, were forced to sit on the grass beneath the groaning, creaking limbs of the ancient bough.

They chattered and chattered, cawing and screeching, laughing and greeting until one particular bird glided gracefully in from across the field. The other birds saw her coming and all their attention went to her. She was as old as the yew tree itself, bald and tough. She made straight for the topmost branch and there she sat until the multitude was silent. The other birds scraped their beaks against the branches they sat on in bizarre applause for their queen.

She opened her faded leathery beak to address the assembly and Mawn found that he could understand her speech and he listened carefully, fascinated, to all she had to say.

Try as he might, though, in later years he could never remember exactly what the subject of her discourse was.

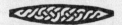

A deep white frost had gathered on the roof of the makeshift shelter where Caitlin spent the night. She was kept warm by a small fire that was tended carefully by watchmen. She was wrapped well in sheep-skins and hide, and the warriors on duty had orders to make sure she did not kick the covers off in her feverish writhing.

When day broke the frost grew heavier still and by the time the party was all awake the sky looked as if it held the promise of snow. This was not unusual for the time of year but so far this season the weather had been warmer than expected and everyone had got used to walking and riding in the sunlight and wearing less clothing.

Ruari examined Caitlin as soon as he woke and quickly pronounced her fit to travel, knowing that the prince was eager to move on and suspecting that she would probably die even if she were kept still.

Then Ruari set himself the task of unwrapping the wound and found that it had drained well in the night. The leg had resumed a normal proportion and the gash that had emptied it was closing and drying out. But for all that, Caitlin had not yet regained consciousness.

Murrough listened to the old warrior's report with relief, thankful that Caitlin would be able for the time being at least to continue the journey. He arranged for her to be seated in front of him across his saddle with her legs dangling on the horse's left flank and her head resting on his chest. This way he could watch over her himself and be sure that she was not suffering too much.

Once he was safely seated behind her on his war-horse, Murrough draped his cloak over them both forming a little tent to keep out the worsening weather. Then, at a much slower pace than before, the company resumed their quest.

The roadway had become very slippery from the frost and this greatly hampered their progress for the horses were more nervous and wary than usual of how they placed their feet on the road's surface. In the dips between hills, where the sunlight did not reach until well into the day, the ice lay even thicker and it crunched beneath their hooves. Mur-rough began to resign himself to not reaching the Tree until at least nightfall.

A breeze rose a few hours after they set off and, before the morning was over, there was a little sleet in the air. The animals breathed swirling fumes and their flanks steamed sweat but this weather was very agreeable to a horse that had a burden to bear and a great distance to carry it.

As the air was just warming before noon the party came upon a gap in the hills where the flat country ended for a while and the road began gradually climbing toward the pass.

When the Saxons broke for rest at noon on the third day of their journey, Seginus began to estimate how far they were from their goal. He reckoned that they could reach the Tree by sundown if they kept up the pace. He checked his calculations and rechecked them, unwilling at first to believe that they had journeyed so fast. But landmarks that were familiar to him confirmed that they were approaching the crossroads where the Quicken Tree stood.

He decided to speak with the thegn. 'Not far from here is an outcrop of rocks,' he told Hannarr. 'There is a gap cut through the hills where we can observe the whole of the valley and all that approaches in either direction. We should rest there and post lookouts, for there are sure to be warriors on the road hereabouts.'

Hannarr saw the sense in this. Let his men rest eight or ten hours now that they were close to the treasure, then they would fight all the better when the pressure was on. He also reckoned on the surprise that their arrival would elicit. 'They will think that we disappeared or that those few wounded that we left behind were the only survivors.'

He went over in his mind all that had happened and searched for flaws in the plan but he could not find any. So all around the rocks that lay about the road, Saxon warriors positioned themselves for sleep and watch-keeping. The rest of the day was quiet. Only one dispatch rider on an old nag galloped down the pass toward Cashel, but he never reached his destination. A well-aimed Saxon arrow took him and he fell.

The mercenaries lost no time in butchering his mount to roast over their fire. There was no written message about his body; whatever news he had to tell was now locked in his skull for eternity.

'It is not wise for you to allow the warriors a cooking fire,' protested Seginus. 'If there is a guard-post nearby they will surely see the smoke and troops will be sent out to investigate.'

'These men have not eaten decent food for almost a week,' answered Hannarr, 'and soon enough some of them will certainly die in battle, so I will not begrudge them their meal.'

Seginus shuddered at what Hannarr considered to be decent food. The monk had eaten horsemeat when he was a boy, but that had been prepared by his father's cook. It was always soaked in wine and herbs and grilled thoroughly on an iron cooking plate. The tough meat that these men chewed on was still blood-red and hardly even warm from the fire.

Seginus went for a walk to test his leg and to find some running water and to escape the smell of horsemeat that hung round the fire. The stench reminded him too much of the burial pyres he had seen in northern Gaul. He walked a long way and was happy with the healing of his bruise, though he decided to let the Saxons carry him a little more.

Hannarr, having eating his fill of breakfast, sought the Roman out, hoping to discover more details of the whereabouts of the Tree. He found Seginus sitting by a spring stirring the water's thin ice covering with a stick.

'How far to our goal?' the thegn demanded, not even greeting the monk.

'We will reach there soon enough,' was all Seginus told him, not wanting to give too much away in case he suddenly found himself of no further use. 'We must be ready to destroy it when we arrive,' he added.

'We need only collect its fruit,' protested Hannarr. 'Why should we cut down the bough also? It will take time. And in those precious minutes we might be challenged.'

Seginus had a carefully prepared answer for the Saxon. 'If we cut the tree and take all the berries, won't that make the fruit all the more valuable? How much do you think the High-King of Eirinn would be willing to pay for the last crop of enchanted berries from the last magic tree in his kingdom?'

'Whenever I begin to dismiss this Roman as useless, he somehow manages to impress me,' the thegn mused. 'You are right, Seginus,' he exclaimed. 'Of course you are right. Now I need only know where the bough stands, so that myself and a few scouts can explore the country around and judge a good time to strike.'

'I will take you there myself,' asserted Seginus.

'You cannot walk yet, dear friend,' replied Hannarr, managing to make his voice sound genuinely caring. 'No, you must leave it to me and my men now.'

'We will go there tomorrow all as one and take our chances,' Seginus persisted, 'or not at all.'

'Roman, you are in no fit state for a fight. You will remain here!' ordered Hannarr. 'I will not have your ill luck following my men into battle again.'

Seginus was about to launch into a further argument when a scout who had been posted back along the road bolted up the slope toward them.

'Horsemen!' he called.

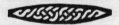

In the lead and on constant watch, Ruari was the first of all of Murrough's men to see grey billows on the horizon, but he thought little of it. He knew that the prince had dispatched other warriors to the Tree and he assumed that this smoke was from the camp of a party of Munstermen patrolling the road. Even as they got closer he never thought to send a scout ahead, for they were now in the heart of their own kingdom and there was surely no safer place for the Prince of Cashel to be than taking the road in his own land. The old veteran gave no sign to any of the others of what he had seen and if any of the horsemen noticed anything untoward they also were silent.

Murrough huddled over Caitlin keeping her warm as he had done for most of the day. Periodically he took her hands and breathed on them to bring the colour back and then wrapped them again as best he could in the folds of her cloak. She briefly regained consciousness at one stage and looked deeply into Murrough's eyes and thanked him, but then she lapsed again into a dark sleep.

The prince was so engrossed in keeping her warm and dry that he did not look up from his saddle for a long time after the sleet had begun to fall, and when he finally did, it was too late.

As the company came level to the rocky granite hill through which the road had been cut in a zigzag path, Ruari began to feel uneasy. Noticing that the prince had not stirred for some time and had covered his head in his cloak to keep out the chill wind, the old warrior decided to obey his survival instinct. He called the party to a halt and sniffed at the breeze. He could smell cooking somewhere nearby. But it was not bacon or beef roasted over the coals that tinged the air. It was not goose or chicken or even a salmon come from the ocean to spawn. The strange aroma tantalised him, for it brought back to his mind long-forgotten things, of a time when he had been a young man and there had been famine in the land and many desperate folk had been forced to eat ... 'Horse flesh,' he said aloud.

At that very moment three arrows cut swiftly through the air. One struck Ruari's mount in the neck and the animal screamed in shock before falling forward and skewing off to the right on the frosty path. Ruari lost the foothold of his right stirrup and slid forward under the mare as she fell. In the next moment the war horse was sprawled across the old warrior, rolling onto him and pinning both his legs fast underneath.

The second arrow grazed Murrough's hand but passed on harmlessly, bringing him swiftly out of his daydream. The third struck his horse in the ribs. It collapsed immediately onto its knees and fell without even uttering a cry. Murrough held Caitlin tightly and drew her close to him so that she would not slip off the animal, but her added weight and the sudden shock of the fall snapped the saddle girths and she and the prince tumbled sideways.

Both were thrown clear, but because he held her so tightly they were dragged down together heavily and they landed awkwardly in the ditch. The fall so entangled them that Murrough had to struggle for what seemed many minutes to regain his bearings. When he released himself from the tangle he lay Caitlin on her back and covered her with her blanket as quickly as he could.

By the time he finally managed to stand and take stock of what was happening, the air was thick with flying arrows and a number of his warriors had already fallen victim to them. Some of the horses had bolted in anguish when they smelled the blood of their kindred and heard their dying cries. Two of the war-horses merely stood stock still and refused to move no matter how brutally their masters kicked and prodded them.

As suddenly as the arrows had loosed forth, their rain ceased and a new menace fell on the diminished company. Eight or ten Saxons wielding broad vicious axes rushed down upon them cutting away at all who were unfortunate enough to fall within the arc of their savage swing. Their shouts turned Murrough's blood to ice.

Gathering his wits, the prince drew his sword and rushed at one foreigner who had just felled a young Munsterman. As he approached the Saxon, the man was regaining his balance after heaving his axe-blade down upon his victim. With a skilful dodge Murrough was able to slip in under the foreigner's defence and strike him deep in the side, slipping his sword cleanly between the fellow's ribs. The Saxon never really knew what had happened, his eyes staring wide, instantly dead.

Then the prince suddenly remembered Caitlin and fell back to protect her. Ruari was still pinned under his horse, yelling curses at the enemy and squirming about trying to get free, but it was clear to Murrough that both the man's legs were broken and possibly crushed. He turned to check Caitlin and, satisfied that she was out of harm's way for the moment, decided to aid Ruari however he could.

But in the short time it had taken for Murrough to focus on the unconscious woman, see that she was safe and then spin his body round again to face the enemy, one of the Saxons had approached Ruari and, with a noiseless cruel blow, struck the head off the old warrior's shoulders. The disembodied lump rolled hideously around the roadway getting under the feet of the savage attackers, the tongue lolling and the eyes bulging.

In the space of next few minutes the prince's company were all wounded or dispersed, some making for Cashel and some for Teamhair and suddenly Murrough was alone with the helpless Caitlin and Saxons were everywhere. He resolved for a moment to make a stand and fight, but realised that if he was killed outright Caitlin would surely suffer an unspeakable fate at their hands. He could not bear to consider that possibility and so he dropped his sword with a clatter and gathered her up in his arms.

He had not run thirty paces when he lost his balance on something that slid in between his feet and tripped them up and he fell hard on the icy road. His burden spilled from his arms and sprawled on the grass at the wayside and he rolled down alongside her.

When he thought to look about him to discern what had caused him to stumble all he saw was a figure dressed in a long scarlet cloak that flapped about in the wind. Somewhere, wrapped deep in the folds of it, warm and protected from the sleet, was the grinning face of Seginus Gallus.

SEVENTEEN

rigen of Alexandria knelt down beside the cleared patch of earth at the gates to Teamhair where, by long custom, those seeking petition of the High-King or the Druid Council would await their summons.

Seated on the ground Gobann held out a hand to his friend and the dark-skinned Christian caught it, dragging them both up to their feet. The two men fell into an embrace and it was a long time before they broke contact to look at each other.

'My friend,' Origen began, 'it warms my heart to see you so close to the end of your quest.'

'And close to the beginning of a new one!' returned Gobann quickly.

'Are you well?' enquired the foreigner.

'I am,' answered Gobann with all the subtle overtones in voice and body that told his friend that he could probably be better. 'I'm sorry that I missed speaking with you at Rathowen,' he continued.

Origen put his palm up toward the poet. 'We all have our duties. And the affairs of state come before all else for one such as you, my friend.'

'Yes, but all this business has quite exhausted me,' admitted Gobann. 'But you,' he added, 'how are you?'

'As well as one can be after a journey such as I have had,' replied Origen. 'Why did God place Eirinn so far from everywhere else on Earth? I was a year gone on the trip to my homeland and then I stayed only a few weeks before returning. So all in all the seasons have turned twice about since I was last here.'

'It pleases my soul that you have come back to us so soon,' Gobann said sincerely.

'My family are now all dead and the patriarch of our community is not as tolerant of the old ways as his predecessor was. He has passed edicts that will in time change the very nature of our faith and I find that I cannot altogether agree with his teaching. The day is not far off when the Roman ways will have a hold over the lands of the Nile.'

'And so, having nowhere else to go, you returned to us,' Gobann smiled.

'Not even Eirinn is far enough removed from the philosophy they teach now in Alexandria, but I thought at least I would find some of the peace here that I once knew.'

'Peace!' exclaimed the poet. 'You came back during the first outbreak of war since the times of Niall of the Nine Hostages and you expect to find peace!' Gobann laughed and slapped his comrade on the shoulder. 'As always you have a natural instinct for finding what you seek!'

'It is true that my instincts may have misled me on this occasion,' ventured Origen, grinning, 'but I could not stay away from this place for long without wishing to see the green valleys again and to stand amid the falling snow and to be shrouded in the eternal damp.'

'What do you mean?' asked the poet, a little puzzled.

'My country is dry and sand-blown. The great river that runs down from Africa waters the soil but it hardly ever rains and there is never any ice. To someone who comes from such a thirsty place,

Eirinn is like to heaven. Here the ground is always moist; the hills green and alive. One cannot go anywhere here without getting damp. I have grown very used to that.'

Both men looked at each other for a moment and then broke into wild laughter.

When their mirth had subsided Origen raised his palm to Gobann. 'Also,' continued the foreigner in a more serious tone, 'I have a dream that I wish to fulfil.'

'A dream brought you back to us?' said Gobann. 'I did not think your people put any store in such things.'

'More a desire than a dream,' said Origen, choosing his words carefully. 'I have heard tell of a man of your race who set sail over the western ocean. Maelduin was his name. I have a wish to follow his voyages and seek out the lands that lie there.'

'Taking a leather curragh westwards is one certain way to ensure that you will indeed be granted eternal damp, my friend,' Gobann laughed.

'Let us share a cup,' said Origen before his comrade had quietened, 'and dampen our thirsts at least. All this talk has left my throat dry.'

'I will drink your brew and you may drink mine,' offered Gobann, searching in his saddle-gear for one of the flasks of mead that Midhna had given him.

'Ah yes,' mocked Origen, 'the famous Irish wine made from bees' piss!'

'Bee dung,' Gobann added in mock-serious tone, 'painstakingly boiled down to taste like piss.'

Again they laughed at their own foolishness and then they sat down together at the edge of the roadway. Gobann poured out a measure of the precious mead. Precious as it had been famous, for its brewer was dead and none now lived who knew his secret recipe.

The poet watched the amber liquid flow and in his mind he likened the fluid to gold. There was not enough gold in all of Eirinn to tempt him to part with a flask of Midhna's mead. And because he knew he could not spare a drop of it, he felt better to be sharing it with his friend.

After having sipped at their drinks for a short while, the two of them allowed their private contemplations to master their thoughts and grasped their cups and lay back on the grass looking at different parts of the sky.

They passed a long time like that, letting their thoughts wander as the liquor took effect. At last Origen broke the silence. 'Are you going to ask me about her or not?' he ventured.

'Who?' answered Gobann as innocently as he possibly could.

'Who!' shouted Origen in disbelief, rising up on his elbow. 'Who!' He took a deep exasperated breath. 'I passed through Britain on my way to Alexandria only because you asked me to try and find her for you! I spent days searching the wild mountains of the northwest for her. Not a day went by when I wasn't close to freezing or in danger of starving to death! And then when I finally tracked her down I was trapped three endless weeks among her barbarous people. And you ask me who am I talking about?'

Gobann shook his head, pretending not to know what his friend meant.

'There was a time, Druid, when you thought of no other woman but her. There was a time when you would have jumped instantly at the chance to talk about her. Gobann, do not think you can fool me for I am certain you will never forget her. '

The poet let no sign show on his face but poured himself another mouthful of the liquor that Origen's people called the Water of Life.

'Have you found another?' asked the monk.

Gobann looked at the ground and then his eyes strayed back to the cup of liquor in his hands. He shook his head.

'We have a saying among my people, Harper,' said Origen, 'that often the best mirror is to be found in the eyes of a friend.' He waited for the poet to lift his gaze to meet his own. 'Perhaps you should try to let her go,' he added quietly.

'I have tried,' replied Gobann, 'but there is not a moment when she does not enter my thoughts.'

'Then perhaps you should seek her out yourself and resolve the turmoil that you suffer through this separation,' advised his friend compassionately.

'My duties do not allow me that luxury,' Gobann snapped, then he was sorry to have used such a tone with his trusted companion. 'Tell me,' whispered the poet, 'how is she?'

'She lives and she is well and she misses you.'

'She told you that?' the poet retorted. Then he carefully searched his friend's eyes looking for the hint of a lie.

'After all the trouble and hardship I took to find her that is the one and only thing she said about you,' answered Origen. 'You deserve each other!'

And then Gobann knew that Origen had spoken the truth.

In the High-King's chambers situated at the centre of the Citadel of Teamhair, Leoghaire and Eoghan met after taking rest from the journey back. They talked long of the past and debated the possibilities of the days to come with their two advisers Cathach and Lorgan the Sorn.

At times it seemed to the High-King as though the Druid Council had somehow arranged everything that ever took place on Earth to unfold according to their own secret plan. And at times this made him furious. But Leoghaire knew that life was a more complex combination of coincidences than even the wisest councillor could arrange.

He had been only a few steps away from the chance blow in battle that left his brother dead and which had led to him, who had never aspired to kingship, being thrust forward as a candidate for over-lordship of Eirinn.

'It was just a chance that it was him and not me,' he thought. 'How can anyone claim to know how things will turn out?'

King Eoghan was of a similar opinion. He did not like any of what he heard from Lorgan or Cathach. 'They talk of the Christians coming here as if it were as certain as the sun rising in the morning,' he thought bitterly. 'It will be a sad day when one such as Palladius has the ear of the High-King and the hearts of the people in his grasp.'

Cathach had always fully expected that both men would resist the Druid Council's plan as much as possible, for it was a bold one and there were many risks involved, not the least of which involved allowing the enemy to settle within the borders of Eirinn.

'Only if we make them believe that we are truly converting to their ways will there be any hope that their armies will not follow the black-robed priests soon after,' stated Cathach. 'If we give any more than token resistance to the Romans they will shatter us as easily as one of their delicate blue-glass bottles. Yet we need their support if we are

331

to be safe from the ravages of the Saxons.'

Cathach put a cup of springwater to his lips and Lorgan took up on his point.

'In Britain the Saxons now dominate the country and the old order is faded almost completely. There is no longer a High-King in that land and the Druid Council sits in the remote mountains of the north where no raiders can reach them. We have been at peace for too long in this land. Our warriors are not up to the task of keeping both Saxon and Roman at bay. The loss of Britain to the barbarian Saxons is proof that we cannot trust them. They were under treaty to the war-duke of that land to protect the realm from the wild Cruitne. But it was not long before they had begun to covet the land of their allies and had broken their word to rise up against King Ambrosius.'

'Poor Ambrosius,' muttered Eoghan, 'he passed away before he could give the kingship into the hands of a worthy successor.'

'The Britons lost too much time in choosing his replacement,' Cathach explained, 'and that ended up costing them dearly.'

'But if we allow the Roman priests to come here and to settle and to convert our people to their ways,' countered Leoghaire, 'how can we be sure that they will send soldiers to our aid when the need arises?'

'We must choose wisely the one who will present our cases in Rome,' answered Lorgan. 'It must be a man who knows Eirinn, is a famously devout Christian, on good terms with the Pope and yet who is not so clever that he will see anything but the highest motives in our actions. A man who has the ear of the powerful in Rome and who believes that the defence of Eirinn is in Rome's interest will easily be able to sway the church and state to our aid.'

332

A face appeared to Leoghaire that fitted that description. It was the man who had spoken to him after Rathowen in his tent. 'I think I could trust Declan,' he thought. 'He is an honest man with a sense of justice.'

'Our cause will be listened to with sympathetic ears in Rome,' added Cathach, 'because of the tragic events in Britain. Ambrosius long begged the Church and Empire for Roman military aid, but it never came. Now the most part of the British kingdoms is under the Saxon thumb and there are no tributes being paid to the Romans for the first time in over three hundred years. That has made the Pope wish he had convinced the Emperor to send a Roman legion to deal with the troubles when he was first asked.'

'He will be the more willing now to consider our necessity when the time comes,' Lorgan observed.

'But it is more than the defence of Eirinn that is at stake here,' Cathach pointed out. 'The Roman Christians will come whether we give them leave or not and next time they will be better organised and a long and bitter war could well be the result. Their ways are alien to us and barbaric. Yes,' he said forcefully, holding up his palm to forestall Leoghaire's objection, 'but it is our plan to influence them subtly in the Druid ways, so that in time they will actually be keeping our traditions alive without perhaps realising it.'

'Their ways are more than alien to us, they are abhorrent!' stated Leoghaire. 'How do you propose to hide the peaceful teachings of Druidic lore within the narrow theology of the Roman religion?'

'Their ways are different,' confirmed Cathach, 'but the basic elements of their faith have the same roots as our philosophy. Justice, love and charity are all emphasised in their holy books. It will not take much effort to convince them that we are all devout converts, for the most of the rest of their practices involve only meaningless mumblings. We will in time come to conceal our rituals within theirs. Once they have established their church and we are sure that Eirinn is safe, we will begin incorporating the greater part of our teachings into the Roman ways.'

'Do we not stand the risk of losing everything,' demanded Eoghan angrily, 'our laws, our beliefs, even the sovereignty of our land?'

'We will surely lose it all if we stand against both Saxon and Roman,' answered Cathach, 'but this way we will have some control over the reforms that are bound to take place. Whether we will it or not we live in a time of many changes. If we resist the turning of the wheel it will trample us and move on despite our struggles against it.'

'There will be sacrifices that we will all need to make so that the plan is successful,' Lorgan added cautiously. 'Each Druid will have to be ready to convert, at least in token, to the Cross, and the kings of the land also must be willing to be Christianed. It is the only way we can ensure the survival of our ways.'

'It will fall to you, Leoghaire,' said Cathach gravely, 'to take the lead and to be the first to offer yourself as a convert.'

The High-King sat for a moment in shock, his mouth agape. 'You talk as if the enemy were on our very doorstep. You speak as if tomorrow the Roman armies will land and murder us all.'

'It will not be tomorrow but a few seasons only, perhaps at most nine or ten summers,' stated Cathach. 'In the little time that we have, we must work very hard and mostly in secret if we are to have any chance of achieving our goals. Our children may lose much of the teachings as a result of our actions, but their children's children will carry on the traditions of the true path, though they may not by that time realise where their knowledge originated or how it came to be passed on to them.'

'With luck and the blessings of the ancient ones, Mawn and Sianan will live long enough to bridge the gap between our old world that is fading and the new world that is to come,' remarked Lorgan. 'And they may be our last hope in keeping safe the purest ideals of our people.'

When the few wounded Munstermen who remained at the gap had been robbed of their valuables and swiftly butchered, Hannarr and his band broke camp. They did not bother to hide the evidence of their presence for there was now no purpose in it. It would not have taken an expert tracker to discover what had happened at the pass that day, nor in which direction the marauders were headed.

Seginus saw to it that Murrough was savagely beaten, tightly bound and thrown across the bare back of one of his own horses. Caitlin, still unconscious, was flung on her stomach across the horse that Streng now claimed. She was secured to his saddle so that she hung before him like a sack of grain.

After the affray almost all of the Saxons managed to find themselves a mount and that was a relief to Hannarr as they would now surely make better speed. Two of his men had perished and seven of his warriors did not win themselves horses, so Hannarr left them to hold the pass, abandoning them as easily as he had the wounded at the loch.

Caitlin's face was muddy, her hair was tangled and sprinkled with frost and grit. Only that the cold reddened her cheeks a little was there any sign that she lived. Her guard, Streng, patted the curve of her backside as he spurred his horse on and the Saxons all laughed together in relief and in joy for having once again managed to keep their lives against all odds.

From where he was secured stretched over a horse's back, Murrough could raise his head just enough to see Caitlin and his blood ran cold when he noticed Streng's hands on her body. He was suddenly so filled with outrage that he felt the power of his fury could burst the bonds about him, but when he tried to move them they did not give way. A trickle of blood fell in his eye and he had to turn away and wipe it as best he could on the flank of his mount. When he looked up again he could no longer see where Caitlin was and so he swore a solemn oath to himself that he would take the life of any man who touched her.

Less than a hour after the fight, Hannarr and his warriors were well on their way and the thegn sent out two scouts ahead to watch the road before them and to find water and food if they could. These men were used to living off the land, to making do with what fell into their hands. That is one of the reasons why they held the Raven in such high regard, for they believed it to be a creature that lived entirely on carrion.

'Carrion. They will be nothing more than carrion when I am finished with them,' Murrough promised himself and he was surprised and a little ashamed at the intensity of his own wrath.

Snow fell from the heavens, brightening the air and dulling the light of the sun. As the Saxons rode on following Hannarr's lead, the warriors took up a song learned from their forefathers. In the way of all the music of that people, it rang with the syllables 'Ho O Ro Ho' beating out the rigid time like a mighty drum. As the men chanted, their thegn recited a storyline, for their songs were not sung in the manner of the Gaels. Each verse of a Saxon song was spoken solemnly and without any dramatic embellishment, the steady pulsing voices dropping in intensity as the storyteller plodded through the stanzas.

Murrough could not understand their speech, but he felt the menace, the resolve, the hard biting tone of the narration, and he shuddered. The snow-filled air swallowed their voices, muffling them and making them sound like a ghostly choir.

After a while the captive prince gave up striving to look about him and he focused on the ground as it passed beneath him. The snow got gradually deeper the further they travelled and the horses often slipped in the slush beneath their hooves. Soon Murrough's hands began to go numb from the cold. His feet were gradually freezing and losing any sense or feeling. He breathed through his mouth so that he could draw in some snow for he was becoming thirsty.

At the head of the procession Seginus rode beside Streng so as to watch over his prisoner and make sure no damage came to her. He could not believe his luck. Surely God was delivering those who had wronged him into his hands so that he could punish them for their insults. His only fear was that the woman, Caitlin, was already too far gone from her wounds to recover, for he wanted her to be conscious when she met her end. He wanted her to feel the humiliation that he had felt. He wanted her to suffer for the way her warriors

337

had treated him and he wanted her to repent her proud words to him.

He closed his eyes and shut out the Saxon chant from his ears and in his head he clearly heard Caitlin rebuking him for his offer of the holy Chrism. 'No woman speaks to me like that,' he said to himself. 'I will teach her a lesson before I see her burn at the heretic's pyre.' That had been the only reason he had argued for her life at all when Hannarr would have left her to his men to do what they would. As for Murrough, Seginus knew that he would be a good hostage to bargain with if the worst came to the worst and the thegn had seen the sense in that also.

As the Roman was brooding over what would be the most satisfying way to punish the chieftainess, the song ended and Hannarr rode up behind him.

'Fall back here with me, Roman,' the thegn barked.

Reluctantly Seginus did so but he kept one untrusting eye on Streng just to be sure no harm came to her. Yet.

'How far?' asked the thegn bluntly.

'Not far.'

'How far?'

'An hour, maybe more.'

'Will this place be heavily guarded?'

'It may well be,' suggested Seginus, 'since your men let so many escape at the gap. By now I expect the whole Kingdom of Munster has turned out to find us.'

'Thank the gods for this snowfall then,' breathed Hannarr, 'for if it makes our passage difficult it will also hamper their warriors. Is there a way across country from here?'

'In this weather!' laughed Seginus. 'You must be

mad. We could ride around for hours without any bearing and never find the Tree. The only sure way to reach our goal is to make straight for the cross-roads.' And then he bit his tongue for he realised he had said too much.

Hannarr nodded quietly and did not let the Roman see how pleased he was with himself for tricking some information out of him. After a short pause he said, 'At the crossroads we will leave the two hostages and the better part of the warriors and ride on to the Tree with only a half-dozen of my best men.'

'Very well,' answered Seginus, rebuking himself for letting the Saxon under his guard.

Hannarr had guessed that the Tree lay not far away from the Cashel crossroads and, satisfied, he let his mount drop back again so that he could issue orders to his men in preparation for their arrival there. He had no intention whatsoever of compromising the size of his force any more than had already been necessary. He had simply been baiting the Roman for clues.

Seginus caught up once more with Streng and was glad that the man had been wounded in the throat. 'At least I don't have to listen to his self-serving prattle or his boorish, empty boasting,' he told himself with relief. 'The archer who took that shot never picked a better target.'

If only Seginus had known who had loosed the shaft at Streng he might have been amused at the brutal irony of her fate, for she now lay across the same Saxon's lap, unconscious.

Mawn was awakened from his half-sleep not by the laughter and talk of Gobann and Origen but by a horseman galloping along the road to Teamhair. As the rider approached, Mawn was sure that he would stop right where they were and deliver them some news of great importance, but the gates to the citadel opened before the messenger and he rode swiftly through, not slackening his pace for a second. When he had passed, the oaken doors were heaved shut again and the road was silent.

Then Mawn turned his attention to Origen whom he noticed in that moment seated in silent thought on the grass beside Gobann. The boy got up and approached the foreigner respectfully, unsure whether it was right to disturb him. Many times when his father had been in a similar state, Mawn had made the mistake of interrupting the blacksmith and he had often been severely punished for upsetting Midhna's train of thought.

'Have you been here long?' ventured the boy. 'I was asleep and I didn't notice you arrive.'

Origen turned to acknowledge Mawn and as he did so Gobann rose from his place and stormed away towards the horses. The boy instinctively ducked as the poet moved past him. He thoroughly expected to be chastised for having broken the mood of their conversation, but Gobann did not raise a hand or even open his mouth to speak. Mawn was surprised by Gobann's lack of reproach. He had learned at a very early age that adults often took their frustration out on children and animals, and it seemed strange to him that Gobann was so silent.

'Do not worry about that one,' Origen reassured him. 'He is not angry with you.' The white-robed brother raised his voice so that the poet could easily hear him. 'He has a argument to settle within himself. Would that he could and save all of us the burden of facing his bitter moods and his loneliness!'

Gobann took his horse aside to brush and groom her. Drugal neighed appreciatively. Her sharp eyes sought out a place to stand where the grass was green and she made straight for it, the poet offering her no resistance, but following with brush and wire comb and the small bag of pigments which he always carried.

'What is your country like?' Mawn asked Origen.

'It is very different from this land,' answered the monk. 'It is mostly a dry and dusty sea of sand which stretches west and east and south further than any man knows. Only a small part of the country is green but it is not the same shade of green that you know.'

'Are all your people so dark?' the boy added, trying to think of all the questions that had been plaguing him about the stranger in the few days since he had first seen him at Rathowen.

'Most of my people are very dark and there are some who are so black of skin that they shine deep blue in the sunlight. Those people have a great kingdom to the east and south of my country called by the Romans Ethiopia.'

'Does the sand-sea run through their country?' gasped Mawn.

'Almost their whole land has been swallowed by the sands, but it was not always so. There was a time when their country was the richest kingdom on Earth and they even ruled my people who were for many generations the kings and queens of the world.'

Mawn could only widen his eyes in awe. He was lost for words. Sianan, who had been dozing by the hedge, overheard snippets of the conversation and now she joined them. 'The great queen who gave her name to this place was one of your people,' she interjected, 'so my grandfather told me.'

'Yes, Teamhair was the daughter of one of our kings,' Origen confirmed. 'Her father was a powerful Pharaoh who my people believed was descended directly from God. But they believed many strange things until the coming of the word of Christ.'

Both children flinched a little at the mention of Origen's faith. The events at Rathowen had not shown Christians in any favourable light and Mawn doubted whether those folk who carried a belief in the Christ were honourable people. After all, they had murdered his own brother on the death tree and their bishop had placed a curse on the High-King of the land.

'When first I saw you I thought you must be a famous Druid,' Mawn revealed. 'I still can't believe that you are one of those Christians.'

'In some ways I am a Druid,' suggested the monk, 'for the ways of our peoples are not so different.' Mawn suddenly listened attentively. He could not imagine that Christians had anything in common with anyone else on Earth for they seemed to bear a malice for all who were not of their faith.

'In my country, the word of Christ was already well known long before it was ever taken to Rome. Our people have kept the Word pure, just as it was taught to us by the companions of the Christ. In Rome, however, they changed the Word to suit themselves. They put much of the true teaching aside because it did not agree with their way of life and so they added much to the story that was never part of Christ's message.'

The children listened politely and took in all that was said, saying nothing but waiting for Origen to finish before asking their questions. 'Truly these two are well chosen,' thought the monk. 'They have the light of learning in their souls.'

'One hundred and twenty winters ago the emperor of the Romans called a great council of the Christian church and representatives came from all over the world to have their views heard, for by that time even though only three hundred and twenty-five years had passed since the birth of our Lord, there were already cracks appearing in the wall of Christ's teaching. Many of the delegates claimed to possess the only authentic version of the Gospels and the Roman emperor was called on to judge who would be the true custodian of the faith.' Origen reached for his mead cup and finished off the dregs.

When he spoke again there was more than a hint of bitterness and anger in his voice. 'Not surprisingly the emperor, Constantine, deemed that the Roman version of the message was the one that came closest to the original spirit of the Christian faith. He declared the Bishop of Rome to be the Pontifex Maximus of the Holy Apostolic Church of Rome. Henceforth the Christian way was to be the state religion of the Empire. Any who dissented from the decisions of the Pope were to be severely punished under Roman civil law. My folk were not troubled by all of these events for a long, long time, but eventually even the hermits in the desert were debating the authenticity of teachings that two hundred years before had been unquestioned. Now the influence of the Romans has spread across the world and no-one really knows for certain what elements of the teaching belonged to Christ and what came after.'

In the midst of some tall grasses not far away Gobann was gently brushing his mare, preparing her for the festival of Beltinne, and she was leaning into the rough bristles as the poet dragged them over her neck and down her foreleg. He worked his way around the animal, grooming belly and flanks and finally the light grey mane and knotted tail. He took infinite care with this last part of the task for he knew that Drugal was very sensitive about her long hairs. Gobann was the only person she had ever allowed to touch them.

Origen had been watching his friend out of the corner of his eye and now dragged his attention back to the children. 'That is why I first came years ago to Eirinn,' he continued. 'I had heard of a community of our brothers who dwelt here and I hoped they would hold some of the older ways of Christianity safe from the influences of the Roman world. When I arrived, I discovered that the old faith of your people was closer to the ancient message of Christ than that of my own teachers. This land is now more like home to me than the land of my birth and the laws and customs of your folk are more dear to me than the opinions of all the bishops on God's Earth.'

Gobann had finished brushing his horse and commenced mixing some of the pigments with which he would paint her. He started with the blue powder that was made from dried plants, turning it over in a small stone bowl and gradually adding water to it as he did so. This would have to stand a while before the colour attained its rich hue. When that was done he set the mixture aside out of the sunlight and went to seek the travellers' well where he would ritually wash himself, ridding himself body and soul of the dust and grime of the Road.

Origen, Mawn and Sianan fell silent. Mawn ached to ask many more questions and his mind buzzed with all the things he longed to know. It seemed to him that when adults spoke they never expressed enough detail or told the whole of the story. He sensed that this was sometimes because there were things they would rather not discuss, but also because they often didn't think the details were important to the telling of the tale.

Throughout the afternoon clouds had begun to muster in little groups across the sky. The small clusters gradually grew as they each melded together, slowly and methodically, without many people noticing. Even Mawn who was usually first to spot such changes, did not detect the gathering storm. He only noticed the darkening sky just as the gates to Teamhair swung open and Cathach strode out to them, dressed in the long white robes that were worn only during the times of the fire festivals.

'Sianan, Mawn and Origen,' he called to them, looking about to make sure that Gobann was not present, 'you have been granted leave to come within the citadel and to take lodgings.'

'I will fetch Gobann!' cried Mawn.

'No, boy!' The old Druid's tone was sharp and firm. 'His case has not yet been fully judged and he must stay here until the Council has given him leave otherwise. Now we must enter Teamhair quickly before he returns. It would not be right if he and I met just yet.'

Cathach took the children's horses by the reins and began to lead them toward the gate. Origen was already at his horse stowing his cup and making ready to move. Mawn and Sianan gathered up their blankets and saddles and followed as quickly as they could.

As soon as they had passed through the gate it slammed shut, encouraged by the rising wind. The timbers thudded together with a deafening crash and Mawn heard Drugal give an anguished whinny and then blow the air through her lips making them flap loudly. He wondered what would happen if the Council of Druids decided that Gobann had failed to keep his géas.

Origen was led away from Mawn and Sianan once they had crossed the inner ramparts of the Citadel of Teamhair. He said some hasty farewells and promised to drop by and visit them in the coming few days, but he knew that it would be unlikely that he would be allowed to see them. The Druids had strict rules that governed their contact with foreigners during their fire festivals. And he was sure that the College of Poets would enforce those laws to the letter where the two children were concerned.

He was given a sleeping place in the house of the King of Munster where he was received as an honoured guest and placed close to the fire. Just after nightfall he was joined by two of his white-robed brethren and they then respectfully went outside in the open air to perform their prayers, so as not to offend their host.

Mawn and Sianan went with Cathach to the house that was called the Star of the Poets and there they were given fresh clothes. Mawn received a rust-brown shirt and bleached linen trousers; all his other clothes except the dark-green cloak his mother had made for him were taken away. Sianan received a long dark-blue shift that tied around the waist and a newly woven brat-cloak of fine-spun wool coloured deepest cherry red.

When they had washed and dressed and their hair had been combed, Cathach took them into the feasting hall. As they walked in front of him he found he could not resist comparing the two of

346

them. 'They are so alike in their manner, in their way of thinking, and yet they could not look more opposite. His hair is the colour of ripe corn and hers the colour of pitch. His eyes are bright and darting; hers are slow and dark. They will make a fine pair in years to come.'

As the three entered the hall all those assembled rose silently and bowed their heads to them. Mawn thought at first that it was Cathach they were paying respects to until he noticed that the old Druid also had lowered his gaze. Suddenly, at an unseen signal, the assembly sat noisily and resumed their chatting as they had been doing before the children were brought in. Cathach led them to their places and sat between them at the great circle of tables.

Mead was passed around and Sianan helped herself, mixing it with water and swallowing it quickly to drown her thirst. She noticed Mawn did not help himself so she poured some for him.

'I don't like to drink it without some water, because it makes me so sleepy,' she explained.

Great flat loaves of bread four hand-spans wide were brought out then and distributed among the feasters. Tearing it into manageable hunks they hungrily devoured it and the bowls of fresh butter that followed. Mawn noticed that this bread was very different from the loaves his mother had baked at Dobharcú. It lacked the rich aroma and it was a creamy colour, where his mother's bread had always been the golden colour of dried hay and was full of unground oats and barley.

They had sat for long enough that two helpings of the bread were delivered, when Lorgan the Sorn finally entered the hall. No-one rose for him but silence spread swiftly across the room as he passed through it. The old man squeezed his way between

347

a gap in the tables and entered the space formed by the circle of trestles. There he stood for a few moments waiting for absolute and utter silence. He did not have to wait long.

'The Council is still debating,' he announced and an exasperated sigh passed around the room, 'but you have their leave to commence the feast.' Faces began to brighten in the hall. Most of the thirty or so poets and judges had been waiting since early afternoon to eat.

'This is the last feast before Beltinne,' continued Lorgan, 'and we have two honoured guests in our presence. So it is fitting that we are reminded of the true meaning of this time before we take the last supper of the dark months.'

Mawn realised that he and Sianan were the honoured guests that Lorgan spoke of and he was surprised that they were receiving so much attention.

Once again the atmosphere in the hall took a sudden change. There were obviously some very hungry men and women here this night. They were not impolite to Lorgan but made no secret either of their wish to get on with the feasting.

Lorgan only laughed good-naturedly and called them again to stillness, raising both his palms for them all to see. Then a harper came and sat beside him and strummed gently at the lower chords of the instrument.

'The time of the Hag of Winter is passing. The darkness is retreating. The world will soon be bathed in light and we are the servants of that light.'

The harper ran his fingers gently up the strings of the instrument. Mawn realised, hearing this fellow play, how great Gobann's talent was and why his harp was so famous. There was simply no comparison between the two.

'The cold months drag on and it seems that the sun is with all for only a short while before the snow begins again to fall. All that has kept us from death this winter is the gift of fire.'

Mawn blocked out of his mind the harper's tune for he did not find that it complemented the tale as he knew Gobann's playing surely would have.

Lorgan continued. 'And just as last year all the hearth fires in the land were put out and rekindled from the sparks of a sacred flame brought into being here at Teamhair, so this year every household will douse their blazes and await delivery of a burning coal from the enclosure of the High-King. This is the festival of fire. This is the festival of life. The kindling sticks are being gathered now from which we will ignite the Need Fire that will provide the smouldering coals.'

Lorgan paused a moment staring at the ceiling where the smoke from the central fire of this hall gathered. He saw something unusual there for it showed clearly on his face and some of his brothers and sisters followed his line of sight to try and discern what it was.

'This year I will stand the closest of all of you to the Need Fire when it is kindled, and this year will be my last for the seasons will soon claim me.'

And then everyone knew what he had seen.

'Eat well then, for you will fast three nights before the feast of Bel, and you will depart here in the guise of darkness. You will speak to no-one save those who share our path and no mead may pass your lips until the new fire is kindled in your own hearth. When you go home tonight do not forget to thank your old fire for its service to you.' Then Lorgan went quickly to his seat and the food was brought out.

There was no meat or fish or fowl on the platters,

only vegetables and nuts and berries and grains and bread. There was broth made from ground acorns and chestnuts and wild roots. Mawn found the meal filling and satisfying. He had never liked the taste of animal flesh and preferred to avoid it if at all possible.

Despite the variety and the quantity of edibles it was no longer a festive meal. Whether it was Lorgan's prediction of his own death or some other reason, Mawn could not tell, but the conversation in the hall was subdued and when each poet had finished their food they rose quickly to depart.

At the door they were all handed a long black cloak that engulfed their white robes completely and hooded their faces and everyone who left the hall was given a long walking staff.

When it came time for Sianan and Mawn to leave with Cathach they were also given robes and staves appropriate to their size and were advised to keep wrapped tightly against the falling snow. Mawn was very surprised at this as there had been no snow for many weeks.

When they got outside though, there was a bite in the air, the bite that clearly speaks of heavy weather. It was fresh and crisp and it reddened their cheeks but it made all three pick up their feet to make quickly for the hearth fire in the sleeping place.

EIGHTEEN

t Teamhair the snow fell heavier than anywhere in Eirinn during the night when the last feast of winter was being celebrated. Great drifts of the swirling, icy whiteness spread across the land, covering the countryside in a thick coating. The very shapes of the hills and plain were transformed so that even someone who had lived close to the citadel all his life could have easily become lost in the changed landscape.

Gobann spent a long while painting his mare utilising many ancient designs and when he had finished he prepared the decorations of his own body before the night fell and the storm reached its peak. He shaved his hair from ear to ear in a line across his head, which was the mark of an initiated Druid, and streaked white lime through the coal-black strands that remained, tying them at the back and working the hair into a tight plait.

Then he used the woad that he had prepared that afternoon to dye his skin deep blue. Using a twig that had been chewed on one end to produce an even, circular shape, he spread patterns of spiral dots all over his skin. With a finer twig he added smaller patterns of zigzags and geometric lines.

Around his eyes he carefully traced lines in dark blue which made the whites and pupils stand out from the rest of his face. His lips he also outlined in blue, taking care not to swallow any of the dye for it was capable of causing a severe stomach sickness.

When he had finished painting the woad he spread the remnants of the dye on the tops of his feet, leaving the toenails unpainted and pink. Then he took more white lime mixed with water and added little dots of it to his skin over the blue paint to make it stand out.

When he had finished, he and Drugal had become brethren. Though they came of different species they shared similar decorations and so they seemed to be kindred beings. Anyone who would have stumbled across the two of them then might have thought himself lost in the realms of the otherworld, for the creatures that stood where the poet and his horse had been bore no signs of the mundane universe.

Gobann checked that none of the motifs had been smudged during the painting and when he was satisfied with the results of his work he draped his cloak about his shoulders and added the final touches of lime to Drugal's decoration.

Across her forehead in the broad flat space between her eyes he painted a curved crescent shape in brilliant white, exactly the same as the Moon during its progression when it was partly obscured: a crescent. The points of it were towards the heavens and suggested horns. This design he had learned during his travels among the wild Cruitne folk and he knew instinctively that it was old beyond reckoning. Painting the curved shape brought sharply to mind the days he had spent with those people and all that had happened when he had journeyed in Alba. As all initiated Druids must do, he had gone to be apart from his own folk for a while and to experience the life and culture of another race.

The feel of the lime stiffening his locks of hair recalled to him how he had by chance met a wandering tribe who called themselves the people of the Blue North. He mouthed the words in their language, 'Garrum tooshcart,' recalling how harsh their speech had first seemed to him and how sweet it now was to his ears. His empty heart drank deep of the memories and he saw once more the face of their chief Druid, the woman he loved ever since those days, Síla Subhach. Síla the merry one, in his own language. Seeing her face again clearly in his mind he added one more finishing touch to Drugal's adornment. Far above the crescent Moon, just under the spot where her mane flopped over her forehead, he placed a tiny white dot. Only someone who knew the poet well, someone like Origen perhaps, would have known that it represented the Evening Star.

When it was well past sunset Gobann realised that he might not be summoned at all this night and so he draped Drugal in her saddle blanket and crawled into a hole in the hedge, packing it tightly with anything that might keep him warm. There he waited out the dawn but he did not sleep. Nor did he eat for, having missed the last feast of winter, he knew that the time of fasting was upon him and that his particular test required of him abstinence.

The night was bitter cold, making it seem that much longer, and the snowstorm grew in intensity until the only sound that echoed through his head was the howling wind tearing at the branches of the hedge and pushing at the oaken gates to the palisade of the citadel.

Drugal gave a cry now and then to let him know she was still alive, but there was only one other voice that met his ears throughout the dark and murky night. Huddled close to him was the otter-skin bag in which was wrapped his harp. Under her covering she was safe and dry and warm and yet Gobann knew that she longed to experience for herself the storm at close quarters. Her strings sang in sympathy with the wind and her timbers creaked almost imperceptibly as she adjusted her position now and then to get comfortable.

If Caitlin's harp was made with the care, though not the craft, of a great harp, Gobann's instrument was one of the most magnificent harps of those days. It had been worked by the hands of two craftspeople, a man and his wife who were famous in their time for sharing their love of fine wood-making. Throughout their lives these masters of the chisel and the plane only ever built one harp together, and it took them a full thirty years to assemble. This was that instrument. On from the makers, the music-loom had passed to their daughter who trained the harp in the correct intervals and the basics of music. It stayed with her throughout her long life of fifty years.

After that the harp was given to the keeping of Malcolm Sweet-Tooth, who was a travelling bard from the Kingdom of Dal Araidhe. He taught her much more of the music. Sweet-Tooth was known throughout the Gaelic world as a master of his craft and was said to possess the very harp that Amergen the Bard had carried with him a thousand years before when the Gaels had first arrived in Eirinn.

Amergen had used his harp to neutralise the magic of the Tuatha-De-Danaan when they sent their spells to confound the Gaels. So it was that Gobann's instrument had come to learn her art from a harp that had stilled sea storms with its

354

songs. That is where she got her love of heavy weather and her secret name which only Gobann knew: Banfa, Storm Woman.

When Malcolm died he was entombed with Amergen's harp lying on his chest and his hand upon its wires and he passed Banfa to his only son the blind harper Colm. This was the same Colm who had fashioned Caitlin's harp. Blind though he was many believed that he was a far better harper than his father had ever been and none who ever heard him play were unmoved. Colm Dhall refined Banfa's talents, sitting at the strings four or five hours every day at either morning or evening. He introduced her to other instruments and the various modes of music. In time, when he felt she had digested as much knowledge as he had in his power to do, he gifted her to Gobann, the poet for whom she had been originally built nearly two hundred years before.

Since Colm's passing none lived but the poet who knew her secret name or who could coax even a simple tune from her. In fact, Gobann rarely let anyone else touch her for she was prone to lose her tuning and behave erratically after the caress of a stranger. Harp and harper were linked by an invisible chain that bound their spirits together. Síla, wise in the ways of such things, had always recognised that she could only take second place to Banfa in Gobann's life, no matter how often he might protest otherwise. She was wary never to comment on the instrument's tone or timbre or on Gobann's rendition of a tune. She well understood how jealous and possessive harps can be of their harpers.

Then came the day when Gobann was asked by the Druid Council to return to Eirinn so that he could prepare himself to be Mawn and Sianan's teacher. The urgency of the plea made it difficult for him to refuse and so he reluctantly left Síla and the people of the Blue North to return to his home.

Now that Mawn had become his pupil, Gobann was not comfortable about having his harp entombed with him at the end of his life. He no longer felt that Banfa was made purely and solely for him to play. 'She is a rare creature and Mawn will need a companion such as her,' he reasoned. 'Perhaps when the time comes it would be wrong of me to be buried with her. Perhaps, if they take to each other enough, Banfa should accompany him on his journey.'

While it was true that a harp became stronger and developed a better tone the older it grew, they were usually left in the tomb with their last harper so that they could die a peaceful death of old age, undisturbed by the troubles of the world. The dampness in the stone caverns where filidhs were traditionally laid to rest meant the wood rotted and the wires decayed slowly but irrevocably.

Harps that continued to be passed on, generation after generation, ran the serious risk of meeting violent ends, through war or accident. Such a death was not good for the soul of the instrument. They were considered to be very sensitive beings and Druidic teaching stated that no spirit should be made to suffer if the suffering could be in any way avoided.

'We will see what is to be done when the time comes, my love,' he whispered gently to her in reassurance. Then he closed his eyes and rested as he knew he must if he was to survive the ordeal before him.

It was not long before the dawn when Gobann was awakened from his sleep by Cathach and two other younger novice Druids dressed in black.

Silently the old man summoned the poet to rise. Gobann managed to remain outwardly calm despite being a little startled at their arrival.

Without a word he rose quickly and went to release Drugal from her leather hobbles. When he had rolled the straps up and tucked them into his saddle he reached down into a feed bag and brought out a handful of oats from the stores he had been given at Dobharcú. Drugal took them from the palm of his hand and nuzzled him for more when they were gone, but Gobann did not offer her any more. He was eager to move on to the next stage of his life and he knew she would be well cared for in the stables of the citadel.

He took her reins gently and led her up to the great oaken gates to where Cathach had retreated. The timbers once more creaked as the doors swung open and the poet entered followed by his horse. Cathach and the novices came after at a distance where no words would chance come between them and their charge.

As they passed the gatekeepers at the innermost sentry post a man came from out of the early-morning shadows and took Drugal by the bit. Gobann let her be led away to the warm dry stables, allowing the palm of his hand to run down her flank as she passed by. Just as she was moving beyond his reach he used his long hard fingernails to scratch softly along her rump and she whinnied in appreciation, turning to look back briefly at her master as the snow once again began to swirl in the rising wind.

At this point Cathach came forward and took the lead, walking swiftly toward a circular stone structure a little less than the height of a man, out of which poured smoke and steam. At the entrance he paused and indicated that Gobann should go inside. The poet ducked his head to enter and immediately bumped it on the moist turf ceiling.

The building was very small, built to accommodate only one person at a time, and the interior was perfectly dark. He fumbled about for a few seconds feeling his way around an iron cauldron in the middle of the floor until he found a stone seat on which he could rest for the next while. He had just sat down when one of the novices brought in a brass bucket loaded with red-hot stones. In the darkness of the little room they glowed fiercely.

The young man tested the water that rested long undisturbed in the broad black cauldron. Then he took some herbs from his pouch and strewed them on the surface of the water. He waited a few seconds for the leaves to sink down into the pot and then he lifted the brass bucket over his head and plunged the stones into it. The cool waters hissed loudly as the burning stones touched the surface and in moments the little sweat-house was full of steam. The novice withdrew and the entrance was sealed with rushes and hay.

It did not take long for Gobann to feel the cold of the night leaving his bones and the sensation of touch returning to his frozen feet and toes. His hair became soaked with droplets of wetness and hung as if it had been bathed in oil.

Before long he had to remove his tunic and trousers and his heavy riding boots. He slipped a bronze armband from his upper arm and he was naked except for the silver sun-wheel which never left its place on a leather cord round his neck. He leaned back against the wall of the structure, closed his eyes and let himself feel the perspiration roll freely down his arms and legs and across his chest.

The scent of wild herbs mildly stung his nostrils as the oils leached from the leaves in the hot water and sweat began pouring over his face. Just as he was beginning to feel the essence of the oils take their calming effect on him, sharpening his senses, the rushes were pulled away from the door and another novice entered with a fresh bucket of searing hot stones for the cauldron. The rushes were immediately placed over the entrance, again blocking the excessive escape of the precious steam into the cold air of Teamhair.

The novice stumbled about a little in the dark then dumped the stones in the water. As the water began steaming fiercely the young trainee's robes brushed against the poet's upper arm and Gobann could feel the shape of a woman's breast beneath them. The novice lingered there for a moment and then put out a delicate hand to steady herself against his shoulder. The fingers of that hand tightened a little around the muscle at the top of his arm, then she moved her body closer to him.

He felt her breath on him and then the bony part of her hip against his arm and his body tingled. A finger touched his forehead and traced down his face. His whole body jolted with the pleasure and the surprise of the caress and then just as suddenly as it had begun the rushes were pulled away from the door again and the woman was gone.

The pre-dawn light streamed into the little hut for a moment and, when the novice was clear, it was sealed up once more. There was the bittersweet scent of new herbs now in the steam.

The seeing herbs.

In the next few minutes his head began to swim and images flashed before his mind, images of spirals and diamonds and circles such as he had painted on his skin.

When he could muster any physical sensations again Gobann found that he was sitting forward, leaning on his knees. As he relaxed and lay back again to let the oils do their work he resolved to find the female novice, for he knew she had made bodily contact at great personal risk and he was confused about why she had endangered her future as a Druid in such a way. To touch one who was to journey to the otherworld was to risk being drawn into that journey also. If the woman was not properly prepared there was a good chance she would not survive the ordeal or, worse, that her soul would be unable to return.

The steam collected as globules of water on his body and he was soaked in the moisture that leaked from the pores of his skin. The blue woad and the white lime washed from him and became streaked in watery lines that ran to the floor. Just as he began to feel that the heat was unbearable the rushes were cleared again and the two novices entered. They passed a silver cup full of well-water to the poet and he drank deeply. Then they lifted him under the arms and helped him out into the deepening snow.

Gobann stumbled at the entrance and was a little startled that he had such diminished control over the movement of his legs. This was not the first time he had been administered the seeing herbs. He knew that they could, depending on the physical and mental state of the seer, have a wide variety of effects and so he began to relax and to cease worrying about what was to come.

As they led him on he strained to catch a glimpse of the woman who had so tenderly touched him in the sweat-house, but both of the novices who supported him were hooded and were much shorter than him, so the poet could not make out which was the girl.

They led him to a large stone basin full of icy

water deep enough that a breeding bull could have stood in it and the water would have only lapped at its chin. They took him to the edge and lowered him in. The shock of the cold made Gobann breathe sharply and shudder, but he did not become more awake. If anything he slipped further into a dream-like state. He began to see the world as if it were shrouded in a strange haze and he could no longer discern whether the distorted shapes that moved around him were human or of the spirit world.

The novices quickly drew him out of the trough after only a few short moments for fear that his body would suffer from the cold, and they scrubbed the remaining blue dye from the surface of his skin. When that was done he was plunged again into the coldness to wash the residue from him.

Once more they helped him out and wrapped him in furs and dragged him to a wattle and daub hut that was nearby. There when he had stopped shivering and had been stripped naked, he was laid out on his back before the fire to be repainted from head to foot by the two novices. This time there would be no gaps in the design where he had been unable to reach; this time he would be totally enfolded in the spiralling motifs that were sacred to this ceremony.

Some tea was presented to him and he gulped it, realising only afterwards that it was an infusion of other, more potent seeing herbs. He recalled that there was only one more stage in this procedure and that was the Feast of the Sights. He propped his head on a roll of cloth that was provided and emptied his mind of all thoughts, drifting into a bright daydream as the novices deftly completed their task.

Cathach looked on their work the whole while,

passively waiting for the decorations to be finished and commenting only when he noticed that the young trainees might be straying too far from traditional bounds in the creation of their motifs. Innovation was encouraged in this work but there were still strict guidelines that had to be followed if the full magic of the designs was to be effective. When Gobann visited the otherworld he would need to be well concealed from some of the denizens of that place. These paintings would help him to melt into the world of spirits.

Whether by instinct or by some chance or perhaps because it had long been planned this way by the Great Council, Gobann was given the sign of the crescent Moon across his brows just as he had given the sign to Drugal. It was as broad as his forehead and painted in dark blue highlighted with white and filled with white dots. The overall effect was that the space above his eyes seemed to shimmer with silver.

The sheen of his blue-black hair was also emphasised by the use of a simple and very clever device. The novices took the strands and rolled them together into bunches of fifty or so hairs. Then, using white pigment made from lime, they painted each bunch of strands with bands of bright white. The overall effect was unearthly and strange, making his hair look as though it was made of the tresses of the tails of many badgers. The very tips of the cropped hair along the front and sides of his head were also covered in drops of white paint.

Gobann no longer had the air of a human but resembled the descriptions of the fiercest Tuatha-De-Danaan in the most ancient of all tales.

It was a long process and the poet was kept perfectly still throughout except for times when his attendants rolled him over or lifted a limb to complete the decoration on every part of his body. By midmorning, when they finally led him dazed and blank outside to continue on the next stage of his spirit journey, he saw the world through very different eyes. All that he beheld was bathed in an odd blue glow.

He perceived that the people who surrounded him were beings of this peculiar light for it swam about them, coursing over the contours of their bodies and giving each person an uncanny stream-lined shape. The flowing radiance reminded the poet of the shape of the spawning salmon that leap out of streams in the spring and in that manner travel long distances inland to mate.

The snow fell heavier now than before and the air was very crisp but the poet was not given any clothes to wear. He was helped barefoot toward his horse. Despite the bitter cold and the deep prints that his feet left in the snow, Gobann did not wake from the half-sleep into which he had fallen.

Drugal had been repainted, watered and fed, her motifs touched up, and she had been fitted with a white leather harness and saddle. The poet's harp was slung from the saddle and the dark otter-skin case was dotted with more white pigment to accentuate the designs already stamped into it.

Drugal's head had been adorned with a set of bright, tiny silver bells which hung on a minute but sturdy branch of applewood, cleverly out of reach of her brow so that with every little movement of her head the bells sounded sweetly. The apple branch was also painted in silver to match the bells.

The Silver Branch was an ancient emblem of acclamation conferred on a filidh by the people of Eirinn. Only the greatest poets were entitled to carry or to hold it. The tradition was that, like the

Speaking Staff that Cathach always carried, all who heard the bells ringing must remain silent until the poet had made a pronouncement. Unlike the staff that Cathach held, no-one, not even the High-King, was immune to the power of the Silver Branch. It was the greatest honour that could be bestowed on any Druid and as such was a sure sign of a wise and learned master.

Nevertheless there were some able poets who took advantage of their right to carry the Branch. The ancient story cycles warned of Druids who, through their greed and ambition, abused the Silver Branch to serve their own petty ends, seeking temporal power or wealth. None of them ever profited by their actions for the Silver Branch was capable of exacting a terrible revenge on those who misused the privilege of bearing it.

The most famous case of this sort involved a poet called Breaga who lived in the time of King Niall. This man had earned the Branch and was highly respected as a reciter of the histories but he was corrupted by a yearning for gold and the responsibilities of kingship. There was never any law to prevent a Druid taking on a royal office or chieftainship but Breaga used the Silver Branch to influence a crucial vote in his favour. He won the rank of chieftain, but his people quickly came to distrust his judgements. Within a year of his election he had started using the Branch to silence all opposition and criticism of his rule. Within eighteen months he was declaring that truth emanated from his mouth alone and within two years he fully believed that he was destined to be High-King of Eirinn and to rule without even the advice of a Council of Princes, not to mention the Druid Council which by now had come to treat him with distaste.

To put a stop to his planned despotic march on

Teamhair his tribespeople very cleverly used the qualities of the Silver Branch against him. Quite simply they refused to speak to him. Since he always carried the Branch with him it was not difficult to pass this off as respectful observance of tradition. In a few short weeks he was brought to his knees, for he could not get any information or acknowledgement from any of his servants or the bulk of his people. He retired from office and took to the life of a hermit, wandering aimlessly on the windswept western coast.

Such was its hold over him that even in his final years, though he was dressed only in rags, he still carried the Silver Branch before him wherever he went. It was said that he could often be heard ordering the birds and the wind in the trees to be silent at the sounding of his bells as he loudly quoted his authority as a great poet and seer of visions.

Gobann was not made in that mould and the Druid Council well knew that he would rarely display the bells, let alone abuse the entitlements that went with them, for he was a humble man.

The poet looked up as he was about to mount his horse and he saw the little branch but he did not immediately recognise it for what it was. His dream journey had already begun.

He was helped by the novices up into the saddle and his feet were placed securely in the stirrups. Then they led Drugal and her precious burden over a field to a man-made mound of stones that had been covered in sods of earth. The poet was by this stage entering a deep trancelike state but he sat high and unmoving upon his faithful mount.

Around the entrance of the mound there milled a great assembly of figures in the dark robes of winter-passing, each with his or her staff, some made of the blackthorn, others of yew and yet others carved of oak or rowan or of the birchtree. Each poet and Brehon-judge and harper and historian and diviner had their own affinity with a certain clan of trees and these they carried as protection at this time.

The days leading to Beltinne held great risks for one trained in the arts of music, law or future-seeing. To wander about without some form of protection or reminder of their own world was potentially disastrous. At such a time most Druids were extremely vulnerable to the many alterations that took place in the world, not just in the subtle variations of the seasonal turns but in every change that relied on the procession of the Earth through its eternal march, winter to spring to summer to autumn. Earth, water, fire and air.

At Beltinne the hidden doorway between the world of the living and the world of spirits was flung wide open and the unwary traveller might find himself crossing that ethereal threshold without realising the danger. If the time of the festival passed by and the doorway shut once more while the unlucky traveller tarried in the otherworld, then there was no way of returning until the next fire festival and even then the way would be fraught with many obstacles and hidden pitfalls.

So it was that a Druid always bore at this time a staff made of their own tree to act as a sure reminder of who and where they were at any given time.

Standing in among the many Druids come to witness Gobann's ritual journey were Mawn and Sianan who waited patiently to catch a glimpse of their friend and teacher. They eventually saw him arrive, his horse surrounded by many younger Druids who thumped rhythmically on goatskin

drums with carved wooden beaters and who
chanted a wordless song in deep resonant tones.
When the procession, led by Cathach, reached the
entrance of the mound, seven Druids bearing long
trumpets made of brass and ornamented with
silver stepped forth from the crowd. Each instrument would have been equal in length to two full-
grown men but their bearers seemed to lift them
with ease as if the trumpets were made of much
lighter material.

The trumpeters arranged themselves around the
little cairn and prepared to perform their part of
the ceremony. Gobann was helped down from his
horse and led toward a small fire. There he was
forced to sit down in the snow and a bowl of
steaming liquid was placed at his lips. Cathach
raised his staff above his head and for a moment
all was so still that Mawn thought even the snow
had stopped falling and the wind had ceased at the
old Druid's command.

Gobann took a mouthful of the brew, but only
managed to swallow a tiny quantity before he violently spat out the remainder of the bitter concoction. As soon as he did so the trumpeters began to
blow on their instruments. It was a sound such as
Mawn had never heard before, totally different
from the music of the war trumpets at Rathowen.
Each instrument played one note and one note
only, but each trumpet owned a note that was
unique to it. Perhaps through some secret of the
design, each instrument was identical in shape, size
and form, though Mawn knew that trumpets which
played mostly higher notes were usually smaller
than those that produced lower notes. The har-
monies were perfect and none of the musicians
strayed for a second from the note that he had first
played.

There was one other curious thing about their playing that Mawn quickly noticed. On the battlefield the trumpeters had many rests interspersed in their music to allow them to take breaths, and their tunes were constructed to accommodate the player's need for a steady intake of air. These trumpeters, however, did not break to breathe but played on continuously and steadily.

This greatly puzzled Mawn and he focused all his attention on the nearest musician in order that he might work out how it was that the man did not seem to need to rest his lungs. It did not take him long to realise that they were cleverly using their cheeks to blow out air while at the same time breathing in through the nose. The effect was similar to that of the bag on a set of war-pipes which held a store of wind that could be forced through the chanter at will, while with the use of valves, the bag itself was being steadily inflated by the piper.

He was so interested in this trick and in learning it that he did not notice Gobann being led into the mound with his harp case. The next thing that Mawn knew was that the novices were sealing the entrance of the tiny cave of stones with the poet inside.

The trumpeters carried on their droning tune and the Druids began to sing words that Mawn could not understand. As they harmonised with the humming trumpets and the intensity of the chanting increased, Cathach approached the sealed entrance of the mound. He raised his staff above his head again and his black winter robes fell open to reveal a dark-blue tunic that was gorgeously embroidered in silver thread with designs of quarter-moons and stars. The cowl fell back from his head to bare his hair to the falling snow and this was the signal for many Druids to step forward carrying kindling and fallen timber.

With great care they stacked the wood all around the mound, covering it with lighter brush across the top and heavier branches near to the ground. When that was done they marched in procession led once more by Cathach back to the house of the Druids that was called the Star of the Poets. The trumpeters stayed until nightfall, being replaced in shifts throughout the day so that there was never a time when the sound of their instruments did not fill the icy air at Teamhair.

When they all eventually retired indoors Gobann was left entombed in the mound among the cold hard rocks in total darkness, seated with his legs crossed beneath him and his hands in his lap. Banfa lay on her back in her case before him and there was a large bowl of crystal well-water placed at his right-hand side. On his left they had arranged a new black-handled knife, called a scian-dubh, with a tempered steel blade half-drawn in its intricate leather scabbard.

He sat there dimly aware of the passing hours, though the constant droning of the trumpets rang in his head and resonated throughout his body long after the musicians had gone to their beds.

Many dreams passed before his observing mind that night; many snippets of trivial information came to him that would be of personal value in the coming years, and toward morning the herbs of seeing gently separated his spirit from the harsh and heavy confines of his body and he took flight high over the hill of Teamhair.

A wind that did not touch the trees or the banners of the citadel for it was a wind come from out of the spirit world wrapped itself around his liberated soul and bore him on its billowing gusts up into the heavens above the snow-laden clouds toward the far south of Eirinn. Gobann had never known such freedom, never felt so alive. He spread his limbs out and stretched them, revelling in the feeling of weightlessness.

He looked down at his legs and arms but saw only deep blue flames where he should have seen flesh. This puzzled him at first but he soon came to accept that all would not be as it once was. After he had become accustomed to this new experience he realised that he was bearing a weight in one of his hands. When he tried to discern what it was he found he was carrying a black-handled knife.

NINETEEN

hen the spirit wind took him up over the Kingdom of Laigin and southwards toward Munster, Gobann could not guess where it would bear him. He knew only that he must trust the wind to set him down in a safe place and then hope that it would return him once more to Teamhair.

The hills and valleys passed by beneath him as swiftly as water flowing from a spring at snowmelt and he quickly lost track of exactly where he was. Then he became aware of another, stranger sensation. The further he travelled the less he thought of himself as Gobann the Poet. That is to say, he was becoming aware that he had an identity other than Gobann son of Caillte. As the countryside of Eirinn changed beneath his soaring spirit, everything that he recognised as Gobann retreated almost completely and some other person, who was much older and wiser and had always dwelt within him, slowly came forward to dominate his consciousness.

Just as Gobann was beginning to come to terms with this disturbing new experience, the spirit wind let him drop from the sky, sending him straight down hurtling toward the Earth. He was not afraid, he did not flinch, but he was for a moment very confused.

In the next instant he was seated on the branch

of a great tree. He looked about him with a new kind of vision. All that he perceived now was in sharp contrast: all the colours of the world were either very bright or very dark. He found it difficult to focus quickly on objects in the far distance, but he discovered to his immediate delight that he could view clearly and in great detail things that were many miles away.

Gobann's attention was drawn suddenly to a very slight movement of the grasses in the field near to the tree in which he sat. He was compelled by some force that he could not command to stare long and hard at the place where he had noticed the tiny rustling. In the next moment he was overtaken by an urge to dive down into the field and seek out the cause of the little disturbance, but just as he was making ready to do so, something thoroughly unexpected happened.

A great black Raven flew out of a nearby tree and made straight for the spot that Gobann had been concentrating on. It disappeared for a moment in the grass and then returned with a small brown mouse wedged in its beak to sit beside the poet. It noisily devoured the still-struggling rodent, cracking the small bones in its beak and gurgling loudly as it swallowed its victim.

It was then that Gobann noticed that he and this Raven were not alone. The tree, large and spreading and ancient as it was, had attracted a great conference, a tribal gathering of Ravens. There were hundreds of the black birds, some small and young—maybe only three seasons on Earth—others immensely aged and balding, having lived perhaps a full century.

This was one of those gatherings that took place only once in every twelve years and they had obviously not planned on so large a turnout for there was not enough room on all the branches for every bird. Gobann could see multitudes of Ravens standing in the field around the base of the tree and many more sitting patiently on the branches of other trees nearby.

Still more birds were flying in from over the fields. On the horizon many black specks were gliding in on the draughts of high mountain air from the west and the well nearby was clogged with black forms nudging and shoving for the best drinking spots. The poet started to feel very uncomfortable, aware that he was conspicuously different from all the creatures around him.

Suddenly Gobann felt the need to scratch a spot on the top of his head. It was a nagging little itch that he had noticed increasing in intensity since the moment he had landed in the tree. Gradually the burning prickle became unbearable as if some tiny mite was burrowing deep into the flesh around his skull. Instinctively he bent his head forward and lifted a leg to claw at the irritation with long talons. When the tingling bite was dealt with it was still a few moments before Gobann realised that he had wings and a beak and feathers and that he had adopted a form exactly like one of the black carrion birds that flocked about him.

When he realised what had happened he felt his heart beat loudly in his body and with an unfamiliar rhythm. He looked about him in panic and screamed at the top of his voice but his fear was lost among the squawking conversations that were taking place around him and none of the Ravens even noticed him.

The poet was filled with terror. 'What has happened to me?' he asked himself. 'And what if I am trapped forever in this body?'

The same old bird who had devoured the field-mouse earlier turned to Gobann and said in perfect Gaelic, without a tinge of accent or even a hint of any birdlike tone, 'Still your thoughts, little brother. There are many here who do not hold any love for your kind. If they suspect that you are not what you seem they could well tear you to pieces. Sit quiet and listen. The conference is about to begin.'

Gobann wanted to ask a hundred questions of the old bird but the creature cackled loudly at him, drowning his thoughts and his voice so that none would overhear. 'I beg you to be quiet,' repeated the ancient Raven urgently. 'We are gathering here to decide what action we will take against your people for the terrible deed they may be about to commit. We are anxious to prevent a great wrong from being done in the name of greed. There are many of my kindred who can see no alternative but to attack all of your people and drive them from the land. They are openly advocating war between our folk. Do not give them an excuse to begin such a conflict, for neither side could ever possibly gain from such a pointless exercise.'

Just as the old bird finished speaking, he motioned with a wing up into the hills in the north. With his sharp new Raven vision Gobann could clearly make out a single black bird winging down onto the plain.

'The Queen has arrived,' the old Raven stated matter-of-factly.

All across the assembly a great cawing broke out in homage to the old She-Raven. The Queen's graceful flight brought her gliding in a great circle around the tree so that she could take maximum advantage of the adulation of her subjects. She turned suddenly and rose on an updraught of air to land perfectly in the topmost branches of the tree.

The countless number of birds all scraped their beaks against the branches where they sat. Those on the ground sought out rocks or hard earth to scrape; those at the well used the stones that were its casing. Gobann felt compelled by an uncontrollable urge to join them in the unfamiliar greeting. The feeling of the bark rubbing against his beak immediately reminded him of the young novice who had brushed her breast against him when he had been in the sweat-house, but Gobann could not explain why.

As abruptly as the scraping began, it ceased, and the She-Raven lifted her voice in a long, slow song; not a song as Gobann knew songs to be, but more like a uniquely constructed poem that used the musical qualities of the voice without an attempt to string them all together. In his poetic way Gobann could appreciate the form, though he did not particularly enjoy listening to it for there was a harshness about the bird's tone that permeated every word she spoke.

The words that she chanted were somehow as familiar to the poet as the common language he daily spoke, but he knew she was speaking in the high and formal tongue of the Ravenfolk. This was obviously an occasion of great solemnity.

'How then shall we live without the great trees to be the perches under us?' she called. There was silence. 'The land of Eirinn is changing around us and we must change with her.'

A male Raven spoke up then whose feathers shone with bright iridescent colours sparkling among the black of his coat. He was, Gobann judged, in his middle age and it was obvious that he had many supporters in the audience. 'How much longer must we live with this threat hanging over us?' he cawed hoarsely. 'That is the real question.'

Gobann could feel the tension in the air as the male bird spoke, but he was not sure if it was because the fellow was being disrespectful to the Queen or simply because he was advocating some kind of radical and unacceptable action.

'Even in our own lifetimes we have seen the irreparable damage that the people of the Gael have done to our land,' he continued, 'are we going to allow them to continue with their desecration?'

The crowd began to mutter and squawk. The poet got the distinct impression that this was a popular sentiment expressed ably by a skilled orator.

'For centuries our folk have sat by idle while the people of the Gael tore the heart out of our country. The last time that we bothered to offer any resistance was when our army mustered to aid the Tuatha-De-Danaan. Are we going to sit by now when the venerable Quicken Tree is under threat? Are we going to watch her cut down for the sake of the petty disputes of the Gaels?'

The Ravens all called out as one, filling the air with their cries. Gobann sat as still as a standing stone. He was feeling very nervous.

'Let us rise then and fight, just as our ancestors fought alongside the Sidhe folk. Let us drive the Gaels from this land forever, so that we may live here in peace and so that our sacred places will no longer be defiled.'

The old Raven who sat beside Gobann had been silent throughout the proceedings but now he spoke. 'We have had many arguments with the Gaels since first they came to Eirinn,' he began, and every bird was quiet again to hear him speak, 'but it is not the Gaels who seek to destroy the Tree.'

Suddenly many caws, including the voice of the

younger orator, were raised in anger to gainsay the old bird.

'My clan have been observing events as they unfold very carefully,' stated the old bird confidently, talking over the mob.

'As always Lom-dubh is watching after his own interests,' asserted the young orator.

'And how can it be in Sciathan-cog's interest, or in any of our interests, to start a war with a people who are not our real enemies?' countered Lom-dubh immediately. The crowd was silent again: the old Raven was imparting some information that they were obviously unaware of.

'It is not the Gaels who would seek to destroy the Tree,' he repeated, 'it is the Saxons from across the sea.'

'Rubbish,' jibed Sciathan-cog the orator. 'In their country we are worshipped as gods. Why would they commit such an act against our kind?'

'They are being influenced by a Christian,' Lom-dubh revealed.

Once again the assembly cawed excitedly. Sciathan-cog could see he was rapidly losing support. He fell back on his last line of defence, slander. 'Are we to believe the words of Lom-dubh the Druid bird?' snapped the orator. 'A Raven who spends his days in the oak groves being fed and coddled and nursed by the poets in their own sanctuary is likely to repeat what they tell him without giving much thought to the truth.' He had the crowd's attention again. 'Show us proof of what you say!' he stormed above the cackling outrage of the assembly.

'I can prove what I say and I can prove that the Druid Council has done all in its power to guard the Quicken. They have dispatched a force of warriors to protect the Tree,' replied Lom-dubh calmly.

'And how will you prove that?' snorted Sciathan-cog.

'I have a witness,' stated the old bird calmly.

Gobann felt the cold sweat break out under his coat of feathers; he twitched his claws and ruffled his wings and tried to look as shocked and surprised as all the other birds in the gathering.

'But before I call him to give evidence,' announced Lom-dubh, 'I require that he be granted immunity from prosecution.'

The entire assembly exploded in protests and insults and mocking caws. Then the Queen spoke up, her voice rising above the din.

'Let no-one of our kind raise any charge against this witness,' she intoned. 'I will personally guarantee his safe conduct from this place.'

Sciathan-cog was forced to relent at the command of the She-Raven. 'So be it,' he agreed. 'Let the witness step forth.'

Lom-dubh spread his tattered wings and then crossed the left one across his breast to indicate that his informant was seated on the branch to his immediate right.

'Your Majesty,' he declared formally, 'may I introduce to you Gobann, son of Caillte, of the Féni who is come to us as a messenger from the Druid Council of Teamhair.'

All the hundreds of pairs of deep dark eyes turned to the poet and there was wonder in every set of them. Not for many generations had they received such an ambassador from the Gaelic people and many had come to believe that the stories of such embassies were only myths to entertain the young ones.

'Speak then, Gobann, son of Caillte,' ordered the Queen, 'tell us what you know.'

The poet waited for a second until he was certain

that he had silence and to make sure that none of his nervousness was communicated to his hosts. Then he drew on his vast experience as a storyteller and related the tale of all that had happened since the coming of Palladius. He spoke of the treachery of Dichu and the coming of the Saxons and of the battle of Rathowen, which many of the birds had witnessed.

He talked of the Druid Council's plans to preserve as much as possible of the old ways and of the Gaels' determination to do all in their power to keep the ancient treaty between them and the Tuatha-De-Danaan. He assured the Queen that Leoghaire had sent a force to protect the Tree and that it would be well guarded and that it was the Saxons who were the real enemy, not the Gaels.

When the Queen heard all that he had to say she sat for a short while lost in her own thoughts, and when she finally spoke Gobann could feel that the mood of the gathering had changed dramatically. 'I believe your words, Gobann,' she stated, 'but I have one important question. If your people have sent a force to our aid, why are they not yet here guarding this Tree?'

Suddenly the poet realised that he and the whole assembly were sitting amidst the branches of the Quicken Tree itself. Not one berry had been so much as pecked by the countless orange beaks and yet the thousands of birds were all striving to get as close as possible to the bough.

Gobann's eyes slowly scanned the horizon in desperate hope, but he knew that some trouble must have befallen Murrough and Caitlin for them not to have yet arrived.

'The Gaels were all captured or slaughtered,' Lom-dubh interrupted, 'but another force is even now making ready to march from the Cashel Rock.'

'Captured!' repeated Gobann to himself. 'Slaughtered!' His heart sank. But he had no time to ask any details for just then a pair of Lom-dubh's scouts appeared on the horizon calling loudly.

The two young Ravens cawed in alarm and flew with all the force of their wings toward the Tree. When they reached the top branches they gave their report to the Queen but everyone heard clearly what they said. 'The enemy is upon us! It is just beyond the rise.'

The old She-Raven had not lived so many years that she could not see that there were two factions that were trying to control the assembly. Lom-dubh, she knew to be an honest bird and wise. But Sciathan-cog, likely as not, had already been negotiating with the Saxons. In any case she did not trust him.

She paused long enough in her thoughts to realise that the safest course of action, for the moment at least, would be to take no action. 'Disperse!' cried the Queen. 'We will scatter to the four corners of the valley and wait to see what the Saxons will do. No-one is to attack unless the situation is certainly without hope and then it will be only when I give the order. Fly!' she screamed.

In a matter of moments the Tree was empty and Gobann was seated alone on the branches. He resisted with all his willpower the desire to fly away with them and not long after they were gone he was very glad that he did.

As he was making himself comfortable on his perch he realised to his everlasting relief that he had once more taken on the spirit form that was closer to his human form. All he could do was sit in the Tree among the dark green leaves and the bright red berries and wait.

For a long time as they rode along in the Saxon company Murrough despaired that he and Caitlin would surely be killed. Then two things struck him.

'If they were going to murder us, why would they bother trussing us up like this?' he thought. He had watched the cold-blooded slaying of three of his wounded warriors before their departure from the gap. 'No, they mean to sell us for a ransom back to the High-King or my father,' he reasoned, 'so we still have a chance. It is surely in their interests to keep us in one piece.'

With that realisation he began to relax a little and run through his mind all the possibilities for escape. 'If even one of my guardsmen makes it to Cashel or to one of the checkpoints along the way, then there will be warriors waiting for our arrival at the Tree. That will be my chance.'

As it happened, not long after he had begun to plan a strategy the small band came within sight of the crossroads. The two scouts that Hannarr had sent ahead galloped back down the road at a furious pace just as the Saxon company were descending onto the plain through a rough gorge. They reported that the road ahead was clear and all the countryside about deserted.

Hannarr halted the company and sought out Seginus. 'There are no guards at the crossroads you spoke of,' he stated. 'Now you must tell me in which direction the Tree lies, for I wish us to pass as quickly as possible or go round if we can.'

Seginus hesitated for a moment. 'I will tell you. But only when I am sure that you will keep your promise to bear me away from this land to safety,' he ventured.

'You have my word,' swore Hannarr, easily and falsely.

'Also I want an assurance that once you have the treasure you seek, you will destroy the Tree.'

'I will,' asserted the Thegn.

'And that you will hand the woman over into my keeping so that she will receive the punishment she so richly deserves for her insult to me,' added Seginus.

Hannarr was beginning to lose his patience. He gripped the haft of the axe Frarod, which he had looted from his former lord, and thought for a moment that he would dearly like to discover whether Romans bled the same colour as other folk. Somehow he managed to hold back, telling himself that when he had the berries then he could rid himself of this foolish Christian.

'Very well, as you wish,' Hannarr replied.

'We must stop for a while at the crossroads then,' the Roman remarked coolly.

'What?' howled the thegn in utter disbelief. 'If we stop there we will surely be seen. It is the only low ground in the area! Indeed the enemy may be laying in wait for us even now. Would you have me make my whole company an easy target for the Irish archers?'

'There is no other way,' Seginus rejoined. 'You must trust that I know what I am doing.'

'How far will we need to travel beyond the crossroad?' asked the thegn.

'We will only know that when we arrive at the place,' answered Seginus slyly.

'By the great God Odin,' roared Hannarr, 'you had better know what you're doing, Roman, or I'll cut you into enough pieces that all the Irish can have an equal share of you!'

Seginus remained stony faced and offered no reply and this infuriated Hannarr even more. He felt that the Roman was mocking him. 'You will suffer for this, you bastard!' he promised Seginus in his thoughts.

'Prepare to ride at the gallop!' he called out to his troops. 'When we reach the crossroads take what cover can be had.'

One of the scouts called out before they broke off and Hannarr just caught his words, 'There is a great tree growing there, that is the only place in which to hide!'

Hannarr had rode a long way on before he realised that this tree was the Tree they had been seeking. When his mind grasped that, he shouted out with joy and kicked his horse harder and finally arrived at the place laughing and whooping in a frenzy.

Streng did not join the others who rode forward. He had lost a lot of blood and his wound was no better, and he did not want to lose his prisoner. She was more valuable to him than the berries of a tree so he held his mount in check when the others bolted off.

The horse that bore Murrough had no-one to restrain it and it eagerly followed the rest, not wishing to be left behind. All the prince could do was to try and relax as much as possible. He knew that if his body was too tense or if he moved about at all he would surely be badly injured by the bumpy ride. He was very vulnerable laid out on his stomach. 'May the gods preserve my unworthy ribcage,' he prayed to himself.

It was not a far ride before the horses pulled up once more. Hannarr dismounted quickly and ran to the Tree. It was not unlike any other rowan that he had ever seen, except that it was immeasurably old and its lower branches spread out almost at ground level. Other than that it was unremarkable. He began to doubt that this was the one they sought or if indeed there was such an enchanted tree.

'Roman!' he called. There was no answer. Seginus had not yet regained control of his horse. 'Roman!' Hannarr demanded. 'Is this the tree?'

Seginus turned his mount about but said nothing. He just stared at the bough and studied it. This was all that Hannarr could take. He ran up to the Roman's horse and grabbed him by the tunic, hauling him to the ground. Then he effortlessly dragged the man over to where the berries lay thick on the grass. When he had got close enough he dropped Seginus down as if he was a bale of hay.

'Is this the Tree?' Hannarr screamed into the other man's ear.

Seginus grabbed a handful of the tiny red bulbs and slowly turned to face the Saxon. 'Have you ever seen any tree loaded full of berries when the snow is still falling?' he asked simply.

Then Hannarr realised what he was looking at. A tree perpetually in fruit.

TWENTY

obann was not sure exactly what was happening to him. He had often listened, enraptured, to Lorgan the Sorn as he told of his experiences when he was first dedicated to the Druid path, but now he wished he had remembered more of what the old man had said.

Seated on the highest branches of the Quicken Tree and looking out over the plain toward the hills, the poet let his mind drift again. Long after the Ravens had become just black dots gathered in far-off trees or circling in the distance, Gobann was still confused by all that had come to pass.

It was as he was letting his mind wander that he began gradually to get a sense that he was not alone. He turned his attention to the right and then to the left. But there was no-one about. So he moved to look behind him.

As he did so he pulled up with a shock. Seated on the branch where he had only moments before been looking was his old teacher Lorgan, smiling pleasantly and holding his hands together in front of him, the fingers intertwined.

'Hello, Raven,' began Lorgan, 'how are you fitting in with the rest of the flock?'

Gobann was too shocked to reply. He just sat with his mouth agape and stared. The poet suddenly noticed that Lorgan was wearing a long cloak made entirely from the feathers of Ravens.

'I can't stay long with you,' Lorgan went on. 'I am off now at last to the great mound that lies over the Western Ocean. I just thought I'd come along and see that you were all right before I embark.'

Gobann was still speechless and bewildered. The world began to feel as though it was swaying under him, so he clutched at the branch on which he perched and dug his nails into the bark until they felt like they would tear out.

The poet realised for the first time since he had been in the Tree that it was snowing heavily all around and that he was covered in snowflakes. He did not feel cold, though he knew that he should.

'I must be going soon,' Lorgan stated again, this time with a little more urgency, 'have you anything to ask me before I go?'

Gobann searched for something to say, then blurted, 'Where did you say you are going?'

'I am taking the ship. The ship to the West, to the lands of Tir-Nan-Og.'

Gobann stared blankly.

'I am going to visit the Land of Youth.' The old Druid paused a moment. 'Like you my body lies in Teamhair but I will not be returning to mine.'

'How do I get back?' asked Gobann, urgently searching the points of light that had become Lorgan's eyes.

'Did no-one explain it to you?' Lorgan countered, shocked.

'No. I was told nothing of what would befall me after I entered the mound.'

'Then perhaps it is better that I say nothing also, except that you must always take the spiral to your left. Follow your questing heart, my son, until the way lies clearly spread out before you.'

Gobann listened carefully to the words, and in the way of a poet he placed the advice in a secure part of his memory where he could draw on it later.

'Lorgan the Furnace of Wisdom I was called when I was counsellor to the High-King. Now Cathach will replace me, and if you should pass this test you will be counsel to the Kingdom of Munster. Learn from the Ravens and trust none but the old one Lom-dubh. He was a great teacher to me in times gone past.'

The wind suddenly rose as it does on the ocean and Gobann was sure that he tasted salt on the breeze and smelled the tang of brine in the air. A horn blew in the distance and it sounded like the signal that the fishermen give when a boat is leaving harbour on a long voyage.

'I must go now,' exclaimed Lorgan urgently. 'May we meet again. And do not forget me.'

As the old man stood up from where he had been perched beside the poet, another aged fellow came and took him by the hand. The pair of grey-beards walked to the edge of the branch, talking together like two men who had long been friends and had shared many trials together. A small curragh came floating through the air, sailing on the falling snow, and it waited for them to embark. There were no oarsmen or crew, but the tiny craft seemed to know where it was going.

The two men sat down and made themselves comfortable, then they both looked back at Gobann as the boat almost disappeared into the hazy whiteness of the landscape. In the not too far distance there was a large dark shape looming through the snowstorm and Gobann could just make out that the curragh headed for this point.

He noticed that the shape seemed to expand a little and realised that the expanded shadow was the shape of sails being set. He knew he was looking on a soul-ship about to set off on a great voyage. In the very next second the snow eased off completely and as it did so the ship vanished from the world taking with it Gobann's beloved teacher.

Directly underneath him there was a great deal of commotion. Men were shouting in a strange language and horses were neighing loudly, but the poet did not take much notice of any of that. His thoughts were still with Lorgan and the other man who had accompanied him. It was a long while before he realised that the other man was King Eoghan Eoghanacht.

Eventually his attention was drawn back to the events unfolding around him. He looked down on the foreigners gathered under the Quicken Tree and he recognised the forms of Murrough and of Caitlin. An overwhelming urge to call out to them came over him and he was just about to do so when he felt a hand touch his sleeve.

Turning his head to see who could have appeared this time, he saw that the Tree was full of little men and women with sparkling blue eyes and bright gold hair. They were all dressed in browns and greens of the most vivid hues, their clothes shimmering in contrast to the whiteness of the snow that had built up on the branches.

The little woman who knelt beside him touched him again and put her hand to her lips gesturing him to silence. Then she broke a small piece of bread from a loaf that she pulled from her cloak. Holding it out in her hand, the little woman offered the morsel to Gobann. He took it from her and devoured it as if he had not eaten for days. It tasted sweet and fresh, like the smell of the first batch of spring honey.

The very moment that he swallowed the bread,

though, a startling change took place in Gobann that was so immediate and so complete that he would later remember nothing but snippets of what came to pass after that. All he would recall was that he transformed into the shape of one of those tiny beings and that he had never before felt so free nor had he ever felt so alive.

Prince Morann, performing his duty at the orders of Leoghaire, did not make directly for the crossroads as his brother had done; instead he took a route over the Eastern Hills, alerting the country as he went so that the Saxons would have less chance of making a clean escape to the sea.

Once he had climbed the range of hills he took only small roads toward the Rock of Cashel, sending out as he went all the newly conscripted warriors to ride on as reinforcements to the crossroads and the Tree. From that gathering point he intended to march the whole army north to aid the High-King if necessary.

He rode on to the King's Hall and the Rock where the King of Munster usually resided. That is how he came to overtake his brother, though he did not expect to, since he knew nothing of what had befallen Murrough's company.

He was still there in Cashel organising troops to help put down the rebellion that Leoghaire expected in the north when the troop of levied guardsmen he had commissioned to ride to the Quicken Tree came galloping wildly into the settlement.

They were yelling about a large party of foreigners, mounted and well armed, marching south directly toward Cashel.

'You deserted your post?' yelled Morann at their captain in utter disbelief.

'We were hopelessly outnumbered,' offered the captain. He was not a regular soldier but one of the wealthier landholders who gave their service in time of need. His guardsmen were little more than peasants, poorly armed and trained and ill disciplined.

'How many of these foreigners were there?' pressed Morann.

'I can't be sure,' was the sheepish reply.

'How many warriors do you have under your command?' queried the war-prince, a deep frown furrowing his brow.

'Only forty, lord,' the captain quickly reckoned.

'And what of the Prince of Cashel and his soldiers? Where did they go?'

'They were not at the place of the Quicken Tree,' stated the captain.

'Why did your troops not hold the crossroads?' gasped Morann.

'We were watching a gathering of Ravens in the Tree,' answered the captain.

'You were not even anywhere near the Tree?' bellowed Morann.

'We were observing from the safety of the high ground. I fear there were just too many of the enemy for us to do anything,' repeated the captain.

'How many?' Morann asked suspiciously.

'I can't be sure.'

'Then you will ride with us back to the Tree and we will count them!' stormed the prince, not wishing to believe a word of it, wondering what could have happened to Murrough to cause him to be almost two days behind schedule.

His thoughts quickly returned to the captain's report. 'This bloody coward may have cost us the

Tree.' He blamed himself for not planning far enough ahead and for trusting the protection of the Tree into the hands of inexperienced warriors.

Despite the great need for haste, there were many preparations to be made and it was three full hours before Morann and sixty troops were ready to set out northwards, and by then the prince was sure it would be dark when his soldiers reached the Tree.

Hannarr was more than usually uncomfortable about having his troops exposed on the open ground. His instincts told him that he was taking a great risk, but there were thousands upon thousands of rowan berries littering the soft grass under the tree and many more in the branches.

What added to the terrible risk of being caught by a patrol of Munster guardsmen was that he had scant few followers left to put to the task of collecting the fruit. Out of Guthwine's original force of three hundred and fifty he had only ten able-bodied warriors at his disposal and no way of transporting the bulk of the precious magic berries.

He quickly resolved to gather as many of them as could be carried and then only if time allowed to cut and burn the tree. The battle-hardened warrior in him began preparing tactics for the whole enterprise as if their labour at the tree was to be a campaign. Summing up the manpower at his disposal, he reckoned there was at least two to three hours of hard work ahead. The voice of reason argued that the risk was too great, but Hannarr enjoyed a challenge. Especially a potentially profitable one.

First he organised his men to gather every available sack or piece of cloth, or anything else that would serve as receptacles to hold the fruit, while he collected all the saddlebags from the horses. Then he set eight of his men to scooping up all the berries that lay around the roots of the tree.

Almost as soon as the party had arrived at the crossroads, Murrough had been dragged off the horse he had lain across and roughly pushed up against the trunk of the great rowan, where he would be out of the way for the time being.

Hannarr surveyed the tough and aged bough, trying to discern the weakest point and the best direction of attack for when he was ready to have it cut down. As he was doing so he began to realise that there were many more riper and fresher berries in the upper branches and this decided him on his course of action.

Despite the enormous risk involved, it would be easier by far to fell the tree and then collect the freshest fruit than to send any of his men clambering about high up in the branches. Having decided the spot on its trunk where he reckoned the tree could be weakened with the least amount of effort, he set two of his strongest warriors to sharpening their blades for the task ahead and Hannarr started gathering kindling to start a fire.

Work was well under way by the time Streng finally trotted down the road at a leisurely pace and joined them. When he had surveyed the scene, he lifted Caitlin into his arms and dismounted. He set her down on the grass and walked around among the warriors, thinking much but commenting little on all that he observed. He took it for granted that he would be excused from any arduous labour on account of his injury.

'Lazy bastard,' thought Hannarr when he noticed Streng, but he let the man do as he wished and did not press the point. He only looked up from his work and scowled at his old adversary.

Streng walked another circuit of the tree and finally, having exhausted the entertainment value of the exercise, approached the thegn and leaned in close to speak, for his voice had lost all of its vitality and was barely audible. 'You're bloody mad,' he stated simply.

Hannarr looked up from the kindling that he had gathered. 'Bugger off,' he replied.

Streng smiled. He had always believed that there was no feeling as good as knowing you were right about something. 'Can't you recognise a trap when you see it?' strained the wounded man.

'What are you talking about?' groaned Hannarr.

'A blind half-drunk milkmaid could tell that those hills are full of eyes watching us, biding their time. I wouldn't be surprised if any moment now an Irish army came charging down that road and slaughtered the lot of us. And your response to the situation?' he chuckled. 'You've got the men picking berries!' He was too delighted to care that his own life was at risk. Hannarr was failing the tests of a good war-leader.

'Shut up,' answered the thegn.

'I can't imagine there's many that are feasting in the halls of Valhalla who got killed plucking fruit!' taunted Streng and he laughed loudly.

Hannarr was tiring of the injured man very quickly, but his words struck a chord in the ever suspicious mind of the Saxon chief.

'Roman,' bawled the thegn, 'come here!'

Streng wandered off, still chortling as best he could considering his infirmity. He went over to where Caitlin lay on the grass and picked her up off the ground. Straining from exhaustion and loss of blood he carried her over to where Murrough lay against the tree and there he dumped her. Then he went off to find some water to cool his burning throat.

'Are you certain that we are not wasting our time with this tree?' demanded Hannarr of Seginus.

'This is the very bough we are seeking,' the Roman declared confidently.

'Give me some proof of its value,' threatened the Saxon, 'or I will waste no more time here. I can feel eyes upon us and I fear being caught out here where there is no place to mount a good defence.'

Seginus looked about him, trying to invent an answer. He knew from what little he had heard that the berries had many virtues when properly mixed but he did not know what was involved in their preparation. And Hannarr was certainly right to think it would not be very long before they were discovered. The crossroads lay open to the surrounding hills. Anyone stopping there could be plainly observed from any of a dozen points along the nearby ridges.

Seginus took a handful of berries from the saddlebag in which he had been collecting them and examined them, cursing himself for not asking Palladius for more details about the Tree. The fruits were indistinguishable from any other rowan berries that could be found in valleys across the northern world. They were totally unremarkable. Some were light scarlet, some were deep blood red and others almost black, but there was no indication that these berries held any of the properties that were attributed to them.

'Roman,' sneered Hannarr, 'I want proof, or we are leaving this place now! And if we leave you will not be riding with us.'

'But the tree must be cut down first!' cried Seginus.

Hannarr reached out swiftly and grasped the Roman by the throat. 'You have been leading us into a bloody trap!' he bawled. 'If you have lied to me about the enchanted fruits, Roman, I will skin the hide off of you and use you for a saddle blanket.'

Seginus was a strong young man who knew many ways to elude the grasp of an enemy but Hannarr was stronger than him by far and as his grip tightened the air was leached out of the Roman's lungs. As the seconds passed Seginus found he could neither fight back nor breathe.

Thegn Hannarr lifted Seginus up by the throat only a few inches above the ground so that his toes barely scraped the Earth and then after what to the Roman seemed an eternity, he let go his hold and dropped him on his back in amongst the pile of kindling.

Murrough watched all of this with a deepening interest. 'Soon enough they will make a mistake and I must be ready for them,' he told himself.

He had been relieved to be put off the horse for a while. His battered stomach muscles ached from the strain of being stretched out over a saddle for so long, but he was much happier to find that Caitlin had been dumped beside him. With effort he rolled over to where she lay and watched her for a few minutes, wishing that he could break the bounds and reach out to touch her.

'I wonder if they will let her live,' he thought.

As if in immediate response to his silent question her eyelids flickered open and she looked him in the face, obviously struggling to focus on him.

'Water!' cried Murrough at the top of his voice. 'We need water over here. She is awake!'

Seginus was lying on his back on the grass catching his breath when he heard Murrough's words. But he did not at first realise their full significance. When the obvious answer to his problem with Hannarr finally came to him, he could have kicked himself for being so stupid. Caitlin's words at Rathowen, the night she had been wounded, came to him again and he remembered that she had proudly stated that she was a Druid as well as a chieftain.

'The girl can brew a concoction that will prove the berries are the ones we seek,' he stuttered at Hannarr.

The Saxon stayed his hand from delivering a blow to the Roman's face. He let the man cower for a moment and eventually moved back a little. 'Then you had better get her to work,' replied the thegn, 'if you value your life.'

At that very moment Streng walked back along the path from the nearby well with a goatskin full of well-water. Seginus, seeing the dripping bag, quickly got up and half-ran, half-staggered over to the man, snatching the skin from him. Then, ignoring Streng's rasping protests, he rushed over to where Murrough and Caitlin lay.

When he got to where the woman lay he carefully removed the wooden stopper and poured the cool clear water over her parched lips and she gulped it greedily. When she had taken her fill, Seginus took out his hunting knife and cut the leather straps that held her forearms together and the ties that prevented her legs and feet from moving.

'Are you all right?' he asked her urgently.

'I have a wound,' she answered vaguely for she had not completely regained her senses.

'Do you know how to prepare the magic

berries?' the Roman pressed her. She did not answer. Her eyes danced around him for a moment until they stilled and she just stared at him with a look of someone who has taken too much mead. 'You are a Druid,' Seginus reminded her, 'you must know!'

Murrough realised his opportunity quickly. He did not understand what had been said between Seginus and the Saxon captain for he did not speak the foreigners' tongue but he saw well enough that deadly threats had been issued and he worked out what had passed between them.

Murrough also knew well the danger involved in dabbling with the berries for he had been told stories of the Tree since childhood. Observing the thegn carefully, he decided that there must be more than the theft of the berries of the sacred tree at stake here, but he could not grasp what that might be.

The Roman somehow had some knowledge about the curative powers of the fruit and probably knew also of a few of their other properties, but he did not know how to go about making the healing tea without aid. That would be to Murrough's advantage.

'She is a Druid and so of course she would know how to mix the sacred brew,' stated the prince. 'But she is too ill to do it herself. If all you want is the healing tea that comes from this fruit, well, she can instruct me and I can then prepare it.'

Seginus looked on the offer with immediate suspicion. 'She can instruct me,' the Roman stated, 'and I will mix it.'

'But there are other herbs that must be gathered,' Murrough lied, 'and the decoction must be tended correctly or it could well become poisonous. I often helped my mother when I was a lad to cook up the tea for those of the kingdom who were ailing.'

Seginus could feel the fingers of Hannarr once again tightening about his throat. He did not trust the prince but he had no alternative if there was to be any hope that the Tree would be destroyed and he might keep his life.

'How do I know you will not brew it up as a poison anyway?' he asked.

'It seems to me that all you need to do is prove the magical properties of the berries,' Murrough guessed. 'There are different recipes that brings out each of the qualities of the Tree's many properties. We will make the healing brew and test it on the Saxon with the throat wound and you will see whether it heals quickly.'

'How quickly will the cure be effected?' queried Seginus nervously.

'It will be immediate and instantaneous,' replied Murrough with a confidence that he did not feel.

'Very well then. I will test it on the girl first,' revealed Seginus, 'so that I know the brew will at least do no harm.'

Seginus took his knife and slit the bonds on Murrough's hands and feet. Fixing a cold gaze on his prisoner and summoning all the menace that his voice was capable of, he demanded, 'What assurance can you give that you will not take this opportunity to escape?'

'What kind of assurance would satisfy you?' asked Murrough.

Seginus spotted the ring that Murrough always wore on his right hand. It was made of gold and had engraved into it the seal of the Prince of Cashel. 'I will take that,' he said, indicating the seal ring.

Murrough hesitated for a moment but finally, seeing no other way to ensure his temporary release, he slipped the ring from his finger and handed it to the Roman.

'That is the seal of my authority as a noble of the royal house of Munster,' warned the prince. 'You must promise to return it to me when I bring you the herbs.'

'I promise,' Seginus swore, having no care whether he kept the vow or not but relieved that he had found a way to placate Hannarr.

TWENTY-ONE

awn suffered less from the cold that night than did most of the occupants of the house of the Star of the Poets. He had lived through several lean winters and knew well the feeling of an empty belly and frozen fingers which country folk took for granted as part of the numerous trials of life.

Sianan had lived a very different life from that of the son of a blacksmith. The life at court of the only grand-daughter of a high Druid was not a difficult one to bear. All the luxuries and comforts of life that her grandsire's position offered she also shared. Cold and hunger were discomforts that had to be endured only when a fire festival coincided with a cold season. Going without food was a voluntary act for her. It was never something that had to be endured for long and so she felt the hours of fasting drag on. In one corner of the hall, shrouded in skins and blankets, she sat shivering and bemoaning in concert with her grumbling stomach and she was joined by many who should have been much more used to this way of life.

The complaining that they all indulged in was as valued a part of the traditional celebrations as the lighting of the fires. Sharing the discomfort among the many of them made the temporary lack of food and fuel much easier for everyone to bear.

Lorgan the Sorn was huddled on a low stool, for

his legs would no longer bend sufficiently to allow him to sit cross-legged like everyone else. He was wrapped in a white wolf-skin that had been a gift from King Niall in the days of long ago when the old Druid had been only a young novice with a quick-witted answer to every problem. At his feet, curled closely together around his ankles, were Lorgan's three faithful dogs, Cailleach, Banatigh and Ainir. They represented three generations of an old and famous breed.

The oldest of the three, Cailleach, was said to be descended of the line of hounds that had served at the side of Fionn MacCumhal the great warrior who lived in the time of King Cormac Mac Airt and of whom so many tales had been remembered. When she was a six-week-old puppy she had been gifted to Lorgan for a poetic eulogy he had composed on a friend's passing. He had been in need of a bed-warmer and she of a regular meal so they hit it off well and became close companions. Cailleach was fiercely loyal to her master and rarely did he travel without her until she had grown too old to run beside his horse all day.

Cailleach gave birth in her third year to ten healthy pups all of which Lorgan had bartered away save for one sickly looking female that no-one had been interested in. In time she became known as Banatigh. This hound was supremely intelligent, a rare animal that always seemed to be watching what was going on, as if taking it all in for future reference. And she had a way with people that Lorgan greatly admired. Banatigh had the ruling of the old poet's home and she did not suffer fools to stay long under his roof. That is why Lorgan kept her: she had always been an excellent judge of character, picking up on things that he never noticed and saving him from many embarrassing or tiresome situations. And that was the reason why she was called, tongue in cheek, 'woman of the house'.

Cailleach never bore any other pups; she had not found the exercise to be a very enjoyable experience and studiously avoided male dogs ever after. Banatigh though, bore three litters, the last of which yielded a rare black-coated hound that Lorgan decided would be a good house dog. He had proven to be right for Ainir turned out to have all the best qualities of her grandmother and mother woven into her character from birth.

These three dogs were more than his companions, they were his only true friends in the world. All of his contemporaries were long dead and even his sons and daughters had passed on. His grandchildren had taken ship with the settlers that sailed to the kingdom of the Dal Araidhe. He was alone.

Sianan had spent a lot of her time with Ainir playing in the Gríanan, the puppy often trotting closely behind her on her long expeditions in and around the citadel. But on a night of fasting when the wind was burdened with snow and even the lapdogs were not given any meat, Ainir preferred the company of her master and the embraces of her family.

Cathach played at the Brandubh with Mawn, seemingly giving all his attention to the boy, but he watched out of the corner of one eye every movement that Lorgan made in the stirrings of his sleep. Lorgan's prophecy of his own death had made Cathach realise that soon he would be the senior adviser in the land. Soon he would have to move to Teamhair to be the High-King's counsellor. Someone would need to be chosen to take his place at Cashel in the court of Eoghan.

'There is still so much that Lorgan can teach me,' thought Cathach. 'I must drink of the knowledge that he carries within him before he passes on.' With the practicality that came of a life of gathering learning from aged teachers, Cathach promised himself that he would spend the daylight hours on the morrow in conversation with the old man.

'He is likely the only man left alive in Eirinn who remembers the days of Niall of the Nine Hostages,' remembered Cathach, 'yet he rarely speaks of those days.' Cathach tried to reckon how old Lorgan must be. It was not an easy thing to do while also keeping an eye on the attacks of Mawn's Ravens. 'He must be over ninety summers old,' he realised. 'Strange that I have never really thought of him as being old at all.'

Mawn picked up a piece and Cathach was stirred from his thoughts to observe the move.

'Why was Lorgan not at Gobann's ritual?' the boy asked the older Druid.

Cathach was a little disarmed at the comment. Mawn had an eerie ability to be able to pick up on what people were thinking. Cathach had heard Gobann speak about the boy's gift but had not experienced it. As a Druid with many years of learning, the old counsellor had grown accustomed to treating such things as unremarkable but there was something about Mawn's uncanny ability, coupled with what Cathach knew about the boy's destiny, that he found distinctly unnerving. He almost felt as though he should guard his thoughts from the boy.

'Lorgan suffers too much from the cold,' Cathach answered finally. 'His hands and feet do not respond well when the temperature drops.'

'He is not long for this world,' Mawn stated in agreement.

'His infirmity is merely a symptom of great age. When one lives so many seasons the body gradually wears out like a well used cartwheel until one day the spokes give way and the iron-shod circle collapses in on itself.'

'Can the cart continue on its journey with only one wheel?' asked Mawn.

Cathach was about to explain that there would be someone to replace the old man when the time came, when he realised that Mawn had expanded on his analogy of the cartwheel in the manner of a very world-wise soul. The Druid was unexpectedly struck by a strong sense that he was not talking with a boy of only nine summers.

Cathach felt an immediate urge to bare his soul to this young fellow, to tell of all his fears and of all the pain of the past that he held inside him, and of all the things that he had buried deep inside his inner being. The desire in him to pour out his feelings was so overwhelming that he was compelled to open his mouth to speak. What held him back, though, was another jolting revelation that came from a subtle implication in the boy's turn of phrase.

'I am the other cartwheel,' he thought, 'the one that may have to carry on alone for a while.' Then he turned his mind to Gobann and he wished that he could somehow penetrate the mound of stones wherein the poet sat, if only to look on him and see for himself that the man had not succumbed to the arduous test that had been set him.

As Caitlin began to regain consciousness under the low enclosing branches of the Quicken Tree, all she felt was pain. Her stomach was badly bruised from the long ride with Streng and her breathing was strained. The next thing she became aware of was that the ground on which she lay was soft with the carpet of grass, fallen leaves and fruits.

Noticing the way the ground hugged her she felt herself relaxing and her breathing was instantly easier. Her hands spread out on the grass and she was certain that at least for the time being she was safe, though she did not open her eyes or even concern herself with anything that was happening beyond her sense of touch.

Even when she began to discern that the ground was lightly vibrating she did not become alarmed but sharpened her other senses to take in what was happening. It took some minutes for her to be able to hear clearly the low humming sound that she guessed was related in some way to the vibrations that her fingers were picking up.

It was not an unfamiliar sensation to her. In the days of her youth and her Druidic training she had often sought out the places where she knew she could encounter this emanation of energy. There were several places near to Rathowen, she remembered, and many around the hill of Teamhair. Sometimes they were marked with a well or a circle of standing stones or a tree or even a lonely cairn of rocks; but each of them had been holy places long before her people had come to this land.

The magic of the Tuatha-De-Danaan remained as strong in Eirinn as it had been for two thousand years and the gateways to their hidden lands were marked at points such as these. There were a few folk, she knew, who could sense where these gateways offered access to the Faery peoples into the world of men and women. She was one of those folk.

The next thing she perceived was the strong

smell of wood smoke on her clothes, as if she had spent a long while before the fire or had rolled in the cold ashes of it. She had the impression that she had not washed for many days and this made her a little uncomfortable, for she knew she had probably soiled her riding gear.

Her five senses ran through a catalogue of observations and deductions before she began finally to wonder where she was. Unwilling to open her eyes, for she was not eager to risk losing the soothing sensation of the humming beneath her, she started thinking back as far as she could to the very last thing that had been in her mind when she had fallen asleep.

In an instant she remembered that it was not sleep that had taken her, but that she had been suffering the results of her leg wound. Eyes still shut she slowly inched her hand down her thigh tenderly testing the flesh for any sign of pain. She could not quite reach her knee without moving her torso but she could tell that the wound was well healed. Only when she was able to tell herself that she would certainly live did she feel ready at last to view the world around her and to quench her curiosity of all that had happened while she slept.

Gingerly and with infinite patience her eyelids parted to let in the light. The first thing that she noticed was the low branches of the great tree that nearly reached the tips of their fingers to the ground and sheltered her from the snow that she could see falling lightly but steadily just beyond. Her last memory was of being stifled by heat, though she knew that was probably from the infection she had taken, and she was a little taken aback to see the snow. It only took her a few moments after that to begin feeling cold.

Beside her she could discern a man lying out-stretched. He was struggling a little as if his arms were paralysed. Her curiosity did not extend to turning her head to see who he was though. There were horses nearby and she was watching them. There were warriors who crossed the path of her vision and seemed to be gathering handfuls of leaves and snow, but she did not ask herself why.

The next thing that she knew was the sound of a man yelling out for help and though she was sure that he was utilising the full force of his voice, she was a little disturbed that it reached her ears as a dull muffled roar, almost as if he were speaking to her from under the ground.

She eventually tried to shift her head but her neck muscles were so strained from her being carried on horseback for so long that she had to move very slowly so as not to aggravate the stiff-ened sinews.

Then she received a shock that she would long remember. A man came ducking under the branches, almost crawling along the grass to reach her in his urgency. When he got up close and crouched alongside her he proceeded to touch her cheeks and then to examine the whites of her eyes by pulling back the lids a little.

The man filled her vision; she could not help but stare into his face and though it took a long while for her to recognise him, when she did she gasped loudly as if an unseen hand had delivered a heavy blow to her guts.

She managed to open her mouth and the man's name was on her lips. 'Seginus Gallus,' she whispered.

She could hear the Roman talking to someone nearby but could not hear clearly what was said, so she tried to sit up and observe the movement of his lips hoping that she could work out what was going on.

As she moved her elbow under her to raise her body she noticed another man behind Seginus. He was perhaps the strangest creature that Caitlin had ever seen. There was a strange light about him that danced in many hues of blue, sometimes totally engulfing his body so that she could only make out the general shape of his form.

He stood upright even though there was only enough room for a man to half crouch under the sweeping branches and he seemed to make no impression on the snow or even to sink slightly into it. Whenever the eerie blueness that surrounded the man softened in its intensity, she could make out dark patterns of green-blue painted onto his skin.

She struggled to rationalise what she was seeing. 'A small man standing no higher than my hips,' she told herself, 'adorned as the wild people of the Cruitne paint themselves, naked and making no mark upon the soft new-fallen snow.' The only possible answer was not necessarily the easiest one for her to accept for she had never encountered the Tuatha-De-Danaan.

She briefly began to wonder what one of the Faery folk could be doing travelling with the likes of Seginus Gallus but there was no obvious answer.

Then as if the tiny man had heard her thoughts he spoke to reassure her.

'They cannot see me,' he began. His voice was clear as the ringing of the goats' bells on a mountainside and it startled Caitlin a little because she could still only hear the Roman speaking in a muffle. 'Do not fear, I have been sent to ensure that no harm comes to you,' he continued.

His voice was soothing and familiar, the tones

reminding her of all that she held sacred. In momentary panic the ghastly form of Fintan's wraith came back to mind, but this was no disembodied soul who stood before her. No, this was something else entirely.

A wave of exhaustion washed over her then and she struggled desperately to keep her eyes open but the little man came and brushed them shut with the palm of his hand and she could resist the urge to drift away no longer. She lowered herself back down upon the grass and told herself, 'I will rest only a short while,' and then once more she slept.

It was a short sleep but one full of many vivid dreams of the kind that are hard to distinguish from reality. In one dream she was a white-feathered swan flying in over the Irish Sea from the lands to the east. As she looked down on the land of Eirinn she saw the smoke from many fires. Where the forests had once stood she saw only scarred empty fields and with breaking heart she glided over toward the hill of Teamhair. As she cast her gaze about the familiar landscape of that place she could not find the citadel. It was not where it should have been.

Winging her way back in a tight circle she carefully scanned the ground again until she found a small hill and a few mounds of earth that were where the High-King's enclosure once had been. Coming to earth she took her own form again and walked the fields around about until she came to a small wattle and daub hut. It was the only structure within the great enclosure that had once been the seat of the Kingship of Eirinn.

A man poked his head out the door of the hut when he heard her footfall and challenged her in a strange dialect of Gaelic that she could only just make sense of. Then she noticed the wickerwork cross above the doorframe and the strange man came out of his hut holding another crucifix before him like a warrior might carry his shield.

When she realised that he was a Christian priest she flew up as a swan again and in a moment her arms had become wings once more and she was sailing away on the breeze winging toward the south. There was a yearning in her soul that drew her in that direction and she had not gone far before she was joined by several other bright swans who came in close and brushed her with their wings as they passed. At the sight of one of them her heart leapt for joy, though he was indistinguishable from all the others and she called his name out loud for the happiness that the sound of the word gave her.

'Murrough!'

'I am here,' answered the prince. 'You will be fine now. The illness is passing.'

Caitlin snapped her eyes open and stared up at him in disbelief, wrenching her mind from the dream state as quickly as she could and striving to take in the world around her. She searched around briefly for the painted Danaan, but the little man was gone.

'How are you feeling?' Murrough asked with obvious urgency in his voice.

'I feel like I have slept too long, but I am much recovered,' answered Caitlin, surprised at the confidence she was expressing in herself.

'Close your eyes and listen to me,' whispered Murrough urgently. 'Do not give any sign that you are awake and feeling well.'

Caitlin shut her eyes and did as she was told. She could hear voices not far off and they spoke the Saxon tongue. She could not understand their speech at all but the guttural sound of it was unmistakable to her after her experiences at Rathowen.

'What is going on?' she asked him, keeping her words low so that she would not be overheard. 'Where are we?'

'We are at the crossroads of Cashel and we are sheltered under the very tree we were sent to protect,' Murrough explained. 'But we are prisoners of the Roman, Seginus, and his band of Saxons.'

'Seginus!' hissed Caitlin.

'You know him?' Murrough asked, puzzled.

'Yes. He visited Rathowen on the evening before Dichu's army came upon us. He claimed to be seeking our conversion to the Cross but we had expected Palladius to send spies to scout out the defences and we were ready to mislead him.'

Murrough put his hand gently over her mouth to stop her talking as two Saxons passed by dangerously close.

'We must be careful,' he warned her when the enemy were out of earshot. 'The Roman means to try to use the berries of the Quicken Tree to make a healing tea.'

'What?' gasped Caitlin trying to keep her voice low. 'He has no idea how dangerous that is.'

'He wants you to prepare the decoction for him so that he can see that it really has the properties that he has been told of. The Saxon chief has demanded the test. They mean to steal the berries and to escape to their ships with them.'

'Where did they learn of the berries?'

'I do not know,' replied Murrough. 'Do you know how to make the healing tea?'

'I know how to make a tea for cleaning the blood and the kidneys,' answered Caitlin, 'but that is

411

made with the berries of an ordinary rowan, not the fruit of this tree.'

'They would have you make the tea and then they will see what effect it has on you.'

'But I do not know how to prepare this fruit! The brew could turn out to be poisonous for all I know!'

'Brewing the tea may buy us valuable time,' Murrough explained. 'It cannot be long before word gets to Cashel about our capture or reinforcements arrive from the Rock to help guard the Tree. If we can hold the Saxons here until then, they will surely be defeated and this Roman captured.'

'What do they expect to gain from collecting the berries?' Caitlin muttered, asking the question more of herself than of Murrough.

'Seginus has told them that the fruit is the source of immortality. The Saxon leader is looking at the berries as a commodity that would be worth a fortune to the right buyer and make his warriors deathless into the bargain. As far as he is concerned, anything that could ensure that he and his men are still raiding in a hundred years' time is worth investigating.'

'We must do something to stop them finding out about the fruit!' breathed Caitlin. 'If they stumble on the secret of the berries by accident it could be disastrous for the Druid Council's plans.'

'What do you mean?' asked the prince, puzzled. 'What secret?'

'My understanding is that the berries only have the power to grant a longer than normal lifespan when they are eaten just as they fall from the Tree, without any preparation whatsoever. Every Druid has heard that story, but the tale has always been put out that there is a special recipe that must be followed before the fruit will have any healing properties. The rumour was that even the slightest deviation from the recipe would render the berries poisonous so as to put off any who might have wished to use the fruit for their own ends.'

'Will it be safe for you to drink the tea?' queried Murrough.

'I am not sure,' she answered honestly. 'Let us hope that it does not come to that. In the meantime I will pretend that my illness is far worse than it really is so that if I am forced to take it they will at least believe the decoction works.'

'I have had them believe that you are incapable of gathering other necessary herbs for the making of the brew,' added Murrough, 'so that they will be forced to release me to do that work.'

'Good,' replied Caitlin. 'That may well be a situation we can take advantage of.'

'I will call the Roman to us now,' he said finally. 'Are you ready?'

'I am,' Caitlin assured him, and as she said those words her hand sought out his and squeezed his fingers lightly. 'Thank you Murrough,' she said sincerely and she raised herself up enough to be able to kiss him lightly on the cheek. She lingered there with her face close to his for a long moment. 'Thank you,' she repeated.

The Prince of Cashel gripped her hand for a second also when she began to release her clasp, he drew it to his lips and gently kissed her on the open palm. Just then Caitlin heard someone approaching so she drew her hand back sharply and Murrough blushed. A few moments later he was gone to fetch the Roman and Caitlin was regretting that her move may have scared him off.

Seginus wasted no time in returning to where the young woman lay; this time he brought a full skin-bag of fresh well-water and another bag full of the reddest berries.

When Caitlin had drunk her fill, the Roman threw her a piece of bread that he had scavenged from one of the guardsmen's packs.

'Can you brew the potion of healing?' he asked her bluntly.

'I can,' replied Caitlin, 'if I have all the other herbs that go into its making, but I cannot go to gather them: my wound is badly poisoned.'

'Tell me what they are and I will seek them out for you,' Seginus demanded.

'I do not know their Roman names, only the Gaelic terms and I doubt that any of these plants grow in your country anyway so how will you recognise them?' she countered.

It was just as Seginus had feared. He could now see no way of getting the task completed without letting one of the two prisoners range free to seek all the ingredients. He weighed up the risks of the exercise against the fury of the Saxons if he failed to produce a proof of the berries' power. Good sense told him that he really had no choice at all.

'Very well,' he relented, 'the prince will go in search of the herbs, with an armed escort. You will stay here and start preparing the brew.' Then he turned to Murrough. 'Do not think of betraying my trust in you, prince, or I can assure you that there will be nothing to stop the Saxons from taking advantage of this situation. And when they are finished with the good lady Druid,' he added, 'I will make sure that she suffers further for your stupidity.'

'He will do as you say, Roman,' flashed Caitlin. 'We Druids always keep our word and I give my promise that he will not try to escape.'

'You have my ring, Roman,' stated Murrough, 'that is my promise.'

Seginus laughed a breathy laugh through his

414

teeth that moved the phlegm in his throat and Caitlin remembered that night in the tower at Rathowen when he had spat at her. 'If only Fintan were here now,' she thought. She heard a voice and knew that no-one else could hear it.

'Fintan is gone,' remarked the little man, 'he has taken the boat westwards. You must rely on Murrough now.'

The Roman saw her eyes glaze over and assumed that it was a result of her illness. He reached down and grabbed her roughly by the chin. 'You should have converted to the Cross when I gave you the chance, then you would not have come to this. So many of you heathens think that you can hold back the hand of God. May this be a lesson to you, milkmaid. Now even your pagan Tree is serving Christ, for nothing on Earth can resist Him.'

Seginus then left to report to Hannarr exactly what was happening; but, despite the Roman's pleading for time, the thegn was not convinced that they should wait around under the tree in daylight standing out like red bulls in a herd of white cows.

'It will be dark in a few hours anyway,' reasoned Seginus, 'and then we will be well covered. With all these clouds it will be a very black night. We can leave at first light.'

Hannarr knew they had stayed too long. Even if they set out straightaway they would not get far before nightfall. And the night would be very dark, too dark for travelling. 'Very well,' he relented, 'we will stay here, but it had better be worth it.'

'You will see for yourself the power of the berries and you will be able to learn the recipe for making the healing tea,' enthused Seginus.

'I said all right, Roman,' bellowed Hannarr, 'we will stay! Now go about your business and leave me alone.'

Seginus rose quickly and carefully moved out of reach of the Saxon, then he went to see if the cooking fire was ready.

Seated on a low rock within earshot of everything that passed between Seginus and the Saxon thegn, Streng chuckled audibly and roughly and strained his voice to say, 'You are a bloody fool Thegn Hannarr.'

Hannarr did not catch exactly what he said for the throat injury had greatly affected the volume of his speech, but he caught the tone and guessed the content. He decided to ignore the man.

TWENTY-TWO

In the hall of the Star of the Poets at Teamhair, as elsewhere in the Royal enclosure, the first full night of fasting was a slow one. Not all of the nobles and chieftains were required to abstain from food—that was something only the Druid-chosen indulged in—and there were many for whom there was no change in the daily diet of mead or ale and fresh meat. But they did not hunt game at this time for it was considered to be a very dangerous season to be out of doors.

If Druids could be lured into the otherworld, then so too could ordinary folk who had not been initiated into the mysteries, for it was well known that the price the Tuatha-De-Danaan paid for their immortality was that they were forever infertile among their own people. To keep their bloodline alive they found it necessary to abduct humans from their homes and keep them in their fortresses to produce offspring who were half human and half Faery.

At this time of year the Faery hunt ran across the country and unwary Gaelic folk could easily become involved in the chase only to find that they returned not to their own enclosure but to the Danaan hillfort at the end of the day. By the time they realised their mistake the gates had closed fast behind them. There were many human captives in the underground palaces of the Sidhe folk.

417

More cunningly a Faery man might take the form of a stag and run the human hunters into a secluded valley where there was a feast prepared for them.

But should any of the hunters partake of the food and mead then they were surely unable to leave the valley again except at the whim of the King of the Danaans.

Whenever a man fell from his horse at this time it was said that if a Faery woman could catch him before he touched the earth he would be bound to her for a year and a day. But time runs differently in the enchanted lands of the Sidhe folk. A year might easily equal a hundred among the people of Eirinn. Many was the wanderer who returned from a seemingly short visit in the Faery country to find the world had changed and all his kin were dead and he was spoken of by the old folk as a legend and a warning to all of the dangers of Beltinne.

This time of year was surely a dangerous time to be out and about but Samhain was even more so for that festival took place in the dark of the year and it was a time when it was not breeding that was on the mind of the Danaans but revenge and the wreaking of havoc among the descendants of the Sons of Mil. Sometimes they broke the truce and took souls captive as slaves.

It was a fragile peace, the one between the Gaels and the Danaans, and no more so than at times when the doorways between the two worlds were open.

Outside the hall of the Star of the Poets the wind was fierce through the night and Mawn stirred often in his sleep, sure that he had heard voices just outside. It was as if there were many people waiting around just beyond the walls, but the door did not open to admit them and no-one entered the hall.

Sianan had curled up close to Mawn just before they went to sleep for they had become used to keeping each other warm through the nights. She woke up with a start when all else was quiet and Mawn stirred also, used to her fitful nightmares but sensitive to them nevertheless.

'I cannot sleep,' she mumbled. 'I dreamt that my mother had returned from the Well of Bridgit.'

Mawn pricked up his ears. This well was something he had never heard of.

'What is the Well of Bridgit?' he asked her.

'That is the place where women go when they have no-one else in the world to look after them and they wish to learn to be Druids,' she answered. 'My father went to the Danaans to study their music when I was born and my mother took a vow that she would not speak a word until he returned. And so she lives with the other Druid women at Bridgit's Well.'

'Do you remember your mother and father?' Mawn gently enquired.

'No,' she replied bluntly. 'I do not even recall what my parents looked like or how they sounded when they spoke.' Tears welled up in her eyes and Mawn felt he could hold back his emotions no longer.

'You are very lucky,' he told her.

'Lucky!' she gasped. 'In what way am I lucky?'

'I remember my mother and my father and every one of my kinfolk. But I am sure I will never see them again. They are all dead and I am left alone now in the world.'

'But did not Gobann go to your village and find you? How could they have all perished since then?'

'The Roman, Seginus Gallus, had something to do with it, though I do not know exactly how he is involved in the deaths of my mother and father.

I only know that the place of my birth is empty now save for the few lost spirits who have not yet realised that they have perished.'

'When did you find out about this?' she gasped.

'I knew they were all dead when I saw my brother, whom the Romans hung on the death tree. No-one told me but I knew,' he said.

'You have never before mentioned that he was your brother!' Sianan exclaimed.

'Gobann told me that a Druid must be strong and sometimes lay aside his own troubles so that the greater troubles of the world can be healed.'

'I am so sorry, Mawn,' Sianan sobbed, hugging him closer, 'you are right. I do not miss my family, really, because I never had a family, but it must be a terrible thing to lose everyone that you love, all in one blow.'

'I will be your family, Sianan,' promised Mawn, choking back a sob, 'and you can be mine.'

Sianan thought about what he said for a second and then added, 'Yes. We will always look after each other, even when we are both old poets. And we will only talk of what hurts us to each other. That way we will be good Druids. Anyway, adults never really want to hear what children say.'

Mawn quickly agreed. 'They do not have as many feelings as we do and they don't know what it is like to be happy.'

Just then, Ainir, Lorgan's youngest hound, came over to snuggle up against Sianan. The puppy also rolled onto Mawn a little as she settled. At first it struck the boy as strange that the dog would leave her master and the warmth of her family to be with Sianan and him, but then a figure walked slowly across the hall and Mawn realised why the pup had stirred.

Lorgan came quietly over to where the children

had been sleeping and he bent down to kiss the girl on the forehead. She closed her eyes as he did so and rolled over to hug her arms about Ainir's neck. Then the old man reached out a hand and touched Mawn on the forehead.

'Bless you both, my children,' he whispered, 'and remember that you can always seek me out for advice. I will be waiting for you to summon me one day.' Ainir stirred and let out a pitiful whine and then crawled under Sianan's covers.

Mawn had no chance to ask the old man what he meant before the Druid rose to his full height and strode toward the entrance of the hall. The next thing that Mawn knew, the snow was blowing in through the flapping door and some novice was struggling to shut it again. The boy went to sleep again and dreamed no dreams until he woke at morning.

Just after the sun rose, Cathach went to wake Lorgan the Sorn for the morning observances. He found the old man still seated in his chair with his chin resting gently on his chest. One of his dogs, Banatigh, had her head in his lap and was trying to nuzzle his hand onto her nose. Cathach looked on that face that was so dear to him and knew that the hand would never stroke his dog's snout again.

Lorgan was dead.

Murrough took as long as was safe to do so seeking out as many different herbs as he could. He was searching only for those that he knew would have no significant effect on the properties of the rowan-berry tea. He wanted to take no risk if Caitlin was forced at any point to drink her brew.

Two Saxons accompanied him, and as they

spoke no Gaelic and knew no herb lore, it was not difficult for the prince to waste time. There were few plants yet blooming and in the snow it was not easy to find anything green, but that aided Murrough in his task.

As the sun was coming close to setting the guards became agitated. They had instructions to return their captive to the Tree before dark whether he had all the ingredients for the tea or not and so they were getting impatient to return.

The prince had a small bag crammed with a few fresh leaves and stems and roots of various native plants and the Saxons were more and more insistent, so finally Murrough relented and they headed back toward the crossroads.

At the well not far from the Tree, Murrough demanded that they collect some of the refreshing water and the three men stopped to drink of the icy liquid. The guards filled their drinking bottles and the prince leaned over the leather well-bucket to scoop water into his mouth.

He had just filled his mouth for a second time when he heard a noise that sounded through every fibre of his body shocking him with every wave of its reverberation. Across the short distance between the crossroads and its water source came the shrill and frantic note of a woman's scream.

Caitlin.

With a rising fear and a sickening feeling in his gut the prince dropped the bucket and the bag of herbs and bolted away from his unwary guards.

It took the pair of foot-weary men a few seconds to react to the fact that he was running off and even when they did they both slipped in the snow such was their surprise.

Murrough did not care that he was endangering his own life by breaking away from the two

Saxons. All he heard was a call for help and everything else seemed unimportant.

In a few moments Caitlin's cry died down and he instinctively knew that she was in no immediate danger. But then another sound met his ears and if there was anything on Earth that could have affected him more than a threat to Caitlin, it was this.

The trees around about and the very earth echoed with the steady pounding noise of broad, iron blades striking deep into the green flesh of a standing bough.

Now all his thoughts went to the Quicken Tree. He ran on toward it, approaching the slight rise where the Tree grew by the crossroads, but with each dull heavy thump that reached him he lost a little more hope. His heart was beating loud in his ears and his hands were numb with an overwhelming hopelessness. He fell hard in a drift of snow cutting his knees on a hidden rock, but still the dreadful beating continued, so he dragged himself to his feet again and ran on.

As he was struggling to the top of the rise he heard Caitlin calling to the elements in an invocation that spoke of the desperation in her heart.

'Wind that is the Air come from the East,
Wave of the Water come from the West,
Flame of the Fire come from the South,
Mountain of the Earth come from the North,
People of the Hills, fair Danaans, come to our
    aid,
Trees of the forest rise and march to help your
    brother who is falling at the hands of
    foreigners.'

The axes crashed into the Tree without any regard for her pleas, but the snow fell heavier and the wind rose and the clouds spat a little lightning.

'What is she saying?' Hannarr yelled at Seginus.

'She is calling on the elements to intervene,' answered the Roman.

Hannarr did not wait for any further explanation; he was a sailor and sailors are superstitious men. He ran over to her and slapped her to the ground with the back of his hand. She immediately stood up again and resumed her chant, this time with more vigour. The Saxon raised his hand again and struck her a second time, harder and with deadly intent. This time her head hit the ground with a thud and she did not get up.

Murrough was rushing down the gentle rise directly toward the Tree when he saw, out of the corner of his eye, the thegn's first blow connect with Caitlin's face. Torn between two loyalties he stopped in his tracks, undecided about which cause was more urgent. When the Saxon struck her a second time something inside Murrough snapped. He turned away from the two axe-men who were spilling the sap of the ancient rowan and headed now directly for Hannarr, his blood fairly boiling, his voice giving full vent to his outrage as he let out a high-pitched battlecry.

He did not reach the man, though. A half-dozen Saxon warriors stood between him and the object of his hatred and the prince was quickly tackled to the ground and held there, his face turned to watch the brutal act unfolding before him.

So it was that Murrough, Prince of Cashel, son of Eoghan of the Eoghanacht, came to witness the killing of the Quicken Tree that had been in the keeping of his clan for nearly a thousand years. Two large warriors held him down in the snow as the axe-men finished their hard task. And gruelling labour it was too, for, though their blades were

424

well honed, the Tree resisted them with every splinter of its body. When the first pair of axe-men were spent, two more stepped forward to continue the work and then two more when that pair was exhausted.

All the while Caitlin lay on the ground and did not move, but she was not unconscious. When Hannarr struck her the second time, the voice that had spoken to her when she first regained consciousness talked to her again. 'Do not rise!' he urged her. 'The savage will surely kill you if you do.' And though she could not see the little man she knew that he was right. She lay where she was and waited.

Whether or not Caitlin or Murrough expected that the Tree would somehow defend itself or that some magic force would protect it or perhaps that a host of the Sidhe folk would ride down the Cashel Road to prevent the desecration of their holy bough, they could do nothing more and both were resigned to watching the Tree fall.

The fresh axe-men worked their way around the trunk, penetrating the inner core of the Tree by stripping away the outer fleshy layers of timber one by one. This was such an ancient tree that the wood was as solid as stone, harder than any that the Saxons had ever cut. It blunted their axes and weakened even their strong arms which were used to heavy toil. It jolted them with every blow.

When the heart of the trunk was bared the great bough began creaking and groaning and the sound of timber splintering cut through the cool air. The axe-men worked on, sweating and straining until the fourth shift took over the work.

They had not been cutting long and they had seemingly made little impact when quite unexpectedly the Quicken Tree lurched over toward its attackers as if in a last desperate bid to stop their hacking. Then with a mighty crash that sent leaves and branches and berries and snow flying in all directions, it fell. The earth shook under its impact and the noise of it falling echoed over the plain.

When all was settled the branches began snapping under their own weight and the Tree rolled onto its side. Somewhere in the tangle of broken timber two Saxons lay dead, crushed and lifeless under its mass.

With one ear pressed forcibly into the ground by his guards, Murrough thought he heard a lamenting cry issue from beneath the soil. He could discern many voices raised in anguish and in rage and behind their angry vengeful words the distant skirl of the war-pipes carried on the breeze down the road from the direction of Cashel. And the tune these pipers played was no lament; it was a battle cry, a stir to war.

He expected that the sound would die off for he held only a dim hope that the armies of the Sidhe would arrive now to take revenge on the savages who had murdered their tree. They had not taken arms in full force for ten long centuries, not since the coming of the Gaels, but this atrocity was surely too much for them to bear.

Caitlin heard the war-pipes too and it put her in mind of the fighting on the battlements at Rathowen when the High-King's warriors had arrived unexpectedly to rescue her garrison. But when, after many minutes, the skirling did not abate she opened her eyes to see if there really were warriors coming to their aid. The first thing she saw seated before her on a branch fallen from the Quicken Tree was the little man she had spoken with earlier. She knew now that she did not have to speak directly to him, he heard her thoughts as clearly as her spoken words.

'Do not fear,' he told her, 'everything on this Earth must die one day.'

'But the Tree was essential to the Druid Council's plan. What will happen now to all we have worked for?' she asked him in her thoughts.

'Never mind about that,' he replied flippantly. 'Look, I have a gift for you.' He pulled out what seemed to be broad, leaf-bladed sword enclosed in a black leather scabbard that he had carried tucked into his belt. 'Take this and keep it well hidden. It has a magic blade. It may save your life.'

She reached over to grasp the sword but just as she would have touched it he drew it back from her grasp. 'Of course you must give me something in return,' he chided.

'I have nothing of any value to give,' she pleaded.

'I know that you do,' he rebuked her.

Caitlin had heard countless tales of the mischievous tricks and difficult ways of the Sidhe folk. Now she remembered that they rarely gave any gift without asking something of value in return. 'What would I have that you could possibly want?' she begged him.

'A little something as a Beltinne gift, something wrought in silver perhaps?' he replied, taunting her.

'I have nothing,' she implored, recalling that it could well be Beltinne by now for she had lost track of time while she was unconscious. 'Everything I own is back at Rathowen.'

'Not even the nut of an oak tree? Or a tiny silver dog? Or a Raven? Not even a wise old salmon cast in precious metal?' he mocked.

Then Caitlin remembered the trinket that

Gobann had given her as a parting gift. She searched around under the folds of her clothes and drew it out. It had not been pilfered by any of the Saxons and was still strung on its leather cord. For a moment she examined it and though she had carried it for days this was the first time that she had really looked at it and she found that it was truly beautiful. For a split second she was unwilling to part with it, but Gobann's words returned to her: 'I do not know who it is for, but I trust that you will know when the time comes.'

Caitlin grasped the silver acorn with its intricate interwoven animals as if she would never let it go. 'I only have this,' she offered eventually, handing it out for him to inspect.

The little man's eyes lit up immediately and he made a snatch for the piece of silverwork, but Caitlin pulled it back out of his reach before his fingers even grazed the surface of the acorn.

'You may have it when I have the sword,' she informed him, 'and not before.'

His bright blue eyes darted furtively about him and finally he nodded his head in agreement.

Like two merchants exchanging goods in a marketplace known for its thieves, they slowly presented their wares to each other, each keeping a firm hold on their own precious object. When the sword was within reach, Caitlin grabbed it and in the same instant the little man gripped his long fingers tightly about the silver acorn. Neither let go of their own treasure until both had looked the other in the eye.

The little man winked and slowly loosed his grip on the sword and Caitlin did the same with the acorn. Finally each of them sat with their new prize hugged close to their chest.

The next thing that Caitlin knew was that the little man was laughing wildly. She looked at the sword, sure now that she had been cheated somehow by the wily Sidhe-man. In a manner of speaking she had.

In her hand was no sword but only a short bladed scian-dubh, the type of black handled knife commonly carried by musicians. It was a beautiful example with a deep rust-red stone set in silver in the handle and many knotwork designs interlaced across the surface of the hilt, but it was certainly not a sword. She realised that since he was so much smaller than her he had easily been able to trick her into thinking the knife was much larger than it really was.

She breathed out loudly and heavily in frustration, lifting her face to where he sat in order to complain to him, but the little man was gone.

'A trick of the Sidhe-folk at Beltinne. I can't believe I fell for such a simple ruse,' she rebuked herself. Suddenly she remembered where she was and she tucked the knife into the top of her boot where it would be concealed.

Then she checked the scene about her, careful not to give any outward indication of shock when she noticed that the Saxons were beginning to prepare a hasty defence of their position.

They too had seen the long column of horsemen galloping down the Cashel Road from the south. Caitlin did not immediately realise that the sound of war-pipes and the line of horsemen represented an impending rescue. Such a possibility was more than she could have hoped for. As the small force came closer there was no doubt that these soldiers were warriors of Munster led by Morann for they carried the green banner of Cashel. The faces of the Saxons showed plainly their fear at seeing them and Caitlin began to recognise that there was some hope of survival for her and the Prince of Cashel.

'This will all soon be over,' she tried to convince herself. 'And though we have lost the Tree, at least there will be no more fighting and Murrough and I will live to tell the tale of all that happened here. And more important, we will be able to salvage a good supply of the berries.'

Hope had no sooner entered her heart than she realised that the Saxons were preparing to fight to the death. All around her the foreigners were gathering fallen timber and creating a barricade with the trunk of the Tree as its main wall. The branches offered plenty of cover from arrow-shafts and because of the plentiful growth on the Tree, any horse-warriors who wished to broach the defences would have to dismount to do so. That would prove a costly exercise for the warriors of Munster.

Caitlin watched the Saxons darting to and fro, digging hasty ditches in which to shelter when the rain of arrows began to fall and bringing out all the spoils they had collected during their stay in Eirinn. Each man began to bury what little he could lay claim to. Every one of them knew that if he were killed, his comrades would certainly know where to look to recover his gold and so, at least, it would not fall into the hands of the enemy.

Four of the foreigners collected all the timber that they could find and threw it onto the small fire that Hannarr had earlier started, transforming it into a bonfire. When it was burning fiercely they stacked wood nearby, enough to last the whole night, for they did not know if they would get the chance to gather firewood again that night and without a fire they would certainly freeze.

Caitlin noticed that the thegn was staring at her and his mind was far away. She thought for a moment that he might have been deciding what he would do with his prisoners. Then she began to shake, realising that Hannarr had, after all, only spared her and Murrough their lives because of their value as hostages.

In her mind she also knew that the warriors of Munster would have their hearts set on revenge and would certainly not let the foreigners get away unpunished for their foul desecration of the Tree. Caitlin was sure that Morann would not even listen to any offer of truce, or talk of exchange of prisoners once his eyes fell on the carcass of the Quicken Tree.

'Perhaps even knowing that the Saxons hold his brother prisoner would not be enough for him to control his outrage,' she thought to herself, running over all the possibilities in her mind. 'As for the warriors, their resolve would certainly harden knowing that the Prince of Cashel was being held. They would likely be eager to fight it out with the foreigners.'

Caitlin tried to see the whole situation from the thegn's point of view, but that did not quiet her anxiety. No matter which way she looked at it, his two hostages had become a definite liability to Hannarr.

As the rush to get the defences in order quietened and the warriors began to settle into their appointed positions, a Saxon grabbed her and bundled her toward the fallen trunk of the Quicken Tree. While the first man held her tightly, another quickly bound her arms behind her back at the elbows, and her feet at the ankles. When the two finished tying her up she was left among the scattered leaves and rowan berries at the most exposed part of the defensive position. She rolled over in the snow and landed up against Murrough, who had been similarly bound.

Clearly Hannarr had decided for the moment to take no action other than to keep them both out of the way. Neither of them spoke; the prince was already working away at his bindings, trying to weaken them. Caitlin immediately crawled from where she had been left, to observe as best she could everything that was about to unfold. The snow was falling heavily again and this limited her vision, though it was obvious which direction the Saxons saw the threat was coming from. All their faces were turned toward the road.

The Gaels were still a good way off and the poor light, coupled with the heavy weather, meant that Caitlin could not clearly make out the faces of any of the mounted warriors. The war-pipes struck up again and now it was an ancient air that they played. This was a sure sign to Caitlin of an imminent assault. Such airs were only performed at times such as this, for they had a greater power to stir warriors than any march could have.

Murrough heard the doleful tune also and knew straightaway that it was his brother who was leading the attack. This particular air was one of Morann's favourites. He had often ordered his musicians to play it at the most inappropriate times, simply because he loved the melody. Besides that, only Morann would have thought to bring his musicians on the few precious war horses available, for it was his belief that the war-pipes were very inspiring to the troops. Murrough would have used all the horses at his disposal to mount every available warrior and then, perhaps, thought about the shortest route that the pipers could take on foot.

On this occasion the playing of the war-pipes

was particularly effective. Their shrill skirling pierced the Saxons with an irrational fear and brought back clear memories of their bloody defeat at the battle of Rathowen when the Munstermen had used these instruments to deadly effect. More than one of the Saxons had seen the army of Laigin waver that day, and they all came to the conclusion that the strange Irish war-pipes carried some magical spell to the ears of their enemies, immediately disabling them.

Caitlin looked out over the field and guessed that there were about two hundred and fifty Munstermen in the force that was approaching the small group of Saxons. The foreigners must have seen that they were outnumbered at more than twenty to one, but none outwardly flinched at the sight of his foes.

All of them stood their ground and calmly awaited their doom. Caitlin got the strong impression that they were no more concerned about the impending threat to their lives than they might be about setting off on a hunt. A few of them even joked with each other and though neither Caitlin or Murrough understood what was being said, both could sense a general feeling of relief among the Saxons.

Murrough watched as Hannarr walked slowly and thoughtfully among his warriors, saying fond farewells, and thought that perhaps Hannarr had decided to fight to the death, for he knew a little about their customs. The Christians believed that, at the moment of death, the soul was elevated to a seat of judgement where all the deeds of that person's life, good and bad, were weighed up.

Then, as a reward for a good life, the soul was allowed to enter Heaven and an existence filled with eternal bliss. If the soul was judged to have led an evil existence it was relegated to the realms of Hell. To a Christian there were only two possible states that the soul could languish in at life's end: eternal joy or eternal torture. These two extremes were illustrated in the Christian symbol of the Cross, which could be perceived either as an instrument for inflicting pain or as the motif that could guide a soul to Heaven. That, at least, was how Origen had explained it to Murrough.

The prince knew from the Druidic teachings he had been given as a boy that the spirit may take on many forms as it passes between existences. That knowledge gave him a certainty that his soul would always be changing, developing and growing. Just as the endless circle of the seasons progressed, stage by stage through many outward forms, so did every living thing.

The Saxons held a belief that had aspects of both the Christian and the Druidic philosophies incorporated into it. Their mythology taught that there was a Heaven known as Valhalla, but only a warrior who was killed in battle would be allowed to enter it. They perceived it as a hall of everlasting feasting, drinking and womanising. Anyone who died as a result of treachery rather than open warfare or who broke the rather flexible honour code of their people was condemned to the realms of Hel. This was a similar place to the Christian Hell: a land full of fire and pain. Everyone who was not a warrior in Saxon society was doomed to return, life after life, until they one day had the chance to perish in battle, and so by that means enter Valhalla.

The longer that Murrough thought on all the possible consequences of what Hannarr might be planning to do, the more uneasy he became. So to take his mind off the subject he sat forward to concentrate on breaking his bonds.

'I wanted to thank you,' Caitlin said, shattering the silence between them.

'You thanked me already,' Murrough answered her quietly.

Caitlin did not say anything more for a while. She worked harder at her bonds though and cursed them, for with her hands so tied she could not reach out to Murrough as she longed to.

TWENTY-THREE

fter the fall of the Tree, thoughts of Heaven and Hell did not trouble Seginus Gallus. He had only one thing on his mind: survival. He knew that once all the precious berries had been gathered in and the Quicken Tree destroyed, the Saxons would no longer have a use for him. He did not trust Hannarr for a moment and he was certain he would be slain as soon as the thegn had the time to deal with him. He resolved to take immediate steps to get himself safely out of the Saxon's reach.

When, just on nightfall, the Gaels appeared in the distance, Seginus was about to make off toward the horses, grab one and try to ride off without being noticed. It was a clumsy plan but time was running out and so he had no choice but to make a run for it. Suddenly he noticed that the Saxons were running wildly about, yelling curses at the enemy. The Roman looked out over the fields and saw to his relief the forces of Munster gathering to attack the crossroads.

The arrival of Morann's army was the stroke of luck that Seginus needed; he could not have asked for a better diversion. As long as the Saxons gave all their attention over to preparing their defences, it was unlikely that any of them would notice him slipping away.

The Roman took a few moments to kneel in the

436

snow and offer up a hasty prayer of thanksgiving. As he stood again he once more he checked that no-one was watching and decided to make off toward the horses. He was just turning to leave when a shout pierced the air.

'Roman!' bawled Hannarr. 'Come here. I have work for you.'

Cursing, Seginus stopped in his tracks and strode through the snow toward the thegn, all the while keeping a nervous eye on the Gaelic warriors assembling on the field before them.

'It is my plan to hold the Irish off until nightfall,' announced Hannarr impatiently, before Seginus had reached him. 'That means only one or two hours.'

'Yes,' replied Seginus, more to let the Saxon know that he was listening, than to agree with him.

'I want you to see to the horses,' Hannarr stated blankly, thinking that the man was no use to him as a warrior. 'Take them over to the well and saddle them ready for our flight. And guard them with your life or we may all be trapped here and then we will certainly die at the hands of the Irish.'

'It is a good plan,' answered Seginus. 'I will go straightaway and do as you ask.'

'At the slightest hint of danger to the mounts, you are to inform me,' the thegn ordered. 'Do you understand?'

Seginus nodded blankly and said an 'Ave' in his head. He could hardly believe that he had permission to approach the horses from the thegn himself.

He decided quickly to take full advantage of the situation and, gathering his few remaining possessions, he headed over to where the horses were tethered. There the Roman carefully selected one that he knew would surely carry him swiftly through the dark hours without need for much rest.

When he made his selection he tied the mare to a sapling and began walking all the other horses over to the well. He returned for his own horse last of all. By that time the sky was darkening and night was coming on and he knew that he must act quickly.

He secured a saddle and bridle on his horse and then went around each of the other mounts and slit the harness girths with his knife, so that all the other packs and saddles fell to the ground useless.

When he had completed this task and he found that he was not yet discovered, he was emboldened. Seginus decided to make doubly sure that Hannarr and his men would not escape or catch up with him. He went round to each horse and released the tethers on all of them one by one, so that they were free to move about.

As it was still snowing and the night was fast drawing on, none of the mounts cared to take advantage of their new-found freedom. Instead they huddled together to conserve body warmth. Seginus did not chase them off either. He preferred to imagine that Hannarr would be relying on them as a last-ditch escape route and he wished he could be around to see the thegn's face when they all galloped off out of his reach in the moment of his greatest need.

Satisfied that he had done all that Palladius would have expected of him in the situation, Seginus Gallus mounted his chosen mare and gave her a firm kick. She carried him off into the gathering darkness, not heading directly south but circling around behind the approaching Gaels, so that in a few hours he would be travelling deep into the heart of the Kingdom of Munster. He still had one duty to perform before he quit Eirinn forever.

At precisely the same time as the Roman was laying wreck to Hannarr's hopes of survival, Caitlin and Murrough were watching the Irish troops forming up to commence a charge on the Saxon position at the crossroads.

Morann had his men break into three distinct companies, each separated from the other by a short gap about four horses wide. Murrough knew now for certain that his brother was leading the attack: this was one of his trademark formations.

The dying sunlight was suddenly and markedly dimmed by a cloud passing over the army. Everyone on the field fell silent at this; the only sound to be heard was the neighing of horses, the stamping of iron-shod hooves and the clatter of harness brass. All the Saxons stood their ground proudly and sternly; some with arrows already strung taut in their bows, some hugging their axes close to their bodies one last time.

The light seeped steadily from the land and another cloud passed across the field. The Saxon bonfire was lending an eerie orange glow to the great corpse of the Quicken Tree, causing shadows to flicker wildly, when Caitlin noticed something moving high up in the sky. Directly above Morann's soldiers, ten or so black shapes were circling in ever descending spirals. But it was not until they were at a tree's height above her that Caitlin realised exactly what she was looking at.

Ravens.

She blinked to clear her eyesight, unable to believe what she saw. The largest of the birds gave out a sudden croaking caw and dropped like a stone directly onto the head of one of the Gaelic warriors. There was immediate panic in the Irish lines. In the confusion and the gathering darkness Caitlin could not make out exactly what happened next but she heard a man's dreadful screams and she guessed that the Raven had targeted its victim's eyes.

Once the Raven chief had opened the attack on Morann's troops, all the other Ravens in the flock also came crashing down on carefully selected opponents. Before long the Munstermen were busy fending off the birds and coming to the aid of their comrades. The struggle with the great black creatures demanded all their attention and the Gaels completely forgot about their impending fight with the foreigners.

Hannarr's jaw dropped open in awe at the arrival of the Ravens. He could not fathom what was happening. 'It surely must be an omen. The Raven goddess has come to rescue us,' he told himself. 'We do not need to run. We will defeat the Irish with the help of the Queen of Death.'

Hannarr raised his voice in a wild call that imitated that of the carrion birds and then charged forward, alone, to where the enemy lines were already in disarray. His warriors stopped for a moment, each looking along the line at the next man until, as a unit, they decided to follow their thegn.

As the Raven attack intensified, each of the Saxons became more and more convinced that they would come to no harm, that they were invincible. After all, they were being protected by the totem animal of every Saxon warrior: the bird of death.

There was only one of Hannarr's company who did not feel the irresistible surge of energy pulse through his body when the Raven attack began.

Only one of them did not experience the excitement of seeing the birds launch their assault. Only one did not charge forward into the affray, confident that victory would be awarded to Hannarr and his outlaws. When everyone else rose from their positions to charge after Hannarr, Streng hesitated. His wound had weakened him and he was too proud to follow Hannarr's lead and his instincts called to him louder than the battlecry to stay put and watch what unfolded.

High up in the sky, above where Morann had placed his companies in battle formation, the clouds abruptly turned pitch black. Streng noticed the darkness immediately for it fascinated him. The surface of the swirling object did not have an even spread of colour but seethed as if some swarm of insects were coursing through the air. The whites of his eyes bulged in amazement when he realised that he was not looking at a swarm of insects or at an ordinary cloud.

What he saw, swirling above the Gaelic army, was the shape of hundreds upon countless hundreds of Ravens, diving and gliding and screeching and squawking. It filled him full of an irrational desire to race forward and join Hannarr. Here was proof that the Great Raven had not deserted them. Like the sagas of the old gods, this tale would end with the appearance of the Bringer of Death. She had come to deliver her loyal followers, come to bring them victory.

'Victory!' he yelled, straining through the damaged muscles of his throat, deciding that his instincts must have misled him. He was about to rush to join his comrades when an acute warning sounded through his body, screaming at him, telling him plainly that to follow Hannarr was to walk into the gaping jaws of death. So, despite all that he saw and all that his eyes told him, he stood his ground.

Caitlin saw the masses of birds also and at that point all hope deserted her. Even when she had been fighting on the battlements at Rathowen; even when she had seen Fintan's body hung on the death tree; even, more recently, when she had been forced to watch helpless as the Quicken Tree was felled, she had never felt so useless and utterly defeated as she did now.

When her eyes first beheld the vast battalion of Ravens she could only think that they would be able to count themselves lucky, she and Murrough, if they were granted a quick and easy death. The Saxons had somehow conjured reinforcements from the animal kingdom. There was no-one who could stand against the weight of numbers of that dark feathered army.

The huge, ugly, black birds started falling from the sky in groups of about ten and Caitlin was compelled, though the sight filled her with horror, to watch them as they made full advantage of the size of their bodies and the strength in their wings. Hannarr's warriors had now almost reached Morann's lines and it seemed to Caitlin that all was lost. The Saxons would only have to wander around killing the Munstermen at will while the Ravens kept them too busy to retaliate.

But just as she was resigning herself to a bloody defeat, something totally unexpected occurred. Instead of falling with all their force upon Morann and his helpless soldiers it seemed that the Ravens split into two companies.

One regiment, numbering around seven hundred birds, flew at the group of ten Ravens that had started to attack the army of Morann. In moments there were black feathers flying in all directions as each of the birds that had stormed Morann's men was literally torn to shreds by the sharp talons and stabbing beaks of up to twenty of their own kind. The first group of birds were being viciously driven off by a much larger force of Ravens.

The other regiment of cawing birds, with just as many Ravens in its ranks, made directly for Hannarr and his warriors. The Saxons were running on headlong toward the Irish lines straight into the mass of vengeful creatures, most of them not comprehending what was taking place until it was too late. In a matter of a few moments the whole battlefield was a confusion of black darting shapes and blood curdling calls.

Hannarr was only thirty paces away from Morann's soldiers when he was overcome with terror at what was bearing down upon him. Then thirty Ravens, each half the size and weight of a hunting hound, landed upon the man who ran by his side. They sliced their talons into the flesh of their victim and tore out the fellow's nose and eyes with sweeping blows. He did not even have a chance to scream.

After that first Saxon fell, it was only a matter of seconds before each was engulfed in a swarming mass of black feathers and wild carrion shrieks.

Without thinking, Hannarr curled his body up into a tight ball, covered his head in his hands and burrowed into the snow. A few moments later when he moved a little to adjust his position, he felt the huge weight of many thronging birds on top of him, pinning him down and constricting his breathing. Their sharp, savage beaks grabbed at the chainmail of his shirt like great pincers, drawing at the iron rings and tearing through the leather jerkin underneath. He could feel his boots being stripped slowly away from the soles of his feet and drew his legs up under him again so that his body occupied the smallest space possible.

The continuous and unrelenting shrieking of the Ravens pierced Hannarr's eardrums and rang like the roar of the ocean in his head. Their violent flapping wings beat along his back like clubs as they fought each other to get at him. Engulfed in a teeming avalanche of ferocious birds with only one purpose: to dismember Saxons and consume their flesh in a bloody feast, Hannarr was certain that he was a dead man.

He wrapped his arms and legs tighter under him in a desperate attempt to save himself. His trousers were already in shreds and the birds were working their way through the heavy leather covering that protected the back of his neck. As he adjusted his position, one of the Ravens managed to reach in under him and strike at his belly but Hannarr closed the gap in his defences so that it could not happen again. There were dents appearing in his helm and he could feel the pressure against his skull.

Then, as suddenly as their attack had begun, the Ravens ceased their cawing and stood back from the thegn. All noise ceased and the field was engulfed in a quiet that was just as deafening as the Raven chorus. Hannarr began to shake. He could not stand for fear; his legs would not lift him. He lay curled up for a long time, unwilling to risk a break in his defences lest the birds' retreat should prove to be nothing but a clever trap.

Eventually, though, after several minutes of utter silence he took a deep breath and, preparing himself lest it should be his last, summoned the courage to look about him. What he saw made him sit bolt upright in shock. A few of the birds called in alarm and fell back out of his range at his movement and the ripple of their disturbance passed across the whole of the feathered battalion. Slowly Hannarr cast his eyes about him. The Ravens had certainly ceased their attack, but they stood, gathered round him in a vast sea of menacing black forms, watching and waiting. Every one of their steely dark eyes was on him, and his face reflected back from every pair as if he were looking into the countless shards of a great mirror that had been scattered in the snow.

All his company were by now dead. Most had been reduced to nothing more than lumps of bloody flesh that stained the soft snowfall. A few of them still had some semblance of human form about them, an arm raised in cold horror; a ribcage picked clean of its meat but still attached to a head that had been left strangely untouched.

As he was allowing all of what he saw to sink in, the birds began parting their ranks to make a corridor, like an army awaiting inspection by its king.

Hannarr let himself lean back and put his hands flat in the snow, pressing their shape into the soft wet whiteness of it.

When he turned his face up again, a human figure dressed in a long black cape was walking briskly through the midst of the birds, making directly for him.

The thegn studied the stranger carefully, trying to figure out who he could be that had control over the Ravens of the air and had suddenly turned them against his Saxon men. Somehow he felt that the figure was familiar. He recognised the walk and thought for a second that he could put a face to the movement of the gently swaying garment. Then he got the impression that this man, whoever he was, must have somehow intervened on his behalf and negotiated his release. Hannarr struggled up off the ground to stand as tall as he could. He made a decision to thank the man and then to ask him his name.

Suddenly the strange figure started to move startlingly fast over the snow, gliding gracefully across it but leaving no mark in the perfect surface. When he got close to Hannarr the man stopped and reached out a thin, bony hand to him.

'Thegn Hannarr Ettenson,' the strange man whispered, the voice coloured by a hint of mocking bitterness.

Hannarr's flesh quivered; his mouth dried up; his fingers went numb and a shiver passed violently through his body. The hair prickled across the back of his head under his iron helm and he could feel his bowels begin to tremble. The figure stepped closer. Hannarr could feel his heart beating in his throat. Slowly, and with infinite care, the strange man in the long cape opened his robes to reveal the face beneath the hood.

At that very second three Gaelic arrows sped through the night, aimed by expert marksmen. Two found their target and thrust deeply and savagely into Saxon flesh, tearing sinew and shattering bone. But Hannarr never felt their barbs, nor indeed did he suffer at all from the rib-cracking impact. He had no chance to explain his treachery or to make amends for it. He was already dead the moment he recognised Thegn Guthwine smiling contemptuously at him from beneath the flowing folds of black cloth.

TWENTY-FOUR

obann had been in an excellent position to observe the Tree crashing to the ground, to feel the rumbling that had rolled across the Earth afterwards and hear the outraged shouts of the spirits who had gathered to its defence. But he had been totally powerless to divert the relentless Saxon blades from the sacred bough.

All around him the spirit people sounded horns and banged drums, sending their call for reinforcements throughout the land. Even they, for all their magic arts, could do nothing to prevent the savages from killing their ancient friend. The Quicken Tree seemed resigned to its fate; it did not fight back, not until the very last, and even then it only made a token effort. Two Saxon lives in exchange for its own.

As it toppled on its side, the leverage on the roots tore them completely from the ground, leaving a gaping hole as deep as a grown man is tall. Gobann was drawn by some force toward this crater to pay his respects to the life centre of the mighty timber creature. He hovered about, having finally begun to get used to his abilities in the spirit form. There at the bottom of the hole, already being covered by freshly falling snow, was an ancient tool that had obviously been buried there when the Tree had been but a sapling. Gobann could not be sure if it had been put there in prophecy or if the implement was meant for some other purpose. He only knew that the Danaans must have had good reason to conceal an axe in the root system of a Tree such as this.

When the first of the Ravens had appeared, many of the spirits who were congregating around Gobann disappeared; whether from fear or because they had some alternative plan, the poet never found out. But he suspected that Sciathan-cog was behind the attack on Morann's troops and that the spirit folk understood this well enough. He guessed that they may have gone off to fetch Lom-dubh and the Queen, but he could not be certain.

As he was pondering these possibilities, a cold wind blew from the south and for the first time since he had taken his new form, the poet felt chilled. Then he realised that the wind was gracefully lifting him up as it had done when he had first set out from the mound. More as a reflex than any desire to remain at the crossroads, Gobann reached out to grab a branch of the Tree but his grip was hindered by an object that he held in his right hand and which he could not seem to let go of.

In a matter of moments he had been swept upwards towards the highest clouds, then far above the falling snow and into the starry night sky. He looked down at his palm and saw a silver trinket: an acorn cleverly contrived so that it appeared that a dog, a raven and a salmon wrapped their bodies around each other in a bizarre embrace.

He remembered giving the jewel to Caitlin before she left Rathowen and he was dimly aware that he had spoken with her at the Tree but he had no clear recollection of any of the afternoon's events. Indeed, it was many years before he was able to remember all that had taken place when he had been among the spirit folk who dwelt at the Quicken Tree and even then he found it hard to accept that he had been so mischievous when the lives of his friends were at stake.

Caitlin's arms were bound very tightly, but she had been slowly working the leather binding down over her elbow joints and she was certain that it would not be long before the thonging had slipped off her arms entirely.

Every once in while she rested her aching arms and worked at freeing her ankles from the strips of hide that bound them. Slowly they too were beginning to loosen and the leather was wearing where the knots had been tied.

Murrough had the same strategy. He was trying to scrape his bindings over the edge of a sharp stone in the hope of wearing quickly through them. He had been working away at them for a long while before he stopped to catch his breath.

'Are you all right, Cait?' he called.

'I am,' she replied, tired from contorting her body to get at the bindings and trying to ignore the pain in her leg wound. 'Did you see if all the Saxons were caught in the Ravens' attack?'

Murrough did not have a chance to answer her. A foreigner's boot connected with his jaw and sent the prince tumbling backwards in the snow. It took Murrough a minute or two to recover from the shock of the blow and the subsequent knocks he received as he rolled along backwards. When he managed to look up, Caitlin was already gone, but he could hear her screams echoing through the night.

Streng had earlier spent a long while trying to

catch himself a horse. When he had finally secured a mount, he cursed loud and repeatedly at the man who had cut all the saddle girths. But Streng was determined not to be taken alive nor to be slain as all his comrades had. He gathered up as many of the precious Quicken berries as he could carry and then rifled the sacks of all the other Saxons, collecting any valuable booty that he could find.

He had no more specific plan in mind than to take whatever would be worth something in the exotic markets of Gaul and to ride away with it. He did not know how, without any crew, he would be able to sail one of Guthwine's ships across the Hibernian sea, or how he would elude capture when the entire country would, likely as not, be searching for him. Gold and booty meant money to him; money meant ale aplenty and as many women as he could manage at one time. He was a man of simple, if large, appetites.

Having gathered all else of any value, he set his mind on the jewel that, of all the treasures they had collected in Eirinn, appealed to him most: Caitlin. His rational thoughts argued that she would be a hindrance to his escape and that if he were to be captured she would be the only cause. But his desire told him to ignore caution and grab her for his own.

'When I have finished with her she will fetch a good price in the slave markets of the south.' He pictured himself auctioning her off to the highest bidder as an Irish princess. 'She'll be worth a bloody fortune,' he decided. 'I'll be able to live in style for a year on the strength of her sale alone.'

With the decision well and truly made, he found some rope to lash her to the horse with and then secured all his other material wealth. As an after-thought, he grabbed the bag full of herbs that Mur-rough had been collecting. 'She can brew the magic potion for me,' he thought, amazed at his sudden good fortune. 'There's not much use in being able to buy as much ale as you can drink if you can't enjoy swallowing it because of an old war wound.'

There was only one thing that he had not counted on in all of his plans, for she was badly injured, and that was that the woman would put up a fight. But fight she did, though her leg throbbed in agony and she could feel her strength draining quickly away.

By the time Streng reached her, Caitlin had almost freed herself from her restraints and he had to waste precious minutes rebinding them. He tied the leather thongs much tighter this time; tight enough that before long the blood had stopped circulating to her fingers and Caitlin was in real pain.

When he had finally trussed her up ready for the journey, she began screaming in earnest and when he slung her over his shoulder to carry her to the waiting horse she gave a kick and the restraints on her ankles snapped. Then she started flaying her legs about wildly.

When they reached the waiting horse he put her down on the snow to take a breath. Caitlin did not hesitate for one second. She let out a kick that was aimed at the man's most vulnerable spot. Her riding boot connected at his groin with a dull thump and Streng almost doubled up in agony, but because of her wound she could not take full advantage of the situation. Somehow the Saxon managed to keep a firm hold of her while he recovered from the blow, but he was winded badly and it took many minutes. All the time she continued kicking and screaming and trying warrior holds on him. Streng was too powerful for her though—even the strongest of Saxon warriors in Guthwine's company had experienced difficulty in overpowering him when they wrestled with him.

However, he gained a healthy respect for Caitlin from the bruising she gave his private parts, and he rebuked himself a little for letting her get under his guard. He began to regret that he would probably have to sell her one day.

'When she's broken in she'll make someone a good wife,' he thought. Streng preferred a woman with a bit of fight in her. But not quite as much as Caitlin displayed.

After a while he got back to his feet and, still holding her by the legs, dragged her through the snow. He paused for a moment unsure of how he was going to mount the horse with her kicking about so much. The answer presented itself readily and Streng felt a shiver of lust pulse through his body as he decided how he might render her unconscious.

In the next second he let go his hold over her legs and she struggled quickly to get up. As she gained her feet the Saxon let go a punch that landed on her cheekbone and knocked her back down on the ground immediately. He waited to see if she would rise again and when she did not move, he bundled her over the horse and bound her legs.

Then he set off, and not a moment too soon for he could hear mounted warriors approaching. He made for the north and tracked along an old watercourse until he was certain that they were not being followed; then he chose a path that would take them eastwards, thinking to meet eventually with the sea. That was as far ahead as he had planned.

He had not gone far that evening when he discerned the distinct sound of flapping wings nearby. Large wings they were, such as a Raven might have. Streng knew that no bird in the natural world ever travels by night, apart from the owl, and this was no owl. It had the smell of carrion about it and it flew, at times, at a great height. He began to suspect that there was more to it than he could fathom, and he remembered the great black bird that had defied Guthwine at Dobharcú.

In the deep recesses of his mind Streng began to work out a way to deal with the winged spy. But as he thought about it there rose a nagging doubt that perhaps the creature was not an enemy at all and that it could be of some help in his escape.

Gobann soared with the soul-breeze high above the world. He turned his thoughts to Teamhair and in a split second he was there, hovering above the sacred citadel that was the symbolic centre of the land of Eirinn.

But he was not yet ready to relinquish his newfound freedom. During the short while he had spent in the spirit form, he began to wonder about the way in which he had been able to travel. He had a few ideas about what was happening and he wanted to see if he was right. As he floated over the citadel the poet decided that this was a good time to try it out.

Gobann closed off all his senses and concentrated on one idea. In his mind's eye he constructed a picture of the valley of Dobharcú as he remembered it when he had last seen it. When he looked about him after a short while, he knew that he had been transported directly to that place.

'I was right!' he congratulated himself. 'I can journey to any place that my heart desires, so long as I can picture it clearly in my thoughts.'

He began to take notice of what was around him. The first thing he saw was that there was no sign of the destruction or of the deaths that Cathach had spoken of.

'Perhaps the old Druid was misinformed,' he thought.

There was a great rush of beating wings the tips of which brushed close to the poet, and a black form swooped down toward the village. It was the Raven, Sciathan-cog.

Then, to his dismay, Gobann witnessed something that would stay with him for the rest of his days. As he floated helplessly overhead, a company of Saxon warriors appeared at the ford. They marched through the waters of the stream and on down the valley toward the settlement. The poet wanted desperately to warn Midhna of the approaching danger but the blacksmith was out of Gobann's reach.

Suddenly the Raven landed on the village green and began to address the foreigners. Understanding the Raven speech, Gobann realised that Scia-than-cog had come hoping to convince the Saxons to follow him on a conquest of Eirinn. This was the bird that had spoken up at the Raven debate informing the assembly that the Saxons were allies of their kind.

Events then began to move much faster than was possible in the real world, as if all that he watched was spiralling rapidly toward a conclusion. The Saxons looted the settlement, set it afire and left. The last image that Gobann witnessed was that of Dobharcú in ruins and the smouldering corpses all piled up in the courtyard. Sciathan-cog was rallying other birds to come to the carrion feast.

The poet closed off his senses again and let only sorrow take hold of him. The stark realisation hit him: it was only by some miracle that he had managed to escape from the village just before the attack. He turned his thoughts to the good fortune that had so many times saved him from death. Gobann often perceived that some other force was at work in helping him and everyone he knew through the dangers of their time, and this was a instance where that help had proved crucial. Through all his studies and his long devotions to the Druid mysteries he had never discovered whether his people had a name for that force.

'Perhaps,' he thought, 'the force is something like the concept of the God that Origen speaks of.'

Then he remembered that he was still subject to spirit travel. When he looked about him and noticed where he had journeyed in his thoughts this time, he was very confused. Below him were mountains and valleys and high green pastures. He was no longer in Eirinn but drifting over the island of Britain. He knew this only because he was looking down on a settlement that he recognised. It was the place where Síla lived and where he had met her.

As he was trying to find some reason for why he had arrived there, an old man came out of one of the long huts that was typical of the houses in that part of the world. He wore a beard and a Roman silver plaque on his chest, but he was a man of the Cruitne tribes.

He looked straight at Gobann and pointed his staff in the poet's direction. 'You are too late,' he called.

Gobann's heart sank.

'You have come too late,' repeated the old man.

The poet tried to call back and ask, 'Too late for what? What has happened to her?' but he could not form the words.

'Síla is gone,' the man stated, as if hearing Gobann's unspoken, urgent questions. 'Gone, never to return.'

The poet was by now frantic; he had no idea what the fellow was trying to say but he feared the worst, that somehow Síla had passed from the world forever. Sickness, war, an accident, childbirth, the myriad possibilities raced through his mind.

'She has gone over the Western Ocean,' the old man called, 'to Eirinn.'

Gobann barely caught these words but when he heard the mention of his homeland he suddenly found that he was back above Teamhair floating near the mound in which his body sat, waiting, temporarily entombed.

Around the mound were gathered all the Druids that had assembled for the rites of Beltinne. It was night and there were no fires burning anywhere in the Citadel.

'Can it be that three days have passed since I left to journey to the Tree?' he asked himself, for it felt as if he had only tarried an afternoon at the crossroads.

He heard Cathach's voice intoning the invocation of fire and then a spark leapt out of the man's hands and into a small pile of dry bracken. Bearers came forward and plunged torches into the flames and then, without waiting for any more words to be said, they started off on their separate errands to deliver the sacred fire to every hearth in every corner of Eirinn.

As the torchbearers made their way toward the citadel gates, a large party of black clothed men and women arrived bearing the remains of all those of the Druid order who had passed away that year. Two of the bodies were still wrapped in the linen bindings that marked them as having only recently died. All of the other remains consisted of boxes of bones.

Only harpers were entombed in stone vaults. When a Druid of another order abandoned life on the earth, the body was left out in the open to rot and to be consumed by the wild animals of the forest. Each year, at the time of Beltinne, the secret burial ground where the corpses lay was cleared of any remains that had not yet returned to the Earth. The leftover bones were stacked around the bonfire, or the bone-fire as it had been called in ancient times, and were thus transformed into ashes.

In this way the dead Druids were able to share one last ritual with their brothers and sisters of their order, and it was not insignificant that the festival of Beltinne symbolised the rebirth of the world after the little death of winter.

It took Gobann a while to realise that the two corpses wrapped in linen were those of Lorgan and King Eoghan. It was very rare that a warrior such as the King of Munster was allowed the burial of a poet, but Gobann knew that there were sound reasons for the Druid Council allowing it on this occasion.

Firstly, Eoghan's heir, Murrough Prince of Cashel, had probably not been heard of for many days and it was not appropriate that anyone else in the Eoghanacht clan be involved in the arrangements. So, very likely, the Druids had been called on to dispose of his body. Secondly, Lorgan and Eoghan were contemporaries; indeed they represented the last warrior and the last Druid in the land who had been alive during the heroic reign of King Niall of the Nine Hostages. As such they both represented an important link with the past. And they had been good friends.

Around the earthen mound in which Gobann's body lay, novices were stacking piles of bracken and heavier wood. The collected bones and the two corpses were reverently placed on top of the mound on a specially constructed platform. The novices then spread a sandy dust on the stones and among the bracken that would, in the heat of the furnace, melt and fuse to give the stone mound another coating of glaze. This was done every year, and every year the layers of glaze got a little thicker. This gave the stones a deep colour and they often sparkled after the rain or could be spotted from miles away as the sun was reflected off their surface.

The ceremony had progressed now to the point where Cathach held in his hand a torch that would spread fire to the fuel all around Gobann's symbolic tomb. In this lengthy ritual, the poet was being introduced into a whole new life. The four elements were invoked in order to prepare him for the hardships ahead. He had first been subjected to a test by water: in the steam of the sweat-house and the washing at the stone basin. After that he had been tested by the element of earth during the three days of his entombment. Then came the test of air when he had taken the soul-flight and then the form of a Raven.

This was the last and potentially the most dangerous test: the test of fire.

Gobann suddenly felt his spirit being sucked down toward the bonfire, down into the mound and for a moment he waited, still outside his own body, watching the flesh-form of himself as it drew controlled breaths. He paused as long as he dared to, unwilling to give up the freedom of the spirit. Then he resolved to allow himself one last look at the world outside. He turned his thoughts to Mawn.

Nothing happened. He was still confined to the stone room. Outside he could hear loud crackling as the bracken exploded in flame, and hissing as the snow and damp around the tomb turned to steam in the heat of the fire. He heard the Druids piling more fuel up against the mound and realised that he was trapped, there was no choice for him but to re-enter his body.

He waited for the next inward breath. It was intuition that told him he must make the attempt on the inward breath. But that breath passed; he missed it. He watched the body breathe out again and prepared himself once more but again he was left locked out of his body. He concentrated all his attention on the seated figure of himself. It only took him a moment to see a great triple spiral carved on the rock wall behind his form. Then he recalled Lorgan's advice to follow the spiral to the left and when he looked again he saw that indeed the carving did follow a course to the left.

He put all his mind onto tracing the path of the spiral maze around to the left toward the centre. As his vision approached the point in the design where the three arms of the spiral converged, his empty body sucked the air into its lungs and Gobann relaxed his spirit enough to be gently drawn in with the breath, and then the room went very dark and he lost consciousness.

It was a long while before he woke from his ordeal and when he did, he found that the heat in the tomb was almost unbearable. He drank some water from the brass bowl that sat before him and then began the slow process of waking his body from its long ordeal.

His arms felt like they were the weight of gold and his legs would not respond at all for many hours. He could not tell if his eyesight was intact at all, for no light penetrated the perfect seal of the mound. His hearing was muffled again and his mouth would not even consent to allow his voice to hum, let alone to form words. Worst of all, his head ached and his neck was stiff and his bones were in agony from three days of exposure to cold and damp. He found that he just wanted to rest but he fought the urge with all of his might, for he knew from all he had been taught that sleep would lead to certain death.

TWENTY-FIVE

t the Cashel crossroads where the Quicken Tree had stood as sentinel for over a thousand years, Murrough was cursing his luck. By the time his brother Morann and his men had finally discovered him lying in the snow near to the dead trunk of the Tree, Streng had already been gone for nearly an hour.

The men of Munster were very reluctant to cross the ground where the Saxons had been slaughtered. Unaware that Murrough or Caitlin were captives of the foreigners, and darkness being over the land, Morann's horsemen took their time in reaching the place where the enemy had spent the afternoon.

When he chanced upon his younger brother at last, Morann grabbed him in a tight embrace and thanked the gods that he was safe.

As the warriors released him from his bonds Murrough quickly related all that had happened in the last few days up to the cutting of the Tree and the kidnapping of Caitlin. Neither man made mention of the Ravens' attack for that was still too fresh in their minds and the night was too dark for such a tale.

When Morann had heard his brother out, he realised that the Prince of Cashel was lucky to have escaped from the foreigners with his life. He was relieved that Murrough was safe, but he was not convinced that Caitlin would survive at the hands of a renegade.

'The Saxon took her hostage,' he surmised, 'to ensure his own safe passage. As soon as he feels that he can do without her he could well slit her throat and dump her. We may never know what became of her.'

Murrough, stubborn as ever, would not even consider the possibility that Caitlin was dead. If there was a remote chance that she could be found he was willing to risk his own life to search for her.

'Give me a good horse,' he begged when Morann counselled that they wait until morning to begin the search, 'and I will track the Saxon myself.'

'It is madness to travel in this storm,' Morann protested.

'I did not ask you to accompany me,' snapped Murrough, 'just to give me a horse.'

'I won't let you go off by yourself in this weather and by the dark of the Moon,' asserted Morann.

'If you will not give me a horse then I will take one,' stated Murrough coldly, grabbing a cloak that was offered to him by one of the warriors.

'You have no chance of finding them,' Morann reiterated. 'It is better that you rest tonight and we all start fresh at first light.'

'They will be halfway to the Saxon lands by dawn,' bellowed Murrough, losing his patience. 'If you want to stay here hiding like a frightened field-mouse, then do so. But do not expect that I will huddle in the straw with you.'

'I will not allow you to risk your life for this woman. Or the life of a good mount.'

'She is a chieftain and a Druid,' yelled Murrough. 'It is our duty to save her from that savage.'

'They have too good a head start on you,' replied the elder Eoghanacht. 'And you do not even know which direction the Saxon was headed. How do you think you will find his trail among all this fresh snow and amid the hoof-marks of all my warriors' horses?'

'I have a very good idea as to where the savage will head. I will catch him. I must catch him,' the Prince of Cashel looked down at his boots, 'before he has the chance to do her any harm.'

Morann saw the resolve in his brother. He knew that once Murrough made up his mind to do something there was no force on Earth could dissuade him.

'Very well,' Morann began, 'I will give you some of my warriors as an escort. Just to ensure that you are safe.'

'Tell them to mount up now then.'

'I have ordered my army to make camp,' Morann explained. 'It will be a long while before any of them can be ready to travel with you.'

'Then I will go alone.'

'These men have ridden at the gallop all afternoon and then witnessed a battle that would make a Danaan's blood run cold with fear. I will not ask any of them to go until they have rested.'

'Very well, then I go alone.'

'You always were impetuous and thoughtless!' exploded Morann. 'Have you given any mind to what will happen if you do not return from this little adventure?'

Murrough grabbed a sword from one of Morann's guards and stormed off to find a horse. 'Enough of this talk,' he yelled. 'I am going, with or without your blessing.'

'Have you even considered for a moment what effect your selfish action could have on the good of the kingdom?' bellowed his elder brother, finally losing his temper.

Murrough stopped in his tracks and turned to face Morann. 'What do you mean?'

'You are the heir to the Eoghanacht. If you perish in some fruitless search, chasing a woman who means nothing to any of us, who do you think will rule Munster at our father's passing?'

Murrough did not answer. He stood perfectly still. Morann read this to mean that his brother was considering what he had heard and might begin to see some reason, and so he pressed his point.

'Murrough,' he rejoined in a calmer voice, soothing and gentle, 'I know that you were never primed for the kingship, and so it is hard for you to accept.' The Prince of Cashel still made no sign of acknowledgment. 'But you have a duty, now that you will one day rule the kingdom, to protect yourself from harm.'

'I do not remember anyone consulting me about becoming heir to the seat of Munster,' stormed Murrough. 'No-one so much as mentioned it until King Leoghaire and our father announced it to the gathering in the Council at Rathowen!'

'Your destiny lies with the kingship of the South,' argued Morann, 'not with some Druidess with whom you have nothing in common and cannot possibly have a future. She is as good as dead and you must accept that.'

'I will accept it when I see her corpse. Until then please allow me some hope.'

'Hope!' mocked Morann. 'What do you hope for? That Caitlin Ni Úaine will want to take you to husband? And what of the hopes of the kingdom? Are you really placing her above your duty? In the name of the Morrigú,' he laughed, 'you cannot be serious!'

Murrough's eyes flared in the firelight. 'I love her,' he said in a subdued tone, and then he turned around again and walked briskly away.

None of Morann's men was willing to go out with Murrough that night. They shared the opinion of their lord as to the dangers of the evening. The common soldiers, country folk and educated men alike reasoned that if the Ravens could launch an assault on the human kind, then the whole of the animal kingdom was to be treated with suspicion. Better to stay by the fire in the company of many comrades than be running about the countryside stirring up all manner of hostile beings.

There was another fear running deeper than even Morann liked to admit to himself and he knew much about the ways of such things. 'What if,' he asked himself, 'the Danaans are finally rising after all these centuries to avenge themselves on the Gaels?' A wild shiver passed through his body but it had nothing to do with the unrelenting snowfall.

With that Morann decided to loan Murrough his own mount. He told himself that at least his brother would have a strong reliable horse that was renowned for its endurance and speed. If he got into any difficulty this would be a good animal to have under him.

'Even if you have no success or if you find no sign of them,' Morann told Murrough as he was saddling the horse, 'meet me here in three days.' The Prince of Cashel nodded in agreement admitting to himself that if he had not found her by then she would truly be lost.

'I beg you to take some food and drink with you,' added Morann, 'and the tinder to start a fire tomorrow night, for it will be Beltinne and those in dire need are excused from waiting for the Teamhair torches.'

Murrough was still furious with his brother and

did not want to waste another precious moment. 'I will be all right,' he snapped. 'I don't need you fussing after me at every turn. Now let me be!'

'You foolish boy!' countered Morann. 'It is I who will have to tell our father of your senseless death from cold and hunger.' He immediately regretted those words, but Murrough did not wait to hear an apology. He swung his leg over the saddle and in a moment was riding off into the night, steering his mount to the east, sure that the Saxon would have made for the sea.

'You foolish boy,' Morann repeated under his breath.

He stood for a long time watching his brother slip into the cover of night and disappear from view. He suffered a deep remorse at not insisting that Murrough take some of his troops on the search. He had a bad feeling about what would become of his brother, a feeling that would not leave him though he tried to put it out of his thoughts.

To take his mind off worrying about Murrough, Morann sent for his three swiftest dispatch riders and issued them messages to carry to the High-King and to Eoghan his father. He ordered them to set out at the first sign of dawn. At that stage he had received no word from the north and Morann had no way of knowing that his father, the King of Munster, had passed away peacefully in his sleep during the last night. Morann had always thought that he would be by the old man's side when the time came.

When he had organised the dispatches, Morann ordered his troops to bed down for the night and that fires be lit all around the crossroads. He posted a heavy watch on every part of the camp. The experience with the marauding Ravens had unnerved him and he no longer felt that he should take the safety of his warriors for granted.

'In the morning we will survey the damage to the Tree,' he decided, 'and retrieve what may found of the Saxons for a decent burial. Then I will send more of my soldiers to Teamhair as Leoghaire requested.'

In his heart he prayed that the High-King had not had need of his troops after all, that there had been no rising in Laigin as Leoghaire had feared there would be and that there would somehow be peace in Eirinn again.

But when he thought on the death of the Quicken Tree and the strange events that followed, his heart sank. He wrapped himself in his bedroll, sheltered under the fallen branches of the Tree, and ran through everything that had happened over and over in his head. But though he tried to convince himself that all would be well, Morann did not end up getting any rest at all that night.

In the middle of the storm when the snow was falling harder than it had for many days, heavier than throughout the worst of the previous winter, Seginus brought his mount to a halt.

He knew from his other travels in this part of the country that he was not far from the Rock of Cashel and he did not want to go too near to that fortress. His mount stood stamping her hooves in the cold and the Roman reasoned that he was probably safe now from Hannarr and his band for it was unlikely that they would follow him this far south. Such a journey would be too risky for them.

Now Seginus had to make a decision, a vital decision, one that could very well save or cost him his life. He knew that there was no other way round Cashel: all traffic going south had to pass by the fortress. If he tried to slip past in the dark there was a chance that he could be mistaken for a Saxon and killed before he had a chance to run. If he waited until dawn he would certainly run into one of the patrols of Gaelic warriors that guarded the road.

In the end he made up his mind to press the slight advantage that he had, and to attempt to pass the Rock unnoticed while he still had the cover of darkness to protect him.

He had not travelled more than two hundred paces, though, before he began to regret his rash choice. Just around a bend in the road Morann had stationed a guardhouse and there were twenty armed men at the post. They all sat huddled around a blazing fire just inside the partly collapsed doorway to an old roofless stone tower.

By the time Seginus saw the guards, they had also seen him and he knew that there was only one way through this part of the country. Along this road.

He quickly resolved to ride casually up to the tower and then break into a gallop when he was close enough. 'Even if they try to pursue me,' he thought, 'it will take them a few minutes to mount up their war horses, and that may be all the blessing that I need in order to get past. Once I am a good way along the road they will surely never find me in this weather.'

He was also counting on the fact that most of Munster's trained warriors were still stationed further north. The soldiers at this post were more than likely farmers who had been enlisted for the duration of the war with Laigin.

Convincing himself to feel confident, Seginus

approached the guardhouse. He gathered his fine Roman cloak about his shoulders and tucked it in under his legs, so that when he spurred his mare on, the edges would not flap in the wind or catch on any low branches.

But his mood soon changed as he came closer to the post. Two warriors in full chainmail and leather armour were already mounted and waiting for him to approach. They were not farmers. These two, at least, were professional soldiers; that much he could tell from the way they sat in the saddle and the weapons and accoutrements that they carried.

A rather fat man, balding and pale, came running out of the tower. His cloak was of very poor quality and it whipped against the top of his head in the wind, but the fellow had an air of authority about him.

'Hold, stranger!' he called and Seginus realised that he was the gatekeeper.

'What is your errand that you are travelling so late on such a foul night as this?'

The Roman's horse was startled and pulled up quickly when the gatekeeper appeared. Then Seginus noticed that the two warriors were taking an immediate interest in him. 'I am bearing a message on behalf of Murrough the Prince of Cashel,' he replied, making no attempt to cover his accent.

'Murrough!' exclaimed the fat man. 'We expected him through here days ago.'

'I have urgent business in the south on his behalf,' insisted Seginus. 'I must reach Ardmór as soon as possible.'

'And what is your business exactly?' one of the mounted men enquired.

'I bear letters from the High-King of Eirinn to the

Pope in Rome,' Seginus lied, his heartbeat racing wildly.

'Why would the High-King give dispatches into the hand of a foreigner?' demanded the other warrior suspiciously.

'Because I speak both the Gaelic and the Roman tongues,' Seginus replied, as if that were obvious. He hoped they did not notice the nervous sweat that had broken out across his brow.

'What message do you bear for Murrough?' asked the other man unconvinced.

'I am to pass that on to no-one save the man for whom it is intended.'

'Who might that be?' pressed the warrior.

'It is certainly not you!' sniped Seginus; then he had an idea. 'But I will gladly show you the letters that I bear if that will prove my story.'

At this point the gatekeeper was beginning to feel the cold and he decided to intervene so that he could get back by the fire as soon as possible. 'Let me see your letters, stranger,' he interrupted.

Seginus knew that few of the Irish could read and fewer still could understand Latin. He searched around in his pack for some of the loose leaves from his personal hand-written Gospel. His hand came across his dagger and the thought crossed his mind that he might have to fight his way out of this situation. Then his fingers brushed against another object. It was metal and quite small; he rolled it about in his hand to discern exactly what it was. He slipped it over his finger. It was a ring. He had almost forgotten that he had Murrough's seal ring, taken as a guarantee that the prince would not try to escape.

With a flourish he produced two leaves of vellum from his pack and the gatekeeper took them in by the fire to get a good look at them in the light.

He was a long while, doubtless warming himself as much as possible while he had a good excuse to do so.

When he came out again he handed the pages back to Seginus with an apology. 'I cannot read,' he admitted, 'and nor can any of my garrison. Do you have any other proof of your mission?'

Seginus paused a moment. 'I only have this.' He gestured to the gatekeeper with his right hand showing off the ring on his middle finger. 'The prince told me that his servants would recognise it.'

'May I see it?' enquired the man.

'Certainly,' the Roman answered warmly.

The gatekeeper took the ring and once more retreated to the fireside. There he found a wax candle and melted some of it over his shield. Then he pressed the flat surface of the ring into the wax and examined the mark that it made.

The ring left a very distinct impression. It was a stylised version of the Quicken Tree, shaped by several Ogham signs combined into one letter. The gatekeeper recognised it immediately as the seal of the Prince of Cashel. He rushed back outside to Seginus.

'That is the sign of Murrough,' he confirmed. 'You may pass, stranger.'

Seginus breathed out in relief and began to feel himself shake with the pent up tension of the encounter. 'Thank you, gateman. Goodnight to you,' he said and reached out to take the ring but he was shivering so much that it slipped from his grasp into the snow. It took the gatekeeper some minutes to find it again and while he was searching the two warriors spoke to each other in low tones. When the man had finally located the ring Seginus tucked it into his bag and made sure his horse moved slowly on.

'Wait!' called one of the warriors. Seginus froze fearing that they had seen through his simple trick. He reached into his bag and grasped the hilt of his dagger ready for a fight.

'My comrade and I are travelling south to Cashel but we could escort you as far as Ardmór if you like,' the warrior offered.

'That really won't be necessary,' Seginus began, but he was cut off before he could say anything else.

'Have you not heard?' the warrior interjected. 'There is a band of Saxon savages wandering around the country sacking villages and thieving travellers. We will journey with you to your destination. It is the least we could do for a stranger on the High-King's business.'

Seginus found that he had no choice but to agree with them, though the thought of being escorted by two of Murrough's own guardsmen struck him as a very dangerous development indeed.

At Teamhair, Gobann slept eventually, though the furnace outside made conditions almost unbearable within the stone mound. He lay carefully down on his side, and he breathed deeply with his face close to the ground where the freshest air was circulating.

He rested two or three hours and then he woke again and continued stretching the muscles of his body and circulating the blood throughout the whole of his system. He tried to remember if he had dreamed anything while he slept but he could recall no strange visions or insights. This was a sure sign that he had passed through a great spiritual ordeal.

Gobann was just beginning to drift back into the dark world of the mound, losing track of the passing of time and even of what might be happening in the outside world, when he heard a tapping on the stone door of the chamber.

He knew that this was Cathach checking to see if he was alive. The poet quickly made his way toward the source of the sound and tapped a return signal with a piece of loose rock.

Then all was silent for a long while, perhaps another hour, perhaps two, Gobann never knew for sure. Finally, when he thought that he could not resist screaming out to the Druids outside to release him, when he was beginning to feel that he was faint from hunger and the lack of light and when his ears ached to hear the sound of human voices again, there was a loud cracking sound near to the entrance of the mound.

Somewhere out there someone was dismantling the elaborate entrance structure that was designed to keep the occupant of the stone mound safe from the heat generated by the bonfire.

Still it was a long time before the rescuers got to where Gobann was entombed. The poet was sitting waiting, humming old melodies to himself when the first chink of light entered the chamber. It was so intense, that first beam of light, that Gobann flinched and covered his eyes and he was tempted to call out in alarm.

Two strong novices came in to the chamber and picked him up under the armpits. They carried him as respectfully as was possible under the circumstances into the light of day.

When the poet emerged from his retreat, there was still snow lying thickly upon the ground and the air was very cold. Cathach approached him and threw a large cloak around Gobann's nakedness and then the poet was bundled off into a house with a fire roaring in the hearth.

He was given warm oat-bread and barley broth much the same as he had eaten at Dobharcú and then he was dressed in fine linen clothes; but the cloak that Cathach had given him when he first came out of the mound, he was encouraged to keep on over the top of them.

It was as he was walking toward the hall of Poets that Gobann realised that the jet-black cloak was of an exceptional weave and extremely soft and light. He looked down at the fabric to try and discern what fibres had gone into its making.

Gobann smiled to himself and thanked the gods for their gifts. His new cloak was made entirely from the feathers of Ravens.

TWENTY-SIX

In the rush to escape certain death at the hands of Morann's warriors, or worse still the Ravens, Streng, the last survivor of Thegn Guthwine's raiding party, thrashed the horse that carried him until her flanks bled. He forced the mare to gallop where the ground was uneven and he kicked her into a trot where she would have walked due to the many stones scattered about.

Caitlin did not stir throughout the night journey but lay across the horse as if she were dead. Streng was glad of the quiet, for he could make better time without having to deal with her trying to escape or lend him some sort of injury.

As the night wore on, the mare began to suffer from the exertion. Streng's solution was to beat her harder, driving her onward through the snow and the steady sleet, and though the storm did not ease and the mare's iron-shod feet slipped many times on the icy ground, he allowed her no respite.

By first light she was completely exhausted and very near to collapse. The mare had not eaten nor been given the chance to drink, though she had sweated constantly under the weight of her two burdens for nearly eight weary hours.

After crossing many fields and brooks and wading carefully through streams in the dark, Streng was forced to find a road. The land was hilly now and the going over the rough sloping ground was too slow for his liking.

They reached a clear path that twisted and turned up the steep inclines about two hours before the dawn and from then on they made much better time, though the hills had turned into small mountains by sunrise.

Streng had travelled in some of the coldest parts of the world and had learned to ignore the elements, but he was beginning to freeze by the time the morning light splashed across the hilltops. He decided to halt and warm himself by a fire. 'Best that I get her moving too,' he thought, looking down at Caitlin. 'She'll be of no value to me dead from the cold.'

If Streng had thought about why he was suffering so much from the low temperatures he would have realised that he was not yet fully recovered from his wounding at Rathowen. Indeed, even if he had been able to rest and recuperate under the roof of his own home in the Saxon lands, it would have been a long while before he would have been fit enough to do any raiding. But he was as stubborn of mind as he was strong of body.

When his stomach began to growl loudly Streng remembered that he had not eaten since noon the previous day. He had been too eager to grab the spoils of raiding and, as a result, the need for nourishment had not even entered his thoughts. He was half asleep from trying to keep the mare on a steady eastward course all night and there was a strange burning sensation spreading in his chest that had nothing to do with the lack of food.

'Once the morning is well advanced,' he promised himself, 'then you can rest a little, but not before.'

So it was that when the sun had been over the

land of Eirinn for a little more than two hours, Streng came across a little stone cottage, its roof covered in green turf, set into a cutting in the mountainside and close to the road. There was smoke seeping out from the roof, for the houses of countryfolk in the eastern provinces often did not have holes or chimneys cut in them. The smoke simply made its way out through the ceiling until it escaped into the air.

Streng stopped the horse on the road for a moment when he saw the cottage. 'Here is a fire and food,' he thought, 'all laid out for me, and no coals to cover when I am done.' Any fear of who might be waiting within the cottage or what danger might face him there did not enter his head and so without further hesitation the Saxon turned his mare toward the dwelling.

They crossed a snow-covered but muddy track that led up to the building and the horse almost fell on her knees in the mire, crying out in her anguish. Despite the noise, no-one came out to question his business; all was perfectly still.

As he got closer to the house, a cow stuck her head out of the wide doorway and bellowed, her breath steaming. The snow fell on her nose, but she ambled further through the doorway blocking it completely with her body.

At that moment Streng knew that there must be someone inside the cottage hiding from him. He slipped from the back of his horse and drew his sword silently from his belt. There was no sign of life anywhere about and nothing stirred in the whole yard but the cow breathing hard in the cold air.

The Saxon scoured the nearby meadows but he could see no-one. Not that anyone would have been outdoors on a day like that, but Streng knew very little about farming and even less about cattle and livestock. He only knew how to slaughter them and cook them so that their flesh was not too tough.

He moved closer to the door of the cottage and tried to peer in through the door, but the cow resolutely stood in his way and the interior was so dark that he could not distinguish anything but the glow from a slow-burning peat fire. The sweet smell of the thick smoke filled the air, making him feel a little dizzy.

Then another scent touched his nostrils, enticing Streng to come further through the door. Whoever lived in this place had just recently butchered a pig for there was a cauldron hanging over the peat fire and the Saxon recognised the aroma of freshly cut pork. Streng had not experienced such a wondrous odour in many long weeks and his mouth began to water uncontrollably.

Everything he sensed around him spoke of danger, told him to be wary and to take no unnecessary risks. But the thin, savoury wisps of smoke beckoned to his empty stomach and he could not resist their call.

He pushed the cow out of his way and plunged into the darkness of the stone dwelling. It took him a few seconds for his eyes to focus and to adjust to the dim light, but when they did he saw a man and a woman huddled together in front of the fire on low wooden stools. They were wrapped against the cold in thick hides and old woven blankets.

They did not stir, they did not move, though Streng knew they must have heard him enter. His pulse began to race; his mind went back to all the strange things that had happened in the last few days, especially what had happened with the Ravens. His battle instincts warned him that he had

478

walked into a trap, not unlike the one that Hannarr had fallen into. However, he could not move, either to attack or to escape. He was rooted to the spot by the irrational fear that to make a wrong turn now would cost him his life.

When he finally dared to, he took his gaze off the strange couple and looked carefully about the room. His eyes began to catch more details of the interior of the dwelling and his heartbeat began to calm again.

On the floor there was the carcass of a pig mostly butchered but still sporting a meaty leg-bone and this sat just to the right of the man and the woman. All the farm implements were hanging neatly on wall racks specially constructed for the purpose. Among the tools there was a very good bow and a bundle of twenty or so arrows. It crossed his mind as being strange that there would be such a fine weapon in a poor place like this, but before he could properly question its presence, something distracted him.

Outside there was a loud and disturbing sound that Streng could not at first identify. His horse whinnied frantically and stamped. A young woman's voice called out. He recognised it as the voice of Caitlin. The pair in the cottage still did not turn around; they did not even flinch, so Streng bolted outside to see what was the matter.

The first thing he noticed when he burst through the doorway into the falling snow was that the cow was gone from sight. If he had been brought up with cattle he would have thought that very unusual, for they dislike snow and will do all they can to avoid traipsing through it.

It was the next thing that met his eyes that cleanly took his breath away, for he had only just that previous moment been examining the bow and it arrows. The shaft of each arrow had a split black feather wedged in its tail to give it stability in flight. A Raven's feather.

Standing on Caitlin's body, on the back of the horse, there was a huge, menacing black Raven. Its claws dug into her clothes, tearing the material in places, and it moved its head slowly about as if it were taking everything in and assessing the whole situation. Sciathan-cog had come to help Streng in whatever way he could. He alone of the rebel birds had survived the battle at the crossroads, just as Streng was the only one of his kind that had escaped.

The bird turned to acknowledge the warrior as soon as it felt him staring at it and then it opened its beak wide, but did not utter a sound. Only a thin rasping wheeze passed from its body as it breathed slowly out. 'The bastard's mocking me!' thought the Saxon. The Raven had his prisoner and his horse securely in its protective grip.

Caitlin had regained consciousness soon after the creature landed on her back and dug its talons into her. She struggled now to turn around and shake the animal off, but the Raven ignored her, treating her as it might an unstable branch.

Streng could only think of the fate of Hannarr and his men and knew that he had to get rid of the bird. The Raven, by some magic, seemed to force the Saxon's gaze toward the dark orbs of its eyes.

At first Streng only saw his own face reflected back through the jet-black glaze, but then suddenly he noticed something moving in the depths of the blackness behind the bird's eyes. He could not identify what it was he felt when he saw the Raven looking back at him, but he thought for a moment that it was in some way related to the feeling of kinship that warriors share who have fought many long campaigns together.

The bird turned its head away for a moment and Streng racked his brain as to how he might entice the Raven away from the horse and from his treasures. Then he remembered the freshly slaughtered pig that lay on the floor of the stone cottage. He carefully sheathed his sword and backed toward the door. The Raven watched his every move, cocking its head before Streng disappeared into the dwelling.

Once inside, the Saxon wasted no time in making for the carcass. But he did not quite reach it before, once again, he suffered a shock. The couple who had sat by the fire were gone. They had disappeared without a trace. There were no windows or doors to the house and the roof looked solid. Streng felt very uneasy and his body started to go numb.

'These sorts of things do not happen,' he told himself. 'There must be a curse on this place.'

Grabbing the leg of pork, he rushed back to the door, fearing all the while that the Raven had made off with his horse and his booty, but the bird was still there waiting patiently when Streng emerged into the light again.

The Saxon held the pork out before it and the bird took interest immediately, watching the food with a hunter's stare.

In a graceful move that exactly mirrored the way he handled an axe in battle, Streng swung the meat behind him and then tossed it towards the far side of a woodpile that lay stacked against the house.

Before it had even landed, Sciathan-cog had taken off from his perch and in a few moments he was tearing at the bone with sharp talons and holding his head back and neck straight to better swallow large chunks of the flesh.

When Streng was satisfied that the Raven was not paying him too much attention, he approached

481

the horse and slowly unstrapped Caitlin. In a moment she was no longer bound to the mare. He made sure she was still well secured before he attempted to carry her inside the house.

He stooped with his load to get her through the door and waited for a split second once inside, just in case some trap had been laid for him. There was still no sign of the occupants. He threw Caitlin down in front of the hearthstone and put his hand on the hilt of his sword. Nothing moved; there was no-one about.

Wasting no time he went back to his horse and took the other bags of booty from where he had secured them. When he had dumped them within the door of the cottage and checked that Caitlin could not move in her bindings, he returned to see to his horse.

As he came out of the door again he was shocked, but not entirely surprised, to find that now the mare was missing. He raced over to where she had stood, hoping to try and track her in the snow, but there were no hoof-prints to be seen. It seemed that she had simply vanished into the air. His eyes darted around the farmyard and he started to sweat.

The Raven cocked its head at him for a second, as if in answer, then returned to its meal. Then as the snow caught in his hair, Streng remembered Caitlin. 'How did I live so long when I am so bloody stupid?' he cursed himself. 'How could I even think of leaving her and all my treasure unguarded in that house?'

But as he plunged once more into the dingy dwelling he found her and all of his baggage exactly as he had left them. He went over to the fire and sat down on a stool to try and calm himself. The rest of the pork was still boiling in the iron cauldron and there was a jug of home-brewed mead by the hearthstone. He picked it up and took a draught, accepting its presence as if he had known all along that all this, the food, the fire, the shelter from the falling snow, it had all been arranged for him.

At the entrance to the hall known as the Star of the Poets, Gobann was met by Mawn and Sianan. Both of them wore the light grey robes of novices, their cowls settled on the back of their necks and leather belts to hold the coarsely woven fabric buckled close to their bodies. Their boots were made of sea-soned cowhide with wooden soles that had been sealed against the damp with many layers of tree sap, which also helped them keep their footing on slippery surfaces.

Over his shoulder the boy carried Gobann's harp case which had been hastily but expertly fitted with a new strap so that Mawn could keep it from dragging on the ground without too much effort.

Sianan held the little branch with the silver bells upon it, and she could not resist moving it slightly every now and then to hear the enchanting sound that they made.

Gobann studied the Silver Branch for a few moments in awe of all that it represented. He dimly remembered that it had hung from the bridle of his horse when he had been riding to the mound of testing, but now he realised that it had actually been awarded to him.

He was suddenly overcome with a mixture of emotions. First of all he felt that despite all that he had been through, he did not really deserve this kind of recognition. After all, he had not really understood everything that had happened to him in the days of his testing and a poet of the Silver Branch was expected to have wide-ranging insights into such matters.

He also felt a deep sorrow; not just sadness for having witnessed the passing of the Tree or of Eoghan or Lorgan or even of the village at Dobharcú. His sorrow was in knowing that it was he who would be called upon to report these things to the court of Leoghaire. It was he who would be required to compose the poem of these times. He would be remembered as the bearer of ill tidings.

'I am truly alone now,' he thought. 'I once imagined that I was alone, but in fact I had many people around me from whom I could draw support and counsel. In those days I was merely lonely. Now I have passed beyond that state of being. It is to me that folk will come in future, seeking advice and aid, begging for my insight and music spells. The rest of my life I will be very busy. I will have no time for anything but my work.'

When that final notion struck him he found that he was really only briefly sad for he perceived that he would be free of many of the responsibilities that other poets were required to fulfil. He began to think himself lucky.

'As for Síla,' he told himself, 'you were separated from her long ago so that you would be able to take this path in life. This is how it was meant to be.' But a voice cried out within him calling him a fool. 'She always understood that I would never be wholly hers, and that our paths did not lie together,' he reminded himself, 'that is why she insisted that we part.'

As he was dwelling on these thoughts, the doors to the hall were opened and he gathered the cloak of Raven feathers about him and allowed himself to be led into the place of feasting.

There were more poets and judges in the hall that night than Gobann could ever remember meeting. Assembled in that place were all the Druids of Eirinn, and many other folk besides. There were some, Gobann concluded from their dress or their speech, that were not of the Gaelic lands. There were women from Gaul and men from Caledonia, and even Origen and two of his novices were seated there in a place of honour. To have Christians seated in the hall of the Star of the Poets was unprecedented.

'Truly the world is changing,' Gobann thought.

Around the hall, set on iron posts, were large lanterns made of fat and linen twine. They burned with long flickering flames that lent a yellow tinge to the walls and to the roof of the hall. The central hearth, which was known as the Fire of Inspiration, was stacked with logs and in the coals at its edge nine salmon, freshly caught, were slowly roasting on flat, iron pans. The fish had been basted with honey and herbs and the sweet smell of the food made Gobann's stomach mutter with anticipation.

Across the embers on the far side of the fire, a young deer had been hung on a spit and the juices dropped noisily in amongst the red heat of the charcoal. Another wide iron dish lay nearby and on it were chestnuts and hazelnuts, the last of the winter store. These gently roasted over the heat and the whole room was filled with the aromas of all this cooking.

As he approached the fireplace the poet was ritually greeted once again by Cathach. The old man touched Gobann on the forehead and blessed him under his breath, then they embraced and stood in each other's arms for several minutes. Cathach laughed a little, which disconcerted Gobann: he had not expected laughter.

The poet was beginning to feel very uncomfortable with the old man's giggles. It was as if the mirth was releasing something stored deep inside himself. Then suddenly a wave of emotion struck Gobann and he felt like he could hold back the burden of his soul no longer and that he had to find some way to let his grief and fear escape.

As if he had been waiting for that very reaction, Cathach suddenly released the poet from his grip and pushed him away at arm's length. He stared searchingly at Gobann and the poet noticed that the old Druid's eyes were wet with tears.

Then Cathach led Gobann to his seat and Mawn and Sianan brought his harp and the symbol of his new status, the branch. The Silver Branch was arranged over the back of his chair so that it rested above his head.

Gobann seated himself quickly and at that signal the whole of the assembled Druids rose silently and stood while Cathach spoke to them.

'He has travelled far,' the old man intoned. 'He has wandered the ways of the spirit road and returned to us from the realm of the dead. He has been given the wisdom of the oldest of creatures and with the most ancient of beings he has shared laughter and merriment. He returned to be a teacher who will instruct the Wanderers. He is Counsellor to King Murrough of Munster.'

With those words spoken, Cathach sat down in his seat and the Druids all followed him. Mawn then brought the harp from its case and just as Cathach had instructed him to do, he placed it in Gobann's steady hands.

The poet did not rise from his seat. He would never again be obliged to do that when addressing any gathering, even if it were a council of all the most powerful kings in the Gaelic world. He rested the harp on his knee and leaned the sound-box back against his left shoulder. Then he ran his rounded fingernails down the wires.

For a moment the sensation in the tips of his fingers reminded him of what it had been like to have claws instead of hands and so he began his poem.

'I was the most ancient of creatures; the black storm that comes at harvest time.

I was buried in the womb-mound, where the spirits gather for to start their journey home ward.

I was wrapped tightly in blue and black and painted with mist and with the rising stars.

My mouth could not eat, but all my attention was given to the little creatures of the field.

My tongue could not speak, yet I talked to thousands of souls, who sought my advice.

My hands could no longer hold the harp, my fingers grew barbs.

In the light of the Sun I was of the Air;

In the light of the Moon I was of the Earth;

In the damp of the snow-storm I was of the Water;

In the twisted wreckage of the Quicken Tree I was of the Fire;

My King rules but does not know that his King has passed forever from this world, or that another greater King has come to Eirinn whose name will be remembered long after we are all gone.

His Queen is in peril of her life, held fast in a stronghold, another Queen will she bear.

When the warriors were set upon by my breth-ren, I stood back in awe and watched;

When the valley was razed by the sea-people, I
    wept.
I found the blade of the old ones;
I found the home of my loved one;
I was in her country but she dwells now in
    Eirinn.'

He had not consciously decided on which words
would be appropriate for this occasion. The images
had come to him from some place outside of
himself, as if some invisible being were standing
close to him and whispering the lines and he,
Gobann, were only repeating them. This was the
power of the Silver Branch.

When he had finished reciting the poem, he took
to the harp and strummed at it. He sought now to
play a new composition on the instrument, a
melody that would not merely accompany his
words but would speak to his audience as if it were
words.

In his heart there was a tune that had never been
played in the hall of the Star of the Poets. He listened to his soul singing a song in harmony with
the harp as he touched the wires tentatively. The
memory of his soul-journey became clearer then
and his fingers grew bolder, striking the wires with
passion and confidence.

The sounds that he brought forth from the
music-loom called Banfa were, at first, like the
distant rumble of thunder in far-off lands. Then
Gobann added flashes of lightning to the melody,
and driving rain to the scene. The calls of fleeing
animals and the cries of frightened children were
suddenly there in that tune. Streams flowed down
to mighty rivers that no Gael had seen, but their
watery roar could be heard in the rise and fall of
the many strands of melody.

When the minutes began to pass into longer measures of time, Gobann coaxed images from the music that were related to the long while that he spent sitting in the branches of the Quicken Tree. The cawing Ravens argued back and forth; their queen, the She-Raven, sat high above the throng, imperious and removed from her subjects.

The final movement of the piece combined the noises of a rising gale with the steady beating axes of the foreigners as they gradually hacked the sacred Tree to death. The gathered storm burst forth within the music as the harp wires rang out loud and strong and tore at the souls of all his listeners. Gobann continued to build the melodious tempest, through the lower tones of his instrument, until the strings were chiming wild and discordant and his fingers moved like the flashes of lightning that struck out at his audience through the tune.

Then suddenly his hands ceased their frantic work and Gobann ended the recital in a frenzied and exotic chord that was more alien to the ears of his listeners than even the tones of Saxon speech.

Only a very few of those hearing it knew that this last phrase, the dying strain of his composition, spoke of a distant time when they would all be long forgotten and no-one would be left who would remember the power and the enchantment that music could embrace.

Mawn had kept pace with the wild music from the very start. Untutored in the forms of music as he was, he did not flinch when the unusual sequences of melody crept in, as some of the older Druids did. He only thought of the wonder of what was revealed to his imagination.

As he often did when the harp took hold of him

in this way, Gobann had shut his eyes at an early stage in the performance. He had consciously closed the world out, putting all his energy into creating a tale told entirely by the instrument. The wires finally stopped their bell-like ringing after some minutes, and only then did he allow himself to come out of the melody trance.

Opening his eyes slowly he took his time to focus on all that was about him in the room. When his vision had settled and he could see clearly, his gaze fell on a figure dressed in the robes of a novice, who stood directly in front of him on the opposite side of the table.

Gobann squinted, as if by concentrating all the power of his eyesight on one spot he would be able to see through the cowl and discern the face of the Druid who stood before him. He was certain that it was the same woman who had pressed her body against him in the mound of testing.

The gifts of the spirit power that had helped him travel swiftly across the land had all but left him now and Gobann felt helpless. He knew that from this day forth he would be bound to the world of the flesh, so he decided to wait patiently until the woman lifted her arm to remove the veil from her head.

As she raised her arm to draw back the covering, the robe fell away from her fingers. The poet was drawn immediately to the spiral designs cut into the back of her hand in a dark blue dye.

His heart stopped for just a second, then he felt it leap into his throat. He bit his lip. He could not speak. His body was numb with anticipation.

She pulled the cowl away from her face slowly, enticingly, until the features underneath were fully revealed.

Then Síla leaned forward across the table that

490

separated her from Gobann and kissed him lightly on the cheek. There was love and longing in the way her lips brushed his face and Gobann was shocked to find himself blushing.

TWENTY-SEVEN

urrough took the road to the east almost as soon as he left Morann's camp at the crossroads. He followed it high into the hills travelling as fast as he judged was safe in the steady snowfall.

When he reached the topmost ridge of the mountains just after dawn, he began to rethink his search. The Saxon would be heading to the sea, of that he was sure. But would he have chanced to take the road? If he had, he would surely be moving at a much slower pace than Murrough had been for he had a burden to bear.

The prince turned in the saddle to look at the path that ran toward the coast. He sniffed at the chill air, sighted a hamlet of clustered houses further down the track, and then checked back along the road he had travelled.

'He will have to rest his mount and take food,' he concluded. 'A Saxon may be able to march for days without rest, but a horse needs to stop once in a while, especially if it is carrying two heavy loads.'

Then he saw, far away along the road he had already traversed, a riderless horse plodding its way up the pass. Murrough did not wait another moment. He turned his own steed and galloped back down the hill.

Streng sat breathless by the fire for a long, long time. It was not just that he was shocked by the disappearance of his horse and the two occupants of the house.

He was aware that he had fallen deathly ill.

Not long after he sat down at the hearth he noticed a trickle of blood issue forth from his nose. This was followed by a steady flow from the wound in his neck, which had opened up again. He leaned his hand on his throat to stem the bleeding but it was quite a while before it ceased completely and he felt he could relax the pressure on it.

He knew he had pushed himself too hard this time and now he had no choice but to rest.

Looking around the cottage he reckoned that he probably could have chosen a worse place to hide. There was a good stock of butter wrapped in a greasy cloth near at hand. There was fresh milk in a wooden pitcher just out of reach of the heat of the fire. There was a boiling cauldron of fresh soup cooking gently over the peat and the house was dry and comparatively warm. A neat stack of peat, enough fuel for many days, lined the wall near to the door.

The pain that had started in his neck at the same time as the bleeding spread quickly to his chest and it was not long before Streng began to feel that he could no longer keep his eyes open. He was weary, not just because of the lack of rest and the injury; he was exhausted to the very core of his soul. He did not try to comprehend the cause of this lethargy; all he knew was that he wanted to sleep a while.

Eventually he dragged himself up out of his chair and made for the doorway, hoping to escape the magic spell that he was sure had been placed on him. On the wall hanging near to the door, the bow and its arrows beckoned him, but he resisted the temptation to take the weapon outside and test his marksmanship with it. Instead he made straight out into the yard. The sickening sensation spread through his body with every beat of his heart. The ground seemed to be moving under him, in much the same way as it might when returning to land after many long months at sea.

He had to steady himself against the doorway and suddenly he realised that he was gravely ill.

Leaning heavily on the door-post, he looked out at the scene before him. The snow had stopped falling and the sun was struggling to light the land through tiny gaps in the clouds. Shafts of light descended on the Earth, illuminating vast swaths of the countryside in the valley below the cottage.

Streng heard a sound nearby, a clicking, gurgling noise. He turned his attention toward the source of it and saw the Raven still gorging itself on the leg of pork.

Unexpectedly it ceased its feasting and cocked a wary head at the Saxon. Streng felt an overwhelming desire to be rid of the creature. He turned to his pack which was just inside the door. Drawing out his axe from its sheathing and raising it above his head, he made a lunge in the Raven's direction.

Without warning the world unexpectedly began to spin around him and he could sense that his legs could no longer hold him upright. He placed the head of the axe on the floor beside him and leaned heavily on the handle until the spasm passed. Then he left the axe propped up against the doorway and returned to sit down by the fire.

Caitlin was still lying bound on the floor, though she had managed to crawl a little closer to the fire. She looked at him through eyes that stung Streng

494

with contempt but he was feeling too weak even to kick her. The Saxon stumbled toward the high-backed stool he had earlier sat on and collapsed on it. Almost immediately he fell into a fitful sleep, his legs stretched out before him, his head thrown back and his hands trailing on the floor beside him.

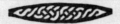

Cieran, who was the bard at the settlement of Ardmór, looked out over the road that led toward Cashel and squinted to see if he could recognise the three men were who were approaching the settlement. Soon they got close enough so that the Druid could plainly see that two of them were warriors and then he feared the worst: Ardmór was about to be attacked by the King of Munster because its chieftain, Brecan, had sided with the King of Laigin in the war against Leoghaire of Teamhair.

'They are soldiers,' he whispered to the man who squatted beside him at the top of the rampart.

Cieran could not, however, make out whether the other rider was a warrior also. 'If they come here you may well be taken to Cashel as prisoners,' stated the Druid. 'And we will all be punished for allowing you to remain here,' he thought to himself.

'If they take us to Cashel we'll never see the light of day again,' sobbed the man, 'and me and Darach might as well be dead!'

'If we only knew where your master is!' exclaimed Cieran. 'I am sure that we could get you safe passage out of Eirinn. We can only hope that he will agree to make a solemn promise never to return to these shores.'

'Do you think that they will exile him?' asked the Briton.

'Without a doubt they will. If he has been captured alive that is,' replied Cieran.

The three travellers halted their horses not far from the gates to the settlement and the two who Cieran had decided were warriors turned their mounts about and rode back in the direction of Cashel. The other rider continued on his way toward the settlement, alone and unescorted.

In a few minutes the man was close enough that they could both see who it was. 'It is Seginus,' the servant muttered in disbelief when the rider got close. 'He is safe!'

The Roman dismounted at the gates and led his horse up to the temporary chapel that Palladius had built just outside the rampart. Once inside the flimsy structure, he knelt and crossed himself and he remained there for many hours, at times silent and at others overcome with emotion.

Darach and Mog, the Roman's two Briton servants whom he had purchased from a trader at Teamhair only a year before, waited at a discreet distance praying also. But their prayers centred on whether Seginus would punish them for prematurely leaving the battlefield of Rathowen.

When their master had not returned from his parley with the chieftain of the fortress on the night before the battle, they had assumed that the Irish had very likely murdered him. They also suspected that their attack on the woman by the stream, whilst they were hunting the stag, may have had something to do with his disappearance. They were only partly correct.

When night fell on the second day after the battle of Rathowen and they had not managed to locate their master in the confusion of the defeat, the two of them decided that Ardmór would probably be as safe a place as any for them to hide. They also reasoned that Seginus, if he was alive, would probably make for that place in an attempt to escape over to Britain or Gaul.

When they arrived at the settlement they entreated Cieran to find them a boat that would carry them and their master safely away to Britain. Cieran readily obliged. He would have done anything to help speed the foreigners from the shores of Eirinn and from Ardmór. He did not like them and he realised that their presence placed the whole community in danger of King Eoghan's wrath.

Seginus spoke to no-one when he finished praying at the wooden chapel and though he had not eaten or rested, he went straight from there to walk to the stone chapel of Saint Linus, ignoring his servants and all who approached him. When he got to the beach he found the doors flung open and the building empty, save for the echoes of the ocean that roared nearby.

The cross that had always stood before the stone altar was lying face down on the floor; all the holy vessels and sacred regalia were scattered around about and the little book of psalms that had been the bishop's gift to the monks of the community was lying open on the flagstones, the pages blowing about in the breeze.

Seginus bent down to pick up the precious volume, his eyes drawn to the fine handwriting and the illuminated borders. As he stood up again his gaze fell on the page that chanced to be open and he read the words aloud in Latin. 'O God, the heathen have come into Your dwelling, they have defiled Your temple and left Jerusalem in wreck. The corpses of Your servants have been given as meat for the birds and the flesh of Your saints has become food for the beasts of the Earth.'

Seginus paused for a moment as the wind rose outside and whistled through the open entrance to the chapel. He took the book and sat on one of the stone benches that had been set out especially for the monks, separated from the seating of the common folk. Laying the binding flat on his lap, he turned the page to read what else the psalmist had to say.

The next leaf was missing and Seginus could not remember the intervening verses, but the last lines of the psalm were there on the next page. 'In the manner of Your great power, preserve those of us who would die without Your intervention. And to those who have worked against You, visit upon them their curses, seven times over. So that we Your chosen people, the sheep of your pasture, will thank You forever. We will praise You through all the coming generations if You but grant this prayer.'

Seginus let the book fall shut on his knees and he wept again. He wept for all the things that might have been, for all the treachery and murder that he had seen. And he wept also for his own sake. He wept for the wrongs that had been done to him and for the two people who had been closest to him in his life.

'Eirinn took my brother,' he cried. 'Eirinn took my bishop also, who was my teacher.'

When the tears had finally dried up, he felt a little comforted. He cast his eye about the chapel and then began the task of putting it in order. Outside, his two servants waited, unwilling to disturb their master, knowing too well that he had a dangerous temper.

It was after dusk before Seginus had finished putting everything back in its proper place. He gathered what he could of the holy vessels of the Sacrament so that he could take them away with him and then he lit every candle that he could find in the place. Closing the double wooden doors behind him, he departed his brother's tomb-house intending never to return.

Darach had taken some of the brass and silver from the chapel and used it to help purchase a boat almost as big as the one Palladius had set off from Britain in. He never told Seginus where he got the money and Seginus never asked him.

The Roman monk suspected that some of the holy vessels had been disposed of for this purpose, but by this time, he did not really care what happened as long as he was able to leave the island of Eirinn and not have to spend another night under its skies.

Within two days the weather had become calm enough that Darach felt confident about setting off, taking a course following the coast from Ardmór up to the northeast. At a certain point, if the weather held, Darach reasoned that they would easily make landfall in Britain.

Cieran gave them provisions and water and made Seginus swear that he would never return to Eirinn. The Roman was more than happy to do so, confident that he would never find himself thrown up on the wild sea shore of this land ever again.

Knowing that if the king's warriors found the foreigners at the settlement all the tribe would be punished for harbouring them, Cieran rushed the Roman and his servants along, encouraging them to depart as soon as possible. He was fairly certain that if he were able to extract an oath from the Roman that he would not come back to these shores, the king might not take such a dim view of the fugitives' presence at Ardmór.

Indeed Cieran was doing all that was expected of him as a Druid, steering the community through times when the warriors were away, and he hoped it was just possible that his actions might save the village from any further trouble. Brecan their chief had drawn attention to himself by siding against the King of Munster in war. 'Perhaps I can bring events back into some kind of balance,' reasoned Cieran.

With a slight breeze and a clear sky before them the three, Darach, Mog and their master set out. Whilst the other two rowed, Seginus sat in the bow staring back on Eirinn and the chapel where Linus lay. Many faces flashed through his mind, peering out of the white-capped sea: Palladius, Declan, Isernus, Donatus, Caitlin, Guthwine, Brecan, Hannarr and Streng. Their forms seemed to be spread out like a tapestry that had been woven into the scene before him.

The hills around Ardmór were bright green with only traces of white where the snow had been. Spring had come at last and patches of the beach were exposed to the sun so that the wet slate sparkled in the light. The Roman let his mind dwell on all that had come to pass since he had set foot in that land, and he could remember very few things that had made him happy or had given him joy. Now, as he watched the island drift further and further out of reach, Seginus thought of how beautiful Eirinn looked and briefly regretted his rash promise never to return.

He took one last long look on the beach where he had landed and where his brother had perished. A figure stood there now, where moments before the pebbles had been deserted and he was dressed in long black robes, waving both his arms over his head.

Seginus Gallus half-stood in the boat, sending the two oarsmen into a panic for a moment, but no matter how hard he strained his eyes, he never knew if the figure on the beach was just one of the novice monks come to farewell him or the spirit of his brother beckoning him to return.

TWENTY-EIGHT

hen Streng opened his eyes again, the snow had stopped drifting down from the sky and the wind had died almost completely. He felt refreshed and much stronger for his short rest. With shaking fingers he gently touched the wound in his throat. The bleeding had stopped and there was no longer any pain.

He looked to his right and noticed that Caitlin was still curled up as close to the fire as she could manage without being within the Saxon's immediate reach. Streng watched her sleeping for a moment. He savoured the colour of her wild red-brown hair and his eyes strayed to the contours of her hips under the travelling clothes that she wore.

He started to feel the desire for this woman rise in him. She moved a little in her rest, her hands still tied in front of her, restricting her movement.

'I have waited long enough for this,' he told himself. 'I'll have her now.'

He got to his feet and with his knife slit the bindings on her legs. She stirred but did not wake. Slowly he edged his hand under her to unfasten the riding trousers she wore and then he swiftly removed her belt. As the leather slipped across the floor under her body, Caitlin shook herself from sleep.

By this time Streng had his fingers hooked around the top of her breeches and was pulling them down over her thighs, trying to get them off her as quickly as he could.

Caitlin fought him hard though, bringing her bound hands heavily down upon the back of his neck and bending her knees to try and prevent him removing her clothes. She aimed to reach his more delicate parts if she could, but Streng expected an attack to that quarter and so he was ready to fend off her blows.

The Saxon changed tack when he found he was getting nowhere with her trousers and he reached up to tear at her shirt, ripping both outer and under garment in one great sweep of his large hand. The sight of one of her bared breasts distracted him from the fight for just a moment. He wanted to make this experience last, to take his time; he did not want to rush any part of it.

Caitlin thrashed about as best she could, trying to get her body in a position where she could roll away from the Saxon, but he pinned her tightly. The harder she fought the more aroused Streng became.

Suddenly she ceased her wild kicking and lay back flat on the floor, breathing heavily. Streng smiled an open-mouthed smile through his yellowed teeth. He saw this as a gesture of submission and it was just what he had hoped for. He leaned over her to take in the sweet aroma of her body; the scent something like a combination of dried herbs and sweat. She did not resist him.

As his nose brushed against her neck she reached around to the side of his head and bit him hard on the throat, drawing blood. The shock of the attack threw him off her and back across the room, as if it had been a snake that had bitten him.

Outside, the Raven, Sciathan-cog, called out in his most urgent warning voice. He could see a horseman approaching and with his far-sight he knew that it was a nobleman of the house of Munster who was passing that way. The Raven wanted to warn the Saxon, to give him some indication of the danger at hand, but Streng did not answer, so Sciathan-cog raised the pitch and tone of his call to an eerie gurgling wail.

Streng sat on his backside holding the new wound on his neck. The sudden thud of the fall set the old arrow wound in the front of his throat to bleeding again, and he had jolted his back in getting up off Caitlin. His temper was beginning to get the better of him.

When he heard the Raven cry, something snapped in him. Though Sciathan-cog was sending an alert to Streng, all the Saxon heard was a mocking call coming from out by the woodpile.

He knew that he could not get near to the woman for the time being, nor did he wish to, so he let his anger pour out at the bird. His eyes fell on the bow that hung on the wall. In a second he was on his feet and he had the weapon in his hands.

In the manner of a professional soldier he tested the bow-string, pulling it hard against his chest and pushing the supple timber away with his other hand.

Caitlin, horrified, saw him reach for the bow but had no idea what he had in mind. For a moment she thought that he was going to kill her with it, but in the next instant Streng had an arrow wedged in the string and he stormed out of the cottage, drawing the shaft to his cheek. All Caitlin could tell was that he was cursing, or so she thought, since she could not understand the Saxon speech.

Only a moment passed before the terrible

screeching of a bird rent the peace of the country-side. The squawking rose to a crazy, frantic scream and then Caitlin distinctly heard a loud crack. The cries immediately ceased and she knew that the Saxon had broken the Raven's neck.

A second later Streng returned carrying the bow in one hand and the carcass of Sciathan-cog in the other. The spent arrow-shaft still protruded from the bird's body where it had struck him deep, disabling his wings.

Streng flung the dead bird on the fire and the flames leapt up sizzling the feathers and filling the cottage with the stench of their burning.

Murrough was riding back down the valley having inspected the unattended horse. He immediately recognised the mare as being one of those that the Saxons had raided from his company some days before, for it bore the seal of the Prince of Cashel. Burned into its rump on the left hand side, there was a small brand about the size of an acorn. It was a stylised version of the Quicken Tree, bearing the Ogham signs that were Murrough's own mark.

He was trotting along looking for a sign of an outdoor fire, thinking that the Saxon would most likely have camped out despite the foul weather. The prince passed by the cottage just off the main path of the road, with its smoky roof and muddy yard, and probably would have continued on his way if it had not been for the appearance of a great Raven. The memory of the attack on Morann's soldiers was still fresh in his mind, so the sight of the bird made him extremely cautious.

Murrough dismounted and tied his horse up in some bushes out of the direct line of sight of the house and proceeded to approach the cottage on foot. If the Saxon was hiding inside, Murrough knew that the sound of clattering hooves would give him away and the renegade would be waiting for him when he arrived.

The prince had not advanced ten paces closer to the house when the bird started screaming at the top of its lungs. Murrough knew it was signalling to someone in the cottage, so he waited, crouched in a clump of bushes, where he was certain that he could not be seen, but where he could safely observe all that happened.

After a short while a large man came out of the hut and Murrough's suspicions were confirmed. 'Its no use, they are waiting for me,' he told himself. 'The Saxon even has a bird on watch for me. I just hope I can get back to my horse without being seen. I'll have to find another way to reach the cottage.'

He was just turning to go back to his horse when an unexpected thing happened. The Saxon drew the bow and let fly an arrow at the bird, striking it hard in the chest. The Raven did not stop screaming though; in fact its cries got louder, piercing the air with its high-pitched notes. The Saxon went right up to the black bird then and grabbed it without any difficulty for the Raven could not use its wings and it could not run.

The foreigner lifted it up, looked it in the eye and snapped its neck cleanly. That done, he turned swiftly on his heel and went back inside the cottage, carrying the black corpse by the throat.

Murrough knew then that he had not been spotted and so he made his way down toward the farmyard. He trod lightly until he could smell the acrid smoke that told him the Saxon had thrown the bird's body among the flames of the fire. After that he moved much more slowly and carefully.

He got as far as fifty paces away from the house when a sound came out of the building that chilled his blood and turned his legs to water. From out of nowhere a woman screamed, a wild cry that echoed the dying pain of the Raven.

Without thinking of the consequences to his own life, Murrough bolted toward the farmhouse, slipping on the snow and rolling in the mud. Such was his haste that when he got up off the ground again he neglected to draw his sword. He was ready now to tear the Saxon apart with his bare hands.

As he finally got to the door he saw through the smoky gloom the form of a woman sprawled against the wall where she had been dumped only seconds before. Her clothes were torn above the waist and her breasts were uncovered. She did not move a muscle and Murrough thought perhaps she was already dead.

'Cait!' he cried in despair. She did not answer or make any sign that she had heard him. Thinking only of Caitlin's safety Murrough leapt through the door and came face to face with the waiting Streng.

The Saxon was already holding his sword and as Murrough reached to unsheathe his own weapon, Streng slashed the prince's fighting hand, forcing him to fall back.

Murrough saw the light of madness in the man's eyes, heard the strange cackle of his laughter fill the dingy cottage and retreated toward the door. Streng lifted his sword quickly then to strike at Murrough's head and the prince was forced to duck and throw himself against the wall.

As he landed Murrough's hand fell upon the haft of Streng's axe. He picked the weapon up swiftly and though he had never before used such a blade, he immediately noticed that it seemed to be very

507

light in his hands, though the axe-head was made of tempered iron.

The Saxon sword pounded down again in Murrough's direction and he blocked the blow with the haft of the axe. Then he deftly lifted the weapon and swung it round him as he had seen the Saxons do at Rathowen. The razor-sharp edge of iron sliced through the smoke and cut the top of Streng's thigh.

Murrough took another swing and drove the Saxon back a little more. Then Streng sprang forward and made a stab at the prince, but Murrough turned the enemy sword away and drove the point into the earthen floor with a parry of the axe. Streng fell back a few more steps to get his breath.

In a great burst of energy Murrough heaved the weapon at his opponent and brought the axe crashing down in a blow that would have shattered the hardest Saxon head. Except that the prince's blow went wide and the blade fell, cutting into the floor.

Streng was quick to take advantage of his enemy's blunder. He used the hilt of his sword to punch Murrough under the chin. The prince fell back still clutching the handle of the axe, but he had lost the advantage. Streng came up to him as close as he could and drove the blade directly at his body.

The thrust missed its mark but tore open the flesh of Murrough's left arm, just below the shoulder. The Saxon managed to push him back against the opposite wall of the house and Murrough could only watch as Streng lifted his blade to strike the death blow. The prince was winded and he was too slow and weary now to stave off the inevitable.

Streng laughed at his foe and said something in his own tongue. Then suddenly the colour left his face, his eyes widened and the wound in his throat began to trickle blood. The blow that he was about to land on Murrough never came.

The prince could not tell why the Saxon had unexpectedly slowed his attack, but Murrough quickly recovered the strength to take advantage of it. He raised the axe and swung it around to slice into Streng's belly. The leather jerkin that the Saxon wore gave way under the cruel blade and he fell forward, bending almost to touch the ground with his forehead. Murrough lifted the axe high again and this time he brought it down in a sweep that was calculated to carve deep into the foreigner's back.

Just before the axe found its mark, Murrough noticed the black hilt of a tiny knife protruding from the Saxon's ribs at a point where they met with his spine. This axe, the fearsome weapon so often used to hack at Irish flesh, now ripped just as happily into a Saxon backbone. With a loud crack, Streng's spine snapped and he fell forward without uttering a sound save for the air escaping from his lungs.

It took Murrough a long while to recover his breath. He had never been at such close quarters with a warrior who knew so well what he was doing. He clutched his injured arm and watched the body of his opponent with a wary eye in case the corpse sprang into life once more. But there would be no more fights for Streng on this Earth.

In the corner of the room Caitlin still knelt, her cloak wrapped around her covering her torn clothes. Her hands were drenched to the wrists in the Saxon's blood and her face was bruised and cut from the beating that the foreigner had given her.

She had managed to twist her way out of her

bonds at the very last minute, while Murrough kept the Saxon busy. As soon as she had freed herself she had reached into the top of her boot for the scian-dubh, the little knife that the Sidhe-man had given her. It had somehow stayed in place through all that had happened to her since the cutting of the Tree, and she thought then that she would have given twenty silver acorns for it had she known how valuable it would prove to be.

Caitlin and the prince faced each other for a while and then Murrough staggered over to her. He moved to kneel down in front of her and as he did so they fell into each other's arms and there they stayed, hugging one another until the fire started to die down.

Eventually Murrough got up and dragged the Raven corpse from the hearth, flinging it out into the snow. He put fresh turfs on the coals and stirred up the fire with an iron poker. When he had done that, Caitlin bound his wounds with strips of cloth from his torn shirt and found fresh water for them to drink.

Then they sat down together and talked for the first time since they had met. They talked of their fears, and their relief at finding each other when they did, of their hopes and their dreams and of how truly fortunate they were to be alive. They spoke also of the Quicken Tree and the Ravens and all the strange happenings that had befallen them, though Caitlin did not mention the little man who had given her the scian-dubh. Finally they discussed the plans of the Druid Council and spoke of Mawn and Sianan and the world that the Wanderers would very likely inherit.

After a long while they both realised that they were desperately hungry and so they ate of the meal that had been simmering in the cauldron and when they were finished their first helping they ate some more, for the Saxons had not fed them well during their short captivity.

Having filled their bellies they decided to rest well until morning and to set out first thing in the morning for the Cashel crossroads. But instead, they talked until night came and they shared some of the mead they found in a jug by the fire. Eventually, when they could talk no more, they fell asleep entwined together wrapped in their travelling cloaks, with Streng's body still lying on the earthen floor where he had fallen to Murrough's death blow.

In the middle of the night Caitlin awoke and she lay for a long time looking into the face of the Prince of Cashel. The firelight gave his skin an orange glow and the bright red of his hair seemed to mix with that otherworldly light, so that she could not clearly make out where his hairline ended and his face began. It reminded her for a brief moment of the blue Sidhe-man for the light gave Murrough's features the same shimmering quality.

Despite her feelings for Murrough, her thoughts strayed to Fintan, even as she watched the young prince in his sleep. She went over in her mind all that had happened to her since Rathowen and how Murrough had so often put his own safety before hers. She felt more than lucky to be alive; she felt she was blessed to be alive, and she knew that she owed Murrough a great debt of gratitude for all that he had done.

They had failed in their mission to keep the Quicken Tree from destruction, that was true, but Caitlin was aware that all things have their time on Earth allotted to them. If it was the day for the Tree to part from the world, then there was no force that could have prevented that from coming to pass.

Unconsciously she began to trace her hand around the young prince's face as she let her mind wander, seeking to comfort him in his sleep. She found herself thinking that he was very handsome and that he deserved a good life and of what it might be like to share a life with him.

She heard in her mind Fintan saying, 'Your way lies with the prince now,' though she could not in that moment remember a time when he would have said such a thing. Just then Murrough unexpectedly opened his eyes and Caitlin touched a finger gently to his mouth to soothe him.

She reached around him bringing her hands up to cradle his head and he leaned over closer to her. As their lips lightly brushed together and they locked in a long embrace, Caitlin abandoned herself to the feeling that she was at last safe and warm and that nothing could harm her again.

They were still wrapped in each other's arms when Morann and his warriors found them early the next morning.

TWENTY-NINE

fter Gobann had recovered from the initial shock of not only seeing Síla again, but of actually being in the same room as her, he tried to settle back into the feast and enjoy what was taking place there in his honour. But try as he might he could not relax.

Seated at the table where she had a direct line of sight to the poet, Síla kept looking across at him and smiling. Each time she did so a shudder rocked Gobann's whole body and he lost track of whatever conversation he was having.

'Why is it that now that I have been able to consider freeing myself from her, she has returned?' he asked himself.

Gobann gazed about the hall trying to control his raging emotions. At the rear of the feast his friend Origen was seated inconspicuously. There were two other monks with him, whom Gobann did not immediately recognise. The poet motioned for them to approach the high-table, hoping that they would be able to keep his mind off Síla for a while. Origen rose, gathering his white robes about him in a flourish and holding the excess fabric under his left arm as was his habit when walking.

The three monks were a few paces away from the high-table when Gobann noticed the subtle nod of greeting that passed between Síla and the Christian. In the next second it struck the poet that

Origen had known all along that she was in Eirinn and had only been pretending that she had resolved to stay in her own country. The only thing that Gobann could not work out was why his friend did not tell him the truth concerning her whereabouts.

The poet did not have to wait very long for an answer. Origen and the other two monks reached the table just as the question was forming in his head.

'Congratulations, my friend,' Origen offered, noticing the frown on the poet's brow.

Gobann did not acknowledge or respond. He just sat glancing between the Christian and the woman from Britain, disbelief giving way to outrage.

Finally Origen could stand the poet's silence no longer. He knew what Gobann was thinking. 'I did as the Druid Council requested,' he protested. 'They knew I was travelling to Britain and felt that I would be less likely than one of their own kind to rouse suspicion among the tribes of the Cruitne, some of whom are not well disposed to Gaelic folk. I passed on to her your messages and theirs and then went home to my own land. She and I arranged that when I returned from Alexandria I would pass through Britain again and that she could then travel with me to Eirinn.'

This much Gobann had been able to work out by himself, but he still did not know why they had gone about things in such a secretive manner.

'Because of your géas,' Origen explained. 'Cathach felt that you would not perform well in your testing if Síla was hovering around to distract you.'

'And why is she suddenly so important to the Druid Council?' Gobann exclaimed sarcastically.

'Because, I am told, she will be Sianan's teacher,'

replied Origen, 'and because you are in love with her.'

'I am what?' stuttered the poet.

'Lorgan and Cathach were both wise enough to know that if you separate a person from the people and the things they love, you will just end up with an unhappy person. Allow someone to spend their life with those they care about and to indulge in the pastimes they love and you will have a person who performs their duties well and survives into their old age.'

'That is not a good argument for the monastic life!' exclaimed Gobann.

'Indeed it is not,' one of the other monks interrupted, and the poet suddenly recognised him from the trial of Palladius after the battle of Rathowen, though he now wore a white robe over his black habit. It was Declan. 'But if the life of service to God and solitary prayer is all that you desire from life then the argument is excellent.'

'Our ways do not stipulate that all monks or nuns should go without the things that are necessary for their physical and emotional and spiritual wellbeing, but there are many who interpret the rule of the monastery in that manner,' added Origen.

'And what of the Roman ways?' queried the poet, recognising now the third monk as Isernus, who had been left in Declan's care. 'The Roman Church is not so obliging when it comes to the wellbeing of its nuns and brothers, or so I have been led to believe.'

Declan took a deep breath before he attempted to answer. 'You are right. Often the life of a Roman monk is unbearably tedious and at times it seems contrary to the teachings of Christ, but I only knew the Roman ways before I came here and to me they seemed right. Now I know that there are other ways, and some are much more as I would imagine Christ would have wanted; in future, I will teach my brothers to respect those ways. There is a community in Britain which was founded by Saint Ninian at a place called Whithorn. Their abbot died recently and they have asked me to come and be his replacement. Isernus and I will set out in the next few weeks if the weather improves; indeed, that is all that has kept us on these shores. All I want from life is to serve my God and to teach the way of Christ and so I am overjoyed to be going to a place where that will be all that is required of me.'

Declan put his hand on Gobann's shoulder as if he had known him all his life. 'But you, gentle Druid,' the monk admonished, 'I can see that for all your wishing to be in touch with the things of the spirit, there are other experiences that you desire from life which the ways of solitude cannot give you. When I first came to Eirinn I did not believe this, but now I know it to be true. The way of the flesh and the way of the spirit are inseparable. Even for one such as me.'

Gobann listened to all Declan had to say and though the man was younger than he was, the poet could sense a great wisdom in the Christian that had nothing to do with how many years he had lived on the Earth.

'Well?' asked Origen. 'After all this, aren't you going to go over to her table and at least talk to her?'

Letting a smile play upon his lips, Gobann took his friend and Declan and Isernus each by the hand in turn and bade them good night. Then he looked to where Síla was sitting and saw that she was still smiling at him. He got up from his seat and went to her and led her out of the feasting hall into the gardens of Teamhair.

Once they were outside she untied the bundle of her hair, where she had knotted the black strands on the top of her head, and pulled the cowl from around her face so that Gobann could see into her eyes as she spoke.

'I have missed you,' she told him. 'But you must have known that we would be together again one day.'

Gobann wanted to tell her all that had happened since they had parted; he wanted to let her know that she had never really left his thoughts, but he simply nodded in silent agreement.

The clouds had begun to break and with them the very last of the winter was falling to the hand of spring. High up in the sky a lone, bright star shone through the blue depths of night. It was the poet's friend, the Even-star, come to remind him of who he was and where his duties lay.

'I am bound now more than ever to the ways of the spirit,' he began, 'and I am responsible for the education of the Wanderers. The world is changing and there is much work that I have to do.'

Síla smiled at him again, amused at his nervousness. Gobann only saw the smile and he was afraid that his message had fallen on deaf ears. 'I have a great deal of hard work ahead of me,' he stressed. 'Too much really. I will need to concentrate all my efforts on that.'

Síla laughed now. 'Cathach and Lorgan sent for me because they knew you would need some help with your task. It was Lorgan's last wish that we share the responsibility for Mawn and Sianan. So it seems we are destined to work together and that you are going to have to learn to concentrate on your duties despite my presence.'

Gobann glanced up at the heavens and the Even-star seemed to shine brighter than ever before. 'Very well then,' he conceded, 'if that it is how the Druid Council has decided it must be, then I can only accept their wishes.'

'And if you had the opportunity to express *your* wishes,' Síla queried, 'what would they be?'

'Let us go in by the fire and sit,' answered Gobann, unable to control the urge to tell her. 'We have much to talk about.'

Long after Gobann and Síla left the feast, Mawn and Sianan went to bed in their own compartment in the hall. Mawn did not sleep for a long while though he was exhausted from the lengthy prepa-rations for Gobann's honour feast. Mawn could sense that the Faidh was upon him and feared that if he slept, he might be given visions again of his family or of the future.

He had begun to treat these episodes of future-sight as though he were being punished for some past crimes that he had committed, for they were always accompanied by anguish and physical pain.

No matter how hard he tried, though, the boy could not keep sleep away forever and eventually he closed his eyes telling himself, 'I will rest them just a short while.'

No sooner had he begun to draw his breaths deep and slow when a scene came to him. There was a conscious part of Mawn that tried to rouse him from slumber so that he would not have to face this ordeal, but the boy was already resting in the dream sleep and it was too late.

His mind was centred on a strange room in a huge stone building. On a throne made of gold there sat an old man in a strange tall hat. His whole body was clothed in white. He even had gloves of white upon his hands. Mawn listened to what the man had to say and it seemed that he spoke of many good things. Unexpectedly the room began to fill with black-robed monks who crowded about the man stifling him and drowning out his speech with their strange singing and their shuffling sandals.

Mawn thought of the Brandubh board. 'The white king is surrounded by the Ravens,' he told himself.

All of a sudden the black-robed brothers withdrew from around the old man, revealing that he too was now dressed in black and his hat, gloves and eyes were all of blackest of black.

Once again they crowded around him, but this time four brothers dressed in the style of Origen's people, all in flowing white, entered the room. They pushed through the black robes and cleared a path. This time the old man had changed form completely. Instead of the form of an old wise man, he had become an ancient dead tree trunk. The white brothers pulled at his branches to drag him to safety but the rotted limbs came away in their hands and the black-robed monks stood around and laughed.

It was a last sight that disturbed Mawn most though, for he then glimpsed, trapped within the hollow trunk of the tree, another man in white. Mawn struggled to make out who it could be who would be locked in such a place. When he finally caught sight of the fellow's face, he gasped and called out in his sleep, 'Origen!'

thirty

urrough discovered later the story of how Morann came to find the farmhouse where he and Caitlin had sheltered.

The farmer and his wife, whom Streng had disturbed while they were cooking their pig, had escaped through a section of the turf roof, which they periodically used to clear the smoke from their dwelling. When the man was sure that his wife was safe, he had borrowed a neighbour's horse and made off for Cashel hoping to run into a group of Eoghan's warriors on the way. He had heard tell of the war and he was concerned that it had appeared on his own doorstep in the shape of this strange uncouth warrior.

As it happened he was lucky enough to encounter a dispatch rider who took him straight to Morann's army at the crossroads. From there the farmer led a party of warriors back to his cottage through the night, only reaching it again long after Murrough had defeated Streng.

When Morann had found them fresh horses and seen to the bathing of their wounds, Caitlin and Murrough mounted and took to the road again with an escort of the warriors of Munster for the long journey first to Cashel and then on to Teamhair.

The way was easy to the crossroads for it was mostly downhill and the horses were eager to get back to their stables, so they did not need much encouragement. Murrough and Caitlin rode alongside each other most of the way, smiling at each other and sharing jokes and occasionally reaching their hands out to one another between their mounts.

With the company taking their time it was past midday before they finally reached the place where the Tree once stood. In the full daylight and with the snow beginning to melt, the scene was much more devastating than Murrough had expected.

The great creature of wood lay on its side on the grass, crushed by its own weight and literally torn from the ground by the force of its fall. There were still leaves and branches scattered all around but every rowan berry had been collected and stored in small timber mead-barrels that Morann had brought with him from Cashel for that purpose.

'Of all the things that I have seen in this war, of all the killing and brutal cruelty, this is the worst,' Murrough thought, looking on the corpse of the Quicken Tree. 'From now on the Tree will only live in my royal seal.' And then he remembered that he had passed his seal ring on to Seginus as a guarantee of his word to return. 'Maybe it really is time for many changes,' he mused.

Caitlin went to view the Tree closely while Murrough was brooding and found that she, too, was very disturbed by what she saw. Poking out from under the trunk of the great fallen bough was a man's forearm and hand, clutching at the Earth even after so many hours. He was long dead of course, a nameless Saxon warrior flattened beyond any hope of rescue or recognition.

The skin was grey and the fingers contorted and Caitlin was immediately put in mind of Fintan as he lay on the stretcher in the place of healing at

Rathowen. Some force of pity filled her then for this foreigner whose life was gone.

'Did he have a wife and a family?' she thought. 'Or a lover at home in the Saxon lands? Was he a father or a brother?'

She went over to the hand and knelt beside the gruesome limb and offered up a silent prayer. Then she reached out slowly to touch the dead fingers and finally to hold the hand as if it still lived.

And then, for the first time since she had been a little child, she wept. This was no mere shedding of a few tears. Now she really cried, loosing all her sorrow and hate and anger, all the emotions that she had been struggling to come to terms with since Fintan's death. The feelings poured out of her like the last sea storms of winter lashing their fury on any vessel unwary enough to ply its waves.

Murrough saw her and left her to her grief, unwilling or unable in that moment to approach her. But when he came back an hour later and she was still sitting clutching the corpse's hand and sobbing, Murrough decided that he should speak with her.

Approaching her as quietly as he could so that he would not startle her with his sudden presence, he whispered, 'Caitlin, are you all right?'

It was a long time before she answered. 'Leave me in peace a while,' was all she said. He did as he was asked and went to find Morann to convince him that they should remain at the crossroads for the night.

'I will not wait any longer,' stormed Morann. 'I have wasted enough time on your selfish adventures. You have your duty to the kingdom to think of.'

'I will not ride this night,' Murrough stated. 'She needs to rest and I will stay with her and guard her.'

'She should be in Cashel where she can be treated for her leg wound and be given proper attention,' Morann exclaimed. 'And you and I should be well on our way to Teamhair to aid the High-King in his time of need.'

Murrough furrowed his brow remembering suddenly that when he had left Rathowen the threat of rebellion in Laigin had been one of the High-King's main concerns. 'Is there any news?' he asked, his tone subdued for he was feeling guilty at putting his own happiness before the good of the kingdom.

'None,' answered Morann. 'There has been no rider from the north in four days. Anything may have happened. Dichu might have returned and slain Leoghaire in his bed for all we know.'

'Can we wait until morning?' Murrough implored.

'It is a waste of precious time!' Morann answered, exasperated.

'One night,' Murrough pleaded, 'that is all I ask. Then in the morning she can travel on to Cashel and I will ride with you directly to Teamhair.'

Morann thought about it for a second. He had planned to take Murrough back to Cashel also, assuming that he would not want to be parted from Caitlin. But he saw that this way they would probably be in Teamhair within four more days, possibly even three.

'Very well,' he conceded. 'One night, and one night only, then we ride directly to Teamhair.'

'Thank you, Brother,' said Murrough. 'Thank you.' And he grasped Morann by the hand until the anger that had passed between them no longer seemed important.

Caitlin stayed by the grey hand until the shadows began to lengthen and the night to fall.

When finally she began to feel the cold, she decided it would be best if she went to take some food by a fire. As she rose her eye caught something lying in the grass.

Just out of reach of the dead fingers, in the strands of green and under a leaf, she saw a strand of black cord. She reached out to it and picked it up, finding that it was attached to a small black bag of a soft and beautiful material the like of which she had never seen before. Intrigued as to what may be inside, she pulled the cords apart and emptied the contents of the pouch into her hand.

The tiny bag held only nine rowan berries, but whether they had been an attempt at pilfering by this dead Saxon or whether they were a gift from some other hand, she did not know. She carefully put them back inside the pouch one at a time and closed it tight. Then she put the pouch in her pocket and resolved to tell no-one of her find. 'This will be my reminder of these times,' she promised herself.

At the fire Murrough had a place prepared for her and he sat with her long into the night until there were only a few watchmen still awake. Finally he could fight off sleep no longer and so he decided to bid her good night.

'I will go to my rest now, Caitlin,' he said. 'Tomorrow you will ride to Cashel and I will go on to Teamhair.'

'I cannot,' she told him simply, shaking her head, 'I am not ready.'

'What do you mean,' he asked, concerned, 'by saying you are not ready?'

'I will be going to the Well of Bridgit tomorrow. I am going to take the vows of the Druid women and spend some months in silent contemplation of all that has happened to me.'

'And will you ever return from the holy well?'
Murrough blurted.

She thought for a moment and then looked him
in the eye with her coldest stare. 'I do not know,'
she admitted. 'At least not yet. After all that has
happened I have realised that somewhere I have
lost a part of myself. I am not sure if I lost it at
Rathowen or at the Quicken Tree or some time
after. I am not even sure what it is exactly that is
missing, but there is an empty space that I cannot
seem to fill.'

Murrough thought that she probably was speaking of Fintan when she talked of something that
she had lost. 'Let me escort you to the sanctuary of
the holy well,' he offered.

For some reason this comment made her very
angry. 'This is something that I must do alone!' she
snapped. 'You cannot go with me.' Then she
remembered that almost the first words she ever
spoke with him were in anger and she did not wish
them to part on such terms. 'I have healed a little
in my body; the wound is clean now and it is time
that I spent a while healing my spirit.'

'May I visit you?' he sighed.

'No,' she answered gently. 'But when I have
found some peace I will return to you, if you will
have me.'

Murrough nodded and smiled to her. 'Find your
peace then and until that day I will wait for you.
You can be sure of that.'

Then the prince thought that it really was for
the best that they spent some time apart as soon
he would have his father and all the affairs of
state to face. 'Is there anything that I can do to
make your time at the well any easier?' he asked
finally.

'Nothing,' she replied. 'But you could wish me a

safe journey and good fortune in seeking my healing.'

He leaned over to her and kissed her softly on the brow. 'You have that,' he assured her, 'You have that.'

Once more they fell into each other's arms and embraced and fell asleep eventually by the glowing embers of the campfire.

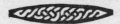

It was almost daylight when a rider entered the camp from the north and was challenged by the guards, who quickly ascertained that he was a dispatch rider from Teamhair.

Morann rose from his bed to receive the messenger and took the man into his tent to hear his news.

No sooner had the tent flaps been drawn closed than the dispatch rider declared, 'Long live Murrough, King of Munster and Cashel.'

He bore the news of Eoghan's death.

Murrough and Caitlin were found and the rider related his news directly to his new king and the woman he wished to make his queen.

'Your father passed away peacefully in his sleep,' the man reported. 'He had spent the day upon the summit of the hill of Teamhair and he took a cold in his chest. By the time he went to his rest that evening he was deathly ill. The fire was built up for him and the Druids administered the herbs of healing, but shortly after midnight his breathing ceased and he passed over.'

Neither Morann nor Murrough spoke for a while as the news took hold of them. Finally it was Morann who broke the silence. 'I always thought that I would be with him.'

'He was in good company,' the messenger told

him. 'Lorgan the Sorn, adviser to Leoghaire, also passed away that night and the two were sent off together at the fires of Bel.'

'That is as he would have wished it,' Morann stated. 'May he rest.'

'The world is changing,' Murrough rejoined. 'Maybe it is changing faster than we can. But it is certainly changing. Go to your rest, messenger, and thank you for your speed in coming. Tomorrow I will ride to Teamhair and swear my loyalty to the High-King and take the crown of Munster.'

Caitlin watched Murrough closely as he received the news and saw the pain that had struck at him at the loss of one so dearly loved and she did not feel quite so alone anymore.

'I will come back to you, King Murrough,' she promised him in her thoughts. 'I will come back.'

EPILOGUE

he Druid Council of Teamhair convened again during the dark of the next Moon, three weeks and two days after the felling of the Quicken Tree. The members of the inner assembly of the Council met in the great hall where Gobann's banquet was held and every important feast celebrated for the last thousand years.

In Lorgan's place at the table of the High-Druid sat Cathach, now the chief adviser to Leoghaire. 'Our task has only just begun,' he informed the Council. 'Yes, we have secured the future of the Wanderers and they are central to our plans for preserving the old ways, but we very nearly lost all that we were striving for because we did not take account of all the possibilities. We must look carefully to the future. It is our duty to the generations that are to come.'

He paused to take a sip of water, then continued. 'We have commenced training the children and they are turning out to be gifted students who take their lessons very seriously. They will take everything they see and hear of our ways into the next generations. We will not be around to guide them then, so they must also be able to survive in a hostile world if they are going to be the living repositories for our traditions. We cannot foresee all that may befall them, but we must ensure that the children survive the coming strife.'

All were silent, contemplating how each of them could contribute to the task.

'We have lived to see the treaty with the Danaan folk tested to its limits,' Cathach went on, 'and the patience of their Druids tried to breaking point. We can only seek their advice more often in future. Why we did not do so before escapes me for they have always held a great deal of faith in the children and the method that we propose for preserving our traditions through the troubles that are to come. They have used these methods themselves, you must remember, to great effect.'

'Murrough has accepted responsibility for Mawn and Sianan,' Gobann added. 'The new King of Munster will safely conceal them within his own household and they will surely feel, in time, as if they are part of a large family. Their lives will be pleasant enough at Cashel, and I feel certain that they will forget this troubled time and one day come to face their destinies. I would not like to be either of them, I admit, but then I do not have half the gifts that either of them have been blessed with. Síla and I will teach them all we can and we will reside wherever the children happen to be. It is our intention to watch over them both very carefully until the time of their initiation as full Druids.'

None could deny, who knew Mawn and Sianan, that they were two remarkable children and that even Lorgan, who had conceived of the plan to use the Quicken berries to prolong their lives, could not have dared hope that they would be so suitable to the purpose.

After the meeting Gobann visited Cathach at his fireside before setting off to Cashel with Síla and the children. The two Druids shared some of the poet's precious store of Midhna's mead and a game or two at the Brandubh, and then the conversation came as ever back to the two Wanderers.

'It is vital that the traditions be preserved by both a male and a female,' Cathach impressed on Gobann. 'Only in that way will the whole of the tale be kept alive. Wherever the Romans have gone they have spread the doctrine of the superiority of the male. The people of Gaul fell into the trap of believing in it and all else the Romans told them and so they were easily dominated by the Christians, so now they have nothing of their past to cling to. It is our duty to redress the balance. The whole of the Gaelic world is relying on you and Síla to pass on your teachings to the Wanderers so that they may in turn pass them on to future generations.'

'Will they really be able to achieve all that we have planned?' asked Gobann.

'We have an ample supply of the Quicken berries, despite the loss of the Tree,' Cathach assured him, 'and they have four good guardians to watch over them, two Druids and a king and a queen. It will be some years before they are really put to the test but I am sure they will live up to all we expect of them.'

'We have not even begun the work,' stated Gobann. 'All of this—the war, the death of the Quicken Tree, the finding of the children—it was all just the first moves in a great strategy. The game will go on beyond our lifetimes.'

'Yes,' Cathach agreed. 'The War Strain will sound down the ages and the Brandubh will be played out for many hundreds of years yet and neither you nor I can know for certain what the outcome will be.'

'In the great game of the Brandubh, are you and

I the players or the playing pieces?' Gobann sighed almost to himself.

Cathach looked at his fellow Druid with an indulgent smile. 'We are both,' he explained. 'We create the game and then we watch it played out, but we are pieces in another larger game. You and I may only hope that the Wanderers will play out a game that we have prepared for them, but who is to say that they will not follow their own strategies and find their own way out of the maze?'

Gobann nodded in agreement. 'All we can hope is that by our guidance their first steps on the Road are sure and steady.'

'Aye,' breathed Cathach. 'The first steps on the great Road to the future. For the moment we are standing at the crossroads, but it may well be that one day you and I will find ourselves back here in this place again. For, like everything on Earth, the Road travels in a perfect circle, traversing the world and binding all that has ever been or ever will be, forever round and round and round.'

PRONUNCIATION
OF WORDS AND NAMES

s I have attempted where possible to retain the ancient form of many of the names in this book, most of the Gaelic or Old Irish words that appear may be unfamiliar to the reader. Below are suggestions as to how the names could be pronounced. I have listed the Saxon and other foreign names separately from the Old Irish and Gaelic.

The inhabitants of Eirinn in the fifth century did not refer to themselves as 'Irish' but identified with their tribal or family grouping or the sub-kingdom in which they lived. In fact there was no word in Old Irish that referred to any sense of greater national identity. This is known from the many manuscripts that were produced in Ireland around that time and later. It was only foreigners, who did not fully understand the clan system, one that considered the peoples of Eirinn to belong to one nation, who used the term 'Irish' to classify them. Thus I have restricted the term 'Irish' to Saxons usage.

During my research for this novel I discovered discrepancies between the Latin used in Rome and that spoken and written in former provinces of the Roman Empire. This was mainly due to a decline in learning on the continent in the fourth and fifth centuries which resulted in numerous scribal errors. Most manuscripts from this time are also full of regional and vernacular terms that have been Latinised, adding to the confusion. This is especially true of many individuals' names. Wherever the Latin language is used in this book I have

tried to represent it as a tongue that was, though
in decline, still a living language and not as formal
as that of later medieval times.

GAELIC & OLD IRISH

Aine:	aynnie
Ainir:	oneer
Amergin:	am-ar-geen
Admór:	ard-more
Ard-Righ:	ard-ree
Banatigh:	ban-a-tee
Banfa:	ban-va
Ban-sidhe:	ban-shee
Bardagh:	bard-ahh
Beltinne:	bell-cheena
Beoga:	be-yog-ah
Brandubh:	bran-doov
Breaga:	bree-aga
Brecan:	brek-an
Brehon:	bre-on
Bridgit:	bridj-it
Cailleach:	kayl-ack
Caillte:	kal-chee
Caitlin ni	
Úaine:	kaytlin (or cotchlin) nee wahnya
Cashel:	kashell
Cathach:	kat-ack
Cen:	ken
Cianan:	kee-an-an
Cieran:	keer-an
Cill-dhaire:	kildare
Cnoc-an-air:	knoc-an-ar
Cnoc-pocan:	knoc-poe-kan

Colm Dhall:	kolum-daal
Conan:	ko-nan
Connor:	kon-or
Cormac:	kore-mack
Cruitne:	krit-nee
Cuaich:	kwatch
Curragh:	koo-rah
Dal Araidhe:	dal ree-ah-dah
Danu:	dan-oo
Darach:	darack
Desi:	dee-siy
Diarmuid:	deer-mot
Dichu:	deek-oo
Dobharcú:	doe-barkoo
Drugal:	droo-gul
Drui:	droo-ee
Druid:	droo-id
Eirinn:	air-in
Eoghan:	yo-ann
Eoghanacht:	yo-ann-aackt
Éremon:	air-ray-mon
Eric:	air-ik
Faidhe:	fay
Feni:	fee-niy
Fianna:	fee-ann-ah
Filidh:	feel-ee
Fintan:	fin-tan
Fionn:	fin
Fomorian:	fomore-ee-an
Géas:	gee-sa
Glas-cloch:	glass-clock
Gobann:	go-bahn
Gráinne:	grahn-ee
Gríanan:	gree-an-an
Kallan:	kal-ann
Laigin:	lah-een
Leoghaire:	leer-ree

Lai Fál:	lee-ah fal
Lochlann:	lock-lahn
Lom-dubh:	lom doov
Lorgan Scorn:	law-gan sawn
Maelduine:	mal-doon
Maoile:	mweela
Mawn:	morn
Midhe:	meeth
Midhna:	mee-nah
Mog:	mohg
Morann:	more-ann
Morrigú:	mor-ee-goo
Múadhan:	morn
Murrough:	morr-uh
Niall:	nee-al
Niamh:	nee-av
Níos:	neesh
Ogham:	ohh-um
Ogma:	ohg-ma
Oiliol:	ill-eel
Oisin:	ish-een
Olan:	ohh-lan
Ollamh:	ohh-lahv
Rath:	raath:
Rathowen:	raath-oh-wen
Riadan:	ree-ah-dan
Ruari:	roo-ri
Samhain:	sahv-an
Scéolan:	skay-oh-lan
Scian-dubh:	skee-an doov
Sciathan-cog:	skee-at-an koge
Sean Nós:	shan-nohs
Senchas Mór:	sen-chas more
Sianan:	shee-an-an
Sidhe:	shee
Sidhe-dubh:	shee-doov
Síla Subhach:	shee-la shoo-vahk

Soghain:	so-hane
Taillc:	chall-uk
Teamhair:	tar-rah
Tir-Nan-Og:	cheer-nan-oge
Tuatha-De-Danaan:	too-ah-ha-day, dahn-an
Torc:	tork

WORÒS OF NON-IRISH ORIGIN

Alban:	al-bann
Allemagni:	al-ee-mahn-ee
Ambrosius:	am-brose-see-oos
Andvari:	and-var-ee
Armorica:	ar-more-ika
Chi-ro:	kee-roh
Declan:	dek-lan
Declinu:	dek-lin-oo
Donatus:	don-ah-toos
Draupnir:	drop-neer
Eboracum:	ebb-or-ahh-coom
Eli:	ee-li
Ephesus:	ee-fees-oos
Frarod:	frah-rod
Gunnar:	gu-nahh
Guthwine:	goot-wine
Isernus:	ees-ern-oos
Linus:	lee-noos
Nicea:	niy-kee-ah
Odin:	ohh-din
Origen:	oh-rig-en
Palladius:	pall-ahh-dee-oos
Pelagians:	pel-ahh-gee-ans
Seginus Gallus:	seg-een-oos gal-oos
Scythian:	skee-tee-an
Thengwulf:	thing-woolf
Vortigern:	fort-ee-gern